For Marie and the three laughing boys.

THE FIRST TRIMESTER

A remote village in the heart of agricultural England, May 19th

Today, of all days, she gave me the news. 'I think I might be pregnant,' she said, as I buttered a piece of underdone toast in my mother's kitchen. Just six little words. Nothing to worry about. She thinks she might be pregnant, that's all. It's not as if she's even sure. That was the first thing I checked when consciousness returned on the cold stone tiles of the floor. 'What do you mean 'pregnant'?' I asked, with as much indignation as I could muster. It's a stupid question, I know, and she didn't bother to answer. She just shot me a look filled with centuries of animosity; a look that any Englishman with a French girlfriend will know only too well.

It's not as if I have any excuse for being so shocked. It must be a full six months since she first asked me if I thought it was about time we started a family. I can't remember exactly what I said, but I must have mumbled some form of assent into my cornflakes. I know I went so far as to say I couldn't see any reason *not* to try for a baby. At the time I thought I was being pretty cunning, but I can assure you that very few women (and none of them French) will bother themselves over the intricacies of such a remark. And, yes, I did agree to flush the condoms down the toilet, but I just think she took the whole damned thing too literally.

What was I thinking? Well, I guess I was banking on my own impotence, or just assumed that everything would blow over. Now I'm left with no alternative but to place the blame squarely with two brothers – first mine and then hers – they were the ones who uncoupled this runaway train when they strutted through our front door, arm in arm with their wives, bearing puckered pink objects which did nothing other than scream for the bottle and as much attention as they could command. Regrettably, they also attracted the interest of my girlfriend. '*Il est trop mignon!*' she'd simper, as she pushed a finger into the shapeless howling machines. I naturally assumed she was pointing out their resemblance to a juicy filet steak. A more accurate translation, it turns out, would be 'he's so cute!'. And I don't suppose I've heard the last of that syrupy line either.

Anyway, that's how we ended up here, hidden behind a locked bathroom door at my mother's place with a pregnancy testing kit we'd slipped surreptitiously into our shopping basket earlier this afternoon at Asda while my mother hovered further up the isle. My hangover is killing me and we're just gawping at this thing, trying to work out whether or not the faintest of watermarks constitutes a positive result. It looks like a pink circle, line or whatever it's supposed to be, but we're still none the wiser.

But I look into her eyes and I know. Know what exactly? I know that she's pregnant. Don't ask me how – her eyes are precisely the same shape and colour as they were yesterday only... now they contain something else. Maybe it's nothing more than a look of fear or vulnerability? No, stop trying to kid yourself, it's the dawn of a biological bloody miracle and the end of life as I know it.

I leave her in the bathroom to decipher the dumb plastic object and head back downstairs to chat to my mother about the weather, the cat and the church choir. I must stay calm. All is not lost. We just can't be sure. Let's wait 'til we're back in Paris, where we can get a proper blood test.

London Waterloo, May 20th

Tuesday morning. I had planned to spend a couple more days in London while she made her own way back to Paris on the *Eurostar* to get on with some work. I was going to visit an old friend and chew coolly over an infinite kind of future, but because *I know*, my life has already changed track and I'm travelling home with her.

Maybe you're shocked that I can't bring myself to tell you her name? If you want the truth, it shocks me too. But you must understand that I'm more than a little angry with her. 'Angry? Hang on a minute... ' I hear you say, 'didn't you just tell us that you agreed to stop the contraception?' Well, that's a fair point – I have no right to be pissed off. None whatsoever. I know I've played my part in all this but, at the time, the idea of having a baby seemed so abstract, so far away. It was almost as if I'd do my thing and somebody else would become the father. Now it all seems so imminent, which must be why I don't talk to her all the way home and blame my mood on the remnants of the hangover. I'm sorry if you think that's unreasonable, but that's just the way things are. These are my thoughts as I sit, stoney-faced, watching the trees and fields roll away from me. I feel as though control over my life is going with them.

Paris, May 21st

No more than twelve hours later, we're standing outside one of the *laboratoires d'analyses* which occupy just about every street corner in Paris. As far as I'm aware, these places don't even exist in the UK, where you'd need to pay a visit to your local hospital instead. Here in France, after a quick cup of coffee and a croissant (and for about the same price), you can nip into your local lab for whatever kind of test takes your fancy: 'Think you might have picked up a spot of syphilis at that dinner party last night,

Monsieur? Pas de problème, please step this way and we'll empty your veins in a jiffy.' That wouldn't be so bad, but we're here for something far more threatening to my deliciously selfish existence than syphilis. Anyway, after a short exchange between my girlfriend and some snooty nurse in a starched white coat, the purpose of our visit is discussed (far too openly, if you want my opinion) and the uniform looks me up and down as if I were barely capable of an erection, never mind impregnation.

One hour later (the longest one of my life by a merry mile), we're back for the results. I'm expecting to be hustled into a back room and given a lecture concerning my future conduct. But no sooner have we stepped through the door than the starchy one is beaming and fog-horning the news that *we* are three weeks pregnant and, before I can even demand a recount, Miss Frosty-Knickers has posted the results on a selection of bus shelters around the city and pushed us back outside onto the pavement.

As I support the mother-to-be in my arms, she's trembling, crying and smiling, all at the same time. Why am I holding her this way? Because I'm a hypocrite? Well yes, but there are one or two other reasons. First, she looks genuinely shocked – happy alright, but undeniably traumatised. Second, I'm afraid she might faint onto the dog shit-laden streets of Paris. And finally, because I may be on the point of collapse myself. Clearly I ought to say something at this point, but what exactly? I think about making a few comforting noises, but I'm afraid I'll start howling like a wounded hyena. The fact is, I really don't know what to say and, in the end, I settle for something like, 'Come on, let's go home and have a cup of tea.' Shameful, I know, but it's got to be better than quoting some dreadful line from a Hollywood movie, as I'm sure you'll agree.

Her name, by the way, is Helena.

When we get home, the first thing she does is to call my mother, who'd become suspicious about all our fumbling around in the bathroom. Helena confessed at the time that she might be pregnant (cue fanfare and another round of scones while son skulks into corner) and as I hear her trilling on the phone, I realise how delighted she is, and that makes me even more churlish. But that's not the worst of it – Helena has handed me the phone and now half my gene pool wants a word with me: *How do I feel?* As numb as a gum full of novocaine. *Am I finally going to start looking after Helena?* I've just made her a cup of tea, haven't I? *And does this mean I'm going to stop messing around and get myself a proper job?* 'Huh' and other non-committal noises. It's obvious she's thrilled, what with me being the eldest child and all that. When my sister-in-law gave birth a couple of years back, I remember my mother asking me whether I found it difficult to watch my brother becoming a father. Not as difficult as it's going to be for him, I thought at the time, before saying something slightly more appropriate like 'Yes, in a way.' I suppose I'd better come clean and admit that I do quite like kids, but only the ones that belong to other people. I'll be the best uncle in the world if you like, but please don't turn me into a father.

Anyway, if you still harbour hopes of avoiding all this, please let me spell out the danger signs and likely sequence of events:

1. You're in a steady relationship with a woman and realise, one sunny afternoon, that you're not having sex with as many women as you once did.
2. A close friend or, more dangerously still, a relative, suddenly starts reproducing.
3. The woman sharing your bed suddenly loses all interest in dancing 'til dawn or making plans for travelling overland to Samarkand. Instead she starts talking about something called 'responsibility'.
4. She throws your condoms out of the bedroom window or insists on stopping the pill. You resist for a while, but one morning you give in because you're hung over or you've

said something inappropriate to one of her relatives.

5. You forget that you're no longer taking contraceptive measures and continue to have sex (with the same woman).
6. Nothing happens for a couple of months and you forget or just assume that you're getting away with it.
7. Because you're getting away with it, you start getting blasé about 'safe periods' and forget to organise a night out with the lads a week or so after her period has started.
8. You get a pointed reminder when she tells you, with a look of genuine hope in her eyes, that she's late.
9. Quietly, you begin to panic.
10. Now she's really late and you have to face up to the awful possibility that all that stuff about drinking too much beer, smoking, degradation of the environment and low sperm counts may just be a load of old bollocks after all.

By now Helena is so busy on the phone that I have another well-earned cup of tea and put my feet up. Staring at the walls of our hopelessly small, dark apartment, I try to imagine the future... Right! That's more than enough of that. Now for something more constructive, like burying my head in the sports pages of the Sunday papers.

Around the world and back again, May 23rd

Helena is still on the phone, chatting to a cousin who lives in north London. Personally, I can't imagine being French and wanting to live anywhere near Turnpike Lane, but then who am I to comment upon what constitutes exoticism for our friends from the continent? Anyway, this cousin lives with a Ghanaian Arsenal supporter and they have these two fantastically beautiful daughters – Celeste and Léonie – really cute kids, but kids that can be handed straight back to their long-suffering and rightful owners the very instant you get bored, irritated or maimed. Anyway, I'm damned sure this cousin has got something to do with the fact that Helena is pregnant.

Not quite as much as me, perhaps, but something nevertheless. Just listen to the pair of them, chirping away like a couple of over-excited crickets. I'm suspicious enough to put down my newspaper and listen. I bet I look about as inconspicuous as a TV detective with chickenpox. I don't get any proof, but at least it hastens the end of their conversation, leaving me free to lecture Helena about making premature announcements to the rest of the world, long before I'm ready to hear the news myself. No one's supposed to hear about this baby for another two months but that's two women that know already (if you exclude the expectant one). To even the score a little, I call my oldest friend back in London. He'll know how to get me out of this fix. After all, he's got two kids of his own and claims he didn't want either of them.

After the cursory preamble, I blurt out my news with all the grace of a rusting bulldozer:

'She's pregnant!'

'Who?'

'Who do you think?'

'Jesus! How did that happen?'

'Whaddya mean, how did that happen? The same way it happened to you, I suppose.'

'Was it planned?'

'No. Well, yes... Sort of.'

'I see,' he says, as I sense disapproval crossing the Channel faster than a new strain of bird flu.

'I thought you two were going through a rough patch and now this... ' His voice trails off before making a probing recovery, 'And how do you feel about it?'

Since I'm talking to another man, I try to make it sound like I know what I'm doing. 'Fine. We're doing fine now.'

'You are?'

'Oh yeah, no problems at all.'

'I see. So, you're not worried, then?'

'Me? No way!'

Only when I've put down the phone do I remember what

happened on the very same day that my friend's partner fell pregnant for the second time. He'd finally saved enough money to make the down payment on a spectacular *BMW* coupé and was about to set off for the showroom when his girlfriend called to deliver the silver bullet. He sighed and lovingly folded the shiny brochures and accompanying technical spec. Then he put them away in the bottom drawer of a decrepit old chest in the attic – forever. My guess is they're still in there somewhere, buried under several strata of kiddies' clothing and an unread volume on the dark arts of child rearing.

I conjure up an image of my friend at home with his two boys. I know he dotes on those kids. I've seen him bathing them and changing their nappies, so why is he so concerned about me? But no matter how hard I try to ignore that part of the conversation, I have to admit the truth of what he said about me, Helena and that rough patch and, before we go any further, I suppose you'll want to know what that's all about. The thing is, Helena and I were going to get married, but I had second thoughts and postponed the wedding a little bit (or cancelled it altogether, if you want to get pedantic about it). I'd probably have gotten away with this disgraceful behaviour, too, if we hadn't told everyone we were about to get hitched. We even gave them a date which, in case you're wondering, wasn't too far off next Saturday. I'd love to be able to explain why I did such a thing, but I'm not so sure that I can. We'd only been seeing each other about 18 months, although we first met five years ago when I had a marketing job in the Far East. Anyway, Helena had come for a visit, we got introduced by her brother, who was working out there as some sort of off-shore engineer, there was a full moon, a bit of a misunderstanding over the sleeping arrangements and somehow we ended up under the same duck feather duvet. Then she went back to France and I stayed under the covers. Of course, we exchanged telephone numbers and all that stuff, but our next fateful meeting was more than three years off.

Paris, May 24th

This morning the thought entered my head. Now it sits there, waiting like a venomous insect preparing to emerge from the cocoon. I don't want to encourage the idea by giving it a name, but it's no use... Medically speaking, I know nothing about abortion, other than the fact that she (rather than he) goes into an unlabelled clinic and what has been done is abruptly undone by a short 'procedure'. Anything else? Well, I do remember once receiving a call from a girlfriend. She told me she was pregnant and I recall being paralysed by fear and incomprehension. Then she said she'd deal with it and I had a pretty good idea what that meant. At the time, I felt only relief that someone other than me would be dealing with the consequences of our irresponsibility and that was the last I heard of it until she called a couple of weeks later and told me the thing had been done. My immediate reaction was one of pure relief. It was just one more thing I was only too happy to push to the back of my mind, well out of reach like all my other unwanted feelings. I ordered another pint and saw the future stretched out in front of me like a broad lawn, unencumbered by children and full of possibilities and choice. But today my mind keeps wandering back to those two brief phone calls. Had I taken some kind of a decision back then, or had I torn out my own eyes? So you see, abortions and I have a history, which may be why the word has come back to haunt me. But I'm not going to utter it to Helena. At least not yet. My plan, coward that I am, is to lie low for a while and see how things develop.

Paris, May 26th

I awoke this morning before dawn with the overwhelming feeling that I've fallen victim of every woman's biological compulsion to become a mother and that Helena has tricked me into getting her pregnant. I refused to show my commitment by getting married, so now she's gone for the next best thing. She wants to be a mother, and why not? That's fine. But why does that mean that I have to become a father?

Now she's gone out and bought a book. It's called *Future Maman* and, according the blurb on the cover, its plan is to walk us through nine months of pregnancy week-by-week. This being France, the illustration on the front depicts a very sexy woman in some pretty skimpy underwear and my attention is drawn immediately to her ample cleavage, rather than the taut, bulging belly conveniently hidden beneath the author's name. The cover of *Future Maman* reminds me I've always professed to find pregnant women rather sexy, although whenever I've said as much to friends, male or female, they look at me as if I'm some kind of pervert. But it's true – I always thought that progesterone glaze held a special allure. So why do I have the feeling I'll come to loathe this book? Probably because I don't want to be walked through nine months of pregnancy. I'd rather it all went away.

Helena has it open at the relevant page right now: Week three of the first trimester, where we're presented with a detailed diagram depicting a small collection of excitable cells, all dancing around a steady, fluid nucleus. Thanks to this charming book, she's now concerned that my consumption of alcohol may have affected the conception in some malign way, so she puts in a call to some jolly green giant of a gynaecologist who happens to live up our street. 'Absolutely nothing to worry about,' he counters with more glee than seems necessary, 'there's nothing like a few drinks to ease the way for conception.' Now he tells me.

What happens next is that, instead of going back to work, Helena gets on the phone to every maternity hospital in Paris. When I question the need for this, she assures me that it's by no means too early. As a matter of fact, she thinks that most of the hospital beds will already be taken. 'But how can that be?' I cry, 'You're only three weeks gone! None of your competitors will have any idea they're freshly up the duff'.

But my protests are met with another of those haughty looks in which French women specialise when conversing with the Anglo-Saxon male.

She's right, of course. Space is sparse in the maternity wards of Paris, which just goes to prove that the wise mother-to-be books her bed at least a decade in advance. I'm mortified to discover that all this is nothing like booking a ticket for a major sporting event (my only point of comparison), which you only do once your team has made it through to the final after months of arduous competition, not as soon as they've scraped through the first round on penalties. The implications of this, which are already obvious to approximately 50 percent of the population, finally dawn upon one aging and particularly dense male specimen in Paris: this city is full of women who have planned their pregnancies with all the precision and confidence of the technocrat responsible for timetabling the trains in Switzerland.

This is enough to convince me this whole pregnancy racket is nothing but a conspiracy. Sullenly, I withdraw from any further conversation and try to face the fact that, barring disasters natural or unnatural, I'm about to have a baby and at least half of it's going to be French. Meanwhile, Helena quietly gets on with what has to be done and, at the tenth time of asking, manages to reserve a metallic bed and a set of stirrups for eight and a half months hence.

Planes, trains, automobiles and a bus, May 27th

A few weeks ago, back in the good old days when the only thing on my mind was me, I booked a trip to Italy to spend some time with a few friends in the hills of Tuscany. The house we've rented is not far from Florence and it has a pool, a large garden, the works. So why do I feel less than delighted? Well, Helena and I were in Amsterdam, for the wedding of two of these friends, Dirk and Carla, last summer. It was a beautiful day, a beautiful wedding and we were head over heels in love. The day after the wedding, I told all and sundry that Helena and I were getting married ourselves. It all seems such a long time ago and I haven't raised the subject of marriage since, which probably accounts for my desire to cancel our little Italian trip altogether.

Helena doesn't want to go to Italy any more than I do, although that has more to do with the travelling than the prospect of a few arduous days lying around in the vineyards of Chianti country. She's afraid of flying and wanted to catch the night train direct from Paris to Florence. But I wanted to do it on the cheap and, stretching in front of us now like a double geography lesson, is a journey involving the Paris metro, a bus to an obscure airport in the middle of the French countryside, a flight to Milan, a train to Florence and another bus which will transport us to Empoli, where I'm hoping we'll be picked up by one of our car-owning friends.

'Exactly how much cheaper is this?' asks Helena, placing a hand strategically to her stomach.

'Quite a few Euros,' I say, in an attempt to deflect further enquiry. 'Come on, we don't want to miss the flight.'

We arrive at the airport in plenty of time for Helena to get nervous and for me to fail to calm her down. From the prefabricated hut masquerading as an airport terminal in Beauvais, we watch as the plane limps in on its inward flight from Milan and disgorges its shabby payload of budget travellers. Helena notices that the pilot is a woman and explains why this has at least given her some hope that we're not about to be plastered all over the Alps: 'As a woman she understands the value of life, which means she'll take greater care of her passengers.' I don't say anything and focus on getting our luggage on board. As a man, I understand that pregnant women don't carry heavy bags.

Helena was right about the trip though. What we save in cash (about €20, since I know you're dying to ask), we're forced to spend several times over on food and litres of mineral water to combat the heat and exhaustion. But we do make it to Italy and even manage to enjoy the journey south from Milan. 'You wouldn't see any of this in the dark,' I say, referring as obliquely as possible to my failure to book the direct night train. I stare out of the window in case I catch a look that suggests she recognises this remark for what it truly is. 'What?' she says. Ah well, at least we're talking!

The Italian countryside, May 29th

There are ten of us in this house – five couples, only one of which is pregnant. After breakfast, Dirk asks why neither Helena nor I had drunk any wine at dinner. I think about lying but I don't bother and, in a rash outbreak of truthfulness, I confess that I'm trying to stop drinking. And Helena? 'Well, Helena is just, um, how can I put this? She's just pregnnnn . . .' But before I can stutter my way through the rest of the sentence, Carla is already upstairs where she's now hugging, kissing and questioning Helena about dates, maternity bras, and, for all I know, my performance at the time of conception. Downstairs, Dirk asks how I feel about it all. Why always that same question?

Helena quickly becomes the centre of attention among the women, leaving the boys free to indulge in a few games of volleyball and other traditional male pursuits, such as jumping on one another's heads in the swimming pool. Relaxing a little, I notice that Helena is positively glowing with health. She looks happy and, as I study her body as it glides gently across the pool, I see no real sign of the tumultuous changes that have already begun inside her. Ah well, if I'm to become a father, I'd better stop lazing by the pool and get off my arse. I don't have a job or a car and we rent a tiny apartment in one of the filthiest areas of Paris. These are not exactly the ideal circumstances in which to welcome yet another hapless mammal into a pitiless world and I resolve to give the whole thing some serious thought – tomorrow.

Unfamiliar birdsong amid the grapevines, late May

In my dream, I'm trying to seduce the blonde from the bakery back in Paris. My body is pulsing with the desire to possess her and, finally, I do. But I somehow let slip that I live with the girl who occasionally comes in a fur-collared coat to buy her morning *brioche*. With apprehension, I watch her face as the girl with flour on her hands weighs up her next move...

I've no idea what day it is today. All I know is that I'm still in Tuscany, the sun is shining, I'm drinking a cup of tea and I haven't had anything stronger for more than a week, which must be some kind of a record. Anyway, we were in Florence yesterday and I watched as my friends drank beer, wine and grappa. They were enjoying themselves without getting drunk and so was I. Yet my deepest fear is not the booze at all, but rather the inescapable fact that Helena bears my child. I feel hopelessly trapped, so much so that I spent most of yesterday staring at the breasts and behinds of the women of Florence and, because of the rules I set, it was a competition that Helena stood no chance of winning.

Maybe I should come clean and admit right now that the two of us were meandering down the well-trodden path to separation. But how can I leave her now? We still have two months to decide what to do with this new life, yet it feels as though the decision has already been made. Somehow, this is about much more than just becoming a father.

Milan airport, May 31st

Italy has been a good break; a minor fantasy surrounded by friends belonging to a relatively unencumbered past. But now it's back to the present and, worse still, the future. In the swimming pool, I managed to avoid altogether the subject of the relationship between me, her and that silent third party. But the late Tuscan spring has eased communication between us, even if one issue remains undiscussed. If there's a decision to be taken about this baby, we'll have to broach it sometime soon, although we both know that only one of us is avoiding the subject. If I do have a kid any time soon, could it possibly become more important than me and my selfish obsessions? I'm having such problems getting to grips with this idea that I resolve to send my brother an email to ask how he coped with such a fearsome prospect. The woman pilot is off duty for our flight back to Paris but we make it anyway. Maybe the beard that flies us home has a couple of kids himself. Who knows?

Paris, June 2nd

Last winter, my brother pitched up in Paris with his wife and three-year-old son in tow – my godson. I'd only met him once before and that was at his christening, when he was nothing but a few limbs and a head poking out of a bundle of linen and lace. So I was a bit shocked when I found out that this bundle had turned into a boy capable of simple oral communication and some charm. I comforted myself with the thought that we'd get along just fine provided he agreed to get straight back on the plane after a last bit of fun at the airport and return to the sweltering, tin pot republic in which my brother chooses to make a living. But that was before my mother dropped her little bomb about fatherhood. Until that moment, I'd been perfectly happy cocooned inside my titanium emotion-resistant armour plating, but as I held the kid's hand in mine, I realised that I loved the way he strained his heavy head when asked if so-and-so was naughty or good. His father was naughty, he replied and I, the unknown and negligent godfather, was nice.

But never mind all that. Right now I need to know whether my brother went through these same self-inflicted agonies when his girlfriend became pregnant. I'm still not ready to reveal too many of my fears so I attempt to write something which diverts his attention away from my weaknesses and suggests I'm perfectly cool about this whole damned business:

Dear brother inferior,
How are you, etc?

Helena and I have decided to keep a journal for her pregnancy. Part of the idea is to collect other people's thoughts on the whole nine-month deal and my particular interest is the male perspective. If you have time, please email your thoughts, especially on the early bits rather than all that drooly stuff when the baby is finally born. For no particular reason, the kind of thing that interests me is whether, once you heard the news:

- *You were scared, proud or just felt plain irresponsible?*
- *You were angry, happy or vaguely resentful?*
- *You felt more or less like stopping smoking, having a few beers or leaving town on the next bus?*
- *It affected your propensity to use contraception in the future, to take up skydiving or buy property?*

Just give me an idea of what went through your head at the time and I'll add your thoughts to our own, objective appraisal.

By the way, did West Ham make it or not? I didn't catch the result!

Yours, etc. Fearless elder brother

P.S. Please don't mention the journal to Helena as she knows nothing about it.

As you'll have no doubt noticed, the line about football is little more than a thinly disguised attempt to deflect his attention from my jangling nerves and give him a concrete reason to react. I know full well that his beloved Hammers were relegated – they always are.

In bed later in the evening, Helena raises the ugliest subject in the world and she asks me directly what I think about the idea of abortion. What's my answer? Well, as usual when I'm on the retreat, I begin by hiding behind the abstract. Opening my defence with a couple of references to the past, I argue that, in principle, I'm against the idea altogether. But Helena instantly sees this for the woolly bullshit that it is. 'Is that your heart talking, or is it really a matter of principle?' she asks. 'It's my instinct,' I say, as if this meant anything at all. The truth is, I'd love to rely on my instinct, but I've been blown about by the prevailing winds for so long now, that I'm not sure if I'd recognise such a thing if it were to kick me wholeheartedly up the backside. I think I left that part of myself on the platform at Paddington station at the age of eleven, along with a plastic bag full of marbles.

I try to calm myself and think the situation through. Has our discussion changed or resolved anything? Not really. So what's the worst thing that can happen? That the baby is born and Helena and I separate before it can get even one candle on a cake? That I'm responsible for adding to the statistics on single motherhood? These are not pleasant thoughts and neither is the realisation that I'm going to have to get back on the phone to my friend in London. No matter how uncomfortable it makes me feel, his advice is usually sound.

'Have you talked to her about abortion?'

'Yes.'

'And what does she think?'

'She didn't say, but I know she wants to keep it.'

'What about you?'

'I don't know.'

'Well, with you trying to give up the drink and both of you going through a rough patch right now, she has to know that you may come out of all this a very different person.'

'And?'

'And you'll have to make a decision on that basis.'

I don't know about you, but this means nothing to me. There's nothing else for it. I'm going to have to try and talk it all through with Helena again. It's either that or flip a coin.

The trouble is, all this is happening at the wrong time. I

can't be too sure what you understand by the term 'rough patch', but he's alluding to the fact that relations with Helena have been less than cordial since I gave the idea of marriage a swift kick in the nuptials. Maybe this suggests to you that each of us played a role in this deteriorating state of affairs, but that wouldn't be true. Helena's behaviour has been entirely consistent over the past 18 months. No, this is my rough patch and mine alone and, to tell you the truth, it's more of a national bloody park than a patch.

Paris, June 3rd

Dirk warned me there'd be days like this and he said that I'd need a big heart when they came. But right now, I'm finding it hard to forgive and forget. Last night I went to a friend's for dinner and my willpower snapped as easily as a piece of dry tinder. I drank some champagne and a glass of red – not much, but enough to spend the rest of the evening in a state of high agitation. Back home, I lied to Helena, got into bed and fell straight into a restless dream: I was still making my way home, half drunk, and the path led through an unfamiliar village, where I came across a girl I once knew. Together we walked down to the shoreline and dived into the ocean. A strong undertow pulled us out into deep waters and then, suddenly, I was back on the street. From the distance, someone who looked a lot like my friend back in London came sprinting towards me, inhaling deeply from expanded lungs. I wanted to say something, but he rushed right past me. When I finally got home, the door of the basement apartment was unlocked and I pushed it open to find nothing but cobwebs inside.

Paris, June 4th

The major event this week is our first trip to the gynaecologist. Helena made the appointment last week and, to my surprise, I find myself asking if I can come along. Perhaps it will make the whole thing seem more real, or maybe this doctor will tell us it's nothing but a bad dream and that I shouldn't eat so many of those rich French cheeses before going to bed.

Her surgery is near enough for us to be able to walk from our apartment and I'm scuffing along kerb-side, not in any great hurry to arrive, when Helena tells me to get a move on. I ask her what's on the agenda and she informs me that it's 'just a check-up', as if we were heading for a routine dental examination: 'Yes, fine, your molars are all still in place. Please see the receptionist and ask for another appointment in six months time.' Yet, as we pad along the worn pavements of Paris, which are positively dribbling with animal piss, I know this is very different. What's more, I suspect I'll be getting to know this short walk fairly well over the coming months.

The waiting room is more or less what I'd expected – all Joan Miró, Modigliani and copies of *Cosmopolitan*. Plenty of expectant mothers litter the deep pile, pale blue carpet and I'm the only man here. We're bang on time for our appointment but, as is the way in this most customer-unfriendly of cities, we're kept waiting for over an hour. This gives me all the time I need to catch up on the latest on the female orgasm and I think I may even be close to deciphering the code of Miró. There's one false alarm when Helena's called to give her personal details to the receptionist, but I stay in my wicker chair and try to find the right expression for the situation – somewhere between art critic and enthusiastic father should do it, I reckon, although an emergency visit to the bathroom mirror reveals more of a Picasso – one of those terrified, green faces with dislocated features drooping uncontrollably onto the floor.

Inevitably I end up sitting next to the woman with a premature baby at her breast. It looks so frail, as if it really should be in a much cosier waiting room for another couple of months. I notice she has a plastic teat fitted to her nipple.

What on earth is that for? Then it registers that I'm staring at the softer parts of a woman in an unusually distracted and biomechanical way. How odd. I try not to gawp and sink deep into a meditation on why it is that, once they turn into mothers, previously circumspect women show no hesitation in breast-feeding their babies in public and couldn't give two hoots about who sees them doing so. I've even observed this phenomenon among long-standing friends of mine when we've shared tents or a hotel room. They went to extraordinary lengths to stop me catching even a glimpse of their breasts when I've spent hours manipulating myself into precisely the right position to do just that. But the minute they've given birth, that's all forgotten. Suddenly they're whacking their tits out all over the place, as if they could no longer wait to show men the purpose for which they were intended all along. Life can seem so unfair at times.

A little later, a nurse appears in the waiting room and the woman and bird-baby are called in to see the doctor. Then the nurse comes back out with the baby in her arms, but she isn't supporting its neck properly and the frail little thing lolls alarmingly backwards and away from the outstretched fingers of the nurse. 'Who wants to look after baby for a minute?' she asks, trying to make light of the fact that she has damned near broken its neck. Jesus, even I'll have a go if that's the best you can manage. But, arms spread like the Madonna in every renaissance painting you've ever seen, all the expectant mothers in the house beat me to it. Helena comes a close second in the race to envelop the innocent one and settles for chatting with the winner. Now everyone in the whole room is beaming at baby and touching their stomachs. Well, almost everyone.

The dangerous nurse reappears and finally Helena's name is called. She leads us into the surgery and promptly strides round to the other side of a large oak desk. This is strange, I think: we're more than an hour late and now this nurse is impersonating a fully qualified gynaecologist. I'm just about to point out that I consider this to be in very poor taste when she starts asking Helena a series of very detailed questions about her periods. I'm incredulous. You mean, this is the doctor? But she nearly killed that baby out there! How can this woman ever be trusted? But Helena is serenely answering this woman's questions, leaving me to panic and seethe alone.

'So, you're about to become a father.'

What was that? Is she talking to me?

'Congratulations!'

She is talking to me.

'How old are you?'

I stumble so badly over *quarante quatre* that, by the time I get it out, it sounds more like four hundred and forty-four.

'A fine age to become a father for the first time' opines the madwoman and I can think of no suitable rejoinder to that.

This is followed by a brief review of the blood test results with which the 'doctor' seems pleased and then Helena is asked to undress before the bogus one starts working me over once more.

'So. You're English?'

I know, I know. I'm sorry. I'm well aware that we're not supposed to be running around interfering with pure French bloodstock and all that, but she had her part in it too, you know. In fact, it was mainly her idea.

'Yes,' I say.

The retort is instantaneous: 'Never mind, you'll still be able to assist at the birth.'

What does she mean 'assist'? If she means watching, well that's fine, I'll be watching with the best of them, unless there's any blood, in which case I plan on passing right out if that's alright with Your Majesty.

'Well,' I say, 'Helena will, um, be doing all of the work, as the woman, I mean.'

I stop talking before I say anything more stupid, though

not quickly enough to avoid the full force of another of those disdainful French expressions which start above the eyebrows and descend the full length of an aquiline nose, before being cast out with the rest of the compost.

Then she's gone again, to a place somewhere over my left shoulder where I sense that Helena is in a compromising position. I keep my eyes focused on the oak desk, searching for the evidence she's an impostor.

'Come and have a look,' she suggests.

At what? I think. Helena has specifically told me there'll be no pictures for at least another month. But now I'm looking at a black and white screen as the doctor points to something resembling a small white worm.

'There it is,' she exclaims. 'It's about eight millimetres long. Can you see the beating heart?'

My eyes are frozen to the screen. Did she say 'heart'? It has a visible heart already? Can that possibly be true? I'm so fascinated by the image that I only half follow the rest of the doctor's observations – 'very small', 'just a few weeks old', 'everything healthy', 'congratulations', 'see you in a few weeks time... '

I find myself pointing ill-advisedly to a large shaded area of dark grey that dominates one corner of the screen.

'What's that?'

'That shows your wife is desperate to go to the toilet.'

I say nothing for the remainder of the visit, not even to correct the doctor's erroneous assumption concerning our civil status. Luckily, all that remains is for a few arrangements to be made regarding our next visit before the doctor issues a final instruction for Helena to avoid cat piss for the remainder of her pregnancy (she has no immunity against something called toxoplasmosis). Other than that, she can't drink for three months, she can't smoke and she certainly can't eat any of those maggoty French cheeses she so adores. I, on the other hand, am perfunctorily informed that I can continue to do all of these things, as if my role in the whole affair were already complete.

So, what about the abortion, I hear you ask? After all, it's only a worm, right? Well, maybe it is but, as it turns out, Helena and I have already had our last discussion on that particular subject.

Paris, June 6th

Did I already mention that you're not supposed to tell anyone about a pregnancy until the first three months have been safely navigated? Anything can happen in the first trimester and even our homicidal gynaecologist has warned us to keep shtum for the time being. So who's in the know? Well, on my side there's my mother (who told my sister); I told my friend back in London – clearly essential if I was to avoid spontaneous combustion – and of course there's my brother, but I'm going to argue that little lot constitutes family and different rules apply. Meanwhile, the baby's mother is steadily working her way through the Parisian phonebook and has told just about everyone *except* her family. Helena's a teacher and I'm not sure whether she's gone quite so far as to make a broadcast to the school at large, but most of her colleagues appear to be privy to the information. Then there are her friends in and around Paris, the cousin in London, most of the population of Holland, plus large tracts of northern Italy. Other than her parents, I've begged her not to tell anyone else, but Helena is so happy she's unable to contain herself. 'But it's way too early,' I protest, 'you're four weeks pregnant and anything can happen over the next two months. I don't want you to be disappointed.' I'm wasting my time of course. Helena is convinced this baby is 'strong' and there's no doubt in her mind that that all eight millimetres of this particular worm will stay the course and duly become eight pounds, eight years old, eight miles high and so on.

Helena sees the world that way. As far as she's concerned, things are either black or white, while I inhabit a zone of almost permanent grey – a place of great uncertainty in which my main priority has always been to avoid anything that smells remotely of commitment. Allow me to illustrate: my mother has just been on the phone again, and she's an absolute specialist when it comes to probing my weaknesses and asking the questions I daren't ask myself. As well as the obvious ones about jobs and my ability to pay the rent, she's just hit me with the other thing that's been nagging away at the back of my head for the past couple of weeks. Yes, that's right – the only commitment which can conceivably rival raising a child – marriage.

It all started innocently enough:

'How's Helena?'

'She's fine, thanks.'

'Have you been to the gynaecologist?'

Only then did I remember I promised to call and tell her all about it. Shit! Two questions in and I'm already firmly on the back foot.

'Yeah, it was fine. Everything's fine.'

'Only you said you were going to call me, and when I didn't hear... ' I hate it when she employs that trailing-off tactic.

'Yeah. Sorry about that. It's just been so hectic lately.'

This wasn't even close to the truth, although I thought it sounded more plausible than admitting I plain forgot. I was also hoping it might make me sound slightly less of a heartless bastard.

'What about Helena's parents?'

'What about them?'

'Have you told them yet?

'No, Helena doesn't want to.' I didn't want to go into detail here and this proved to be another major, tactical error, allowing my mother to head the conversation where she probably wanted to take it all along.

'What are they going to say?'

'I don't know. I expect they'll be delighted.'

'But you're not married!'

'Lots of people have babies without being married.' By now I could feel the quicksands sucking at my ankles.

'That's not what I mean and you know it. They're going to think you're not committed to Helena.'

At this point, I started adding what I imagined to be a bit of gravitas to my voice in an effort to limit the damage: 'Oh, I don't think they'll be worried about that. After all, her brother isn't married and his girlfriend's pregnant for the second time.' I made sure there was plenty of emphasis on the word 'girlfriend' but it made little difference. By now she was truly on a roll.

'The brother that doesn't like you?'

'It's not that he doesn't like me.'

'But you went down in his estimation when you pulled out of the wedding, didn't you?'

Ah yes! Helena's brother. As far as I'm concerned he's the one who should be shouldering most of the blame for this mess in the first place. When he left Asia, he took his girlfriend to Barcelona where she fell pregnant. So they packed once more and moved back to Paris where I happened to be visiting friends. Anyway, I got invited over for a glass or two to celebrate the birth and I had a feeling that Helena might be there so I prepared a little speech before I went: 'I'm sorry I didn't call but you know how it is. It was never going to work, you know, what with us being 11,000 miles apart and me not remembering your name.' Only things didn't quite work out the way I'd planned – pretty soon we were ignoring everyone else at the party and, after two glasses of champagne and an uneaten curry, we picked up where we'd left off in Asia. The fact that she couldn't speak English and I was operating on my long-lost school French must have helped, because I insisted upon lunch the follow-ing day and she thought I meant breakfast. You can probably guess the rest.

Paris, June 7th

Today we're off to spend a couple of days with Helena's parents and, over a breakfast of *All Bran*, with which I secretly hope to replace the moral fibre which appears to have gone missing from my body, I ask Helena whether she intends to give them the news. 'No' she says firmly, 'it's still too soon.' I resist the temptation to point out that since the rest of Fifth Republic already knows, there's a danger they'll hear it from another source and it might just be better coming from us. Instead I sip at my coffee and wonder whether the delay will buy me more time to concoct a decent story before I'm confronted by Helena's father.

Her parents live in Normandy, not far from the D-Day beaches. I wouldn't mention this, but lurking at the back of my mind is the idea that their proximity will somehow make them more sympathetic to the idea that their daughter is now pregnant to an Englishman and ex-Ally who has asked her for her hand and promptly reneged on the agreement without proffering anything remotely resembling a coherent explanation. I board the train in Paris with the expression of a donkey that has outlived its usefulness and suspects it's on its way to the pet food factory.

Although Helena insists she won't be imparting the fateful information to her parents, I know that she will. I can tell by the way that she denies it all the way out to Normandy while I watch the dairy cows of Camembert country fly past the windows of the train. At the station, we're picked up by Helena's father. He looks really pleased to see his daughter and even manages to smile at me. The fact is that Helena's father is an amiable, gentle soul and this lifts the donkey's spirits just a little as I attempt a smile of my own.

We've been in the house for a full fifteen minutes before I leave the bedroom in which I've dumped the bags and remained hidden for as long as I dare. Meanwhile, Helena has been talking to her father and when I sit down at their crowded kitchen table, her father immediately gets up and leaves.

'He knows,' says Helena, her voice an excited half-whisper.

'You told him?'

'No, I think he just guessed.'

'How?'

'He keeps smiling at me in a knowing way.'

'Maybe he's just pleased to see you.'

But her father is a paediatrician at the local hospital. For the past 30 years, he's been looking into the faces of women who've just given birth or are about to do so and he's still smiling when he returns from the garden with the heads of a few dead flowers which he's lopped off with a chillingly large pair of secateurs. Maybe he just smiles more than I remember?

In the evening, the four of us (or should that be five?) head out to dinner and Helena starts to behave in a way that's guaranteed to give the game away. First she refuses to sit at the table to which our waiter directs us. Why? Because the people at the table next door are smoking. Helena's parents have seen their only daughter enjoying an after dinner cigarette often enough, but tonight they say nothing and we move tables. Then her father orders a bottle of wine. First I refuse a glass then Helena follows suit. Still they say nothing. We start ordering the food. This is never a simple process with Helena but pregnancy has complicated it tenfold. My preferred method for selecting an item from a menu is quite simple – I choose the starter that I fancy and I order it. Then I repeat the process for the main course. But Helena prefers to regard the menu as a lengthy list of individual ingredients, any of which she's free to combine according to her own taste. What's more, she's convinced that such cross-fertilisation is acceptable across an array of starters, main courses and any number of set menus. For example, she may prefer to combine the duck from menu A with the asparagus from menu B, and have the whole lot in a sauce which belongs to the *menu de dégustation*. Surprisingly, this kind of request is often tolerated in France, whereas in England, you'd politely be told that the chef has enough problems sticking to the one page of his *Delia Smith* and requested to kindly stop fucking with his head. Perhaps Helena's parents are less embarrassed than I am by her gastronomic quirks and foibles because they don't even blink when she orders prawns grilled to extinction as a starter and follows them up with an overdone steak in a sauce she read about in a women's magazine earlier that week. In spite of all this incinerated flesh, we get through the meal with Helena's parents still labouring under the illusion that their daughter is without child and about to come to her senses by dumping the Englishman over a cup of decaffeinated coffee.

D-Day arrives a little later than usual in Normandy, June 8th

In the morning we get rumbled. Helena's mother and I are contentedly watching two muscular tennis players that used to be women grind each other into the red dust of *Roland Garros* while Helena and her father chat in the garden. At one point they pass through the periphery of my vision and I sense they're both beaming but it's tie-break time at the French Open and the armchair and I seem to have melted into one.

Shortly after the Williams sisters have been hosed down, I discover Helena has confessed all to her father. He got the ball rolling by asking whether she'd changed her mind about not wanting children. Perhaps he'd suspected all along. As we straddle our bikes for a ride to the beach, however, Helena still insists that she's not ready to tell her mother. 'Fine,' I grunt, 'but surely you can't expect your poor father to keep the secret for the next eight months?'

By the time we're back from the beach, Helena's father is preparing a small shoal of mackerel for the barbecue and informs me that he's got a bottle of champagne on ice. Champagne? Does that mean he sees this as an event worth celebrating? I hadn't expected that! Unfortunately for Helena, however, her father thinks his wife should be told why the rest of us are making merry. Once again I try to impress upon Helena the inexorable logic of his argument and finally she snaps.

'OK, you tell her then.'

'Me?'

But Helena is adamant and sheepishly I inform her father the task has fallen to me. He smiles again as I retreat to the bookshelf to look up the vocab necessary to compose a couple of sentences along the lines of, 'Sit down, please. Here are the smelling salts. You'll be needing these once I tell you what I've done to your daughter this time.'

Back in the garden, Helena's father jemmies the champagne cork out of the bottle with an announcement about there being something to celebrate.

'Oh, what's that?' asks his wife.

'Some good news!' he says.

Suddenly everyone is looking at me, including the damned mackerel and I stammer it out: '*Oui, c'est ta fille... Elle est, um, enceinte.*'

As soon as the words are out of my mouth, I realise I've made a huge error. I'm supposed to address Helena's parents, both individually and as a couple, as *vous,* although they get to use the more familiar *tu* when speaking to me. This is one more aspect of a French love of hierarchy and formality that I'll never fathom, much less get my head around grammatically. Yet I know I've made a serious mistake because Helena has spent hours with nothing but me and a book of French verbs for company and now she's kicking my shins under the table. I'm so busy contemplating an afternoon's detention that I barely notice the kerfuffle my announcement has caused. Helena's father is alternately pouring and swigging champagne and her mother is leaping up and down so erratically that I'm beginning to worry about the proximity of the hot coals on the barbecue. Despite the confusion, I'm refusing the champagne and, bizarrely, Helena's mother is rubbing it into my wrists as if it were new fragrance by *Chanel.* Helena has tears in her eyes and, before I know what's going on, I'm being kissed and congratulated, which is not at all what I'd anticipated. What is it about babies that the mere mention of them is sufficient for people to overlook the most serious errors of etiquette?

Caen, June 9th

I'm kicking back in the garden as Helena takes another of her increasingly regular naps. Her father suggests a game of chess and, in the name of family spirit, I agree. Naturally I let him win the first game within about ten moves. I figure this has to be a wise move, in case it was all a bit of a show yesterday and his true intent is not so much to win a game of chess but rather to tear me limb from limb. Either way, I see no point in further provocation. I try a little harder in the second game and it takes a full twenty moves before he's reduced my side of the board to something resembling the face of an amateur boxer minus his gum shield.

To avoid further humiliation, I start to talk about the future and soon catch myself saying I'm about to make my return to marketing. I am? So how come I swore blind I'd never contemplate any such thing? Then someone pretending to be me says that Helena and I are thinking of buying a house when, in truth, I spent a full twenty minutes dismissing the idea out of hand only last Thursday. As I pointed out to Helena at the time, French bank managers are not renowned for financing swanky, left bank apartments for ageing, unemployed neurotics in full mid-life crisis. I round off my fanciful monologue with an addendum about buying a car and, as I ramble and rave, Helena's father just sucks on a pipe and occasionally nods. I'd almost prefer him to call my bluff. Exercising remarkable restraint, he has never brought up the subject of me chickening out of the marriage and I don't want to tell any more lies for which I'll have to account on my deathbed. So how do I repay him for his hospitality, for not asking the question to which I have no answer, and for the barbecued mackerel? Do I get down on my knees, beg forgiveness and offer to do the washing-up? I do not. I demand another game of chess. Perhaps he's just taken pity on me for being so patently self-delusional, but late in the game I finally force one of my rooks behind his defence and put him inadvertently into checkmate.

On the train home, my thoughts turn to the situation that Helena and I are facing back in Paris. The fact that her parents now know renders the whole situation that bit more real. For an hour, the train rumbles through a series of Norman stone villages. Every time we stop, I watch as parents wave goodbye to children who are returning to work in the big city. Is this the future for me? Surely not. I've no idea how to put another's needs before my own and as far as supporting anyone else is concerned, my negligence knows no bounds. I haven't done an honest day's work for a very long time, I'm living a dream, a fantasy that I won't have to go back to corporate whoring. But now there's a baby on the way. A nipper! Before I know it, there'll be shoes and clothes to buy. Another few months and it may even need to be fed something other than the milk of its mother, something that will cost money. And where's it going to live? With its parents, I suppose, but they live in a glorified shoe box with nowhere for the innocent one to lay its head.

Back in Paris, I postpone, yet again, any serious thought regarding these issues by opening my email. Buried among all the advertising for legal highs and dick enlargement (the last thing on my mind at the moment) I find an email from my brother. I hesitate for a moment. Do I really need this right now? Oh, what the fuck:

Dear older yet smaller brother,

Nice to hear from you, and congrats once again. I don't really have too many clear recollections about the pregnancy but, for what it's worth, here's a response to your questions...

1. I was never really nervous about the baby despite our unmarried status. Of course, I had all the usual male doubts about whether I'd be able to cope with all the crying and nappy changing once the thing was born, not to mention the money it takes for feeding, clothing, schooling and so on.

This is not exactly a promising start although there's some small comfort in knowing that he obviously felt the same fears as I do. I also take a cheap snigger at his use of the word 'thing'.

2. I did a piss-poor job of proposing to my wife, saying something like 'I suppose we'd better get married then' – not exactly what she'd imagined from her knight in shining armour. I never did buy her a real engagement ring.

Yeah, well don't worry about it, mate. Believe me, it runs in the family! You may not be Casanova, but at least you got round to it eventually. I retreated even faster than Napoleon at the Russian front.

3. We got into the baby thing quite early, reading a book entitled 'What to expect when you're expecting' and imagining the kid as he passed through his various stages – from the size of a lentil to an olive, through to that of an orange, all of which we were able to monitor on the ultrasound. This proved to be a convincing demonstration that he was already with us and I remember once seeing his hand waving to us and feeling a flush of pride. This was followed somewhat later by some live action, the highlight of which was watching his elbow lifting the skin of his mother's belly as he rolled over, just like something out of 'Alien' as John Hurt is about to have his guts exploded by the emerging creature.

Is this permissible? Comparing your son to a bunch of vegetables and then a vengeful, slimy monster? I turn to see Helena stretched out on the bed and think better of it. Maybe it's the kind of thing you can get away with after the birth? Perversely, it makes me feel a bit more human.

4. We spent a lot of time painting the kid's room and buying furniture; a baby chair for the car, clothes, bottles, pram, etc., all of which kept us busy beforehand.

Yes well, the less said about that the better.

5. I also remember when we first found out we were having a boy and seeing his neat little organ staring out from the screen. I didn't want to let on, but I was quite disappointed because I was really hoping for a little girl. 'Course, I'm real happy with the boy now.

Ah good! Clear evidence of deceit! Things are beginning to look up.

6. Having a baby was the straw that broke the camel's back for the smoking thing – I'd been having chest pains for some time and I knew I'd have to quit.

Yeah, alright. Don't you start. I'll get round to it eventually.

7. Responsibility was an issue – I'm not, was not and probably never will be very responsible, so I did worry whether I'd be able to handle it all. As it turns out, I needn't have bothered and of course I can cope, even if his mother does most of the work.

That's true, too. Compared to my brother, I'm a model of responsibility and, selfishly, I take further comfort from this – he's an excellent father and if he can do it then so can I. By now I'm beginning to feel pretty smug about my chances.

8. Did I ever consider backing out, dumping the wife and letting her go it alone? Surprisingly, no. Not for one moment. If I thought about it at all, having a kid seemed like a natural progression. My biggest fear was whether I was up to it and how I was going to fit the needs of a baby around my impermanent lifestyle.

As I read that first sentence, a moment's reflection is followed by a sharp pang of guilt. Had I ever considered such a thing? Hell no, not really. Well, OK then, I suppose I did, but only for a couple of days and not a second longer than that.

9. Overall, I was calm and spent quite a bit of time reassuring his mother and helping her overcome her cravings and fears and slowly coming to terms with what was happening inside her (which took the best part of six months). We got into the growing baby by listening, reading, positive thinking and trying to keep the atmosphere calm and tranquil by singing to the baby and playing brain-forming classical music.

Brain-forming classical music! What the hell is he talking about? Just when I was getting used to the whole idea, he hits me with this shit – listening, reading and getting into what? Helena and me are just about talking. Will that do?

That's about it as I recall, but I'll let you know if I can think of anything else. Cheers and love to Helena...

Helena is rudely awakened as I crash shut my laptop. 'Everything alright?' she asks. 'Just fine,' I say and head moodily for the bathroom. The person brushing his teeth in the mirror opposite calls me an asshole and insists I'll never pull this one off.

I think Helena's already given up on the idea of us ever having sex again, at least for the duration of the pregnancy, and by the time Mr Moody gets back from the bathroom, she's asleep again. Yes, I know I'm supposed to be the one who finds pregnant women sexy and all that, but she's already beginning to put on a bit of weight. It's not as if she's getting any particular cravings or downing six gallons of *Häagen Dazs* at a single sitting, more that she generally likes to eat a lot. Normally she'd go for a run a couple of times a week around the small patch of green that passes for a park in this city, but she hasn't done any exercise at all since she got pregnant and has added more than a kilo already. Not much, I grant you, but just the wrong side of enough. I'm still in the doghouse so I haven't said anything about it yet but I can't help feeling that it's not quite fair on me.

Paris, June 11th

Sneaking another look at *Future Maman*, it surprises me to discover our baby now has a tongue and that its facial features are already forming, along with the skin and the vertebral column. At least I can take comfort in knowing we won't be giving birth to an invertebrate... Jesus! How can anybody read this stuff? This week's charming instalment describes the potential effects upon the foetus of, among other things, AIDS, syphilis, toxoplasmosis and hepatitis, and provides a long list of the causes of spontaneous abortion. And that's not all. It also tells you what to do if you find blood in your underwear. (I've checked mine already and they seem to be clear but if you're not so lucky, you should get onto your doctor right away.) The chapter ends with a piece about something called the cytomegalovirus. I don't even want to know what that is. Just the sound of it is enough to wipe out an entire family before breakfast. I think I'm going to put this book down for good and just let nature take its course.

The reason all Anglo-French joint ventures are such a bad idea, June 12th

Tonight we're having dinner with Inès, a distant cousin of Helena here in Pigalle, and, to make matters worse, the cousin is pregnant and her smug, balding husband (yes, of course they're married) is a salesman for a mechanical escalator company. I've met them a couple of times before, the last time at some dinner party where the husband pressed me quite unmetaphorically up against the wall for more than an hour while he tried to sell me the benefits of the world's fastest moving walkway. It's at Montparnasse station, right here in Paris, just in case you happen to be more interested than I was. All I can remember about our conversation is that the damned thing is divided into three pieces and it slows down right at the end to prevent some old dear and her pet chihuahua getting slammed into the ticket office at 150 kilometres per hour.

Anyway, in the hope of avoiding all the baby talk, I've already manufactured an excuse to be late and when I arrive, shortly before dawn, Mr Escalator greets me and shows me around their model home: 'And this is the baby's room,' he says, pointing to a small palace tucked away in the west wing of their beautiful bourgeois apartment. I think of the equivalent at our place – an outsized hole in the skirting board from which Helena currently runs her nascent ceramics business. 'Not bad,' I sniff.

Not bad? It takes us fully half an hour to walk back to the dinner table, by which time my morale has sunk lower than a sausage dog's nuts. We rejoin Helena and the Escalator's wife who are nibbling olives and talking about nausea. Now there's a subject I know something about, although right now I prefer to keep my counsel and focus instead on polishing off an excellent aubergine dip.

At one point Cousin Inès gets up and heads for the kitchen. For the first time, I see her in profile. My God, she's huge! 'How many months is that?' I manage to stammer once I've regained control of the muscles in my lower jaw.

'Six and a half,' she exclaims, patting proudly the shelving units which have replaced a once slimline belly.

I want to ask Inès how it feels, whether it hurts or whether the metro doors have ever closed on her new storage system, but I can feel Helena's eyeballs boring into my neck and manage to bury myself back in the nibbles just in time.

Mr Escalator is clearly feeling even more pleased with himself than usual and recounts the story of their beautiful wedding (he knows all about our own aborted plans, which is presumably why we're hearing this story in the first place). He's thrilled about becoming a father, he's delighted with the bottle of *Chablis* which I'm not drinking, and he's just ecstatic about the dinner that he's whipped up all by himself – gazpacho, grilled pomfret with endives and peach pie for dessert. Pretty good it is too, I feel forced to admit.

But when he starts bleating about the chances of the French at this year's Rugby World Cup, I feel obliged to draw the line. My inferiority complex is not insignificant even without him doing his best to stoke its smouldering embers, but by now I've had enough and launch a vicious counter-attack. First I establish my credentials by delving back into the past, citing the wonderful Blanco, Sella and Jean-Pierre Rives. Then I draw him carefully towards the trap door by praising the ball-handling skills of *les Bleus* in general and, as he begins to puff himself up into a shape prouder than the cockerel which adorns the shirts of his idols, I take aim with the sucker punch: 'But it's the mentality of the French players that worries me so – whether they truly have the spirit necessary to win after so many deflating losses – against the English, of course, but also against the *irlandais*' (and, French style, I lengthen the pronunciation of this word beyond all reason in order to prolong the agony). 'And both of these,' I continue, 'within the recent confines of the Six Nations tournament.' Before my host can even think about drawing breath, I quickly add a list of other famous French defeats – against the Australians in a long gone World Cup final, against Wellington at Waterloo and, of course, against Henry V at Agincourt.

Now this kind of insult to French pride is bad enough, but when it comes from an Englishman it's almost unbearable. I get away with it, but only because of the bond forming between the two women who are elegantly polishing off the peach pie at the other end of the table, while we two go at it as if the Hundred Years' War were just getting started.

'What was the matter with you in there?' asks Helena as we walk home.

'What do you mean?'

'You know perfectly well what I mean. Why were you so aggressive?'

'I was just having a little fun.'

'Fun? I don't think we'll get invited back.'

'You don't think so?' I try to suppress the stadium-sized cheer welling in my belly.

But Helena's right. I behaved appallingly and it's all born out of jealousy and a loathing of my own inadequacies. Mr Escalator will undoubtedly become a gentle, caring father, a model husband and all round provider. He already has a job, a fantastic apartment and a bedroom (plus matching potty) set aside for his baby that just reeks of new paint. I, on the other hand, have none of these things.

I used to have a job, and quite a good one at that. For many years I was on the payroll of a marketing services company which produced expensive but very cheaply-bound reports for a series of high street retailers. At one point I was even invited to join the executive 'bored', although this was probably a case of mistaken identity. Anyway, it was as my career neared its premature end that I met Helena for the second time and immediately began preparing a move to Paris, where I planned to do little other than indulge my fantasies of writing Oscar-winning screenplays and drinking wine, while Helena continued her hard labour at the *lycée*. Then came that marriage proposal, after which we spent the best part of twelve months darting about between London and Paris, disturbing the sleep of any fish that survive in that stretch of the Channel, and doing our bit to keep the ailing *Eurotunnel* afloat. It was very romantic, as I'm sure you'll understand – weekends lazing about on the *rive gauche* for me and an introduction to the pleasures of Bermondsey and the Isle of Dogs for Helena.

I told her how I'd grown bored of my job, and about my one idea for a film, and she encouraged me to follow my dreams. Once installed in Paris, she probably expected me to open the laptop and take up where Proust and Sartre had left off, only I felt more at home lounging in the pavement cafés observing the local fauna. Finally I produced a short story for my niece and nephew. Intellectually, I doubt it satisfied even these two pre-teens, but it nearly did for me. After a few weeks off with nervous exhaustion, I enrolled on a screenwriting course at the American University in Paris (largely because the homework comprised nothing more arduous than regular trips to the cinema) and that's how I got started with this damned film script.

But one evening in the company of Escalator Man has confirmed that the game is up now. I'll have to earn some money soon because babies start costing you a fortune long before they emerge from the womb. Not that this means I'm prepared to listen to Helena's views on the subject. What happened to all her Bohemian ideals anyway? Six months ago it was all, 'Come on, let's throw everything into the back of a truck and move to Provence!' What truck? What everything? And anyway, what would I do in Provence? Write odes to lavender and sunflower oil? But all that was several long months back. More recently, our daily dialogue goes something like this:

'I really think going back to work would do you good. Perhaps you could find something part-time.'

'Doing what?'

'The things you're good at.'

'Like smoking *Gauloises* and getting a bit of service in a Parisian café? Who's going to pay me for that?'

'No, not that,' Helena will say, with more patience than I deserve. Then she'll mention the marketing word, and I'll run screaming from the room.

Part of the problem is that Helena has noticed the inadequacy of our apartment and our lack of a car. I've offered to affix a baby seat to the back of my bike, but that suggestion was greeted with about as much enthusiasm as a mouse with its legs tied together reserves for a burly tomcat. She's also becoming suspicious about the effect that my stunted and stuttering screenplay is having on my mind, and it's true that, lately, I haven't been getting out that much. I prefer to stay at home and spend my time endlessly rewriting scene one and swearing at the Albanian labourers who are demolishing the apartment opposite. I'm way too stubborn to admit that Helena may have a point about the screenplay. But she's right, I'm driving her, and most likely myself, completely mad. At some point I'm going to have to stop writhing as pointlessly as a lugworm on a fisherman's hook and start looking for some kind of a job.

Reluctantly, I pull out my old CV. Hmmm, this is going to require quite a bit of creativity. I'll start first thing in the morning.

Paris, on the morning after Friday 13th

How could I have allowed it to happen? I guess I'm underestimating the hold this addiction has over me. People told me not to go to the party but I thought I could go and stay out of trouble. I guess I must have lied to myself again. Drinking my *Coke*, I was all right for a couple of hours until someone pressed something stronger into my hand. I unclenched my jawbones, relaxed my grip and promptly lost all control. I got home at around five in the morning. I'm tired and hung over alright, but worse than that, I'm totally confused.

Paris, June 16th

Today marks the start of the seventh week of pregnancy and I'm hoping to spend as much of it as possible under the covers without answering any unpleasant questions about why it takes a week to put a CV together. To pre-empt any such eventuality, I'm already brandishing our copy of *Future Maman* when Helena walks into the room and I launch straight into a set of carefully prepared diversionary tactics.

'Do you want me to tell you what it looks like now?'

'Go on then... '

'Well, he measures between seventeen and twenty-two millimetres.'

'He?'

'What?'

'You said 'he'. I thought you were sure it's a girl?'

'No, I think it's a boy.'

'Is it still too early to tell?'

'Yes, but the eyes are forming already and he, or she, now has eyelashes, fingers, toes and the beginnings of a cerebral cortex.'

'I hope he's better endowed than his father in that respect' says Helena.

Her comment sets me thinking and, as Helena reads up on some stuff about the presence or absence of zinc, fluoride, iodine and a host of other vitamins and mineral salts, the intellectually towering conclusion I reach is the following: If the baby is already forming all these bits and pieces, then, inevitably, it'll end up taking after either me or Helena. A logical enough deduction, you might say (if you felt like avoiding the word crude), but the implications of this, my very own share of the inheritance of centuries of great philosophical thought, are, to borrow a phrase from Descartes himself, simply gob-smacking: this thing, this baby, shorter still than half the length of my little finger, already has almost half of the equipment it will need for its seventy-odd year passage on earth (if you discount the DVD player, two mobile phones and a pair of *Adidas Stan Smith*). Otherwise, most of its limbs, facial features and tics are rapidly nearing completion and it already resembles one or perhaps both of its parents. I may be slow, but at least the true wonder of all this is beginning to penetrate the low-lying fog which permanently envelops my brain.

The evolution of polite Parisian society since the last millennium, June 17th

Helena gets back from school in a bad temper.

'How's the CV?' she asks abruptly.

'Well, I've printed it off,' I say hopefully.

No reply. No wonder she's in a stinking mood – yet another spate of strikes is affecting daily life in France and it has taken her almost four hours to do the round trip to the suburbs. Also affected are the post office, the railways, the refuse service and the schools themselves (where the teachers are threatening not to allow the annual *baccalauréat* examinations to proceed). The French have closed just about everything today, other than their precious *boulangeries*, which would probably remain open through a nuclear war, and the streets of Paris are alive with demonstrators and the wail of meat-wagons carrying their intimidating cargo of cropped, baton-wielding police from the CRS corps.

This stand-off has been dragging on for weeks and Helena refuses to join her colleagues on strike although the walk to work isn't doing much for her health and she regularly returns home with a face like a thoroughbred forced to give rides at Blackpool beach. My suggestion that she rest on the bed does nothing to improve her mood.

'Look,' I say firmly, brandishing a paper given to us by the psychopathic gynaecologist, 'it says here you've got to get lots of rest.' Helena just looks at me, her eyes underlined with tiredness. I might just as well have informed her that the earth is no longer round. Undeterred, I push on and reel off a long list of things (explicitly highlighted in bold font) that she shouldn't be doing, including long, arduous commutes into the suburbs.

'Just how do you suggest I get to school then? We don't have a car.'

I decide against offering her my bicycle and settle instead for putting the kettle on and trying to keep a low profile.

'Anyway, I'm not going back,' she says.

'But you've only got two more weeks till the start of the holidays!' As well as having a shorter working career than the average male praying mantis, teachers in France get more holiday than you squeeze into a fattened-up Christmas *Filofax*.

'No. I mean I'm not going back to that gynaecologist.'

Even if I haven't yet finished reading all of those articles in *Cosmopolitan* about what it is that women are looking for in men (other than a six pack, the Swiss bank account, three orgasms a week and a modicum of common sense), I'm taken aback by this piece of news. But I must be quite pleased at the same time, because I hear myself endorsing her decision with the speed of a spiked greyhound at Walthamstow dogs. 'Yeah, did you notice she only had one eyebrow? The woman was clearly unstable and she hated the English.'

'It's nothing to do with that,' says Helena, wearily. 'She's private and the insurance company won't cover the costs.'

Despite her exhaustion Helena will now have to go through another round of phone calls to find a doctor that doesn't keep toddlers in her fridge freezer, and since I'm going to be of very little assistance in this process, I resolve not to burden her with all the issues which, although important to me, can probably wait for another decade. Ah well, there goes my list of light conversational topics for dinner, such as the saturated fat content of the three great Normandy cheeses, my little treatise on excess proteins and their effect upon the mood and, of course, the Gisele Bündchen guide to a perfect figure.

In a hapless attempt at redemption, I hit the all-night video store to distract Helena's attention from some of my more obvious failings. But her eyes roll to the heavens the minute one set of celluloid gangsters begins disembowelling their on-screen rivals. She simply cannot understand why anybody might consider any form of violence as entertainment, especially when you consider what's going on out there somewhere for real (just outside the *Assemblée Nationale* here in Paris, for example, where the police and the citizens of France are currently beating each other over the head with an assortment of the finest French sausages). Entertainment without violence – is such a thing possible? Not for the male half of the planet, it isn't.

This reminds me of how I'd once tell anyone unlucky enough to live within five miles of the fortified ramparts of my shabby bedsit that I considered it totally irresponsible to bring children into a place as despicable as planet earth in the late twentieth century. As it turned out, my true motive was either to impress or to explain away why I was unable to hold down a relationship long enough to contemplate parenthood. Anyway, by the time the main character in this film is bludgeoned with a baseball bat and then buried alive, I'm beginning to wonder if perhaps I wasn't right all along. Once in bed I place my hand on Helena's belly although I'm not sure if this is to reassure myself or to protect the peace and innocence of the unborn.

Paris, June 19th

Helena's all-time favourite film is one that should never have been made in the first place because it's about ballet dancing (rather than football). I confess there's one other, exceedingly small, reason which may account for my attempts to deny its existence: when I was a kid, my mother persuaded me to take ballet lessons. That's right, while most of my friends were out straining their groins and kicking lumps out of each other with football boots still fashioned out of real cow hide, I was pulling on a pair of unmanly tights and hoping that my friends wouldn't spot me in a tutu in the back of our old family *Ford Corsair*. I hated it so much that even my mother's steely determination to turn her son into a once-weekly daughter endured for only twelve months. Now, of course, I wonder what would have happened had I continued and almost regret giving it up. Even having to pack out my tights with a bunch of midget bananas and endure everyone calling me a 'poof' has got to be better than my current pickle – no job, a leaky CV, a swollen liver, and two and a quarter pages of a film script that wouldn't make the grade on Australian daytime TV. As the dancing begins, Helena is in raptures and I fall headlong into my preferred cocktail of childhood regrets, until an alien thought unexpectedly worms its way into my head. It's about twenty millimetres long and made of pure, expanded DNA. From its warm, cosseting bath of placental fluid it knows nothing of the potential opportunities and disappointments which lie ahead. Maybe, just maybe, I can make a better fist of being a father than I have done a son.

French homework, Paris, June 23rd

Like every French man, woman and child I begin the new week with a visit to the *boulangerie*. Absolutely nothing comes between the French and their daily baguette. I don't know whether it's actually illegal for bakers to strike in France, but if they ever do, I'm sure it will incite a revolution to rival anything that happened back in 1789. Within one block of where we live there are no fewer than five bakeries, each with its own speciality loaf and rabid band of devotees. Personally, I prefer to flit between them as I love to imagine them cursing into their dough and trying endlessly to counter my infidelity.

This morning I'm out on the street early, weighing up the relative merits of the *la Flûte Gana* and *la Renaissance*, both ostensibly mere loaves of white bread, but each with its own secret recipe and a history longer than that of the Fifth Republic itself. Only in France could a combination of yeast, flour and water spend a few minutes in the oven and arise ennobled as the *Renaissance.* Maybe I've been in this country too long, but only this morning does the true absurdity of these names hit me. I'm sure you can get your choppers around the *la Reformation* or *la Belle Epoque* somewhere in Paris and, for all I know, there's a short, stumpy and lopsided loaf out there somewhere all dressed up in full military regalia and calling itself *le Napoléon*. Still, I can't complain – the bread is always fantastically good and fresh. Can you imagine arriving at the bakery counter in *Sainsbury's* and, instead of the usual seedy white bloomer, demanding a sliced wholemeal *Tudor and Stuart*?

I eat no more than half of my still-warm prize on the way home and we sit down to delicious breakfast of bread, *confiture* and coffee. It's Helena's last week at school before the endless summer holiday and she's about to conduct an oral exam for a bunch of Parisian history students: Question one: In which year did the *Baguette Baron Haussmann* first appear on the streets of Paris, and what gives it that special, malty taste?

Despite the fortification of breakfast, Helena's on the verge of collapse. I really don't know how she's going to get through the rest of the week. Her tiredness is making her more and more short-tempered (at least I think it's the tiredness, rather than me) and at the same time, she's trying to work her way through an order for some of her ceramics. She shouldn't be doing this at all but every evening she locks herself in her *atelier*, crafting a series of cups and saucers that she's determined to deliver on time. A few days ago, her father (now fully recovered from the shock of being outmanoeuvred at chess) instructed me to prevent Helena from working with any toxic enamels, but she refuses point blank to wear an old *Mickey Mouse* gas mask which I just happened to find in our neighborhood skip.

I'm convinced she will have run out of steam by the middle of the week, so being visited by my past is probably the last thing she needs, but we're about to be descended upon by a number of my old boozing pals from London and just about everywhere else I've ever had too much to drink. The timing couldn't be worse as none of these friends has any idea that I'm trying to quit and, to cap it all, we're supposed to be visiting the new gynaecologist this week for the first ultrasound, the very thought of which fills me with trepidation – I can't get the image of John Hurt's alien delivery out of my head, as evoked by my charming brother, and I've been thinking about *Rosemary's Baby*, the Polanski film in which Mia Farrow gives birth to the son of Satan via John Cassevetes (or was it the other way round?). I can still remember the bumph in the *Radio Times* twenty-five years ago, which described the film as every woman's nightmare because it preys upon their fear of giving birth to a monster. Now that fear is becoming my nightmare too.

I dare not broach this subject with Helena and I don't know whether she worries about it as much as I do. But worries about what, precisely? Well, do you want the full list or the abbreviated version? Out of pure superstition, I refuse to pronounce the names of diseases and potential deformities which run freely around my skull like rats in a slimy bucket. Will we know in a few days whether any of them is set to affect our baby, or will we have to wait another few, excruciating weeks? I hope I'm not starting to sound protective here, but Helena's gone off to the swimming pool for an hour, so I think I'll sneak a quick look at *Future Maman...* Why is there no book called *Futur Papa,* by the way? Maybe we men aren't supposed to show any interest or emotion until the baby forces its misshapen head out of the womb? Or do they emerge feet first?

Here we go – '*week eight: weight 2 – 3 grams, length 3 centimetres. Face continuing to form*' (those eyelashes must be longer than Sophia Loren's by now). '*Nose and ears already visible, palate forming, salivary glands, the heart and vascular system already complete.*' It seems you can even hear the blood being pumped to minute capillaries if you happen to have something called a *Doppler*. I turn the page. Shit! Look at that – a picture of a baby, and I mean a real baby, rather than some bloated, cartoon grub. Of course the head is still three or four times too big, but at least it no longer looks like an extraterrestrial in tears because it's missed the last rocket home to Mars.

I search fruitlessly for the golden paragraph which states unequivocally that Helena's mood and my life are going to radically improve by next Wednesday afternoon, but instead I find out that she's facing the likelihood of a series of cramp-like painful sensations in the stomach, something the French call *fourmillements*. What the hell are they? It's not even in the dictionary, although it does inform me that a *fourmi* is an ant and that *fourmiller* is the French verb you need to use when insects are swarming all over your peanut butter sandwiches. Ah, here we go, the first ultrasound: 90 percent of any serious malformations will be revealed, we'll find out the risk of spontaneous abortion and we'll discover whether we're going to have twins. Twins! At the first sign of twins, at least one of them is going straight back to the manufacturer, I can promise you that.

In the middle of the night Helena is awake in a state of some suffering. 'Whassamadder?' I whisper from my underground lair deep in the land of nod. '*Fourmillements!*' she cries. Expecting to find the bed swarming with tiny, biting beasts I spring out of bed faster than a fox pursued by the massed ranks of the English aristocracy. Helena stares at me incredulously. 'What are you doing?' she asks calmly, 'it's only pins and needles.'

Paris, June 24th

Just two days of school left. My forays into *Future Maman* have warned me time and again she'll be exhausted throughout these first few weeks and this is now etched onto her face like a primitive wood carving. Even though she's fortunate enough to be conducting the oral examinations in our very own neighbourhood, I can only watch as she levers herself agonisingly out of bed in the morning and back into it when she crawls home for lunch. I practically have to push her out of the door again as soon as she's left an impression of her perfect bite in a fresh, green apple. The last thing she wants is to test a group of bored pupils on the Cold War and the geopolitical issues facing America. This morning, one of them told her that the population of the US is 'probably around 2 million'. And we Europeans scoff at the Americans for knowing nothing of foreign affairs? Even without another human life rapidly taking shape in my belly, I couldn't be arsed to get out of bed if that's the best they can do.

There's no avoiding the fact that Helena and I have descended into a modest cold war of our own lately. I prefer to believe that the last rites of the school term are at fault, rather than my erratic behaviour, and I'm doing all I can by helping with the cooking, but even my finest prawn risotto fails to alleviate her mood. The trouble is that I'm so damned edgy as I await my friends and a test of my own. I know I should keep my mouth shut until the weekend, by which time Helena will have had a couple of days to recuperate; I know she's tired, I know I've been playing my own less than vainglorious role in our little war and, above all else, I know that anything I say will antagonise her further. All I need do is give her a bit of room to talk while I do the listening, and I can do that, right? Hell no, I wade right in.

Kingdom of one, June 25th

I've prepared a seven-hour monologue and start to deliver it on the eve of her last day at work. As soon as her eyebrows reach the upper viewing deck of the Eiffel Tower, it's clear Helena has got the gist of my introduction: 'It's been very difficult, especially for me... You have to understand how I feel, burble, burble, etc.' But I'm not so sure how much of section two she captures – a masterpiece of finger-pointing, intended to make her feel guilty about her temper, taking out her frustrations on me, and the disastrous effects of her egotistical behaviour on our relationship. This, I duly conclude, is bringing our respective bad points into sharp focus and causing us to drift apart at the very moment we need to pull together. Not bad for someone who's cancelled a wedding, hidden a drinking problem and lied about their entire personality before moving to Paris and turning her life upside down, eh?

Luckily for Helena (and luckier still for me), I'm just about to launch into my illustrated back catalogue of her most selfish acts and get in an early claim for canonisation when I hear the unmistakable sounds of snoring from the couch. Not even outrage can keep the poor girl's eyes open and I'm forced to deliver the rest of my speech to a slug and a few half-interested pigeons down in the courtyard.

Paris, June 26th

Helena's up early and I've already asked whether she remembers any of our 'conversation' from the night before. 'Yeah' she says, 'the bit where you were feeling sorry for yourself.' But before I can ask which particular bit, she's out of the door for the comparatively light relief of forty *Bac* students lined up against a wall waiting to tell her about the atrocities in the Balkans. When she gets home in the early evening, however, her eyes are brighter than I've seen them for some time. School is over and the miracle has occurred without me having to force it. She's light on her feet, talkative, cooking dinner, diving into her *atelier* to finish work on her crockery. In short, she's a different person and this lifts the strain from my own shoulders. We're talking again, touching and almost treating one another as two human beings.

Paris, June 27th

My friends will want to know why I'm nursing an orange juice rather than slugging back my normal ration of beers. But far worse than that, I'll have to tell them that Helena's pregnant. Why do I envisage this will be so difficult – after all, they know most of my faults already, so there's simply no point in pretending or lying to these people. What I'm dreading, I suppose, is one of them telling me that, this time, I've really gone too far.

The first of them arrives in the early afternoon. Vincent is a Frenchman who lives in the twilight zone at the foot of Brixton Hill and I listen as he relates the latest developments in his own life, which is, of course, the life I'm trying hard to leave behind: struggle out of bed, arrive late at work, drink coffee, eat lunch, leave early, forty winks, dinner, drinks, party, bit of shut-eye, wake up hungover, rinse and repeat. As Vincent talks and I hang on to my news, I'm as nervous as a cat in a poodle parlour. Eventually, I can contain it no longer and it simply spurts out of me like water from a snapped faucet: 'Helena's pregnant!'

Immediately I focus my attention on a small patch of Parisian pavement somewhere between my scuffed brogues and, for a short geological era, I hear nothing other than wailing sirens and the yapping of designer dogs which never allow you to forget you're in Paris.

Then Vincent says: 'A father? You're going to become a father?'

'Well, yes. I guess that's the general implication here.' I look at his shocked features. Another long pause follows before I go back to my study of the pavement.

'But that's fantastic!'

'It is?

'Of course it is! Congratulations! How does it feel?'

'Well, I'm pleased, naturally, but... '

'I'm sure you'll make a fantastic father, you know.'

'I will?' I can't tell you whether my eyes carry a look of hope or mere incredulity – you'd have to ask Vincent – but then he starts to tell me that this is the condition to which he has always aspired – not pregnancy itself, of course, but being close to someone that gets pregnant and preferably by him. He just hasn't recruited the right woman yet. It turns out that he even knows what his two daughters will be called – Estelle and Marina. Hmm. I'll make a mental note of Marina;

I quite like that one, and now at least I can go back to Helena with one suggestion, instead of just saying no to all of hers.

Vincent seems so pleased about my impending fatherhood that I try out the announcement on my other friends the minute they arrive. To my amazement, I get exactly the same reaction – hugs, kisses and optimistic notes on my suitability for parenthood. Do these people know me, or are they all drunk and deluded? One of them even goes so far as to say that this is exactly what I need in my life. I ponder her words carefully. Could there possibly be an element of truth in this?

If so, then there's no sign yet that this particular animal is about to shed its old and unwholesome skin. While Helena stays home, we hit the bar and late in the evening, I look down to find an empty beer glass in my hand. There was no pause for thought – the only thing I remember inserting into the space between one drink and the next were the words 'Why not?' If impending fatherhood is to turn me into someone or something else, then that needs to be shared with whoever it is that lives inside me and orders all the beers. As for becoming a responsible father, well, those were not Helena's words when I staggered back home in the wee hours smelling of stale hops and grain.

Hung over under the late June skies, not far from Reims

After very few hours of sleep, I've joined Helena at the party of one of her colleagues out here in the middle of nowhere. The dependable mother-to-be was up with the lark and arrived at the appointed time by car while the unreliable father had to catch a train because he overslept and finally pitched up at least two hours after lunch. At least the journey gave me plenty of time to reflect upon the way in which last night ended – I was sitting outside a nightclub called *Nite Folies*, debating whether to take the plunge and staring at the doors as if they were the gates of Hell itself.

The hosts of this party are a gay couple who are gradually renovating an old farmhouse that one of them inherited from his grandmother. It's a large, sprawling property with an expansive garden, at the bottom of which runs a small stream. Helena's in heaven and impatient to give me a guided tour of what our own future should look like, while I'm focusing on the faults and all the maintenance work required by a place like this. I hardly need tell you that this earns me nothing more than a dirty look and a barbed comment about my inverted priorities.

It's a beautiful day and I spend most of it lying in the tall grass with nothing more than an ear of corn for company. I watch as young parents play with their children, running amok in the fields, taking off their shoes, scuffing along the river bed or climbing cherry trees, wicker baskets in hand. Despite my hangover, it strikes me that one or two of these odd little creatures do appear to possess a bit of personality and may even be quite likeable and I'm just getting used to this idea when my idyllic reverie is rudely interrupted. Standing between me and the sun is a miniature monster of indeterminate sex (owing to the carroty ringlets which obscure everything bar a pair of plump, rasping lips). Gratuitously, the ginger thing takes aim with a pink water pistol and directs a fierce jet of water straight and true into the nape of my neck. From somewhere behind the plant life overhanging its face, I can hear the giggles of something that's clearly having a really good time. Where are its bloody parents? No sign of the bastards. If this were the US, and not the People's Republic of Asterix and de Gaulle, I'm sure it wouldn't be out of the question to kick their butts and then sue them. But, in my semi-toxic comatose state, I let it slide. Besides, the cold water running down my back brings me a lot closer to wakefulness than I've managed on my own today.

The party is French in a way that only the French know

how: the food is amazing and the toilets prehistoric, there's barely any alcohol being consumed and all the talk is of politics and sex. I used to believe that the French do little other than philosophise and make love. Now I'm convinced this is merely something they would love the English to believe. After dinner we all sit down for a game of 'Psychiatrist', a game which the French use as an excuse to ask each other a bunch of dirty questions otherwise forbidden by their fantastically rigid society.

Before we depart, Helena takes me on a refresher tour of the property, designed to remind me of the highlights of the house and make me feel as depressed as possible about our own darkened chamber back in Pigalle. She needn't have bothered adding to the misery of my hangover and, to avoid any possibility of further torment, I fall asleep as soon as the car door is shut.

A major turning point in the plot, June 30th

The short, northern summer appears to be over; it's pissing with rain and Helena's off to register at the maternity hospital in the dreary eleventh *arrondissement*. I'm feeling knackered and fancy a bit of lie-in. 'Do you want me to come with you?' I ask. Her voice says 'No, it's only paperwork,' but her expression says 'Aren't you interested in seeing where your baby's going to born?' Sighing, I pull back the curtains and hear myself saying 'Of course I'll come,' before I hide the truth by staring out at the rain for as long as I dare. We catch the metro and walk from the stop at Belleville to a place that will become my second home less than seven months hence. By the time we get there, our umbrella has been turned inside out by the weather and my expandable map of Paris has disintegrated into a single lump of dripping wet pulp.

It doesn't look too bad at first sight; a greyish building enlivened no end by row upon row of green and purple plastic window frames. At reception we're given a form and

I offer to fill it in because Helena hates forms and, for some perverse reason, I rather like them. Maybe I just welcome the relief that comes with a few certainties. So no, Helena's never been stricken by any of the potentially fatal diseases on offer, she suffers no allergies and does not have a family history that puts the baby at risk. This leaves only the small matter of her poor choice in paternal, genetic material, but other than that, the form considers me to be more or less irrelevant.

We're called into a tiny decompression chamber off the main waiting area. This metallic cupboard is inhabited by a small landfill of paperwork and an elderly woman with a kindly face. She checks our paperwork and helpfully points out a few of my spelling mistakes, before we get right down to some serious French bureaucracy. There are three essentials that, as the father, it's my solemn duty to perform: the first of these was accomplished one night a couple of months back; the second is to recognise the consequences of this act down at the town hall; and finally there's a declaration of birth to be made no more than three days after the baby is born.

This all seems such a long way off that I'm thinking of catching up on that last half an hour of sleep in my virulent green chair before I'm inexorably sucked into a labyrinthine explanation of how to complete the registration of the baby. This seems like a minor detail, but just as I'm in the midst of transmitting my disinterest via a whale-sized yawn, the kindly woman impresses upon me, in no uncertain terms, the importance of both remaining acts. If we don't recognise the baby as our very own, the poor little blighter will be forever deprived of a long list of civil rights to which it would otherwise be entitled. And what might those be, I hear you ask? The right to talk in a ridiculously exaggerated accent for the rest of its life, the right to block French motorways with flocks of unshaven sheep, or the right to demand a lifetime of subsidies from the EU in order to continue producing killer bacteria disguised as cheese in some unwashed corner of rural France? But I keep my mouth firmly shut. If there's one thing I've learned since arriving in this country, it's that you do not play under the wheels of the almighty steamroller of officialdom and survive.

As the two women talk and I try to look like I'm listening, the phone rings non-stop. It would appear that our host has two full-time jobs: a) tuition on the importance of French paperwork; and b) making appointments for tuition on the importance of French paperwork. Her preferred approach to this dual task is to let the phone ring for about ten minutes before picking it up. In this way, she can get through at least a couple of subclauses of French law and its application to the Parisian infant before interrupting herself to take a call. The poor woman! As soon as she replaces the receiver, it starts ringing again, something which would drive me completely nuts.

After seven hours of official procedure, the fun finally arrives when she pulls a wodge of literature from somewhere deep in a pyramid of papers. On top of the pile is a pamphlet entitled *la préparation à la naissance* and we're now taken through a lengthy list of prenatal services which range from the essential to the downright bizarre. In the first category, there's a discussion on the avoidance of pain with the anaesthetist and a host of other preparatory sessions for the birth, including relaxation, chats with the midwife and videos of a typical birth (all of which I shall naturally be going to great lengths to avoid). Then there's a forest of literature on what to do with the baby once you get it home (put it to bed, perhaps?). All perfectly normal, you might think. But just as I think I've got my head around that little lot, she's suddenly trying to sell us the benefits of acupuncture, prenatal chant (eh?), something called 'the words of men' and another little item (for which I can offer no translation) called *l'haptonomie*. To me, none of this sounds like the kind of stuff a group of blokes might get together and discuss over a pint at the *Dog and*

Duck. Take 'the words of men', for example, which entails half a dozen lower primates sitting around in a circle (whether they are holding hands is not clear from the pamphlet), discussing their emotions, their experiences of pregnancy ('Yeah, well, my Shirl's up the spout, innit?') and attempting some form of bonding without the use of any fixative or other hallucinatory solvents.

Who's she trying to kid? We don't even do that after a few shots of tequila in some murky nightclub, so we're unlikely to try anything so risky, utterly sober, within the confines of a well-lit public hospital. But just as I'm about to dismiss the whole idea out of hand, I look up to find Helena and her new friend smiling at me in exactly the way benevolent country folk smile at the village idiot. This conspiracy goes way deeper than I ever suspected.

I hide among the remaining sentences of the 'words of men', which states, in bold font, that 'to be born as a father is the fruit of an indeterminate period of gestation'. 'What on earth does that mean?' I plead with Helena. But my question is intercepted more quickly than a rogue missile: 'That, after nine months of pregnancy, the woman goes into labour and emerges as a mother. For the man, whose body remains unaffected, the transition from rock ape to father can take a little longer.' I look into the two sets of eyes which have me pinned against the lurid walls of this infernal antechamber. Yep, they're talking to me alright, and I resolve at once to hold hands and share my innermost fears with the first male I meet on the metro home.

After this latest setback, I don't much feel like going into detail on the subject of *l'haptonomie*, to be honest. All I can say is that it involves using your hands to share your emotions with the baby while the poor little devil's probably trying to get a bit of kip in the womb. Even if he could understand what's going on (and frankly I doubt it), I don't suppose he'd be interested in sharing what's going on in my head this morning.

Approximately seven years later, we are shown the door

by a woman who has left kindly far behind and moved straight through hard and on into sadistic. As we're leaving, she presses a bunch of goodies into my hands and we start opening them up on the metro. Welcome to the baby industry! The first thing that squirts its way out of the pack is a promotional baby bottle which, between us, we manage to drop onto the highly unsterilised west-bound platform of metro line nine – an inauspicious introduction to parenting. Also included in our bumper welcome pack are a number of baby publications and assorted pieces of advertising. The magazine covers are the exclusive territory of blonde, dentally perfect mothers, paint-by-number fathers and blue-eyed, genetically modified babykins, all of whom appear to live in a suite at the *Ritz* to ensure that Junior spends his entire childhood in idle luxury. Meantime, back in the real world, it's still pissing down, I have an almighty headache and I need to lie down.

I'm just drifting off into a dream full of baby artefacts and naked barbarians chanting homicidal nursery rhymes when Helena pops her head around the bedroom door. 'Are you 'aving a nappy?' she asks. It takes a moment before my befuddled brain works this one out: 'It's called a nap,' I say, before my head hits the pillow once more.

I wish I'd stayed asleep too, but my dozing is interrupted by a call from someone describing herself as a friend. Apparently she's been reading my film script and her comments are not encouraging. In fact she thinks I should bin it without delay. I may have been thinking precisely the same thing for a couple of days, but my response is still as sharp as a porcupine's bum.

This evening Helena and I have tickets for a new play called *Un petit jeu sans conséquences*, which does make me wonder whether the playwrights of Paris have been looking over my shoulder these past few months. Anyway, it looks like being the final nail in the coffin for my screenplay, as the play is everything that my own effort is not – concise, witty, one scene leading directly and logically to the next, and the whole thing brilliantly acted and excitingly staged. I leave the theatre thoroughly depressed and, back home, I pick up my script and lay it ceremoniously to rest underneath a pile of unpaid bills.

Paris, July 2nd

Without my writing, there is a small hole in my meticulously unplanned days until the *Tour de France* starts at the weekend. This race is an absolute godsend for idle, unemployed loafers such as me: Three weeks watching abnormally proportioned men chasing each other around France on bicycles and every glorious kilometre of it covered live on French television. It's an event that has fascinated me since I was a boy and this is my chance to watch the whole damned thing – a 3,500-kilometre orgy of buckled wheels and denials of drug abuse, featuring a troop of cartoon characters shorn of all dignity and bodily hair wearing polyester shirts. It all starts in two days' time with a six and a half-kilometre sprint around the streets of Paris.

Until then, there's nothing for it but to start looking at job ads while Helena disappears into her *atelier*. She's not her usual enthusiastic self today – she feels sick and is overcome by a desire to go back to bed every time she looks at her cups and saucers. Perhaps Junior has made up his own mind about playing with those toxic chemicals? He may only stretch to a total length of twenty-eight millimetres but he's already determined to make his presence felt and get Mummy exclusively focused on his needs. Obviously he's going to be providing me with some tough competition in this respect and, for this reason alone, I'm sure it's a boy.

Helena, who still thinks it's a girl, has been wracking her brains to think of a few more names:

'What about Lola?'

'What about it?'

'Do you like it?'

'What, the car?'

'Car? What car? I'm talking about a name for your daughter!'

'Oh sorry! No.'

'Why not?'

'Dunno. Not enough syllables maybe.'

'This is our child, not a game of *Scrabble*. What about Pearl?'

'Definitely not.'

'Why not'?

'Reminds me of shellfish.'

Big sigh. 'OK. Ella?'

'Too old-fashioned.'

'Aurélie?'

'No.'

'Well, you suggest something.'

'What makes you think it's a girl?'

'I don't. I just happen to like those names.'

'Well a boy called Lola is going to have a lot of trouble in England, even if he can get away with it here.'

'What have you got then?'

All I've got is Emil from one of my favourite books when I was a kid. Helena's clearly stumped by the fact that I've finally conjured up a suggestion and heads back to her chemicals. Shame. Now I'll have to go back to that list of jobs in the newspaper.

Paris, July 3rd

On the metro, I bump into a friend who's brought her young baby along for the ride. Under normal circumstances, I'd give the pair of them a wide berth and make an enormous show of rolling my eyes and tutting. But it's different today and I think I know why. I watch as little Cleo pushes herself upright in her pram, looks at me and coils one or two tiny fingers around the edge of my seat. I shouldn't allow it to happen, but I'm bewitched as she stares me down. Her eyes are the colour of the Atlantic Ocean, her skin so pure and unblemished that you expect it to be completely transparent. Her expression conveys nothing but wonder and innocence and I haven't a clue what she's thinking as she scans my own face which bears more furrows and lines than a tract of overworked arable land. She wraps all her tiny fingers around one of mine. The skin of her hand is damp and cool. She makes a grab for my watch. To her, time means nothing, at least not in the way it does for me. It's just another random object to be explored and then chewed between toothless pink gums.

'Are you still with us?' I suddenly realise her mother is addressing me.

'What?'

'Getting broody, are we?'

'Not at all,' I retort, although I'm more interested in Cleo's perspective of the world for the rest of the trip than I am in my own. My God! What's happening to me?

Le tour des femmes de France, July 5th

This weekend life will return temporarily to normal. Normal, that is, for a teenager trapped in the body of a middle-aged man. And the happy set of coincidences that have precipitated this? Well, Helena's off to spend the weekend with her parents in Normandy while I receive an old friend from England and we get to watch an orgy of sport from the comfort of a darkened living room. The centrepiece of this major session of reality avoidance is the *Tour de France* and because this is the centenary year of the gruelling event, it starts right underneath the Eiffel Tower. When my friend gets off the *Eurostar,* we spend a couple of hours checking out the most advantageous viewpoints along the course. But, back at home, when I try explaining the logic of this to Helena, she looks at me the way the last of the great polar bears might contemplate the antics of *Winnie the Pooh* right before passing into extinction. 'But you're French,' I protest, 'you must be interested in *Le Tour*.' Still no reply. Instead, she finishes packing her bag before disappearing for the station at St Lazare.

Within seconds, my friend and I are in a bar, cracking open peanut shells and analyzing last season's sports action in excruciating detail. I have a cold beer in my hand, but don't ask me how it got there as I won't be thinking about that until tomorrow lunchtime at the earliest. We position ourselves strategically in that corner of the café which offers the most advantageous viewpoint, not for watching *Le Tour,* I might add, but for eyeing up women as they pass by. Please understand that this is strictly for the benefit of my friend who has recently divorced and is still suffering from a deep soul sickness and a lack of regular sex. I'm just here to help nurse him back to health. After all, it wouldn't be fair to let him drink alone, now would it? I know where my responsibilities lie and they start again on Monday the minute Helena gets home, right?

'There's something about French women, isn't there?' muses my friend as he hides behind a glass of *Kronenbourg 1664*.

'Oh yes,' I admit, from a purely ethnographical point of view.

As if to emphasise the point, a group of American teenagers crowds suddenly into the bar. The boys are all knotted vowels and back-to-front baseball caps, while the girls, who sport enough railway track on their teeth to carry you clean across the Rockies, are, like, dressed to kill. In fact they wear very little – bare midriffs, plunging necklines, exposed calves, thighs and backs. Their eyes are flashing in all directions except ours, I note with only the barest trace of disappointment. I know they're young but there's something unmistakably different about American women – something they lack and French women have in abandon. I can't quite put my finger on it (and Helena wouldn't let me anyway). Is it nonchalance, or a certain hauteur? Something about the way they hold themselves or the way they walk? I don't know, but my friend sums it up nicely with a remark that 'even ugly French women have class'. He's right, too, and this reminds me of a conversation I had over drinks with three French women barely a week ago. One of them casually asked the Englishman to describe a typical French woman. I felt like a student who has mugged up on only one subject but turns over the exam paper to discover he's come up trumps. 'Well,' I said, as if I was about to start talking for the whole of England, 'I can't talk for the whole of England, but... ' (and here I stopped to insert a lengthy pause, just to ensure all parties were duly riveted), 'she's refined, sophisticated and beautiful. Wrapped in a *Hermès* scarf, she tends to look a lot like Jeanne Moreau or Juliette Binoche. A cool dark exterior, belied by eyes which smoulder and glow like top quality coal. She's Catholic, *mais pas trop*, can talk a bit of politics and a lot of cinema and, unfortunately, she prefers sleeping with French men rather than the English.' With my fanciful portrait barely begun, I noticed my audience had already spilled most of their apricot juice and were giggling into the sofa cushions. Helena (for yes, she was one of the three) gave me the look that I forgot to include in my caricature and said; 'Well, I guess that might describe about 2 percent of all Parisian film stars.' Is it really possible that my world has shrunk to such a degree?

AWOL, July 6th

Before Helena gets home, I enjoy one of those days I feared had gone forever. It begins in bed with a minor hangover, a big pot of tea and every English Sunday newspaper I can find at the newsstand, but the real action starts after a brief lunch of whatever's-left-in-the-fridge. The men's singles final is on the radio while the first stage proper of *Le Tour* is live on TV, including a massive pile-up just one kilometre from the finish with wheel sprockets and snapped collarbones all over the road. At some point I think I hear the phone ringing although I'm far too busy to answer. But the caller persists and I pick it up just as events on Centre Court in faraway south-west London draw to a close. It's someone called Helena and she wants to know whether I'm enjoying the weekend. Automatically, I start to scan the living room in case any stray beer cans have escaped my notice.

Paris, July 7th

My reality check arrives when Helena rolls back into town with a face like a summer squall. The paranoid part of me wonders whether she'd installed a video camera in our bedroom before leaving or perhaps secreted one about my very own person. Or maybe my system has triple-distilled the alcohol into pure guilt? Either way, I don't find out until later why she's returned on the offensive.

Things become clearer when Helena lets slip that her mother has offered to buy her a car as a pregnancy present. This immediately gets my back up because, as far as my diseased mind is concerned, it implies that we can't afford more than our current ration of two, hand-pumped wheels. Helena and I have been through this argument so many times: She thinks life would be easier with a car. I believe that a combination of metro, bus and bike is more environmentally friendly, less stressful and, above all, cheaper. Her attack focuses on the last, and weakest, of my arguments and the whole thing develops into a row over my inability to anticipate the needs of our nascent family. I try to explain why I'm reluctant to part with the money for a machine which I hold responsible for the demise of mankind and conclude that the decision to buy a car has bugger all to do with her mother.

But this just opens the floodgates and it becomes clear

that, while I've been lounging on the couch, Helena has been subjected to a series of caring parental questions about her choice of partner. They've also made clear their belief that Helena shouldn't sell the small property she owns in Paris to buy, jointly with me, a larger one. 'Why not?' I ask, flabbergasted that such things have been discussed in my absence. The response is unambiguous, unanswerable and could so easily have fallen from the lips of my own mother: 'Because you've shown no commitment to the relationship.' We've been round the houses a few times on this one, too. I argue that leaving my place in London and moving to Paris represents a commitment to the relationship and Helena's standard retort is that all that was undone when I chickened out of the marriage. Forced onto the ropes, I come back with the contention that a baby represents a far bigger commitment than a piece of paper. And so it continues until the neighbours are forced to call in Kofi Annan to peel us apart, but not before Helena has struck an ugly low blow about my preferred position within the household being usurped by another baby.

An interior world, July 9th

It's time for the first ultrasound proper and my mood has not improved by the time we leave for our appointment with the replacement gynaecologist. The journey by metro is a nightmare and when we resurface somewhere near Bastille, the streets are choked, hot and polluted. She may be exhausted, but at least Helena is willing to break the silence which has descended between us. In ten days' time we depart for her brother's house in the south of Spain and now she wants to know why I hadn't shown any interest when she was making plans for our summer holiday. Rather than rekindle the flames of yesterday, I keep to myself the thought that the unemployed don't take holidays and we lapse into silence. We're a full ten minutes late for the appointment. This isn't going to be fun and I'm sure the doctor will be worried about the mental health of this baby fully six months before it's even born.

I haven't thought much about the ultrasound and I don't expect to be moved by the experience. I don't know why, but I imagine that all we'll see are a few grainy black and white shots of a shadowy semicolon lurking about in the womb and, as we sit, solemn as a funeral cortege in a waiting room with more plant life than Kew Gardens, I'm still so mad with Helena that I can't even bring myself to look at her, never mind get excited about something we've created together. Instead, I just sit in the steamily oppressive atmosphere and stare at the enormous tropical fronds.

Eventually we're ushered into the surgery where we're given a lecture about the importance of being on time, which adds a further ten minutes to the proceedings. Me? Well, I'm thinking that if we don't get on with it, I'm going to miss the massed sprint finish anticipated at the end of today's stage of *Le Tour*. If time is so precious, why don't we just get started and stop arguing about how late we are?

Once we've spent three hours postulating on the date of conception, Helena slips out of her trousers and gets onto a bed upon which the pillows have been replaced by computer screens. Cold, clear blue gel is applied liberally to her belly, followed by an implement which looks like some kind of joystick. The screen flickers hesitantly to life and I settle into the only position which enables me to watch the show and avoid eye contact with both the doctor and the mother of my child. Then I get the shock of my life.

I'm looking at a baby – a fully formed, live, kicking human being. And I mean kicking! This baby must think it's competing in the *Tour de France*; it's pedalling more furiously than a world-class sprinter with the entire peloton up its backside. I can feel Helena looking at me but I don't return her gaze because I can't take my eyes off the screen. This isn't at all what *Future Maman* had led me to expect. From a cursory glance at the book, I was anticipating something quite docile – a cross, perhaps, between a newt and a tiny, inanimate bird.

I didn't expect it to be doing anything so soon after its tiring journey across the border between nothingness and existence. But this baby is already doing a lot more than merely existing. Right now, it's reclining in a bath of amniotic fluid, waving its arms and legs like a complete madman and, as we zoom in, even its fingers and toes are visible to the naked eye. I study the head, and it, too, is human. No question about it. OK, maybe it still looks a little as if it were wearing a crash helmet, but at least one that fits. Occasionally the baby appears to prop itself up and smile for the camera. I sense Helena trying to catch my eye but I'm completely captivated by the sight of an unborn child. Now Helena's giggling and crying for joy. 'Hold still,' says the doctor, in a vain attempt to keep the image steady.

As she rolls her outsized deodorant stick across Helena's belly, the computer allows the baby to be appreciated from a number of different angles. A full complement of appendages is counted and the head measured. Then she tells us the femur is already 6 millimetres in length.

One of us speaks and I think it's Helena: 'What about the sex?' she gasps.

We agreed we would ask about this, back in the times when we still talking.

'Too early to tell,' says the doctor. 'I could guess but it wouldn't be reliable.'

Then I stammer out the question which has been bursting for release ever since we walked into the surgery: 'Is he, I mean, she... Is everything alright?'

The doctor snaps off a switch on the computer. Suddenly one half of the screen is filled with a graphic display of the baby's heartbeat. It thunders across the screen just as it would at the climactic moment of any episode of *ER*. I hold my breath through another short series of peaks and troughs. 'Heart's fine,' she declares, as if announcing the safe arrival of the 08.53 from Charing Cross. Bizarrely, I can't stop myself from wondering whether this woman ever gets excited about anything – sex, chocolate éclairs or perhaps some extraordinary combination of the two? But before I can take this thought any further, she pulls another set of graphics up on screen:

'All perfectly within the norms.' I exhale and finally glance at Helena just in time to see a degree of wildness disappear from her eye.

An image of the baby reappears on the screen. Apparently he was not delighted about being replaced by a set of graphics and now he's gyrating like a champion dervish. 'Can't you feel that?' I ask Helena, before I remember that, officially, we're still not talking. 'Not a thing,' she says. I find this hard to believe. There's more action going on in her belly than you'll encounter at an oversubscribed health club. Even if the screen does exaggerate the size of the baby (which is still only five and a half centimetres long) the on-screen commotion is such that I'm tempted to tell him to take it easy. If I were a woman, I'd take one look at the screen and insist upon lying down for the remainder of the pregnancy.

Helena is deliriously happy and on the verge of tears once more. Our disagreements and grudges have been temporarily washed away by this small screen trailer of forthcoming attractions. Throughout our emotional buffeting, the doctor has been attempting to conduct a precise scientific exercise. Now she's about to shut down visual communication and put Junior back to bed for another few months. He looks knackered too, as he lolls back once more in his amphibious armchair. Good night, little fellow. Nice to meet you. See you again soon. We'll find you a name just as soon as we can, I promise. Bye now, take care and don't do anything silly in there.

The screen goes dead and I feel an inexplicable sense of loss. We're given a set of commemorative photos – nice but not the same thing at all. On our way out of the surgery, I notice the painting on the wall. Inevitably, it's a Miró – some sort of disassembled woman with her legs spread wide apart and a bunch of abstract swirls and curls charging around in the area of her sex. What is it about gynaecologists and Miró? Maybe I'll find out over the course of the next few months but, right now, I couldn't care less.

Helena and I hack our way through the waiting room jungle, leaving behind the receptionist who somehow manages to maintain an antarctically unfriendly demeanour in the swelter of the waiting room. Blinking hard, we emerge once more onto the sunlit pavements of Paris. Same old hot, dirty streets, but now we know Helena is carrying something that changes the world and we know that because we've seen it with our own eyes. Until now, it had been an uncertainty, a concept, an idea, a page in a textbook, a circle on a pregnancy testing kit, a notion, a fear, a worm, no more than the distant rumbling of thunder. But not anymore. Now it's a baby with two legs, arms, a head, torso, fingers and ten toes. All present and so far correct.

Helena's still clutching Junior's first photographic portfolio as I steer her into the first bar we come across, which just happens to house a large TV screening the end of today's stage of the *Tour de France*. We sit down and order coffee and mineral water.

'Did you see him?'

'Yes, I saw him,' I say, watching the lung-bursting efforts of a lone Frenchmen as he attempts to keep clear of the peloton less than five kilometres from the finish.

'It's a miracle!'

'I know. This guy's been out on his own for almost 75k.'

'Did you see his little legs?'

'Yeah, they're turning to rubber but he's only got a couple of kilometres to go.'

'He's going to be a proper little cyclist.'

'Well, he's not doing too badly right now, even if they're sure to catch him before the end of the stage... '

'Catch who?'

'Him,' I say, gesturing at the widescreen TV.

'*Quel imbécile!*' mutters Helena darkly, although I don't think she's talking about the poor French cyclist. But she's so elated that she doesn't even mind my world being dominated by 200 advertisements for *Lycra* charging around the French countryside. Instead she goes back to a study of the data printout furnished by the gynaecologist. The Frenchman doesn't make it. He's swallowed by the bunch a few hundred metres from the line and eventually flops onto the tarmac, gasping like a beached sardine.

The workings of an Italian seafood restaurant, July 11th

There's no doubt the ultrasound has had a profound effect on me. Had I not seen the contents of Helena's belly, I'd probably be happy to look no further into the future than the end of *Le Tour*. But the evidence that my greatest responsibility is no longer to myself is becoming too difficult to ignore. Granted, it's not as if the baby already needs a new pair of shoes but, like it or not, I'll be turning provider a few, short months from now and that can only mean one thing: it's time to look for a job. Wearily, I connect up to the net.

'Cheri, what are you doing?'

I close down the BBC sports page double-quick time. 'Looking for a job. Why?'

'I have to go back to the gynaecologist for a blood test.'

'Need me to come with you?'

'No, not worth it.'

'Are you sure?' I hope the sound of my relief is not audible.

'Yes. I'm going to look for some baby clothes and a pram on the way home. The sales are on.'

Baby clothes? Pram? Shit! I open a job website and, by the end of the morning, I've decided there are two outfits on the planet for which I'd genuinely consider working, provided the transfer fee is sufficient. Then I reconsider one of them. I couldn't play for Chelsea. There's no sense in lowering my sense of self-esteem any further just yet.

A few months ago, my old boss visited Paris with an offer for me to return to marketing services bulging in his back pocket. It was a perfectly good job which we discussed over dinner. So what did I do as he detailed the multiple benefits of this generous package? Well, with a mouthful of pasta and several glasses of red wine rampaging through every capillary in my body, I began to gesticulate wildly and most ungratefully, even going so far as to pronounce that 'never, but never, would I return to feed off the stinking carcass of big business'. Yes, I'm sure those were my exact words. It makes me shudder to think of them. He looked at me steadily across the table and asked what I intended to do once the money ran out.

I stuffed another forkful of slippery clam linguine into my mouth to gain a bit of thinking time. Then I vaguely remember telling him that Helena and I were thinking of moving to the south of France (at which point Helena almost choked on the errant heart of an artichoke). We'd get by, I told him. God knows, we'd probably even find time to grow our own root vegetables.

He was pretty polite about the whole thing, as I recall, and didn't even mention the fact that I wouldn't know one end of a turnip from the other. The last thing he asked me, rather prophetically as it turns out, was 'But what if you have children?'

I remember all this as I wade my way through a muddied list of unappetising opportunities in the marketing sector... There's even one which may merit consideration (if I can *Polyfill* enough of the holes in my lamentable CV). They're on the lookout for the usual suspects:

- *Customer oriented* (largely an ability to avoid swearing, moaning or burping whilst on the phone to a client).
- *Autonomy and team spirit* (not bothering the boss with stupid questions when he's asleep and taking it like a man when he bollocks you for another of his

monumental fuck-ups).

- *Inspiration and creativity* (doodling and scribbling at your desk without revealing too many of your deep-seated insecurities or substance abuse problems, or otherwise illustrating the workings of your inner psychology, plus an intuitive ability to extract soft drinks from the vending machine without the use of coins).
- *Trust and transparency* (the boss is allowed to lie to you, but not vice versa).
- *Energy and fun* (a willingness to work your nuts off to unrealistic deadlines and show up at the pub, where, just before last orders, you swallow six pints in as many minutes with the alkies from data processing and chase them all down with a few tequila slammers).
- *An ability to write in English with sharp analysis and pragmatic conclusions* (churning out reports through the thickest of hangovers while the boss sleeps it off and enjoys what the French call a 'fat morning').

Suddenly, it all comes flooding back to me – the reason I fled marketing services in the first place and why I said what I did to my old boss in that restaurant: midlife crisis or not, deep down I truly believe that I'm through with marketing and all of its over packaged by-products and brands. All that creativity wasted by so many talented people, fuelled by nothing more exotic than hot air and the profit imperative, trying to flog you an extra packet of biscuits. They're prepared to dedicate entire lifetimes to launching line extensions of a branded peanut, beer, or an industrial-strength toilet paper. It's the intellectual equivalent of landfill.

But then I remember those frantically pedalling limbs, and the defenceless nakedness of that tiny creature in Helena's belly...

Dear Sir,

I note with interest your advertisement in the most recent edition of 'Marketing Bollocks Weekly'. I've recently moved to France with the avowed aim of a return to the energetic, fun-filled days of my previous life in marketing. As you can see from my wholly fictitious CV, I've had only the one nervous breakdown (well, two if you count that six-month drinking binge in South America), but I'm as good as clean these days and the Prozac has removed all rebellious thoughts from my head as effectively as any frontal lobotomy...

After fully six minutes agitating over my application, I half-heartedly press 'send' and hope that the intended recipient has already buggered off on his two-month summer holiday.

When Helena gets back (short of a couple of pints of blood), I assure her our future is all but secured and suggest a trip to the cinema. But she's too tired, so I call up a friend. He wants to see an old Italian movie called *Life is difficult* and I don't bother to protest.

The French Alps, July 12th

There's not much point in worrying about jobs this weekend as Monday is Bastille Day and, yet again, the whole of France is on holiday. It seems that the only people working today are the riders in the *Tour de France* and, boy, have they got some work to do. In front of them now are three stages across the high Alps; a total of 633½ kilometres, including several climbs that would kill a mountain goat, never mind an amateur, twelve-smokes-a-day cyclist such as myself. There's little else on French television this weekend and the traverse of the Alps is likely to be the *plat principal* of this year's race, the section which shakes out the two or three potential winners and leaves the rest gasping for oxygen, water, an ambulance or a vial full of stimulants. Even watching it on the box is something of a marathon

– about six hours a day – as I carefully explain to a disbelieving Helena.

The Parisian Alps on Bastille Day

'You're not going to watch it again today, are you?' asks Helena, as she finds me ensconced in front of the box at 10.30 a.m. ready for the start of the final Alpine stage.

'Oh, no,' I lie, 'just the start.'

We are leaving the city for our summer holiday in two days' time and I have a lot to do before then. Luckily, I can do most of it with one eye on the television.

'I don't suppose much will happen today,' I reason, wolfing down an obscenely early lunch of sardines on toast in case it all happens while I'm not in the room. To think that the next time these cyclists pass through the Alps, I'll be up to my neck in nappies and bottles. Anyway, we're about to see the future up close and in the sharpest of focus as we'll be staying with Helena's brother and his girlfriend in southern Spain for three weeks. They already have one child, with another well on the way.

Paris, July 15th

I have mixed feelings as I prepare for the trip. From what, exactly, am I taking a holiday? Half of me thinks I should remain in Paris and sort out our future, while the half that bought the air tickets thinks, 'Sod it, let's lie on the beach in Andalucía for a couple of weeks.' I'm sure you know enough already to realise that this particular argument didn't last long.

Neither of us will miss the building site that's steadily developing beneath our apartment windows. We live on a particularly noisy and polluted street that feeds one of the main east-west boulevards in Paris. The main advantage of the flat (or so we thought before signing several kilos of paperwork) is that we live *côté cour*, which means our rooms are at the back of the building, overlooking a small courtyard and set back from the main thoroughfare where the locals practice for Le Mans. We reasoned that a lack of light would be more than compensated for by the fact that we are protected from the diesel din at the front of the building. But that was before the landlord of the building across the courtyard decided to turn the place into a minor industrial estate. He claims this is mere renovation work, but early every morning his Eastern European chain gang grinds away with an extensive selection of hardware, and the cranium-piercing screech of steel tearing through steel is not the gentlest sound with which to replace birdsong. Nor is it easy to enjoy breakfast if you're watching your croissants leap clean off the table to the melodious tones of a jackhammer. Even Saturdays bring no respite.

For the first few days, I was able to blot the aural assault from my consciousness, but now there's a heat wave and we're faced with the choice of death by cacophony or asphyxiation. Because she's now at the end of her third month, Helena's already finding sleep harder to come by. She's taken to yelling out of the window, demanding to know when the work will stop. But the migrants just stare at her, unable to comprehend a word of French and unwilling to defy the orders of their employer. Their tar-stained features show a measure of sympathy for the wan figure waving like some desperate medieval princess in her tower. But they're under their own kind of pressure and, after a few hapless shrugs of the shoulders, they go right back to their hammering, screaming and smelting.

But tonight Helena is in tears, her resistance broken. The last straw is the clattering of plates from the restaurant which operates a kitchen behind doors that open onto the courtyard below. I try to calm her; 'It's just one more night, Helena. Then we'll be gone. Don't try too hard to sleep; just relax and it'll come.' Mercifully she's already asleep when I check a few minutes later.

Goodbye to the factory, July 16th

We're awake and packing before the ferrous woodpeckers have even stirred. One look at Helena's face is all I need to tell me that the metro and train combination I'd planned is likely to be received with the enthusiasm of a condemned man whose last act is to buy a winning lottery ticket. So I hail a cab and we bid goodbye to the steaming streets of Paris from the back of an air-conditioned taxi.

Helena's brother and family have been visiting friends in France and we've arranged to meet in air-side limbo at the airport once we've been sucked through check-in and customs. In the departure lounge, I pick up a cup of coffee and smoke a cigarette. Then I notice a soft play area where a few small children are playing on a rocking horse. Up and down the slide they go – tumbling, grinning and crying. I catch myself thinking this little playground is an excellent idea, which is strange because, under normal circumstances, the only thing I can think of at an airport is to set myself up at a bar with a tumbler full of anaesthetic, the back pages of a non-taxing newspaper and a desire to avoid contact with any member of the human race not immediately resembling a barmaid. I'm just about to start mourning my loss when I catch sight of Helena's brother, his heavily pregnant girlfriend and their mop-headed boy who is clutching a small, stuffed rabbit. He looks at me and I look at him. Clément is a shy boy but he takes my hand and leads me directly to the soft play area. Tentatively, I place him on the slide and guide him down. Once we've repeated the procedure several times, I start wondering whether this is how it really feels. Can it be so simple and gentle? Of course not! Today I'm little more than a temporary, hired uncle, but soon enough I'll become the father and main gunslinger and filling the vacant spaces in my head will be my own child. I wait for the cocktail of expectation and terror to finish pulsing through my body. I don't know if I can do this. Am

I alone in this fear, or do all prospective fathers experience such crippling doubts?

Two and a half hours later, all eight of us (if you include unborn children and worn-out rabbits) are disgorged into the terminal at Seville airport. Instead of charging outside in my habitual manner, I'm forced to watch the slow, precise operation that's required with a child in tow. Parenthood is not just an eighteen-year-long test of your patience, it seems, but a logistical exercise to rival the organisation of the *Tour de France*.

I love Spain. As soon as we emerge from passport control, I breathe in deeply the smell of black tobacco, the sound of hissing espresso machines and the incessant clink and tootle emitted by the one-arm bandits to which the Spanish are undyingly addicted. It feels good to be back and my thoughts turn naturally to a first, lengthy siesta.

Helena's brother, Pierre, has an engineering job on the coast, not far from the Portuguese border. They live in a small seaside resort to which a goodly number of urban *Madrileños* escape every summer. Their small garden contains a mandarin tree and a children's swimming pool. The beach is five minutes' walk away, there's no traffic and I've already forgotten the sounds of the building site back in Paris as I fall into a deep, uninterrupted sleep.

When I re-emerge into the harsh Spanish sunlight, Helena is playing, or perhaps I should say practising, with her nephew in the garden. Cécile is relaxing in the shade, hands folded neatly across her swollen belly. The talk is of pregnancy, as it will be for the next few days. I snatch the odd piece of conversation – the things you can eat and those you cannot, whether you can drink the tap water in Spain and how long you can sit in the sun.

Helena swaps our copy of *Future Maman* for a huge hard-cover entitled *J'attends un enfant*. Unlike the dodgy drawings in our book, this one contains lots of photographs and we are soon introduced to a colourful embryo and learn when it officially turns into a foetus (very quickly, as it happens, and probably when you are least likely to be paying attention). Then Cécile asks whether we'd like to see photographs of the birth. Helena recoils but not as quickly as I do – I'm down at the bottom of the garden long before she's finished the question. I'll probably have a look alright, but very quietly in my own time and certainly not when anybody is watching.

Through all of this, I try to imagine Cécile's six and a half-month belly transposed onto Helena's body, something which causes me to shudder. I realise I'm afraid of the birth, that I don't understand how it all works. How is it possible that Cécile will be able to squeeze another human body out of her slender frame? Helena has disappeared, so I chance my arm with a few questions:

'Cécile, how much does a baby weigh, in kilos?'

'Oh, usually between three and four.'

I cannot visualise this other than by imagining myself at the fishmongers:

'I'd like a whole salmon, please... '

'*How big?*'

'Oh, I don't know, maybe three and a half kilos. That one, perhaps?' And I point to one of the slithery monsters lying dead on a slab of ice.

'*That one? That's only a couple of kilos, son!*'

'Well it looks plenty big enough to me. OK, give me something a little larger then. Not too big, mind.'

The man in the rubberised blue apron dredges us something up which looks like it's been lifted straight from a Jules Verne novel and grins. '*That's your baby!*'

'My baby?'

'*Want me to gut it for you?*'

I'm going to have to look at those pictures...

'Cécile! Why is this baby facing down?' I rush over with the book open at a drawing in which the baby is quite clearly the wrong way up.

Cécile looks calmly at the picture, then at me, and laughs. 'Because they're designed to flip over before the birth!'

This idea appals me although I try not to show it. It doesn't make any sense. 'You mean they can survive like that, in there,' I'm pointing rudely at her stomach by now, 'upside down?'

'Of course.'

'Holy shit!' I put the book away. I'm not ready to deal with this.

Life and death in Spain, July 18th

We've spent the last couple of days doing very little, although I'm showing an inordinate interest in the activities of little Clément – watching his rhythms, when and what he eats, how much freedom the little emperor allows the rest of the household, whether his parents get any sleep, the extent of their social life, that kind of thing. Cécile and Pierre strike me as remarkably attentive and patient parents. They have to be – in the last forty-eight hours, Clément has fallen on his head at least twice though this is not the fault of his parents. It just happens to be the heaviest part of his anatomy and therefore that bit which hits the deck first. Maybe it's just because he's a little sick? Whatever the truth of it, he sleeps little and cries a lot and his mother and father are never far behind – feeding and watering him, picking him up, dusting him down, wiping away tears, putting him to bed and watching over him through half-shut eyes as they search exhaustedly for some sleep.

I look at Helena. I'm on the verge of telling her I've made the most terrible mistake, that I really can't do this because I'm too selfish, too lazy and too irresponsible. I'm almost prepared to admit that I'm too damned scared before I notice the smile on her face and the tenderness with which she follows her nephew's progress around the garden and anticipates any clumsiness that might result in another tumble. Then something falls into place in my own head. I won't be the only parent of our child and, what's more, it's likely I'll be playing the supporting role rather than the lead. I can see how it's always the mother who provides for the primary needs of a child. After all, they carry it and feed it for nine months before Daddy gets to even hold the results of his own primary instincts. What Helena needs from me is not to become a one-man kindergarten, but rather to provide a helping hand and a safe and stable environment for the baby. I don't have to do it alone; I'm not the star of the show and she'll always be there when I fuck it up. The downside is that I won't win any Oscars for doing it right. I just have to get it done, like everyone else.

In the late afternoon, Pierre and I head to the beach on bicycles while the girls and babies follow in the car. Clément is still recovering from a bout of gastritis which probably accounts for the fact that his nappies smell like a couple of hectares of the finest agricultural compost, but this is quickly forgotten in the salty air of the beach where he's introduced to a fine young Spanish lady named Maria. She's eighteen months old and deeply suspicious of anyone not immediately recognisable as her mother. In an attempt to win her confidence, I begin sifting clam shells out of the boiling sand. As I place them in a row upon her thigh, she gazes at me as if I'm the last remaining double agent from the Soviet bloc. Her chestnut Spanish eyes are so profound that you could stare at them a lifetime and never reach the bottom.

The shell game is interrupted briefly when Maria catches sight of Clément's willy. This must be the first time she's seen such a thing in her short life and she cranes her neck for a better view. Unable to restrain her curiosity, she reaches out to grab the offending article and Clément, who fails to understand what all the fuss is about, resists the first female advance of his life and runs headlong into the simpler pleasures of the surf.

By the time we reach home, I've discovered another of the delights of having children. Clément has successfully transmitted his infection to the rest of the household and his father is the first to falter. Pierre has not even dismounted his rusty steed before he vomits into the first available receptacle (which happens to be a bucketful of my carefully selected clam shells). He's forced to retire as I relax and allow the evening sun to gently penetrate my skin. Idly I boast of an iron constitution and the fact that I'm rarely ill.

Three hours later, I'm bolt upright in bed because an unseen and malicious enemy has my stomach in a vice-like grip. My head is pounding and I'm sure that if I get so much as a whiff of a chorizo sausage, I shall empty the contents of my stomach in less time than it takes to say 'iron constitution'.

'*Qu'est ce qu'il y a, chéri?*' asks Helena.

'I'm dying!'

'Dying?'

'Yeah, you know, the state you enter shortly before you're buried in the soil.'

'Is it liable to be protracted?' asks the woman who is obviously familiar with the inability of the male of the species to tolerate any pain whatsoever, unless it's in the name of winning an extended sports event.

'This is no time for jokes, Helena. Can I please have a glass of water?'

'Is that your last request? No priest or cigarette, then?'

'Water's fine.'

'Have you written your daughter into your will?'

'I'll do it tomorrow, if I survive the night. Promise.'

An Andalucian cave, July 19th

I haven't done that or anything else so far today, because I've been asleep for the last twenty-four hours. The massed ranks of all Iberian bacteria have abandoned my stomach but only because they've decided to invade my skull. Pierre and I crossed each other on one of our many trips to the bathroom and exchanged the type of greeting which must have been prevalent before primitive man learned to communicate via the spoken word. Neither Helena nor Cécile has yet been afflicted by the same malady. Perhaps pregnancy makes them immune to whatever it is we're suffering from? It must be the hormones, I muse, before drifting back into the comfortable kingdom of unconsciousness once more.

Over the Pyrenees in a dress, July 21st

One look at Helena's face is enough to confirm that she's become the latest victim of whatever it was that Clément cooked up with that *Kiddie's Khemistry Kit* of his. She looks as reduced as Fay Wray in the palm of the original King Kong. Cécile has also succumbed to the belligerent bug and, at seven months pregnant, that must be one hell of a stomach ache. Yet the feebleness which attacked my joints has now fled and I manage to walk all the way round the bougainvillea bush in the garden before the lure of *Le Tour* becomes too strong. Six hours later, as the riders are thirteen kilometres from the finish on the last dance uphill, Lance Armstrong is leading the main contender, German Jan Ullrich, when he suddenly weaves too close to the side of the road. In the most bizarre moment of this fantastical event, he manages to get the handlebars of his bike caught up with an old lady's handbag and tumbles to the deck, bringing the leading Spaniard down with him. Ullrich avoids the spilled lipstick and poodles and continues. Surely this is his chance. But he stops and waits for Armstrong to get back on his bike and rejoin the battle. What is he thinking? Germans are not supposed to behave like that. Has the man never heard of national stereotypes? Perhaps he's too plain knackered to take advantage of his rival's misfortune and, clad in mink stole, stockings and stilettos, Armstrong inevitably rejoins him at the front. Within another ten metres, he's pulling ahead once more. By the time he reaches the top, he has all but ruined Ullrich who finishes one minute behind, by which time

Lance has ill-advisedly introduced the word 'awesome' into the Spanish language. The gentleman German now needs a miracle before they reach the finish in Paris. As a native of England and one who has been raised on the sights and sounds of gallant losers, I know it'll never happen.

After several days of sporadic puking, meanwhile, the tension is beginning to rise in our little house by the beach, imperceptibly at first, but then to such a degree that even the Englishman in front of the TV is unable to ignore the evidence. It starts when Helena begins to panic about the state of her unborn. The reassuring pain in her breasts that confirms Junior's presence has disappeared, but Cécile's suggestion that she's over-dramatising is not the spoonful of honey that Helena craves. Hurt when she'd rather be hurting, she retires to bed with the Rock of Gibraltar that has now taken up residence in her stomach.

The hunt in Andalucía, July 22nd

By now Helena's in a state of advanced panic. The cup of tea I proffer, more in hope than expectation, makes not the tiniest dent in her desperation. There's a real wildness in her eye and because I'm way out of my depth, I do what any real man would do and call desperately for Cécile, who promptly administers a dose of no-nonsense shut-up-and-go-back-to-sleep-and-you'll-be-fine-tomorrow. I catch most of her speech, a small fragment of Helena's ultra-colloquial reply and decide my best course of action would be another short walk around the bougainvillea bush. As I'm sure you understand, this is motivated purely by prudence on my part and a desire to let the pregnant women figure it out between them and is in no way related to any form of cowardice.

A call is made to the gynaecologist in Paris who, from a distance of almost 1,500 kilometres, diagnoses early contractions. Even to a Neanderthal like me, premature contractions seem unlikely. Helena's symptoms are no different to those suffered by the rest of the household and neither Pierre nor I are expected to give birth at any time soon. Cécile's furrowed brow suggests she's deeply unimpressed by the doctor at the other end of the continent and, as I hide between the lurid pink and orange blossoms, she tells me I shouldn't be intimidated by the anxieties of a pregnant woman at the first sign of trouble, otherwise I'll end up being swept downstream to disaster faster than a kayak in the spring melt. 'Who me?' I ask, dusting down my jeans. 'I was just checking for rare Spanish beetles.'

Cécile's irritation with Helena's histrionics is increasing by the minute, but we're under instruction to score an anti-dilatory called *Spasfon*. Cécile and I remain sceptical about the necessity for this, but in the name of reassurance, we check in at the local pharmacy. They've never heard of it and insist there is no local equivalent. Back outside, I shove little Clément into one of those oscillating toy cars which, in return for a €1 coin, plays an irritating electronic tune and sends the poor child into a temporary delirium. The car is a miniature *Porsche*, which reminds me that I need to put aside some cash to buy Junior a pram otherwise I'll be transporting my kid around in a seaside bucket and spade. At least I've discovered how to make small children smile, even if the price to pay is carrying the damned 'Birdie Song' around in my head for the rest of the week.

Back at the ranch, Helena is in final rehearsal for her deathbed scene. Her last request? Why, a single slice of cooked ham, of course! Other than *Spasfon*, this happens to be about the only thing we don't have in the refrigerator, but I promise to search for some at the local supermarket just as soon as it reopens. Helena resumes her languid passage into the afterlife and I hit the kitchen to prepare lunch for the survivors.

With lunch on the table, Pierre gets back from work and enquires after the health of his only sister. I inform him that her post-mortem will follow hot on the heels of a dessert of yoghurt and prunes. Little brother is distinctly unimpressed by my attitude and decides to check for himself, while Cécile and I dive headlong into an enormous bowl of pasta – the first time I've so much as looked at solid food in almost forty-eight hours. As my snout nears the bottom of the bowl and Pierre's dish goes cold on the table, I sense a growing feeling of unease. At first I think I may just have overeaten, but no, as I'm wiping the last of the tomato sauce from my mouth, little brother returns to the table with a face like tropical storm.

'You know what,' he asks rhetorically, voice barely under control. 'When pregnant women want something, it's our duty to provide it.'

Duty! Now there's a word that's guaranteed to get my goat. Every mealtime, when I was a kid, I was force-fed a diet of duty and how-to-behave-like-a-responsible-adult. As my defiant, oily features emerge slowly from the penne, I try not to betray the irritation erupting inside. 'Is that a fact? So what does she want?' I ask in a voice which could tear skin.

'A piece of white ham,' he answers, as if these words were hitting the dictionary for the very first time.

I'm furious with Pierre, but not half as furious as I am with Helena. How dare she betray me over a single slice of Hispanic swine? I came here in the hope of recovering my friendship with her brother after the furore over the aborted wedding. When he found out what I'd done, he called to tell me precisely what he thought of my U-turn and I had no answers, no explanation to offer and just sat on the other end of the phone, clucking and wobbling like some backbench Conservative jelly. While his parents were either kind or befuddled enough to say nothing, Pierre was determined to uphold family honour. He told me it was time to 'assume my responsibilities and grow up a little'. And we've barely spoken one word to one another since, until we met at Orly airport one week ago. Now Helena has handed him a nice sharp knife to finish the job.

By now I'm boiling with rage and the only way I can cool off is by sinking my teeth into a perfectly formed Spanish peach. But little brother hasn't finished yet: 'I think she'd like to talk to you,' he says, gesturing vigorously over his shoulder. I'll bet she would, and not about the bloody cycling either. She probably expects me to hunt a wild boar in the National Park down the road, kill it, wipe its arse and then serve it up in a perfectly ironed Spanish waiter's outfit. Well bollocks, I'm not moving. I finish my peach and fill the silence with the sounds of insolent sucking.

Of course I know that now is not the time. I know she's not well, that she's pregnant and I shouldn't. That's why I'm counting to ten as I take the walk down the corridor. No good. I count again, this time in Spanish. Still fuming! I try it in French, but linguistic limitations mean I get no further than seven and once I do reach the bedroom I explode like a bunch of cheap Chinese fireworks, totally ruining Helena's white linen deathbed scene with a volley of self-righteous, self-pitying, snivelling claptrap, all aimed at making her feel guilty for undoing a friendship with her brother which I fucked up in the first place.

For some reason, and let's put it down to a lack of spine, I have my back to Helena throughout this tirade. When I do turn around, the pale face on the bed is blinking and exhausted. She feels exactly as I did forty-eight hours ago. At least she's bearing it in stoic, female fashion. Damn it, I'm not going to! I refuse. I cannot and will not give in...

Several seconds pass before I pick up a small bore rifle, a hunting hat and head for the hills. Five days later, I'm back with 200 grams of prime, acorn-fed ham and in my absence things have clearly been happening. Helena, adding a few grains of dry white rice to her daily portion of restorative piglet, is apologetic (God knows why, but I say nothing). Pierre is talking to me as a friend, rather than some Mafiosi conducting a vendetta against the animal which has permanently besmirched his sister's reputation, and Cécile is smiling and presiding over the whole lot of us as sanctimoniously as the Queen of Sheba. What the fuck is going on here?

Helena's finally back on her feet this morning, Clément's missing rabbit is discovered down the back of the sofa and two couples are preparing to retreat a little into their own hermetically sealed worlds. Helena and I have decided to take a break from the tensions of family life to tour the southern fringes of Andalucía and everyone smiles as we bid our farewells. Even the local boar population appears to have forgotten the bullet and honk loudly as I reverse out of the drive and point the car eastwards in the direction of Seville.

United again in our small French hire car as we drive through the baking plains of the Rio Guadalquivir, Helena and I share observations on the past few days. She focuses on the delights of rearing a small child (and don't bother asking me what they might have been), while my attention has been drawn more to the strain of tending to the little buggers' every need (and Cécile and Pierre's relationship, unlike our own, is fully serviced by a housemaid-cum-babysitter).

Helena is also keen to draw my attention to the perfect lifestyle which Clément enjoys with his parents and integrated rabbit in a town free of pollution, with nothing more noisy next-door than a half-baked Alsatian that can't be arsed to bark in the heat. I turn up the radio in the hope of finding a song that will distract her attention but it's already too late and, as I struggle to find a wavelength with a sufficiently strong signal, Helena runs the rule over Pierre's job (respectable), house (large, airy, well-equipped) and car (a two-litre, sixteen-valve injection job that's even got me thinking employment may have an upside) and I'm shamed into silence. Finally, the radio hones in on a tortured, soulful Flamenco singer and I manage to persuade myself he's wailing in tune with my own miseries: what am I doing down here in Andalucía on holiday in a hired *Renault Clio*? I have no job, no house, and no car of my own. Surely I should be back in Paris, fixing up the future? After all, the baby cannot be expected to live forever under the caramel-coloured parasol with which I intend to resolve our immediate accommodation problem. Why was I born without the bodily parts necessary to take our predicament seriously?

In the midday heat, I loll on the sand as the future stretches in front of me and shimmers. One or two objects are visible in the distance but everything else is lost in an indistinct haze. We're not talking about it, but I suspect the return to Paris is already on Helena's mind. I know it's on mine, but whether or not I should return to a job in marketing services seems far too complicated a subject to contemplate as the salty water laps at my ankles. I know the discussion is coming and I know Helena's going to argue for a move to Toulouse but I'm not ready. I know nothing of that city. What would I do there? Why is she so confident that everything will be alright in the end? Surely she's been watching too many movies? The only certainty in my life is that I'd like an ice cream. To me, it feels more like I should forget my dreams, swallow my pride and return to what I know best.

So what is it, exactly, that I know how to do? Well, if I were to explain it to an alien on a junket from a distant solar system, I'd probably tell him that what I do for a living is assist a variety of voracious multinational corporations to make people aware of dreams, desires or preferably fully-formed and packaged products which they're not yet aware that they want. If that's a little unclear, why not try this: the imaginary company I'm servicing makes ice cream and they have a fantastic new idea, for example an ice cream that glows in the dark. But they're not quite sure whether the children to whom they intend to sell it are going to want to walk around town eating something that looks like a small nuclear reactor sitting on top of a perfectly normal ice cream cone, much less whether anyone is willing to pay for it. My role is to talk to the teens and their cash-dispensing parents and ask them exactly what they like and dislike about the new *Kryptonite Mangun* and, should one of the pubescent punters happen to come up with a new angle on the product during our discussions, like 'It's well tasty and the radioactive strawberries zapped my zits double quick time,' then my recommendation would be to use this as a tag-line to advertise his enriched uranium by-product slap bang in the middle of *Neighbours,* on the grounds that it will attract hoards of teenagers with faces like a slice of pizza and too much disposable income for their own good.

Still think this is far-fetched? Perhaps. But only this summer, one of the world's biggest ice-cream manufacturers launched a range ice creams named after the 7 *Deadly Sins*. You can decide for yourself whether lust, revenge and jealousy are desirable attributes in a teenager whose hormones are playing havoc before he's stuck a tongue into all those E numbers.

I'm finding it hard to convince myself it's a good idea to go back to this type of work. In fact, I'm convinced that only another of the Seven Deadlies, gluttony, will persuade me to do so. But the other way of looking at it is to think of the amount of money required to support a young family.

Yesterday afternoon, for example, I took a drive with Cécile to buy little Clément a new pair of shoes. 'How often does he need re-hoofing?' I asked.

'Oh, about every three and a half months,' she answered, as casually as you like.

Christ! I thought, before checking the price – €35, and that was in the sale! Then I remembered a conversation I'd started with Pierre in the middle of a chess game because I was trying to avoid an outbreak of genuine fisticuffs.

'Don't worry about the shoes,' he said, 'the real cost is all the love and attention they require.'

And with that, he splattered one of my remaining pawns and put me handsomely into checkmate

We reach Seville and turn south towards the old city of Cadiz. All around us lie fields the colour of ochre. There's almost no vegetation and it hasn't rained down here since the Spanish Civil War. The only sound is that of the sun burning holes in the roof of our *Clio*.

Costa de la Luz, July 24th

I'd never noticed it before, maybe you have, but the surface of our planet is simply crawling with those minor pests we refer to as children and babies. Admittedly, Helena has been stopping to look at every single one of them since we left France and that could be why they're so visible all of a sudden. You've already met Maria, but I could introduce you to thousands just like her, right here on this beach. Maybe it's just Andalucía, but the place is infested with kids bawling their little lungs out – howling because Daddy won't build them a sandcastle or blubbing because fat Uncle Pedro trod on their sea shells. I might even feel some sympathy for the parents, only most of them are worse than their kids. Of course, I'm not going to turn out like any of them because I'll remain supremely well-balanced. Oh sure, I'll be giving the nipper all the care and attention he deserves – I'll even buy him the odd pair of shoes – but it's important to retain a balance in life, and avoid turning him into one of those mollycoddled little bastards, don't you agree?

Beach babies and the end of the tour, Vejer de la Frontera, July 26th

We've landed in this little walled and whitewashed village up in the hills somewhere between Cadiz and Gibraltar. It's a beautiful place and quiet too, at least until dusk falls at which point all the local teenage boys start using the narrow cobbled streets as a raceway to impress the girls with their scooters. Watch out, *niños*, it might start out as a snog and a fondle round the back of some fourteenth-century castle, but it all ends up in a semi-detached in the suburbs of Orpington with a 'baby on board' sticker in the rear windscreen of a sensible saloon and puke all over the leatherette seats.

Anyway, the streets of Vejer are just teeming with pregnant women and toddlers who are trying to escape from their prams and make a dash for the town walls and the spectacularly perpendicular drop into the surrounding countryside. Then there are those parents for whom the worst appears to be already over, walking around town with youngsters who lie somewhere between the ages of tantrum and heroin addiction. You know the type – their haircuts are sensible enough and they remain self-conscious enough to agree with Mummy and Daddy in public, but they've already begun to sprout haphazard limbs and no longer retain control of their moods or bodily functions.

As we wander around town, Helena stops to study each and every child under the age of three as if there were any substantive difference between them. We're nearing the end of her third month now and she's finding it pretty uncomfortable walking around vertical Spanish villages in temperatures reaching 36° in the shade. Maybe it's only weariness that causes her to stop and goggle at all these kids?

I suggest spending a bit of time down at the beach. From my point of view, this would mean a nice twelve-kilometre burn-up in the hire car followed by a bit of peace and quiet lazing around in the surf with the latest reports from *Le Tour*. To my relief, Helena agrees. We pick up supplies, then set off down the hill, where I slip down into third to overtake a lengthy caravanserai of German tourists with the underpowered engine screaming for mercy. Helena lets loose a volley of abuse over the bass-driven sounds of the stereo. I can't quite make all of it out, but it's got something to do with her not minding if I kill myself, or even her, but before I slam all of us into an oncoming bus, would I please spare a thought for the one passenger who's too young to wear a seat belt. Duly chastened, I take my foot of the gas, push the car into tourist gear and smile as considerately as I can at the Germans.

Down at the beach I pull out a copy of *El Pais*. I doubt my Spanish is up to reading much of their analysis of the Iraq war, but that's not what interests me. The papers here are full of the climax of *Le Tour*. Paris may seem like a million miles away, but the race will be settled over the rain-sodden pavements of that dank northern city this weekend. There aren't any children on this particular stretch of the beach which means I may even be able to unwind a little...

Claudia is twenty months old. Her parents have parked her buggy right next to Helena and, as I conclude a fascinating article about the forthcoming world swimming championships, I'm suddenly aware of two little eyes boring into the back of my neck – an area I'd reserved exclusively for the rays of the afternoon sun. Someone is trying to feed her a packet of crisps but, for some unknown reason, Claudia seems to be more interested in the man who lines up shells on the legs of babies. Things take a distinct turn for the worse when Helena strikes up a conversation with all three of them, which would be fine were it not for the fact that Helena can't speak a word of Spanish and needs a translator. That's why she's elbowing me in the ribcage and asking me how to say 'I think the bulge in her nappy suggests it's about to overflow!' I give Helena my filthiest look, but all to no avail and, after a couple of minutes spent discussing feeding times, breast milk and maternity bras, the penultimate stage of *Le Tour* begins to exert an irresistible pull...

The commentator thinks Ullrich is going too fast in the rain. No sooner has this thought exited his mouth than the German falls off his bike. He was going too fast in the rain. Lying in a puddle, Ullrich loses thirty seconds before getting back on his bike. He's managed to tear a large hole in his sponsor's *Lycra* shorts and will now finish second to Mr and Mrs Armstrong for the fifth time in a row. Not long afterwards, Lance slithers home like a yellow Texan sea snake and, after three weeks, it's all over bar the last stage which is little more than a parade up and down the Champs Elysées. What an anticlimax!

I wander back to the beach, where there's no sign of Claudia or her parents. But there is one increasingly large belly, which I spot from the bar. It's by far the whitest thing on the beach because Helena has a very fair skin, which is resisting the Spanish sun for as long as it can. Eventually it will signify its discomfort by breaking out into a series of frowning brown freckles. Helena stands up and waves. Her pale slender legs look like alabaster pillars which are too slender to support her small baby balcony and I'm overcome with fear at the sight of her fragility.

Sea food and run, July 27th

We spend the next couple of days following the rhythm of the rest of the coastal holidaymakers – getting up late in the morning, over a breakfast of coffee, raw ham and nebulous white bread, attempting to decide which beach to visit. Once we have set up camp near the shoreline, Helena reads and I walk along the beach. Eventually, we will eat a simple lunch of fried fish, lemon and salad. We talk little and only about the books Helena is reading, rather than about the future. I don't read. In fact, I'm not really doing much of anything. I've become more lizard than human – panting and baking on the hot sand and at regular intervals padding my way to the surf to cool off in the water before returning to my body-shaped indent in the sand.

In the evenings we eat gazpacho, fish soup, more salad, clams, mineral water and fruit in inexpensive restaurants. Helena looks happy, unless I order shellfish and then she looks worried. Helena has a problem, you see, and if I order paella, she'll hide her face behind a napkin as I top and tail the prawns and remove any exoskeleton from the plates in front of us. She'll eat these animals alright, but not if they are wearing anything at the table. Crabs are her nemesis and whatever they did to her when she was too young to scream, Helena can't now remember, but I think it's something she should look into and, hiding another pile of pink armour, I suggest a spot of hypnotherapy to get to the bottom of her phobia of things that move sideways. It's not that I mind dealing with the shellfish, but it can be embarrassing when the table next door orders crustaceans and Helena gets up to ask if they wouldn't mind changing their order, or perhaps moving to another restaurant.

Scrambled eggs, July 28th

After another two days fending off babies and crabs, we're driving further south to the port of Tarifa. I don't know how long we'll stay in this town, but we need to hide in the shadows for a while. My brain feels as if it's sitting, sunny side up, on top of my skull.

We leave after breakfast and drive through the first cloud that I've seen for what feels like months. The mountain sierras come down to meet the sea near here, and the road is lined with gigantic wind turbines. As the mountain mists swirl across the road in front of me, the supernatural atmosphere is heightened by an imaginative electronic music set on the radio, where some kind of machine is singing that 'there used to be another way of living, another way of sharing, another way of doing things'. I'm sure it's right, too, but can I find it? Or do I have to go back to marketing, which involves almost no sharing and is barely living at all? Helena and I don't talk as the car swings through another series of foggy curves: Helena because she's a little frightened in this lunar landscape and me because I don't have any questions, let alone any answers.

Tarifa old town, July 29th

This is a great town. Sure, it's full of surf hippies, dreadlocks, baggy shorts and marijuana, but the sharper urban set is well represented too – Madrid, London and, if you discount us two, Paris. My guess is that we're all here for the same reason, which is that Tarifa is a frontier town. Just twelve kilometres across the Straits of Gibraltar is another culture, another continent and another way of doing things. I've never been to Africa, but this morning I can see the unmistakable rise of the Atlas Mountains through the clearing southern skies. I have a sudden yearning to get on the boat and make the crossing but I'm overruled by Helena, who has a sudden yearning for lunch followed by a hotel bed on which to take a prolonged nap.

After unloading our bags and swallowing some pizza, I leave Helena to sleep and book myself onto an afternoon boat trip. A rather commercial looking outfit is offering a trip out into the Straits to spot dolphin and whale. They claim it's 95 percent likely that we'll see at least one species. Too many years in the business of marketing is enough to make me suspicious but I decide to go for it anyway. At worst, I'll get a good view of the Moroccan coast and a ride on a boat.

The narrowness of the Straits amazes me, as does the enormity of the oil tankers that pass through these waters nose-to-tail and cut across the bows of high-speed ferries shuffling between the two continents. There are also plenty of Spanish police boats patrolling the coast on the lookout for ragged refugees on makeshift rafts, desperate to chance their arm on the continent of Christianity, *Cornflakes* and consumer democracy (for those rich enough to enjoy it). To me, it seems highly unlikely that any self-respecting mammal might care to make its home in these turbulent waters.

But then comes another slap in the face for my cynicism as we're tracking a school of pilot whales to the port side of the boat. There must be about twenty of them, rising rhythmically out of the water, exhaling and then dipping under again. They appear to be completely undisturbed by the presence of the boat and a dozen goggling, lobster-red tourists from the frozen wastes of the north. They're serene and quite beautiful and I'd be quite content to watch them inhale and exhale for the rest of the day, but the captain soon tires of their stately progress and veers off towards the African coast. The relief on the other side of the water looks almost identical to the Spanish coast and somehow this surprises me, although I don't know why it should. As we complete our turn back to the Spanish mainland, we're joined by around fifty bottlenose dolphins, the ones like Flipper, as the captain adds helpfully over the tannoy. By now I'm hanging over the front of the boat. (I know I'm supposed to call it the aft, but I can't bring myself to use such a ridiculous term. After all, I've spent even less time at sea than *Captain Bird's Eye*.)

The dolphins take my breath away. They are barrelling along right underneath me and if I can't help smiling as I watch, I swear to God the dolphins are actually laughing. Underwater, they roll onto their sides, take a sneaky glance upwards to check that we're still gawping, before spinning sideways, lunging forward and then breaking the surface like synchronised silver torpedoes. It's almost as if they are taking the piss out of our cumbersome boat, laden with its cargo of gangly, unwaterproof humans. They remind me once more that it's time I gave up smoking, if for no other reason than the fact that they look like single, steel-grey and supremely healthy lungs, quite unlike my own which have taken a hammering for the last twenty-five years. The dolphins toy with us for a further five minutes and then, as unexpectedly as they had arrived, they're gone again. As I turn back to my fellow passengers on the boat, I feel strangely deflated. I'd really prefer to swim all the way back to port.

On the road between Tarifa and Ronda, July 30th

Back up in the sierra, we quickly climb to over a thousand metres and Helena has a few more suggestions for the baby's name:

'What about Sidonia?'

'You've been studying the map, haven't you?'

'What do you mean?'

'I mean Medina Sidonia, that small town about 100 kilometres west of here.'

'Yes.' She's sheepish now.

'So, you still think it's a girl, then?'

'That's what you want, isn't it?'

We roll into Ronda in the early evening and check into a hostel so cheap that even I'm satisfied. The town itself is split into two halves, deeply divided by a ravine which plunges 100 metres down into the Rio Tajo. The main feature of the town is an eighteenth-century bridge which traverses the gap and enables one side of the town to talk to the other without everybody having to shout across the narrow gorge. We eat at an expensive terraced restaurant which overlooks the bridge and watch the sun as it sinks into the surrounding fields. Reading my furrowed brow, Helena can tell I'm getting increasingly worried about our expenditure on the trip, so she tells me my delicious broad beans and blood sausage are a nice way to celebrate three months of her pregnancy. Women can be very clever sometimes, can't they?

The insects of Ronda, July 31st

The unfortunate thing about the sights of Ronda is that they're all displayed vertically. For example, we have to climb down a stone staircase carved into the side of the gorge by a Moorish king and then we have to climb back out. Apparently the king had his slaves running up and down the staircase ferrying water to troops busy defending the town against the Spanish. Anyway, I'm knackered by the time we get to the bottom, never mind getting back out again. In part this is down to the heat, although dolphin therapy has yet to wean me off the *Benson & Hedges*. I wait at the top of the well for Helena who is not far behind. This is surprising because it took her an age to get down this hellhole in the first place. 'You're quick!' I say. '*Ah, oui,*' she pants, 'I climb like a goat, but I go down like a cow!' This makes me laugh so hard that Helena has to carry me back out of the well.

Further down the gorge we visit the old Arab baths. In this heat I could do with a dip myself but they no longer contain so much as a drop of water. Then, with the temperature still rising, I make a serious mistake. I suggest a short-cut through the fields to get back into the main ice cream and *Coca Cola* zone. We get about half way when a colourful and imperious Spaniard rides out of the seventeenth-century dust, halts his even more imperious steed and reprimands Helena for not wearing a hat. We have been warned repeatedly by all the baby books of the perils of sunburn during pregnancy and here we are marching through fields in a temperature which I estimate to be at least 35°.

By the time we reach the next oasis and the welcome relief of some iced water, the sun has boiled us silly. Helena is red in the face (from anger rather than sunburn) and we sit in the bar in silence for some time until I return to my senses and discover that the joint is, for some unaccountable reason, about to screen *Being John Malkovich*.

I've no idea now whether it's the absurdity of the movie that does it, but in the middle of the night I'm awake, sweating and in a panic. In my nightmare, I'm trying to protect Helena from an invisible evil force. We're running around the garden of my childhood in grass taller than ourselves when I see an enormous locust coming through the grass at a tremendous speed. It must be twice as big as I am. Fearing the worst, I force myself to look at its face. To my horror, I see its jaws are made of wood. This terrifies me bolt upright and now I'm sitting here in bed, frantic, but dead still, in the sweltering darkness. As my senses regroup, I become aware of the sound of a single mosquito patrolling the room for blood. Armed with a copy of The Gideon Bible, I chase it around the room as if I were Peter Cushing hunting Count Dracula himself. I swear to God I'll never again kill a living creature with such lust.

Ronda, August 1st

It's even hotter today. We resolve to move at a slower pace and pay a visit to the Palacio de Mondragon. Covertly we dip overheating toes into the water which runs in elaborate patterns through beautiful gardens. Upstairs, I visit an exhibition while Helena enjoys the ceramic tiles and an extended history lesson. Then we retreat from the sun and return to hide in the dark of our hotel room before we're given another dressing down by Don Quixote.

There's a flamenco performance in Ronda this evening and Helena (representing the more adventurous side of our relationship) tries to convince me it's worth spending €50 on the tickets. I think it will be inauthentic and full of tourists. We agree to resolve our dispute over drinks on a small plaza near the hotel. By now it's seven in the evening and there's still no sign of the afternoon cooling off. Helena attempts to make it to the post office for a single stamp but gets only halfway across the cobbled plaza before she returns, looking like someone who's attempted a marathon in the Sahara desert.

I ask Helena whether it's likely we'll regret not going to the Flamenco performance. She merely shrugs her shoulders at my unanswerable question and peels the banknotes from my wallet. We sit down with the free drink offered with the ticket. I look around and fear the worst. There appears to be just the one Spanish couple in the audience; the rest are English, German and American. I even spot a pair of those milky blue eyes that immediately mark out the Dutch. This is going to be awful.

A little later than advertised, the musicians appear on stage. Two young women in traditional dress, each with a brilliantly-coloured flower knotted into her hair, are accompanied by a man with a guitar and a ponytail. They are aligned behind three microphones at the back of a hard, wooden dance floor which, for the time being, remains empty. The guitarist begins to strum a few of those aching, half Arab chords and the women begin to moan – the sound emanates from somewhere deep inside, a place to which the rest of us have no access. At times it seems barely human and I wonder whether their song is perhaps proof that it is possible to combine Christian and Islamic culture to harmonious effect, after all. The result is astonishing – the sound of the deepest vacuum as it's filled with bitterness, longing and regret one minute and unbridled joy the next. As I sit with my eyes closed, I can feel birth, death and all that lies in between.

It's almost midnight and the room is as hot as an Afghan cave. Suddenly a noise like a rifle shot jolts my eyes back open. Now there are two dancers on the floor. He wears a suit as black as charcoal, she an immaculate dress which falls for miles from its perch on the rise of her breast, although it soon starts to ebb and flow with a life of its own. Every so often, I glimpse calves of steel flashing beneath the turbulence of her skirts which she controls with grace and the utmost precision. Her face is hard with pride under jet-black hair and briefly I wonder how it is that her make-up doesn't run, but that's my final thought for the night before I'm transported to a place where there's no need for intellect – a place ruled by blood, iron, dust and bile. Without resistance, I allow myself to slide into a maelstrom of pain and carnality.

They dance together not as you and I would dance together, circling awkwardly to find the spaces in which we cannot hurt one another. No, this is where man and woman come together in a primordial place beyond guilt or fear, a place where two parts of a single whole fuse to experience all the body has to offer. Around them, the rhythms grow ever more fractious – that biting discordant guitar, the underground wails of the women, the tautness of their percussive palms – cutting across the movement of the dancers before rejoining body and soul for a single moment of the purest sex.

We are entranced by this bewitching expression of the human condition. I cannot comprehend how feet can move like feathers yet sound like thunder, how arms can become bows and fingers a hail of unerring arrows, expressing more than is possible with a lifetime of words. I've never seen such a powerful incarnation of womanhood. She dances with the grace of an eagle, the bite of a serpent, the sensuality and ferocity of a tigress. She weakens and bleeds me, before replenishing my soul with hope, love, power and the realisation that I'm alive.

THE SECOND TRIMESTER

Sick on the road, August 2nd

The turning point comes as we begin to wind our way slowly back towards the coast and, whispering in the middle distance, Paris. Today marks the beginning of the fourth month of Helena's pregnancy and women are now pointing at Helena's belly and smiling. They all ask the same questions: how many months? Do we know the sex? Is it our first? My own question, about whether the size of her belly is normal for three months, meets with nothing more than a fifty-kilometre dose of passenger seat silence as we descend from the heights of Ronda.

For most women, the onset of the fourth month marks the beginning of the 'quiet' period of pregnancy as they gradually become accustomed to the squatter in their bellies – a bit of a respite before the onslaught of the final trimester. (At least, I think that's what I remember reading in *Future Maman*.) Right now, the book lies buried at the bottom of our suitcase, covered by a fine layer of sand and untouched since our arrival in Andalucía.

In my own head, today also marks the point of no return. There's no going back now. I can be as scared and unprepared as I like but, for better or worse, I can be reasonably sure this fatherhood thing is going to happen to me.

As we reach the outskirts of the Grazalema National Park, the road is climbing again but not as fast as the mercury. The gauge which measures the temperature outside our dusty *Clio* already reads 35° centigrade. Yesterday I heard that this park is full of little rivers and streams and forms part of what is referred to as 'wet Andalucía'. Wet? We've already crossed a couple of bridges, but the only thing moving in the river beds below was a bit of scorched grass blowing lazily in the hot wind. We stop for coffee, water and a little local advice. Helena swallows a refreshing plate of cold prawns and peppers as I explore the possibility of finding somewhere to swim in this sizzling mountainscape.

By the time we get back into the car, the temperature has reached 39°. We drive through the whitewashed village of Grazalema and on towards El Bosque. The tar on the road surface is beginning to melt and a voice on the radio reports that large tracts of southern Spain and Portugal are on fire. At the bottom of a deep ravine, we find a river, which, in an effort to escape the sun, is carving its way through the rocks at a tremendous speed. The water is deliciously cool and we sink below the surface, moaning and bubbling in the shade like a couple of old carp. Suitably chilled, we crawl back onto the river bank in what looks like a slow-motion replay of a defining moment in the evolution of man and, under an old fig tree, enjoy a lunch of pork ribs, chorizo sausage and oily, spiced potatoes.

On the move once more, the road becomes an endless series of the slow curves which lull Helena into a state somewhere between hypnosis and nausea. The temperature has gone beyond 40° and the air conditioning is straining away at full blast but offering little relief. We pass through another remote town without stopping. No one is out on the streets. They must all be hiding in darkened cellars. The road is much slower than I expected and there seems to be no end to the rolling hills and the haze dancing across the road. 'How much further?' says Helena, choosing her words carefully to ensure maximum economy. 'Not much,' I lie, before pointing out another piece of desiccated carrion lying in the roadside, its withered legs sticking in the air like a flagpole abandoned by some misguided invaders many decades ago.

We're trying to get to the town of Alcalá de los Gazules,

where the map has convinced me the road flattens out and will lead us, straight and true, back to the beach. But the temperature is still rising, my head is beginning to throb and Helena is getting dramatically paler. 'We'll stop in Alcalá. Get a *Coke,* I promise.' 'Huh?' says Helena. The heat is draining everything of meaning, and words of more than one syllable are becoming indistinguishable and pointless. We lapse into silence once more. The only sound is the drone of the air conditioning. I'm not even sure I'm awake any more, although I think I just saw a signpost indicating that we're still 5 kilometres short of Alcalá.

'Stop the car!'

'Huh?'

'Stop. Now!'

I can't summon the effort to say 'Huh' one more time. Instead I brake so abruptly that the *Clio* stalls. The thought occurs that I'm almost past caring as Helena spills out of the passenger door and zigzags behind the car. I watch in the rear view mirror as the sight of her vomiting brings me to my senses. Then I fall out of the car with the last of our water and a hat. Helena looks a little green around the gills but claims to feel better. I manage a feeble joke about her wasting the chorizo we ate for lunch but she just stares into the distance. We pour the remaining water down the back of our necks and get into the car. The temperature gauge reads 47°.

As we finally pull into Alcalá, Helena says 'Ironic isn't it, me being sick today?'

'Why?' I'm still not prepared to chance anything longer than a three letter word, just in case my brain bursts open like a sickly sweet, overripe water melon.

'I wasn't sick once in the first trimester.'

'And?'

'I'm sick on the first day of the second.'

This does feel oddly significant in some way but, right now, I'm incapable of reasoning why. Instead I pull in at the next red and white sign. The heat has sapped our energy, strength and any remaining sense but the *Coca Cola* returns them all in a single shot of sugary brown fizz, just like it says in the ads. Only then do I allow myself to reflect that what we've just done was stupid and risky.

Back on the coast, I check us into the hotel closest to the beach and flick on the TV news: southern Spain is suffering a remarkable heat wave. The temperature has reached 52° in Seville and Córdoba, a number of people have died and the tanned weather girls in floral frocks are telling everyone to stay inside and be careful. Perhaps I'm hallucinating but I even hear a special message for mad dogs and Englishmen: stop playing the fool with the life of your unborn child.

A good hot meal, August 3rd

Straight off the Sahara, the hot wind has blown us into a town north-west of Tarifa, where the Mediterranean opens up into the Atlantic. It's a spot favoured by the bronzed, athletic set, most of whom are wielding surf boards. Still operating on a strict diet of monosyllables, Helena and I tiptoe down to the beach as the wind picks up fistfuls of sand and flings them at our unprotected skin. The only refuge is to be found in the surf or at one of the ubiquitous *chiringuitos* (a type of Spanish beach hut invariably sponsored by *Coke* or *Pepsi*), which are full of surf hippies sucking on elongated spliffs. Lazing on the beach is a relief and the wind blows any words from my head long before they've had a chance to solidify on my tongue.

Early in the evening, we head for the nearest town to seek shelter from the ferocious elements in what looks like a Moroccan bazaar. It's the first weekend of the August holiday and the migrant population is in the mood to party. Helena and I loll on floor cushions embroidered with gold thread and watch the sun setting as the surf dudes tuck into whisky and hashish sundowners. They're a cosmopolitan bunch, united by a love of those wispy beards that hang from their chins like strands of permanent spittle.

As we make a move for dinner, one of the beards hears Helena and I conversing in our habitual cocktail of English and French. He's called Manolo and his girlfriend's name is Mercedes, so it doesn't take too long to figure out that they might be Spanish. Manolo is keen to practise his English and presumably to impress Mercedes, who doesn't speak much of anything, but has beautiful green eyes.

'Where you from?' asks Manolo, just to get things rolling.

'England. And Helena here is from France.'

'England! I just come from Oxford,' gobbles Manolo.

'Oh yeah, what were you doing over there?'. I find it hard to imagine that such a genteel English town has much to offer in the way of surf, even if there's surely a plentiful supply of dope.

'No. No surfing,' says a suddenly serious Manolo. 'You see, I am nuclear physicist.'

I look at the beard, the shaved head, the pirate shorts and the girlfriend and figure it's just about possible, but decide to proceed with caution. At this point the four of us are approached by a dealer flashing a lump of hash the size of a duck's egg.

'No. Is OK,' hisses Manolo, before turning his attention back to me. 'Yes, I was working for a food company.'

'A food company?'

'Yes, testing the food for radioactivity.'

'Radioactivity?' By now I'm figuring that repetition is the only way to proceed in a conversation that's going places I'm not sure that I want to go.

'Sure. Is a lot of radioactive food since Chernobyl.'

'And how did you like England?' I venture, before he tells me something I really don't want to hear.

'Oh, I like very much England. But the food not so great.'

'Oh? Nuclear fallout?'

'No, no,' laughs Manolo, 'England fish come from Atlántico,

no radioactivity there!'

'Cool,' I say because it feels like the kind of thing I should be saying in this town. 'Manolo, do you know of a restaurant somewhere near here? Somewhere we can have a nice, safe dinner?'

Manolo points happily in the direction of a restaurant which overhangs the beach and, before we part company, I ask for the name of the town into which we have stumbled.

'He has no name.'

'What?' I ask, gazing around at the fair-sized conurbation.

'No name, no. Is just one *chiringuito enorme!'*

In the town with no name Helena and I eat fresh grilled fish and by the time we've polished off our enriched uranium dessert we're feeling beat. Not so Manolo, Mercedes and the rest of southern Spain – they're just getting started. Most Spanish in summer mode start eating around eleven in the evening. But the summer evenings truly begin after a shot of coffee, a digestif and a quick shower. In this false calm before the storm, Helena and I drift innocently off to sleep. But around two in the morning, we're rudely awakened as things really begin to kick off with a cacophony of slamming doors, parties on balconies, break dancing in the hotel courtyard, shattering glass, shrieking and the viscerally uncoordinated sound of the truly pissed as they fornicate the night away.

The chiringuito, August 4th

As we sit down to toast and coffee, Helena's face is not a portrait of serenity. The only thing that stops her from exploding is the fact that the party still hasn't finished and she won't be able to make herself heard over the noise. It's now 9.30, and surrounding us at the breakfast table is a small squadron of horseflies and a number of party animals at the fag-end of a big night. They're indulging in a breakfast of beer, cigarettes, hashish, plus a bit of coffee on the side, and trying to ease their sleepless way into the new day. They're cackling and shouting things at each other that none of them will remember by the time they have been to bed and woken up again later this evening.

Helena is appalled because she can't believe anyone would want to abuse themselves in such a way, and I'm appalled because I've spent extended periods of my life abusing myself in exactly this way and a small part of me regrets that I won't be joining the party. As I sit here and watch, one month sober almost to the day, I'll admit that it looks uncomfortably like insanity yet I can still feel the pull towards the abyss.

The nocturnal ones head back to their burrows and we make for the beach which is almost deserted. For the rest of the day, I shuffle like an old crab between the hot sand and the cold water and nothing much is said.

We know what's coming later and figure there's little point in hitting the sack early. Instead, we join the party goers in the early evening at the *chiringuito*. I plant myself in a deckchair and point it out to sea. In front of me, a thousand stars are playing in the night sky, while behind me candles flicker languidly in the breeze and Helena is rocking gently in a hammock to the ubiquitous beachside beat of Bob Marley as the spliffs burn red, gold and green in the night all around us.

The bullfight, August 5th

But one more night with the living dead is all we can bear. I reload the *Clio* and point the air conditioning northwards. It's a long drive back to Mazagón and I want to break it in Cadiz, the home town of someone I once knew in a village near Barcelona. Andres was an alcoholic and, rather unwisely, he ran a bar that served as the social centre of the village. Well, by about lunchtime, he was usually too drunk to run anything other than his own ailing circulatory system – his wife and four dark-eyed daughters were the real engine room of the place. Andres just stood there misty-eyed, beer in hand, talking incessantly of a town he had abandoned for Catalonia thirty-five years previously. Although I understood barely half of what he said, I liked Andres and always felt a certain empathy with him even if, at the time, I didn't know why.

Cadiz is almost an island. The city is connected to the mainland by a thin strip of land which is now little more than a motorway. While Helena sits in a shaded café terrace, I go for a wander around the town. I search for a while, but fail to find the ghost of Andres patrolling the alleyways of the old town, though the streets still resonate with the sounds of what must have been an exciting childhood. Then I set off to see what is one of the most spectacular cathedrals in Europe, but it's closed today and all I'm offered is the opportunity to climb its tower for a fee of €3 and in a temperature approaching 40°. I decline, and trudge reluctantly back through the old port to find Helena. It's time to go back to Mazagón.

I'm not really looking forward to part two of our stay with Cécile and Pierre. I happen to know they're expecting more visitors this weekend and my fear is that family tensions will soon resurface. I'd prefer to divert the panting *Clio* to the airport in Seville and get straight on the plane. I've already spent too long away from home and I'm longing for a little bit of space to call my own as well as an excuse to escape further scrutiny of my increasingly erratic behaviour. But I can feel the expectant mother beside me squirming with excitement at the thought of seeing young Clément again and resolve to hold myself in check for just a few more days. We pull into their driveway, soaked in sweat, in the early evening and I'm secretly delighted to find no one home. I roll my swimming trunks up in a towel and head directly to the beach.

Back at the house, we start by circling each other a little warily although a resolve to make it work seems to have affected us all. Despite the excess of politeness and respect that permeates our barbecued mackerel supper (why does that oily blue fish always seem to accompany delicate dinners in this family?), everyone is relaxed by the time we reach dessert and a degree of warmth has returned to our table. After dinner, the girls retire and I tempt fate by suggesting a game of chess. Pierre thinks twice after a hard days' graft, moulding and shaping a new coastal gas terminal, but he relents after a nip of whisky and a quick shot of caffeine.

I get the white pieces and start off in aggressive mode – the only way I know how to play. I figure that if you're going to go down anyway, then it's better to do so in an attacking rage rather than meekly defending the skirts of your chaste queen. I'm expecting Pierre to devour the men of my static defence as rapidly as a swarm of starving locusts devours a field of fresh corn, but somehow it never quite comes to pass. Cheekily I slay a bishop here, a knight there; before greedily submitting to the exchange of queens he offers halfway through the game (so much for defending the honour of virgins).

Half an hour later the board is decimated, I'm still a couple of pieces to the good and the cicadas watching from the surrounding trees are abuzz with excitement. What's got into me? I'm playing like a man possessed and thinking fully two and a half moves ahead. By now we're into the early hours of the morning and I'm finally in a position to whip the ass of the son of the father who beats me but loses to the son. If only I can hold my ragged troops together long enough, I should be able to press home my advantage. I might even be able to make it look like I know what I'm doing.

I ponder the motivational miracle that is revenge and arrogantly tilt backwards the brim of the preposterous leather hat I purchased in a moment of idle fancy in Ronda. I'm no longer the whipping boy – I'm a cold and calculating matador with untold resources hidden beneath my suit of lights. I stare at my prey and ponder how to finish him off with maximum aplomb. Who knows? Much more of this and I may even come to believe in myself as a father. I scan the garden amphitheatre where row upon row of white handkerchiefs are fluttering in the breeze in recognition of the skill and daring of the torero. The only thing standing between me and utter glory is the small matter of outmanoeuvring the last remaining castle defending his king against my unshaven crew of bishop, knight and other bit-part medievalists. Ungallantly, I demand the bull's resignation. Pierre looks at his watch and then at his empty whisky glass. He probably can't be arsed to be chased around the chess board all night by such an amateur and, after a moment's reflection, he sighs and knocks over his king. It's all over and, revelling in the applause of the aficionados and their simmering black-eyed wives, I rip off my jacket to reveal a still taken from the scan of our unborn.

Why rabbits do not take cruises, Mazagón, August 6th

Little Clément is sick again today. It's only a cold but we all fear the worst. To cheer him up I pick up his favourite soft toy. It's a rabbit called Quito, from the Spanish 'conejito', the English equivalent of which would probably be 'Bunnykins'. In the Spanish vernacular, however, it may also be translated as 'little pussy' and, no, I don't mean the one with the paws, although I decide against sharing this with either Clément or his parents.

I've already been warned about messing with an object invaluable to the little one's sleep, but I think it might be fun if the rabbit joins Clément in his paddling pool. After all, what are uncles for if not to overstep the mark once in a while and release their temporary charges from the iron fist of parental discipline? I place the rabbit in a small bucket and plot a westerly course across the pool. Pierre looks on without saying too much, perhaps for fear it may come across as sour grapes after his humiliation on the chessboard. But my purpose-built bunny-boat proves woefully inadequate for the crossing and capsizes when the adventure has barely begun. Quito sinks in a trice and, ignorant of the true proportions of this calamity, I start laughing like a hyena as Clément begins to cry. Pierre, face set harder than Abraham Lincoln's on Mount Rushmore, snatches the rabbit from the depths and without waiting for the band, marches both it and his son inside.

Five minutes later, as I lounge in a garden deckchair, Helena spells out the extent of the damage. The boy is overtired, it's siesta time, he can't sleep a wink without the pussy-rabbit and his father is livid. Demonstrating a complete lack of knowledge about the importance of stuffed animals in the world of small children, I offer to dry the bedraggled object out in the sun, to wring it out manually or even to buy a new one. Helena suggests that I take a long walk and, before you know it, we're all back to square one. Only this time, I'm clearly to blame. As I close the front gate with me on the outside, the only sounds coming from inside the house are those of a rabbit being frantically blow-dried and Clément wailing in his cot. Why didn't I head straight for the airport when I had the chance?

I'm given another severe reprimand by Helena when I slink back into the garden an hour later: Clément's parents have taken out an injunction order and if I'm seen within twenty-five metres of the rabbit, I shall be arrested immediately and subject to deportation. I base my defence on the fact that Quito was clearly complicit in the crime by agreeing to board the boat in the first place and I cannot be held solely responsible for his lack of seamanship. But all my arguments are rejected out of hand and I resort to sulking in silence. I'm pissed off with all of them, but especially with Helena for siding with a fucking soft toy. Later in the evening, dinner is a little tense, but Quito is as dry as a desiccated coconut. I know this because, when no one is watching, I break parole and viciously ram my forefinger into the little bastard's furry stomach.

Maybe Helena has made an appeal for clemency on my behalf because I appear to have been granted a stay of execution and I'm mournfully savouring the last of my alcohol-free rum and raisin ice cream when Helena asks Cécile whether she plans to have an epidural for the birth of her second child. This prompts a long conversation about the birth of Clément (a twelve-hour affair in a Parisian hospital). Pierre was there throughout, apparently, in their private room, listening to a few CDs and chatting as Cécile went into hard labour. The bit about the CDs surprises me a little – I mean, how do you decide what music to listen to when your partner is in agony? I try to imagine the scene:

'Pierre, Pierre, please, I can't stand the pain.'
'Just a minute dear, I just have to change the compact disc.'
'Get the doctor, I need another shot of class A narcotics.'
'Just a jiffy, darling. Be with you in a mo'. What do you fancy? Metallica or a spot of Charles Aznavour?'
'Please, I just want to die.'
'Hold on then, I'll put on Handel's Messiah.'

Cécile assures us that, after nine months of bearing the almost unbearable, it's fairly normal for women to want to abandon the whole thing at the last minute and opt for something more relaxing, like suicide. It was Pierre's job, and it will soon be mine, to coax her back from the jaws of death into one final effort. I'm watching Helena's face throughout, especially the part where Cécile insists she can't wait to go through it all again. As a man, I simply can't understand how any woman could contemplate putting herself through such an ordeal, but Helena wears no particular expression and betrays no emotion as the story of the birth reaches its bloody climax. I know I'm supposed to be there too, so I'll just have to ask the doctor if he will please anaesthetise me, top to tail, at the same time as he does Helena.

The evening heralds the arrival of Cécile's brother, Thibault, and his new bride, who've flown in direct from Central America. We've met once before and I happen to know that two of their favourite sports are drinking and smoking. Much as I like them, I fear staring bleary-eyed into an empty tumbler before the end of our holiday. Before retiring, we discuss the possibility of a trip to the sand dune park of Doñana, through which the Rio Guadalquivir dribbles its way down to the sea. The newlyweds and I decide to pay a visit in the morning, which means setting off before sunrise, but the cocktail cousins are unconcerned by the thought of a hangover and, late in the evening, I set the alarm for the first time in months.

Longitudinal drift, August 8th

The minute I hear distant voices I shake myself out of the damp sheets and Thibault, Aurélie and I are soon stealing off through the dawn like three burglars caught on a grainy CCTV video barely a couple of hours after our heads had hit the pillow. It's a beautiful walk through the dunes down to the beach on the fringes of the national park. It's still way too early for conversation and the only sounds are the cicada singing themselves to sleep and a breeze blowing gently through the thorny bushes which have made their mobile homes on the sands. We dive into the cool sea.

As the Latin cousins start to swim back in the general direction of Central America, I pick myself up and walk along the beach with only my footprints for company. After no more than a couple of hundred metres, I'm overcome by a sense of utter solitude. Effervescent waves of exhilaration start to pulse wildly through my veins. I've no idea where it comes from but it's a fantastic feeling. Quickening my pace, I peel off my T-shirt and abandon it on the beach. The only sound is that of the surf breaking against the shoreline. As the sun warms my back, the tension of the past few days lifts from my shoulders as though I were shedding a layer of old skin. I follow that line where the sand is permanently saturated by salt water and my feet sink a little further into the sand, leaving a more solid imprint. It's strangely gratifying to turn and to watch myself leaving a trail and, meeting with no resistance at all, my thoughts return to those childhood fears, only this time I'm overcome with a feeling of contentment.

I no longer have any wish to return to Paris. I want to stay here, close to the sky and the sea. Suddenly I'm close to tears and have no idea why. I struggle to hold them back. A single drop of salty water rolls down my cheek. I fall to my knees and sink hard into centuries of pulverised shell. It feels as if a body far more powerful than my own is pinning me to the spot. I have no desire to fight it.

Adiós to Mazagón, August 9th

Thibault is singing and playing the guitar, Pierre is teasing a set of bongos and everyone's talking ten to the dozen. Lamb cutlets are smoking away on the barbecue, champagne is uncorked and I watch as it gradually replaces the empty bottles of wine and beer which already litter the table. Helena's youngest brother has flown in from France to join the party and is regaling us with tales of a heat wave in Paris, and Helena is enjoying one last dance with her nephew before he fades and is sent to bed exhausted. I'm taking pictures and, from the head of the table, Cécile surveys the whole scene like an overindulgent aunt. Hearing the fuss, Pep and Carmela arrive from their house across the street and we fall into a free-flowing conversation that will continue long into the night.

Pep, a teacher, tells me about his son who lives in Madrid. After a stint writing for a newspaper in Seville, he chucked it all in to write a film script and, for the first time in weeks, my own, lost project crowds fleetingly into my mind. It's hard not to notice the light in Pep's eyes when he talks of his son. I ask if he's a product of the educational system of Mazagón and he nods quickly before averting his gaze. 'Then you must be very proud,' I suggest, knowing full well that this is not the kind of thing a stranger says to another man in Spain. Pep hesitates and considers his answer. Although 'hmmm' is the only sound issued by way of official response, a long look into the bottom of his whisky glass tells me all I need to know.

Eventually, I look at Helena in a way that conveys the question 'Do you fancy a couple of hours of shut-eye before we head to the airport?' She understands instantly and we slink off from a party that's barely getting started. My only hope is that, before long, we'll be back in Spain.

Walt Disney versus the real world, August 10th

As we prepare for take-off, Helena reaches out for some form of reassurance. I look at her terrified face through eyes which resist my attempts to open them fully. The pilot has given us the route and the direction of the wind, has introduced the crew, hopes we'll have an enjoyable flight and all that other meaningless guff that's supposed to reassure the nervous traveller. But the only way he could reassure Helena is by slipping into a little red cocktail dress and talking in a fine falsetto voice until we've all landed safely in Paris.

'Talk to me,' says Helena, as she always does when we board an aircraft, 'please, talk to me!' Her terror is the only thing keeping me awake as the plane lifts its sticky feet out of the liquid tarmac on the runway. What am I talking about? God alone knows – for all she cares it could be the chemical composition of kerosene. She just needs to hear words, the sound of a voice, anything to distract her from thoughts of imminent catastrophe. Long before the plane has reached cruising altitude I'm fast asleep and I doubt that even crashing into the Sierra Nevada would awaken me.

Which is more or less what I think has happened when I finally come to a couple of hours later. Helena is surrounded by what at first glance appear to angels, although it turns out to be a Spanish family heading for *Disneyland*. As the plane gropes for the runway, She is talking to all of them at the same time. The mother holds her left hand, the father her right and the youngest son reassuringly strokes her hair as Helena tries to explain why Mickey Mouse has a *Pepsi Cola* ad stuck permanently to his arse. I'm still trying to make sense of this sight as the plane lands at Orly and the whole family, plus adopted daughter, bursts into wild applause.

It's 40° on the streets of Paris, but the humidity makes it feel more like boiling point in Hell. I heave our sand-filled suitcases into the boot of a taxi. The sweating driver fails to lift so much as a little finger to help but sneeringly adds a few Euros to the fare for our bag. I pick up a copy of the *Independent* at the airport and, as the cab swings through the southern suburbs of Hades, I read that the swelter in France is such that the state electricity company is worried about its nuclear reactors overheating. As nobody knows what will happen if they reach a temperature of more than 50°, they've been spraying them with water in an attempt to cool them down. I wouldn't have thought a garden hosepipe would be of much help if that little lot goes up, but what do I know about nuclear engineering? The streets of Paris are completely deserted this morning, as all the locals are still at the coast or in the country. To convey the magnitude of the summer exodus from the city all I need say is that four of our five neighbourhood *boulangeries* are closed. I mean, where is a man supposed to buy his little piece of French history? Well, sod it, we're all toast if one of those reactors goes up.

Treat her like a lady, August 11th

It's Helena's birthday, but she has a visit to the maternity hospital lined up to spoil it for her. I'm not going with her as it's nothing interesting like a video conference with Junior, just another round of tests and a check-up. In return, I promise to take her for dinner and a movie in the evening and return to my yellowing copy of the *Independent*. Opening the review section, the first thing I find is an article penned by some shrink claiming that therapy for addicts is useless unless they're willing to confront the pain they're trying to avoid by taking that first drink, drug or extra slice of cake. If only I'd known what I was unleashing when I downed those first four pints of fizzy, urine-coloured lager at the Ye Olde Red Lion at the age of sixteen.

Helena gets back looking hot and bothered.

'Everything OK?' I murmur, barely looking up from a report on England's latest humiliation at cricket.

'The doctor thinks I'm a bit overweight.'

'Oh? How much overweight?'

'About three and a half kilos'

'That all?'

'What?'

'I mean that's not much, is it? How much does the baby weigh anyway?'

'About twenty-five grams.'

'I see.'

It's already too late of course. The damage is done. In fact it was done back in Spain when I asked whether her bikini was the same one she'd worn so gracefully on our summer holiday the year before. Helena fully understood where my tactless questions were headed and her body language strongly suggested I hadn't got away with it. Not a nice birthday present, especially when you consider the conspicuous absence of any other.

'So, you think I'm fat, then?'

I'm in a no-win situation now. Whatever I say will only make things worse. Better by far to distract her attention by pointing out that the *boulangerie* has just reopened or that the curtains are on fire. Of course, I try anyway and succeed only in compounding the error: 'It's not what I think that matters, chérie, I'm only repeating what the doctor says.' But I already know that the cheap little bistro I was going to try and get away with tonight will no longer suffice.

As soon as we arrive on the left bank of the Seine, I ask which film she'd like to see. Back in the times when our sex was purely recreational, we spent a lot of time in the *Quartier Latin*, where a number of movie houses show films from the days when most men were gentlemen and men like me were in prison. Anyway, tonight I'm pushing for Cary Grant and Katharine Hepburn in *Bringing up Baby*, not because I see it as in any way educational, but more because I know there's no way I'll get away with anything remotely action-oriented after my comments earlier this afternoon. But Helena favours an old Billy Wilder and, in a last ditch effort not to ruin her birthday, I agree almost gracefully. The film stars a rubbery Charles Laughton on superb form as an exuberant barrister on the point of pegging it after a lifetime's excess of cognac and cigars and, despite some old biddy reeking of Pekinese dog reeling off the entire plot in the queue, the film is so funny that we emerge from the cinema all smiles and I'm finally convinced that I've done the right thing by giving up on my own witless film script. The only problem now is that I wouldn't mind trying my hand as a loudmouth lawyer.

We're hungry and Helena, who's been forbidden to eat raw fish, selects a Japanese restaurant around the corner from the cinema. She watches with envy as I order a board full of slimy, fresh sashimi. Just in case, she consults with the waiter about her condition. He confirms the opinion of every gynaecologist on the planet and compels her to order a range of brochettes but this is not the real reason her birthday turns sour.

It kicks off when Helena asks after the birthday present I have yet to buy her. This morning, after I casually mentioned not having had an opportunity to buy her anything, I gave her a collection of shells that I found on the beach in Spain. I'd mounted them beautifully in a handmade wooden box and labelled each one with a name chosen to remind her of some of her favourite places like Ronda and Mondragon. But this is not quite the same thing, apparently, as getting out of bed and nipping down to the *Galeries Lafayette* to buy something with hard cash.

'Perhaps it's not the same in England.'

'What do you mean?'

'Perhaps there, you do not think of a girl on her birthday.'

'Helena, I asked you what you wanted this morning and

you said a ring. I'll buy you a ring.'

'So where is it?'

'I didn't have the time.'

'You mean you had other priorities.'

'I will buy the ring, but I want you to be there to choose it.'

'I don't want to be there. I'll take anything you choose, especially for my birthday.'

This makes me angry because it's simply not true. I've bought Helena gifts in the past and she's rejected all of them. I once spent an entire weekend trawling through every pair of knickers in London (if you'll pardon the expression) before finally choosing something English that a French woman would allow close to her body. I'd never done such a thing before and found it at first embarrassing, then educational and finally quite exciting to be surrounded by garments I cannot begin to explain (let alone undo). But, in the end, the garment I chose turned out to be 'made of the wrong material' and, much to my frustration, she refused even to try it on. It hurt to have the whole lot thrown back in my face. At this point, I know I should shut up and not bring up any more presents from the past, but instead I remind her of the black leather handbag I bought her last Christmas, which has never been seen since. This brings no more than a gesture of resignation – is it her fault I'm a man with so little understanding of her tastes?

Still I persist: 'I made you a present with my own hands.'

'It's not the same.'

'Why not? Because it didn't cost a lot of money?'

'No. It was a nice memento of our visit to Spain. *C'est tout.*'

'You mean it's not good enough.'

'*Ce n'est pas ça.*'

And so it continues until the tears fall into her rice bowl and I can no longer hide my exasperation. I wish I hadn't eaten so quickly – then I'd have an excuse not to look at the birthday girl sobbing on the other side of the wasabi. The meal is ruined and we spill back out onto the teeming streets to walk through the beauty of Paris by night without a word passing between us. We cross the Seine as it cuts its silver path through the city and on out to sea. The medieval *Conciergerie* is illuminated, the stars are out and a thousand lovers are patrolling the floodlit bridges like intoxicated sentries. How many nights have we spent walking through this very same scene, gazing in wonder at the city of light and whispering dreams we could no longer keep to ourselves?

One of us, and it probably isn't me, suggests we take a look at *Paris Plage*, a temporary beach installed on the banks of the Seine for the month of August. Maybe we're just missing Spain or maybe it's hard being back in the city when the future seems so uncertain. Those few Parisians who haven't fled the city for the summer are sitting half naked under the stars, drinking beers, strumming broken guitars and rolling joints. The sand is full of *Marlboro* butts and smells a bit musty. I notice it doesn't return my grip the way it did in Spain. 'Come on,' I say. 'We're dead tired, let's go home.'

Long after we have both fallen into a deep slumber, the phone rings and awakens me. I'm completely disoriented, it's pitch black, stiflingly hot and I no longer know whether I'm in Spain, England or some distant tropical jungle. My skin is wet with humidity. I can hear Helena talking in English but I can't make sense of her words. Before I know it, I'm asleep once more. In the morning, neither of us will remember who called in the middle of the night.

Paris, August 12th

Helena's parents have offered us their house while they're away on holiday. I'd like nothing better than to escape from the city again, but I should start looking for a job. Helena tells me there's little point before September and I know she's right. Nevertheless I feel guilty about lounging around on the beach when she's three and a half months pregnant and Daddy remains idle. Helena is determined not to spend the rest of her school holiday in the city but she's far too clever to try and bludgeon me onto the train. Instead, she invites my sister to join us on the Normandy coast. I take the bait willingly and put away my CV for another couple of weeks.

What real babies do for a living, August 13th

Tomorrow night we're having dinner with Helena's parents. En route for Mazagón, they're in town for one night only and I'm not looking forward to the event because I know they've bought Helena a present the approximate size and shape of an old *Renault Clio*. Now I'll be forced to endure dinner looking exactly like the miserable cheapskate I am.

As I sit and practise spitting out the right verb endings for phrases such as, 'I remain forever in your debt' or 'Your generosity knows no bounds and contrasts markedly with my own,' Helena calls Cousin Inès. She and the Escalator are due to give birth to a minor mechanical device in a few weeks' time and Helena wants to know how things are progressing. My grammar studies are rudely interrupted by an awful howling and shrieking from the bedroom.

'She's had it!'

'Had what?'

'The baby!'

'What baby?'

'The one that made her bulge around here,' says Helena, reappearing from the bedroom and gesturing at her belly. 'Or hadn't you noticed?'

I ignore the reproach, but I still don't get it.

It transpires that Cousin Inès was on holiday when, without warning, she began throwing up all over the pristine beaches of Brittany. At first the doctors thought it was food poisoning, but when the vomiting continued into the night, she was taken into hospital for observation. There they discovered she was suffering from a rare liver disorder and were forced to whip out the baby before the illness threatened the life of both mother and child. Baby Agathe was prised perfunctorily from the womb just a few days ago and fully one month premature. 'Come on, we're going round to see her', says Helena. I haven't seen her move so fast for a good three and a half months.

We get round to their apartment right in the middle of feeding time. Inès is sitting on the couch – a mother where once there was formerly a girl – while another, tiny human sucks at her nipple. I'm embarrassed by this open display of femininity and try to find a position from which I can talk without staring at her exposed breast. But Inès has no such inhibitions and demands that I come out from under the coffee table because she can't hear a word I'm saying.

Agathe is as frail as a featherless bird that's fallen from its nest. She also has a remarkable amount of silky brown hair for one so young and I'm almost tempted to ask whether she's wearing a wig. Agathe continues her mid-afternoon snack and we get the full story of the birth as I focus on a study of Agathe's tiny delicate feet. I could fit them both into the palm of my hand and spend the rest of the afternoon marvelling at their organic perfection.

As the story of the birth draws to a close, I open my ears a little. Apparently the whole thing happened so precipitously that little Agathe spent the first hours of her life without a name. Her parents had prepared a list of boys' names, but were not at all ready for a girl. I find this a little surprising as there are only the two alternatives, as far as I'm aware, but 'Agathe' was suggested by a nurse who eventually got sick of carrying around an anonymous bundle.

The hospital stories are over but before I can breathe a sigh of relief, Inès produces a huge stack of photos. Most of them feature her lying in a hospital bed with more tubing running in and out of her body than you'll find in a chemistry classroom. First up, there's a nasty little shot of something I assume to be the severed umbilical cord. I almost throw up at the sight of this piece of plumbing and ask why it's wrapped in pale blue cling film. Inès tells me it isn't, that it's supposed to be that colour. I show the photograph to Helena who flinches but doesn't say anything. With all these extraneous body parts lying around, it's little wonder Inès looks like she's comatose or in a state of deep shock.

Quickly, I rifle through the rest of the photos until I find what I'm looking for – Mr Escalator himself. Was he conscious? Did he run away from the final scenes of a drama he co-authored eight months previously? More importantly, will he provide me with an excuse to do likewise? Ah, there he is... But no! He's beaming broadly enough to convince me the French have just won the Rugby World Cup final against the English, in the last minute. How can this be? I've heard people say that the birth of a child was the most exhilarating moment of their lives, but I always assumed they were lying through gritted teeth. How could that possibly be true?

'How is he?' I ask the mother-as-milk-bottle. 'I mean, was he badly traumatised?'

Helena kicks me under the table but Inès only laughs: 'Far from it. Since the birth, he's been on cloud nine.'

I return to the photographs and scrutinise the features of the mechanical one. Here's a man in the prime of his life. The next eighteen years have just been written off as surely as a *Deux Chevaux* that's been driven into a brick wall at 40 kph. Yet he's smiling. Then Inès adds that he can't wait to get home from work, and that clinches it as far as I'm concerned. Now I know she's lying -there's nothing in this man's life that could possibly compete with the joy of selling a moving walkway.

About half an hour after our arrival, little Agathe has finally had enough to drink. Inès puts her breast away as if it were a piece of crockery going back into the cupboard and scribbles something on a notepad. Helena asks what she's written and it turns out to be a log she's keeping of when the baby sleeps, awakens and feeds. The little detail that lodges in my skull like a piece of shrapnel is the news that Agathe wakes up every two hours for a feed. Naturally, I ask what her father does when this happens and I'm told he gets up to help.

Helps with what? After all, it's not as if he can produce a breast full of milk.

The moment Helena's been waiting for ever since we arrived comes when Agathe is peeled from her mother and handed to her. It's the first time I've seen Agathe's face as it's been buried in Mummy's softer parts ever since we arrived. She has pale bluish-green eyes and looks surprisingly human, if a bit stoned after all that milk. As she takes Agathe into her arms, I can sense some of Helena's impatience over her own pregnancy melting away. Then the two women come up with the most appalling idea.

'Why don't you hold her?' asks Helena.

'Me? No. I mean why... Why, um, me? No, definitely not. I can't, I mean, I don't know how... '

'Like this,' says Helena.

Has she forgotten what happened the last time I tried to steady a simple toy rabbit? I'm still protesting as Agathe is placed firmly against my shoulder by Inès. I freeze. Agathe's eyes reopen momentarily to check she's in safe hands and I'm on the verge of telling her she's not, that her life now hangs by the barest of threads, when she wraps an arm around my neck the way in which a sleepy lemur might wrap its tail around a tree. Then she lets out the most almighty yawn. So that's it! I'm not a danger to children and society at large – I'm just becoming another of those sleep-inducing, blanket-boring, leathery old armchairs known as adults.

A few minutes later Agathe is returned to her rightful place at mummy's breast and I start making my excuses. I can't deny that the visit has been a nightmare, but at least an educational nightmare.

Why certain English people will always feel uncomfortable in France (part I), August 14th

The first thing I did this morning was to check that Helena hasn't given birth overnight. I'm relieved to report that she hasn't, so despite dinner with the in-laws, the rest of the day should be a breeze.

I don't know whether it's the coming of another ice age or merely the end of summer, but the temperature in Paris has cooled to something approaching comfortable and I wheel my bike out of the courtyard for the first time in weeks. The streets reek of diesel and I dread to think what it must have been like in the capital at the height of the heat wave, which has already roasted 5,000 people to death this summer in France. After no more than a few strokes of the pedals, I'm gasping for oxygen, though this may have something to do with the fact that I'm still smoking and probably about as fit as Luciano Pavarotti on Boxing Day.

In the evening we settle down to dinner in a garden restaurant selected by Helena. Straight away, I notice how the high walls will make any early escape both problematic and more than a little embarrassing. Her parents look tired but relaxed. Relaxed because they've spent the last two weeks on their annual holiday in the Alps, and tired because they've driven non-stop to arrive on time, or maybe just because they've been working all of their adult lives and they don't know how to stop.

Our meal is a relaxed affair. We chat about the family down in Mazagón and I forewarn them as best I can with a few mug shots of the rabbit, but along with dessert comes the moment I've been dreading, when Helena's mother pulls a set of car keys from her handbag. *Voilà* – the present! I've tried to rehearse for this by saying 'Thank you' or at least looking suitably contrite. But, as the keys hit the tablecloth, I say nothing. I don't even know where to look. Part of me wants to express my deep gratitude (because there's no doubt that we'll be needing the car) and the rest of me wants to explain that it is my intention to become a good husband, partner and father, but I'm just not ready to get started. Sullen as a shamed child, I merely stare at an untouched crème brûlée in front of me, afraid of saying the wrong thing in front of a group of adults.

Over coffee, Helena's father gives us a second set of the keys for the house in Caen and tells me we will be doing them a favour by sitting the house, as he's worried about their garden withering in the summer heat. Their unending generosity makes me feel even worse and all I can think of, by way of response, is to volunteer my services with a watering can.

In transit, August 16th

Less than forty-eight hours later, we're on the Normandy express and on our way back out of the putrid city. The gift of the car has brought my unease to a head and, as the train rattles through cholesterol country, I broach the unpleasant subject of our financial situation and my lack of a job. All I have to show for my past efforts is a fast-dwindling pile of cash, a deep-frozen pension and one lousy savings policy that's currently riding the waves of the stock market about as well as a polecat windsurfs.

On the train, we add up what's left in the kitty and Helena says 'not much, is it?' No, it's not, but it's still enough to persuade me that a further couple of weeks on holiday isn't such a bad idea. I make up my mind to give our precarious situation some serious thought as soon as we arrive. A firm resolution, then? Why yes, until it evaporates on the beaches of Normandy barely six hours later.

Why certain English people will always feel uncomfortable in France (part II), August 17th

It's market day in Caen and everyone wants to stop for a chat with the stall holders: '*Bonjour, Mesdames, Messieurs,* how are you today? The children? The garden? *Ah, très bien!* And what about the neighbours' dog?' What about it indeed? As the sun continues to arc lazily across the sky, they discuss, individually, each of the pork chops on display before finally selecting a couple which, to my untrained eye, look identical to all others from the ribcage of the same animal. Sixteenth in the queue, and wanting to beat everyone else about the head with a piece of black pudding, it occurs to me that I'm demonstrating the impatience of the true Parisian here, but I can't help it – this is taking forever. Haven't these people got anything better to do on a Sunday? Does little Marcel here want to go to the beach or is he happier here, sticking his baguette between my shoulder blades until I can stand it no longer and put the little bastard to the sword? Just buy your bloody *saucissons* and get the fuck out of the way! Not that the pompous stall holders are in any hurry to offload their swine and put an end to the elaborate French service ritual. And why do the French all shop in couples? Is it purely to double the length of the queue? I need to calm down and remember that a love of food runs deep in the blood of every French man and woman, just as a pint or a stiff G&T does in that of the English.

Once we've finally fought our way to the front of the queue and are about to head home for a midnight snack, we run into one of Helena's old boyfriends. He's in the market with his wife and daughter and, wouldn't you know it, they're in the mood for a chat. Now I'm expected to pretend an interest in the doings of a young, provincial family and, just when I think things can't possibly get any worse, we get invited to dinner. Shit! All I want to do is to go back to Paris and live in abject disharmony with a bunch of rude but exceptionally efficient supermarket cashiers.

An hour later, we pitch up at the old boyfriend's place with a bunch of the closest thing we can find to flowers from the wizened garden. I resolve to keep a wary eye on Helena's past in case he produces a pair of handcuffs or suggests a half-naked romp in the rose bed and, to avoid any possibility of conversation, I begin constructing a series of vertiginous cardboard towers which are promptly knocked down by his daughter. This delights the child – a muscular two-year-old named Lea – and doesn't appear to bother her mother, so the two of us turn the living room into a wasteland while Helena and the love interest start chewing over the state of the world. Lea and I continue stealing hors d'oeuvres from the table until my playmate is finally sent to bed, although I get to stay up late and attempt to come to terms with my jealousy.

Much to my displeasure, the past turns out to be a nice guy called Guillaume. He owns a couple of shops that sell windsurfing equipment and, before Lea was born, he liked nothing better than to jump in his van and drive 2,000 kilometres south to, of all places, Tarifa. Not that he gets many opportunities for that kind of escapade these days, for one small but glaringly obvious reason.

Guillaume is everything I'm not. He's dedicated, hard-working, steady, entrepreneurial and generally well-built. He has an opinion on anything that matters and much that does not. For a while we discuss the ways in which he's trying to expand his business into England. A couple of minutes into the subject, I catch myself warming to the theme and wonder whether I'm not going stir crazy without a job. Helena seems to think so, which may be why she appears to prefer the company of Guillaume this evening, who, far from the voracious seducer and predator of my imagination, is Citizen Sane, leading a normal, healthy, family life: he's married, has a small property and responsibility for a number of employees, gets up in the morning to have breakfast with Lea. He comes home in the evening, a little tired perhaps, has dinner with his wife and relaxes with a glass of beer, wine, apple juice or whatever takes his fancy before a sound night's kip. Helena assures me that this is the way a high proportion of humans behave, but I'm not so sure. It all seems a bit unlikely to me.

On the way home, I foolishly bring up the subject of cigarette smoking. Despite all my efforts, I haven't quite managed to forget all my elaborate speeches about the absurdity of smoking with a young baby in the house. I have no idea where I'm going to find the will or the courage to stub out my last cigarette, but I know that if I don't, the grim reaper or the taxman will do it for me. Helena has heard it all before and just looks at me as if I were an anteater swearing off ants.

Children past and present, August 18th

My sister is catching the boat over from Portsmouth tomorrow. She has two kids, neither of whom has seen the sea since the school holidays began a month or so back. Helena's cousin Nathalie has already made the trip over from Turnpike Lane with her two girls in tow and, if I didn't know better, I'd suspect it's all part of Helena's master plan to get me thinking there's nothing abnormal about becoming a parent. If so, she hasn't yet understood, because I'm already looking forward to seeing my playmates. My sister's children know me as the 'bad uncle' because of a short story I once cooked up with them in the starring roles in which they defied their parents from cover to cover and got to use a series of previously forbidden adjectives, although I'm hoping my sister will have forgiven me by the time she gets off the boat.

The beach house is only twenty kilometres from Caen but Helena's thoughts are already a thousand miles away. This place has quite a history. It was here that Helena and Cousin Nathalie spent the endless summers of their youth and one look at Helena's face this morning is all I need to tell me that once she opens the gate, it will be like stepping through a portal into a lost childhood.

I can see the years falling from her shoulders as she eases into her mother's *Renault Twingo*, a car so stub ugly even the French can't be bothered exporting it to Britain. I've chosen to cycle out to the coast on a bike which belongs to her father and I drop down through the pre-war alleys of Caen until I reach the canal towpath which connects the city to the ferry port of Ouistreham. It's hot and I stop to take off my shirt. My wheel is pointed magnetically north and the breeze at my bare back is blowing lost memories from the tangled pathways of my youth. I guess it's just that kind of a day.

Halfway to the coast, I encounter a young boy standing in the middle of the towpath. He hasn't heard the approaching whir of wheels and stands there staring out across the canal, utterly motionless. I'm close enough now to see his dishevelled blond hair. He's wearing an old woollen sweater that looks strangely familiar and he doesn't turn until I'm almost upon him. Then I nearly fall off the bike. He looks exactly as I did at that age! He must be about ten and his face is a mixture of curiosity and fear – a cocktail I remember only too well. He watches as I pass, both of us open-mouthed with surprise. I think about turning round and telling him everything will be alright, but he'll have to work it out for himself – I just hope that he doesn't wait as long as I did before getting started.

Now I part company with the canal and the memories it's imparted and rejoin a road heavy with holiday traffic. I need to concentrate on avoiding cars and caravans as they transport wide-eyed children to the hotels, gardens and sand castles containing their multi dimensional memories of the future.

Nathalie and Helena are lying in the garden by the time I get to the house, lost in past summers of milk and honey. Now one of them is pregnant and the other has two young daughters. Helena gets up to show me around a house which appears to have been wallpapered with the very tissue of her memories. When she shows me where she slept, undisturbed by anything other than dreams of dolls and gingerbread, tears well in her eyes at the sight of a bed now full of young Celeste's toys. I sense Helena is feeling the loss of her childhood every bit as keenly as I had mine down by the canal. Maybe we're both hoping to recover some lost part of the past once our own child is born.

Celeste and Léonie are playing on the grass. They have neither time nor capacity for sentimentality and are presently engaged in the serious business of immediate gratification of their needs, which means grabbing plenty of attention from some of the larger, garden animals. Their father, Jonah, has crossed the Channel overnight and has had little sleep and even Celeste bouncing up and down on his chest fails to bring him back to life. So it becomes my job, for the next couple of hours, to provide props and entertainment, games, chocolate croissants, and regular doses of orange juice as Daddy dozes under an old apple tree in the garden. At least this gives me a good warm-up before the arrival of my own niece and nephew. The girls pull me to the ground and stampede my skull and occasionally some of my more tender areas, before ordering the donkey back to its feet for yet another ride. I'm soon rendered breathless and remain utterly incapable of administering anything that sounds like reproach.

Celeste is almost four and perhaps the prettier of the two girls. Her eyes are further apart and her beauty almost Egyptian. She likes to wear a tutu or the robes of a princess, as well as a bit of jewellery and bright flowers in her hair. Léonie, two and a half, doesn't like wearing clothes, hats or anything else. Her personality is dynamic, forceful and just a little vicious.

Late in the afternoon, I haul myself from the dust after one last wave of attacks from Léonie and reach automatically for a cigarette when I am immediately reprimanded by her sister.

'What are you doing?' she asks incredulously.

'Er, smoking a cigarette,' I reply, with as much conviction as I can muster.

'*Mais qu'est ce que tu es bête,*' comes the retort of someone enjoying only her fourth summer. 'Don't you know that will kill you?'

I look at my shoes, but they don't have an answer either.

To my relief, Nathalie comes to the rescue when she tells

the miniature inquisition to leave me alone. I don't find out that she has an ulterior motive until she directs me to the back of the house and asks if she can scrounge a fag. She still likes an occasional smoke, but buying her own is clearly out of the question when faced with the anti-tobacco commission as represented by her daughters. I hand her one from what is to be my last (or possibly penultimate) pack. Nathalie checks that we're not being watched and, nervously, I strike a match which catches between my fingers and burns me. It's the first time I've done such a thing in twenty-five years of smoking and it underlines the fact that Celeste is right and I've been wrong for a very long time.

It's time to pick up *that* car and, in a small back country village, I'm formally introduced to a small, grey *Renault Clio* by a silver haired farmer called Lenormand, before a band of much younger Lenormands take me through the paper work. The transaction takes place in their kitchen and I feel as if I've mistakenly wandered onto the set of a sitcom where a bunch of English actors are playing a formulaic French family. The place is full of flies and there's an overpowering combination of odours, among which I detect cheese, wine, garlic and finest Normandy cowpat.

Out of the darkness, August 19th

The car is still working when I make the journey out to Ouistreham harbour to meet my sister. She lives on the border between Hertfordshire and Essex and has endured a long trip to get here with her offspring, involving trains, taxis, a six-hour ferry crossing and a spot of projectile vomiting. No wonder she looks pale as she staggers through customs. Clutching her left hand is Lily, her eight-year-old daughter who is carrying more *Toblerone* than you would think anatomically possible. On her right arm, and wheeling his very own suitcase, is Lily's nine-year-old brother, David.

David is autistic or, more accurately, he suffers from

Asperger's syndrome. I hate to introduce him in this way, as if the condition were his defining characteristic. But sadly, and for all practical purposes, I suppose it is, as he spends most of the day counting or cataloguing numbers – the length of CD tracks, dates of birth, car registrations, street numbers, that kind of stuff. As well as a mathematician, he also happens to be a talented jazz pianist.

'Hello David! How are you?' His medium-brown gaze falls upon me as the data associated with his uncle's face clicks into place: 'Fine,' he says, before asking how many minutes it will take to get to the house, the name of the street and the number of the house. I give him the figures and, just for fun, translate the name of the road, incorrectly, as the 'Street of the Piglet'. As usual, he looks at his mother for confirmation, because kids like David rarely recognise it when people are pulling their leg. When my sister nods and smiles, David permits himself a little chuckle and it becomes our joke for the rest of his stay. It's largely thanks to his mother's efforts that David is piecing together at least some understanding of the emotions through which all of us must learn to navigate. It's a lifetime's work and as we steal back to Caen in the fading light, I reflect that I shouldn't be worrying about having a child, but rather praying for one that's well equipped to deal with the storms that lie ahead.

One perfect sandcastle, August 20th

Our plan is to drive to the house by the beach and throw all the children together in the hope that they'll get along well enough to allow us to lounge in the sun with the newspapers my sister has brought from England. But first we have to persuade David to eat some breakfast, which is never easy, as counting comes more easily to him than sustaining his own organism. No such problem with Lily – she's wolfed down six chocolate croissants by the time David has reeled off a list of his favourite ragtime tunes and allocated each to its appropriate wormhole in the numerical universe. It must be hard for Lily – she knows her brother is not like other brothers. She sees him standing alone in the school playground every morning and is forced to watch on as other boys tease him for his refusal to play football. She may not fully understand why, but she knows he gets extra help at school and, through it all, she watches his back and remains his best friend. Lily understands him better than anyone else and sometimes she misses out on the attention that David demands and, one way or another, always extracts from his parents. But just for today, as she and Celeste paint their lips and practise for supermodeldom, she's as happy as Nathalie and Helena, who are talking babies or whatever else it may be that occupies women for hours under a parasol, or David and Léonie, who are fighting over the last *Coke*-flavoured ice lolly as my sister mops up the tears.

And so it goes on for a few, perfect days until I catch myself thinking that Helena and I will soon be adding to this unruly throng. As I wonder what our own child will look like, I realise that a small part of me is happy with this turn of events. Will it have blond hair or brown? Helena's hazel eyes, or my own murky mix of blue and green? Will she have the character of Celeste, Lily or Léonie, or will he turn into a pocket calculator like David? I don't mind, which is just as well, since we won't get so much as an inkling for another five months.

The geometry of family, August 21st

My sister takes her leave at the blustery port and I kiss the kids goodbye as they depart for the boat. Lily's mouth is so crammed with triangular chocolate and bubble gum that she just grins me goodbye. David promises to call me as soon as he gets back home with some missing information relating to an early Madonna CD before checking the precise duration of the voyage one last time and turning towards the exit.

I watch them walk towards the customs gate and notice again how skinny David is. He's all elbows and knees, and moves like a Junior *Mr Bean*. My sister walks just behind him, as always, arm half-cocked. They turn and wave one last time, each with passport in hand. I thought I'd be a little relieved when they left, but I'm not and now that they're gone, a small hole has been punched in my summer holiday.

A brief history of addiction, August 22nd

Helena is beginning to talk about the return to her school in the rough and ready suburbs of eastern Paris. We're staying in Caen another week, but I can't wait to get home now the kids have all left. I'm beginning a dangerous dialogue with the gleaming bottles of wine and beer on the supermarket shelves and I need someone to tell me that I'm not going mad. It's been seven whole weeks since I touched a drink and I want to go back to Paris in the hope of finding a friend who, like me, is trying to resist the allure of a glass or two chilled to perfection. Helena thinks I'm crazy but we soon reach a compromise – I'll catch the train tonight and return, in good time for the wedding of one of her old school friends, tomorrow afternoon.

First I need a copy of *L'Equipe*. Reading this sports daily is as close as I ever get to practising French and my only motivation to learn. Ever since I was a nipper in long woollen socks, I've spent hours poring over football league tables, cricket averages and other, instantly forgettable, statistics. This may be less harmful than a number of other obsessions, but it seems I was born wearing the pyjamas of compulsion.

The evening is filled with caffeine and the laughter of sober friends and it's well after midnight by the time I get back to our apartment in Pigalle. It's strange to be back after the luxury of the house and garden in Caen – I feel like a mouse that's been chased into a hole in the skirting board by a burly tomcat, after it's had a month-long run at a cheese nibbles factory. I go through the post. Nothing but bills and a postcard from Helena's family in Spain. It feels like months since we left Mazagón. Carefully, I check my emails. The only thing I've read in the past two weeks (other than *L'Equipe* and the beer ads) is a report that a new virus is rampaging across the net. I delete four or five messages offering to thatch my head with nylon, or sell me *Xanax* at a one-off price aimed at the mildly suicidal, but there are also two messages from real human beings, one of which turns out to be from an old colleague and is mysteriously entitled: *DO YOU WANT SOME WORK?* Well, that's a very good question: do I? I'm too tired to consider the question tonight and flop onto the bed and fall asleep faster than a narcoleptic with a *Valium* habit.

At the crossroads of yesterday and tomorrow

The action on this plane is divided into two sections: while my family gathers in economy, a rave party is in full swing in first class. I'm ignoring most members of the former and head to the front of the plane where I know at least three girls who are partial to a bit of stroking, fondling and kissing. But somehow I get lost in transit and end up at a pensioner's party at my old office, where all my lives finally run into one. I want to know where the girls are, but Helena won't tell me. I wander deep into the throng of the aged, before someone hands me a tulip glass filled to the brim with brandy. Without pause for thought, I down the unctuous liquid in one. I stare at the empty glass in disbelief. How did that happen? Then someone jumps up onto the table and points a porky finger at me. He screams that I haven't even had seven seconds of sobriety, never mind seven weeks. Then the brandy fumes reach my head and huge viscous droplets of amber sweat begin to ooze from my saturated pores.

The dream wakens me at four in the morning. I drift off once more, only to end up oversleeping. Back on my feet, there's no time for coffee and no time to reread that email, although I do manage to print it off. I brush my teeth in a hurry and fall into the only suit that remains from my days of employment. On the train I pull the email from my bag. It wants to know whether I'm interested in doing a bit of research for an American telecommunications company. They want to run a few simple interviews – pop psychology for big business – something I used to be able to do with my eyes closed and a thumping hangover. The only snag is that, this time, I'd have to do it in French. I decide to call the Americans on Monday and one edition of *L'Equipe* later, I'm back at the station in Caen where Helena is waiting for me in the *Clio.*

As we drive to the wedding, I tell her about the email.

'So what are your reservations?' she asks.

'None, other than my vow never to return to that particular planet.'

'You mean planet earth?' says Helena, with a level expression.

I shift a little uncomfortably in my seat and continue to stare out of the windscreen.

'Hmmm' says Helena, patting her stomach in that way that she has. We drive the rest of the way in silence.

It's six in the evening by the time Helena and I roll up at the garden reception and, to my relief, the wedding turns out not to be a wedding at all. This friend of Helena's disappeared off the map some time ago, only to resurface in Argentina. There she met a young man on the streets of Buenos Aires and, a few days later, they were distributing invitations to their wedding. Other than her frantic parents and one sister, no one from France could make the trip and that's why, six months later, we've all been invited to celebrate the marriage back at the family home in rural Normandy.

Very quickly, I get together with all the kids for a game of football in the trimmed and immaculately decorated garden where we're joined by two or three other social misfits (including a guy with a Marseillaise accent so thick I can barely discern one word from the next) and we proceed to kick lumps out of each other as the bride's mother watches her garden being shredded more quickly than a set of dodgy government papers.

Eventually we're called in to dinner and there's no way out – I'm going to have to make some form of polite conversation without leaning on alcohol. Luckily I'm seated at a table with the man from Marseilles and we spend a lot of the time talking about the sagacity of Abramovich's investments at Chelsea. On the other side of our table is the bride's sister, who is also patient enough to listen to my awkward attempts at human communication. I want to explain that I'm not mentally retarded, that it's my reluctance to slug back a couple of bottles of wine before dinner that has returned me, spluttering and self-conscious, to my teenage years and the point at which my emotional development was put under house arrest for the best part of three decades. But this isn't the kind of confession that helps a party to swing, so I swallow my discomfort with a gallon of *Perrier* and resolve to keep my nerves under as much control as possible.

My not drinking doesn't go unnoticed. It's the usual story: you refuse the aperitif, so the French say, 'Ah, you don't drink. I understand. Have a glass of wine instead!' Not one of these people has ever heard of an Englishman that doesn't drink beer and it's not as if I'm as fortunate as Helena, who can point to her stomach before spreading her palms in some universal gesture of resignation.

The one person at our table who says nothing about all of this is a nice old man called Serge. He's lost his voice as a result of throat cancer and I'm sure I don't need to tell you how he got that. Thanks to a tracheotomy, he talks sparingly and, because I don't have the vocabulary to fill all the empty spaces, we're at about the same level conversationally. But this is an arrangement that suits us both and provides plenty of time to reflect on the nature and effects of addiction.

By about midnight, we've almost finished eating and the

speeches begin. First up is the bride herself: rather than pretty she's handsome, vivacious and dark haired. Her eyes are olive green and well spaced, and they flash with the right mixture of darkness and light. She's a little thin and her skin is pulled taut across prominent cheekbones. As she talks, she pulls intermittently on a cigarette. Her sister told me that, at the wedding in Buenos Aires, she burst into tears at the thought of spending the rest of her life in Argentina and there are further tears when, later, she chats briefly with me and Helena – she's sad that she won't see us again for such a long time, even though she's never met me before and hasn't seen Helena for ten years. To be honest, I'm a little concerned by her wild and romantic nature.

Her husband is handsome in a way that you'd expect Argentinian polo players to be handsome – dark, brooding and a man of few words, although the ones he does use have been chosen with extreme care. His speech alone sounds strong and determined enough to carry his wife through any hard times that may lie ahead. As he finishes, someone hands him a rose the colour of blood. He puts the thorny bloom between his teeth and folds his arms around the frail frame of his wife. His love for her is obvious and you can see that her parents love her too – right now they look like two small dams, constructed from a tremendous amount of twigs and holding back an awful lot of water.

At around three in the morning, I wander out of the marquee and into the depths of the garden. It's a clear night and there's a real chill in the air. The stars are all out, throbbing away in the deep indigo sky, watching and waiting to see whatever it is that will happen to each of us once the party breaks up. After a while, I go back to find Helena. This time I don't ask whether she's ready to leave, because she's so pale and drained that I doubt she's capable of an answer. I peel her elbows from the table and instruct her to mouth goodbye at anyone crossing our path. The bride's mother leads us by flashlight back into the field where the *Clio* awaits.

The moon glints in the cloudless summer sky. It's so cold in the car that I'm forced to turn on the heating. Not that they can feel it back in the wedding – most of them will be dancing till dawn.

New York, August 25th

After breakfast I get straight on the phone to the American telecommunications company. Inevitably my call is picked up by an answering service, which announces the name of the company (a word combining the world of the brand so neatly with Darwin's theory of evolution that you're almost tempted to believe that one is the inevitable result of the other) and little Miss *Audix* requests that I punch in the extension number of my 'party'. My prospective employer is straight on the line with a voice that could mix concrete. And, as if I'd never been away, it's straight down to business:

'Hi, thanks for calling me back.'

'Sure, no problem,' I say, in my best American accent.

'Do you have some costs for me?'

'I sure do,' I hear myself say, sickeningly. Then I reel off a set of figures that I concocted on a page of *L'Equipe* while in the tub.

'That sounds fine.'

Now I'm worried. His response means one of two things: either there's a danger he will give me the work, or I'm seriously undercharging for my services.

'Can you tell me a little bit about your experience in this field?'

'Sure. I learned the trade in London twelve years ago, got transferred to the States for a couple of years... ' And the rest of it comes out as one long sentence without commas or full stops – my entire career as one single and uninterrupted event. As the words escape from between my teeth with the hiss of a pressure cooker, I think of what is not in my verbal résumé: the sabbaticals, the depression, the partying, the vow never to return to marketing.

'And how's your French?'

'Well, I moved here ten months ago and I live with a French woman, so it's pretty good.' Another statement which obscures more than it reveals.

'We were hoping for a native speaker, but that seems fair enough. What about your experience in the telecoms market?'

I reference the names of three behemoths in the sector and await the next question.

'Do you know what a 'voice over Internet Protocol' is?'

I've no idea, nor any desire to pretend that I do. 'No,' I say firmly.

'Ah,' says this, the latest and finest product of an evolutionary chain that goes all the way back to the primeval tadpole in the slime.

'That's the litmus test, really. Hey listen, thanks anyway. Why don't you email me your details and if anything more general comes up, we'll give you a call.'

And with that, the line to New York goes dead faster than a dodo at the fag-end of the seventeenth century and I'm still clutching the receiver seconds later when it finally sinks in that I'm free to go water the garden.

I tell Helena about the call and she looks vaguely annoyed. She wants to know whether it's essential to have an encyclopaedic knowledge of telecommunications equipment in order to talk to a few industry boffins. I don't bother her with the details, but if your client happens to be an American with a penchant for micro-management, then the answer to this is a resounding yes. I stare at the numbers in front of me. I calculate that they would have paid the rent for a couple of months. Maybe they'd even have stretched to a pram and a few other essentials for Junior. But I'm also calculating the cost in terms of my fragile hold on sobriety. I'd once been sucked deep and hard into the airless vortex of marketing, brands and profit multiples and the bottom line is that I almost never made it back out. Part of me can't help but feel relieved that extension two-zero-five has called my bluff.

But I have to admit that being out of work for almost a year worries me more and more. I suppose I just assumed that once I was desperate enough, I'd walk back into marketing whenever I wanted and without any side effects. Today I've been warned that this may not be the case. A few days of the summer holiday remain before I fold away the beach towels for another year, throw them into the back of the car and drive back to the city – a phenomenon known to the French as *la rentrée*. It starts as a massive traffic jam on the *périphérique* around Paris on a Saturday and ends when you crawl back to the office, dressed in a grey suit on the first Monday morning of September. Only I don't have a grey suit, much less a job, and I don't know how I'm going to find one that doesn't fill me with bile and self-loathing.

I tell myself I'm not yet ready to go back to work, that I need more time to figure out what I want to do and how I'm going to explain all this to Junior when he comes naked and screaming out of the womb. I can't exactly stuff him back inside and ask him to give me a few more months to work it all out. Damn! I need some air or, better still, a cigarette.

I step out of the house only to realise I'm out of smokes. I'd been toying with the idea that the packet I bought for the wedding might be my last but I hadn't really meant it, had I? I wander down to the *tabac* on the corner of Piglet Street. Shut. Now I'll have to walk right into town. Damn it!

Why not stop right now? I turn back towards the house before changing my mind again. Not drinking is bad enough. I can't give up today. I'll give up soon enough.

When, then?

I don't know. In a month or so. But before the baby is born. Yes, for sure. I don't want to greet him with a *Benson & Hedges* hanging from my lower lip.

Why not now, then?

I don't know where this question is coming from, nor even who's asking it, but it stops me in my tracks. I look up and, in the distance I can see the *Abbaye aux Dames,* one of several old churches still standing in the rebuilt city of Caen. When they surprised the Germans that night in June, 1944, the Allies knew the French were hiding out in here and the *Abbaye aux Hommes* on the other side of town and somehow they managed to avoid bombing these monuments and their precious cargo of terrified human souls. I look at the magnificent façade of the building in the evening sunlight.

Why not now?

And before the nicotine can worm its way any further into my thoughts, I turn on my heels and head back to the house where I try to interest Helena in the track and field meeting which starts in Paris tonight. But she can't understand why hours of preening and posing might be required before eight steroidal freaks start running in a straight line for ten seconds, grunting like stuck pigs and, less still, why I might be interested in seeing the same race in slow motion (their facial muscles drooping grotesquely like candles in a howling gale). Part of the reason is that my own, spectacularly untuned body is going into critical withdrawal, but I won't tell her about that until tomorrow in case I have to run to the petrol station at four in the morning.

Breakfast epiphany, August 26th

Well before breakfast, Helena catches me in the act of sticking a nicotine patch on my upper arm. I bought it almost three years ago, when I happened to find myself in *Boots* with a guilty conscience and a sizeable hangover. I must have been travelling with them ever since, but I've never quite come to the point of actually taking one out of the packet. After a bowl of *All Bran,* I warn Helena that I may be even more bad-tempered than usual over the next forty-eight hours.

Lost, August 27th

The pharmacist had warned me that nicotine patches can cause nightmares and I remember spending much of last night lurking in the undergrowth of a Hieronymus Bosch painting wearing little more than a leopard skin. I tried to hold out for the rest of the night, but the dream was so disturbing that, long before dawn, I ripped the colourless, odourless patch from my skin. At the end of the dream, I would appear to have passed most of the night in a basement flat which conveniently doubled as a ferry terminal, where I'd been waiting for a boat to take me out of a place full of winos and weirdos. But the ferry never arrived and suddenly someone was pressing a glass of champagne into my hand. I gulped it straight down, compressing the grapey bubbles at the back of my throat. Then I slammed down the glass and reach automatically for a packet of full strength, non-filtered cigarettes.

The Princess in the tower, August 28th

We've been invited to dinner by the sister of the bride from Buenos Aires. Régis and Olivia live about fifteen miles outside Caen and a good kilometre or so from the nearest village. Helena, who has always said she'd like to live in the countryside, is appalled by their isolation. Their house is beautiful; sculpted from old Norman stone, with walls as thick as a castle and windows so high and wide you could easily lever the odd princess out of them. Much to Helena's disappointment, their two-year-old daughter Ella is away for the night, but she agrees to stay for dinner anyway.

We're shown over the property and I reflect on how little time it would take to show anyone around our place – a couple of strides in either direction and you'd fall headlong into the courtyard or ram your nose into a windowless brick wall. But here, we're required to rent a tractor just to get from one end of the garden to the other. The property is really three houses in one, two of which had their roofs blown off in an almighty storm. The reconstruction of the place is a long-term project and the prospect of redecorating such a big old house is making Helena's mouth water. Before she gets too excited, however, I steer her to the edges of the estate and point out the neighbours – three cows, a flock of sheep and a lone rabbit.

Régis has fired up a barbecue and, as I join him, he's about to pile an alarmingly large proportion of the French countryside onto the grill. We're outside to escape the girls, partly because Helena is being shown around young Ella's bedroom, which is about the size of Hampton Court Palace and fitted with everything a two-year-old could possibly have heard of, never mind want, but mainly because Helena and Olivia have fallen into a conversation about childbirth and I could sense the whole topic heading in a singularly unpleasant direction. Those bits I did catch before throwing myself down the stone spiral staircase concerned Ella's position in the womb and the attempts of the doctor to manually invert her.

There's no room to eat in the kitchen and the dining room has no floor so we sit down to dinner in the makeshift abattoir where Régis has suspended a single, naked 60 watt bulb from the remains of some decrepit old rafters. At least the conversation has taken a lighter turn (unless you happen to be a cow or a pig).

I'm still busy with the last of my pork chops and another length of spicy merguez sausage as darkness falls and I notice Helena sneaking the odd nervous glance over her shoulder into the gloom and stillness of the countryside. I know where her fear comes from: when she was a very young girl, her father temporarily moved the family to Réunion Island, where they lived in an isolated house in the country. The only other building within screaming distance was the local lunatic asylum. Anyway, one hot afternoon, young Helena was at home alone with her baby brother when a schizophrenic inmate from across the way showed up uninvited and wearing a grin borrowed from Jack Nicholson in *The Shining*. After very little in the way of neighbourly pleasantries, he told her he'd be back later that evening (after a nice cup of cocoa) to slaughter the entire family and suspend their bodies from the washing line. Helena has been waiting for him ever since. I've tried to persuade her that he's locked up somewhere in the southern hemisphere or buried six feet under but she remains convinced he's still out there somewhere, roaming the French countryside, looking for Helena and her babies with a sawn-off shotgun and a crazy chocolate-stained grin.

After the short commercial break, August 31st

On our way back to Paris, the car hums through the low-hanging cloud. My head may be empty but the roads are full, which gives me plenty of time to review the latest burst of outdoor activity from my dear friends in the marketing business. I marvel at the sheer quantity of crap they can tie into the end of a simple summer vacation – pencils, a new suit, a new car, a haircut, a change of shrink and, while we're at it, how about an entirely new personality? Their messages have gone up in neon all over France and at least ten million people have mindlessly coordinated their watches in order to belt home to the capital city at precisely the same time, which provides everyone with an opportunity to kill the entire family in a motorway pile-up before autumn even gets started. Those of us who do make it back spend the rest of the evening staring into each other's apartments and trying not to think about the infinite wait for summer to return.

Paris, September 1st

The last night of summer also happens to be the night upon which Helena first feels movement in her belly. Is this normal, I wonder, or is Junior just pissed off about missing the summer. I have no idea, but it's all Helena wants to talk about as she heads off to school, leaving me lounging in bed with a cup of tea and a copy of *L'Equipe*. Not quite everybody is facing *la rentrée* to work on this damp and grey Monday morning.

French homework, September 3rd

I arrive neither bright nor particularly early at the French National Employment Agency, or *ANPE,* as it is affectionately known in these parts. I take ticket number 63 and slouch in the haphazard queue. The advisors have just started talking to number 42, so I have quite a while to wait. On the crumpled form I was given way back before the summer even started, I find a paragraph which translates into something suspiciously like 'preparing for your interview with the counsellor'. Might as well do that then, since I'm here:

The first question is easy enough:

What have you been doing for the past few years?

I skip any references to alcohol and give them the official version.

What are your principal skills?

I ignore the voice at the back of my head which wants to write 'Day tripping to fantasy worlds' in the large space provided for my answer. Instead, I try hard to remember the sort of guff which used to impress me when I was sitting on the other side of the desk.

Educational qualifications and other skills?

My memory stirs. I'd once attended university. Now what was that all about? Then the form comes up with a real curve-ball:

Please specify the type of work you are looking for.

Next question please.

If you do not know, please state the sectors that attract you.

Shit! I haven't really thought about that. No, sorry, no idea. I look up at the counter. Still on number 42. Good. That gives me plenty of time to think of something. But I'll fill in the easy ones first, if you don't mind...

Do you have any particular hobbies or interests? If so, please specify briefly below.

That's more like it, but to which of my current obsessions can I admit? Well, there's professional football for starters and how about writing stories for the under-fives. What else? Probably best not to mention marketing at this stage, they'll find out about that soon enough. How about hosting game shows, intergalactic travel and do-it-yourself psychotherapy? That little lot should keep them quiet for a while.

Then, out of the blue, it occurs to me that I might consider telling the truth, if not on the form itself, then at least once I get in front of the counsellors. I look up and check them out. Sure enough, they're not biting the heads off numbers 40, 41 and 42. I've never seriously contemplated the idea that there may be a job out there that I'd genuinely enjoy. I pause to reflect upon my natural instinct, which had been to lie throughout the form. Then I tear through the rest of the questions like a whippet:

Would you like someone to help you with your search for employment?

Yes.

Would you like someone to assess your competencies?

Yes, please.

Would you like some advice?

Well, I think I need some, don't you?

What did you say?

Sorry! I said, yes. Yes please. I'd like that very much indeed.

Good. Then please sit back down and await your turn.

OK, thank you.

And stop biting your fingernails.

Like I said, I just assumed that the day Junior dropped out of the womb, I'd run back to my old pals in marketing with my tail wedged well and truly between my legs: Stay of execution over, here is your fattened salary, company car, medical insurance and a bond entitling you to a reasonably-sized spot in the company cemetery if you keep your nose and arse clean. Now, please put your head back into this tailor-made noose...

No! I can't. I refuse. For once in my life, I'm going to stand up for myself. I jump to my feet, roll up my sleeves and start pawing at the floor. This is it, I'm ready. Let's do this thing! Out of the corner of my eye, I see the ticket counter rolling lazily onto number 45. I pause. Numbers 46 through 62 are looking at me a little strangely. Embarrassed as a newly shorn ewe, I sit back down behind a large buff file and pretend to thumb through a few employment offers.

An hour or so later, a grey-haired counsellor called Maurice is staring at me so incredulously that I'm convinced his eyebrows are about to lose all contact with their earthly moorings. He's already informed me that most people do come in here with at least some idea of what they might like to do and now he's demanding to know what I've been up to these past few months. To tell you the truth, my patience is beginning to wear a little thin. 'OK, you really want to know? I'm writing a screenplay.' I hadn't planned on telling him any such thing but Maurice looks strangely relieved and, for a few minutes, he buries the eyebrows in his computer screen.

Eventually, Maurice persuades me that I really ought to have a second choice, just in case the screenplay doesn't work out. I notice how he's making a real effort to sound sympathetic when he says this and I'm just about to start feeling a little sorry for him when he pulls out an enormous hard-bound book which, he explains, lists every possible occupation from Acrobat to Zookeeper. This is a two-volume affair known as the *Fiches Rome* and Maurice wants me to become intimately acquainted with the twin sisters just as soon as I can. He's sure there's something in there, even for someone like me. But that's it for today – Maurice has noticed number 64 pacing the floor behind me like a tiger about to end a self-imposed hunger strike and has decided I need more help than he's either willing or able to provide. He'll be sending me to a specialist, someone who can help me define my very own 'project'. Ah yes, of course, a project! As a nation, the French are obsessed with the notion of projects and they can range from the relatively straightforward, like planting some geraniums or finding a job, to the highly complex – reforming the French social system, say, or plotting against the President of the Republic. It isn't the complexity of the project that matters but, to count as a member of the human race in this country, you have to have at least one project on the go, otherwise your friends start digging you a box-shaped hole in the ground.

I'm finally disgorged with an appointment to see the specialist, a telephone number for a couple of French lessons, a half-eaten cheese sandwich and the beginnings of my very own project. I hurry straight down to the *mairie* of the ninth *arrondissement* where Helena is waiting to register the baby. I've already been here twice; once to schedule our wedding and then to cancel it. Shortly after I committed the second of these acts, Helena's parents solemnly declared to all and sundry that their daughter and I no longer shared any projects, although that all changed when Junior went and got himself conceived. Now that's what I call a project and what's more, it looks like being a truly French project. This morning I spoke to some old trout from the British Embassy in Paris, who told me our baby will not get British nationality until our conjugal situation is 'normalised'. 'He's not a British citizen,' she said, when I had the temerity to ask for an explanation, 'not if he's born to a French mother, in France!' Only the way she told it, 'he' sounded more like 'it', France not unlike the municipal garbage dump, and the French a nation of horseflies. When I complained about her tone, she invited me to press zero and take it up with Queen Victoria herself.

Poor Junior! As a passport-bearing Frenchman, he'll have to fill an entire lifetime with projects and other, utterly nonsensical Cartesian ideas.

The dawn of man, September 5th

Whatever happened to the summer? Already those aching blue skies seem so far away. The minute we arrived back in Paris, the weather got straight into its autumn clothing, forcing us to follow suit. It's freezing cold, the drizzle won't stop and, as I trudge off for my follow-up appointment with the careers counsellor, I have an enormous ache in the head. I know it's purely psychosomatic, but I feel lousy as I slump heavily opposite the counsellor. I peer at her suspiciously while she finishes a call and a stack of paperwork associated with whoever just got ejected from this warm, fake leather chair.

Madame Ferrat isn't the kind of counsellor you'd find at an English social security office. First, she has a terrific figure, to which a couple of expensive looking black garments cling for dear life, her hair is an immaculate blond bob and her jewellery is gold and tastefully hung. We're halfway through our conversation before I realise she's quite a bit older than her appearance suggests.

Within a few minutes, she has extracted my story more efficiently than a bookie taking a fiver off a housewife on Grand National day. Throughout our conversation, her cool blue eyes appraise my plausibility and transmit messages back to the silicon chip that resides at some central point between her earrings. We talk about screenplays for a full thirty seconds before she wraps up that particular subject by making it clear she regards that type of activity best reserved for the evening once the baby has been put to bed (and no, it didn't take her long to find out about that either). Madame Ferrat is certainly not in the business of indulging my fantasies. Her job is to find me a job and she's not about to let me get in the way of her exercising her duties.

She sends me packing with instructions to make a complete list of my competencies and to go through the *Fiches Rome* with a fine-tooth comb, stopping only when I've found something of interest and, preferably, for which I'm qualified. Then she warns me that France is not the same as the UK: prospective employers in this country are far more interested in the right kind of training or a fistful of diplomas than they are in the blag, bullshit or capacity for self delusion of weird zoological anomalies like me. Somehow I fail to be overwhelmed by this latest revelation about my hosts and, on my way out of the door, Madame Ferrat hurls a date at the back of my head, upon which I'm expected to rematerialise in her presence, fully prepared and as motivated as a pink rabbit on *Duracell*. Madame Ferrat is not the kind of person for whom you don't do your homework.

I head straight to the video shop. By the time I get there, my head is throbbing so hard that I just pick up the first two films that come to hand. The rain is still falling outside, so Helena and I crawl into bed to watch a film featuring two of Hollywood's finest at their surgically enhanced best, in a syrupy tale of love against the odds in Paris. The dialogue soon has me cowering under the covers, where my mind wanders and I start to reflect on how I came to be here in the first place...

It was in February, slap bang in the middle of the longest winter of my life, that I met Helena for the second time. Every Friday I'd leave work early, catch the evening train to Paris and spend the weekend with Helena, sober and in love. I'd return on Monday morning and spend the rest of the week drinking and hiding from my clients. I was living for the moment when I could catch the train back to Paris and abandon that part of my life which I could no longer bear. My double existence could never last and it came crashing down as soon as I made the move to France, where I had too much time on my hands and nothing better to do than listen to the thoughts that pursued me through the night and try to answer the questions weighing heavily on my mind: *Why did you leave a perfectly good job? What are you going to do now? You don't exactly have a plan, do you? As a matter of fact, you don't even speak French. Do you like what you see when you look in the mirror?*

The truth of it was that I'd resigned from a well-paid job and moved to France with no prospects and a CV that read like a textbook on despair. I knew I had to change. But how? For a while I did nothing, other than torture Helena with my excruciating attempts to master the French subjunctive. I've no idea why she didn't throw me straight out of the house but while I thought things could only get worse, she was convinced they would improve and it's one of those extraordinary things that we choose to call coincidence that, on the very day I made the decision to put down the bottle, the baby was conceived. The momentous event occurred after an evening spent at the apartment of Helena's aunt – a generous, gentle woman who also happens to be a psychiatrist. I'd taken a back seat as the evening festivities began, due, in no small part, to a hangover which was still chipping away at the base of my skull from the night before. But, by the time most of the guests had already left, I was still arguing with the aunt and one of Helena's brothers about whether addiction is a disease or some sort of moral failing. To oil the debate, we cracked open another bottle of champagne. Already distracted and foaming at the mouth, I was completely incapable of resisting its allure. Helena and her aunt refused and the brother and I drained it quickly and without reflection.

By the time we arrived home, I was quite drunk and feeling lower than ever. Tears rolled down Helena's cheeks as I described my feelings of failure and impending doom. I picked up the half-finished glass of red which had somehow materialised in front of me, sniffed at it and put it back down. Helena watched me, her eyes a little swollen. Then she said she was no longer prepared to listen to a voice shot through with such self-pity. She got up and moved towards the bedroom. I thought she was going to pack her bags. I wouldn't have argued if she had. Instead, she got into bed and asked me to join her. I can't tell you why I agreed. But that night, with my own life at its lowest ebb, between us we started another.

A kick in the works, September 8th

I'm back at the *ANPE*, ready for a marathon session with the *Fiches Rome* in preparation for my next meeting with the Ferrat. I look at the cover of the imposing double volume, rifle the thin leaf pages and decide to invest in a cup of over-sweetened, government-subsidised coffee. Even in English, the *Fiches* would take longer to review than the Lord Admiral's fleet. My first task is to understand the way in which they're organised. Essentially, they are a classification system which employs a series of numerical codes to sort and order every conceivable job or profession. The way they are ordered is so hierarchical, so typically French, that they make the Egyptian pyramids look like a pile of bricks which have been tossed randomly one on top of the other.

But by the time I reach the unmelted powdered milk congealed at the bottom of my polystyrene coffee cup, I believe I've cracked the code and, happily, can discard one volume entirely as it's largely commercial and there's really no need for me to bother the captains of French industry with my CV. There are many reasons for this and I'll spare you the unnecessary detail, but just to give you an idea, until fairly recently I thought physics was something to do with the shape of a woman's body.

The jobs in the remaining volume are grouped under a number of different headings, each of which is given a double digit code. A further three numbers define the precise duties and competencies required by a particular profession, the type of training entailed and where the work takes place. Recklessly, I dive into the first category – pastry maker, dog shampooist (not really my thing, but I want to start off in broad scope mode), lawyer, *chocolatier,* carrier pigeon and arms dealer – each merits its own meticulous description, equal in length to all the others and there are thousands of them. What diversity, what a mosaic of interlocking pieces! Why on earth didn't I undertake such an exercise when I first had the chance all those years ago?

Lit and loaded after six or seven cups of genetically enhanced caffeine, I emerge from the *ANPE* cave snarling and clutching a fistful of poor quality photocopies. My problem is not so much that I've found something I'd like to do, but rather that I've found too many of them and I'm not sure whether there's enough life left in me to make a start. I head home to tell Helena all about how I've hacked my way, bare-chested, through the employment jungle, and found the key to professional fulfilment.

I cross her at the front door. She's on her way back from the swimming pool and looks a little pale, but I press on regardless.

'What have you got then?' Helena says, as if I've come home with a new tropical disease.

'Look,' I say, fanning out the photocopies as proudly as a poker player producing a royal flush.

Helena starts to leaf through the *fiches*. By the time she's finished, she looks like the exasperated parent of a child that's started to rewrite its Christmas list with Santa already halfway down the chimney. She hands back my dreams and disappears to lay her aching body on the bed. In my excitement, I've forgotten to ask how she's feeling.

I continue to prepare for my next meeting with the Ferrat by attacking the other, more daunting task that she set last week – a complete list of my competencies. This takes me the rest of the afternoon and, much to my dismay, the list covers less than one side of A4. Never mind, perhaps it will stretch to the bottom of the page once translated into the long-winded language that is French.

My musings are interrupted by a shout of excitement from the bedroom. I've been so absorbed in my task that I catch myself wondering whether Helena has had a sudden flash of inspiration about our future.

'He kicked me!'

'What?'

'He kicked me... '

'Who kicked you?' Quickly I scan the room for rogue Italian footballers.

'The baby! Who do you think?'

'Ah, yes, of course. Where?'

'Put your hand on my belly,' says Helena, guiding my trembling fingers to the only part of her anatomy that might conceivably house another human being. 'Can you feel anything?'

I feel only the racing of my own pulse.

'There! Did you feel it this time?' Helena makes a minor adjustment to the placement of my fingers. Suddenly I feel a slight tremor underneath her skin.

'Yes!'

'You felt it?'

'I think so. I felt something like a little kick, yes!' I look at Helena's face, which is filled with a mixture of childish wonder and delight.

'He's a little footballer,' she says, as a smile the size of France rampages across her face.

I stay by Helena's side for a while and continue to press my fingers lightly into the softness of her belly. Slowly she drifts off to sleep while the presence of Junior continues to register like a tiny earthquake on the needle of my stubby and somewhat rudimentary monitoring equipment.

The light fades slowly outside our apartment as I lie beside the two human beings with whom I now share a bed. Despite his increasing visible presence around the apartment, I've barely thought about the changes this baby will soon ring in my life and I remain absorbed in the struggle to find my own path. Is this selfish? In terms of the attention I'm failing to lavish upon Helena, it is. Is this my way of preparing for the future – by sticking my head in the sand? I haven't picked up our copy of *Future Maman* for weeks, I'm only vaguely aware of the changes which continue apace in her body, her moods and her eating habits, and I've done nothing to accommodate them. But as we approach the end of the fourth month, her body continues to silently adjust itself to the new life within.

Even my mathematical abilities are sufficient to do the calculation: Junior will be born in around twenty weeks' time. Will I be ready? It doesn't really matter, because he or she (and we'll find out next week) is already thundering over the curve of the horizon and soon enough I'll be unable to ignore this presence any longer.

From fantasy to reality (and back), September 10th

I arrive at Madame Ferrat's with renewed vigour. I lay my cards on the table and explain that the *fiches* I've selected represent the fields in which I'm generally interested rather than a set of concrete job applications I intend to write anytime soon. This is such abstract nonsense that I feel sure any French person will be duty bound to swallow it hook, line and sinker, but Mme Ferrat just smiles indulgently and asks to see the list of competencies which I've translated into French with a little help from Helena.

'These are not competencies,' she declares, after the most cursory glance at my list, 'they're character defects – you'll have to redo the list.'

I protest, naturally, but what she wants is a list of all tasks I've actually performed throughout my long and ignoble campaign in the marketing wars. Then she turns her attention back to the *fiches* and expresses mild, yet barely concealed, surprise at my eclectic selection of future lives. 'What's this?' she demands, holding up the last page as if it were a piece of rotten meat.

'Ah, yes,' I say, 'I've always fancied working in a national park, you know, somewhere up in the mountains.'

'Really?' This is the only official word of retort from the other side of the desk, but, by now, she's looking me up and down – but mainly down – as though I were a tramp stationed outside the *Ritz*.

'Well, you know, just for a few months, anyway.'

I'm beginning to wonder whether the Ferrat really has my best interests at heart or if she's been for a chat with Helena. Now my depressingly efficient counsellor picks up the *fiche* that most closely resembles the job I did in the past and steers my attention to her computer screen. Together we search a couple of employment websites and she very quickly rustles up a couple of jobs for which I might reasonably apply and expect to receive more than a four-letter word by way of response. One of these is a multinational pet food conglomerate that's looking for someone to liaise between its marketing department and the mongrel population of France. 'What about that?' she exclaims. I don't answer and lower my gaze from the screen – I hate dogs and I'll be damned if I'm going down in history as the man who helped perfect the world's first self-digesting, curry-flavoured dog biscuit for Fido the Flatulent. The Ferrat looks at her watch. My allotted hour is almost up and she's already thinking about her next victim. She tells me that the pooch plan was only ever intended as an example and her final instructions are to redo the list of competencies, search all job websites, wash thoroughly behind my ears and come back next week with a list of potential employers. I signal my assent by nodding haplessly. I know she's only doing her job, but I'm disappointed. I came here to change career, not to end up back in the big doggie bowl of marketing.

Never mind, some friends are arriving from London tomorrow and I'm not going to spoil the weekend worrying about all this bollocks. On Monday I'll dream up some sort of a strategy for getting what I want out of Mme Ferrat. I'll be back at work soon enough, so why not relax a little and enjoy life while I still can?

Frayed nerves, September 12th

My friends have left their two children in the soft play area at *McDonalds* and they arrive wearing the manic look of a couple of escapees from Colditz. For the last couple of days they've been in the Champagne region, eating, driving around and visiting the local cellars and when I open the front door, my oldest friend is standing there clutching a case of champagne and grinning like a well-oiled coyote. I know now that I should have just closed the door and got an early night. But I practically swung the thing off its hinges and they stepped right inside to continue the party and extol the joys of life as available in shapely green 75-centiletre bottles. The very sight of them filled me with sadness before they'd even crossed the threshold.

Their first suggestion is that we crack open a bottle. They can't understand why I might want to give up drinking and, just for a moment, neither can I. Surely one glass can do no harm? These two have seen me dead drunk on more than a few occasions. But, as we discuss my abstinence over nibbles, they're not sure if, in the larger context of being British and everything, an inability to coordinate drunken limbs and tongue constitutes reasonable grounds for total self-denial of the noble French grape or the Great British pint. With a look of genuine concern, my friend (who knows me as well as anyone on our crowded little planet) leads me quietly out onto the streets where we go for a drink and a quiet chat – one of those man-to-man deals without the girls. Throwing caution to the wind I take a seat in the neighbourhood bar and order a tomato juice loaded with celery salt and *Tabasco*.

My friend's theory is that my problem is not alcohol at all but rather the emotional immaturity; the relationship failures; and all the other disappointments that I chose to hide from view; that eventually caused me to seek solace in the bottle. My own argument is that it works precisely the other way round – my problems begin with the attractive frothy head on the beer, and by the time I catch sight of the bottom of the glass, I've already succeeded in doubling them. But, as my wise owl of a friend concludes the argument for the defence, I'm all for casting aside my doubts and the tomato juice in favour of something altogether more pissy and lager-like.

I resist, but watching the pair of them enjoy a couple of glasses of cold, sharp Chardonnay over dinner only encourages the animal buried deep inside: *Come on! It looks good, doesn't it? You see those droplets of water forming on the outside of the glass? Right! It's chilled to perfection! What are you worried about? Of course you can have one or two glasses. Stop fretting! We'll deal with tomorrow when it arrives. It's not like you're busy at the moment, after all. You, an alcoholic? Don't be ridiculous!*

Determined to push my luck, we leave the girls and head to the *Styx*, a seedy underground joint down on the *Grands Boulevards* and barely fifteen minutes' flight from my perilous perch on sobriety. It's midnight on Friday and I know what to expect – thumping techno music and not a sober soul in the house – and before I'm properly through the door, I run into an old acquaintance who is sweating and swigging vodka cocktails with equal proficiency.

Just for a moment I'm totally unnerved. What am I doing here? No, let me rephrase that – what am I doing here sober? I run for the cover of the bar. When I get there, I order a *Coke* without vodka and the barmaid looks at me as if I've taken a wrong turning for a Seventh Day Adventist convention.

Fortified by the rush of sugar and caffeine, I forge my way towards the dance floor as half-naked torsos spill across my path. Ecstasy eyes, deep yet superficial, quickly scan my face like burned-out searchlights. The steps on the dance floor are as fast and metronomic as the music and everybody in the house waits for the DJ to force the music upwards to yet another artificial crescendo. The entire darkened chamber is aglow with fast-burning cigarettes. Now what? I can't remember ever daring to put so much as a single toe onto a dance floor without first saturating my cells in liquor. I close my eyes and wait for my feet to be swept along by the metallic rhythm. But my heart isn't in it and a diminished voice within pleads that if I'm going to start drinking again, then please don't let it be tonight.

Night and day, September 13th

I scan my skull for hangovers. Negative. After a long lazy breakfast of relief, coffee and croissants, I suggest a walk down to the Left Bank. As we sip coffee and water at a café on the Boulevard St Michel, I learn that, by some strange quirk of fate, today is the day that the hardcore of Parisian night-life have chosen to exercise the right they share with every other French man and woman to demonstrate on the streets of Paris. The old city will smile just as benignly on the ravers as it does the farmers, accountants, or whoever else happens to be stomping down her regal boulevards looking for freedom of speech and the opportunity to swear publicly at a few gendarmes without fear of reprisal.

Another hour passes and it's beginning to look as if the party animals have failed to get out of bed on time for their little window on the great advent calendar of democracy. They're protesting against a government led by an overweight and vaguely obnoxious prime minister who evidently disapproves of their late-night consumption of narcotics and has kept himself busy closing down a number of their favourite after-party haunts. As far as I can tell, the way this works in the great Fifth Republic is that, while the French economy continues to stagnate, the party crowd gets to protest about the repressive tactics and girth of the prime minister and enjoy a few hours partying in the sunlight until the government continues its clampdown as soon as the sun sets. With a bit of luck the dancers will disgrace themselves too, just to show that the fat cats were right about their lack of morality all along.

By the time a large number of police motorcyclists pull

up and start showing us just how shiny a pair of boots can be, it's the middle of a stinking hot September afternoon. Maybe it's the past catching up with me, but by the time we settle into another enticing pavement café, my resolve is beginning to waver once more. I'd dearly love to quench my two-month thirst with a single bottle of ice-cold beer, just like the one the placards have nailed into my subconscious: A couple of chiming glasses, just dripping with condensation, have mysteriously landed on some idyllic Barbadian beach while a deeply tanned couple with immaculately coiffed, golden locks are lounging around in their underwear, laughing at each others' jokes. In the background, a spotlessly uniformed waiter is grinning as widely as Louis Armstrong. The beer itself looks as transparently innocent as a ray of carbonated liquid sunshine and a couple of hectares of ice cubes are clinking around in a handy silver bucket along with several kilos of sharp-coloured citrus fruits, just to convince you the whole scene is as healthy and wholesome as tea with the vicar, only seventeen times more sexually suggestive and without any hint that it'll all end in tears. As the sun begins to sink languidly below the horizon and another perfectly cloned couple looms into view, ready for vacuous conversation and the prospect of some androgynous group sex, I close my eyes to the tricks of the ad agency (by now I recognise the house style of the agency *Devious, Conniving and Bastard*). It's not these images that I need to remember right now, but rather the interminable slate grey mornings I spent imprisoned in my own skull as something inhuman tried to beat down the door.

I'm not out of jail yet, either. Now my night owl friends want to visit the *Brahma Bar*, one of the most glittering and overpriced stars in the nocturnal Parisian firmament. Helena and I have been there a couple of times before, back in the days when even a perfectly mixed gin and tonic had nothing to add to our mutual, all-natural high. But this evening, as my friends scrub up cleaner than a pair of cardiothoracic surgeons,

I practically have to beg Helena to accompany us:

'Come on, it'll be fun.'

'What's fun about spending the evening in a giant ashtray?'

'You used to like it.'

'So what? I used to enjoy wetting my nappy and burping.' Helena stretches one hand languidly towards a nearby paper-back (the tactical manoeuvre) and the other for her belly (the strategic reinforcement).

'The others will be disappointed.' I'm getting desperate now.

'Are you going to drink?'

''Course not.' Then comes the inspiration: 'Not if you come along.'

Helena leers at me like a zealous police inspector who is fully aware of the truth but has not one shred of the evidence necessary for a conviction. Sighing more audibly than a disgusted walrus, she levers herself gingerly off the mattress, muttering something ugly and unnecessary about blackmail. Then she pulls on a pair of her finest pregnancy pants and waits as I lower her feet into a pair of cork-heeled shoes – not exactly *Christian Lacroix* but comfortable, unlike the anorexic winkle-pickers selected by one half of the couple from London. Beautifully shod she may be, as she staggers out of the apartment, but she's also quite lame.

Packed into the *Clio* like designer sardines, we head to the fashionable end of town. It's midnight on Saturday and most people around these parts are about to start dinner, although one glance at Helena's face in the rear-view mirror confirms my suspicion that she's already thinking about breakfast.

We get the eye from the bouncer, of course, as one of my friends is black and there aren't a lot of black people in the *Brahma Bar*. Maybe they're expected to provide the music and do a bit of washing up, I don't know, but after a lengthy wait and a series of filthy looks, we just about make the cut. What you will find in the *Brahma Bar* are a lot of people with money and an equal number of people looking for ways to relieve them of it. Tonight, the latter are represented principally by a hoard of bottle blondes from the old Soviet bloc. Looking and smelling as if they have all fallen face-down into the cosmetics counter of a low-end department store, they're hanging around wherever they're likely to get an expensive cocktail spilled down a prominent, glitter-sprinkled cleavage. Unfortunately for the girls, however, the men with the seriously large piles of readies are in the restaurant downstairs, eating the Japanese *Kobe* beef at approximately €56 a mouthful.

Helena is in no mood to be jostled by the Ukrainian mafia and makes it absolutely clear to our painfully superior waitress that she expects to be seated forthwith. The snooty one shoots us a look that would kill a cockroach stone dead at a hundred paces and demands an apology from Helena for using word like 'forthwith' in a place like this. But then Helena points to the silent but influential fifth member of our party and, much to her obvious disgust, the waitress is left with little choice but to usher us downstairs among the self-styled elite.

My friends are suitably impressed by the whole scene, especially when they catch sight of the three-story high, fake marble Yogi who presides over this sorry mess and wisely keeps his back to one of the walls. I order three soft drinks and a glass of Chardonnay, the price of which requires me to put in a call to an offshore bank in the Cayman Islands for an extra line of credit. Since conversation with our friends on the opposite side of the table is nigh on impossible over the sound system (the CD is naturally available in the foyer upstairs), I end up watching people at the surrounding tables. Right next door, for example, a couple of bulimic and upwardly mobile advertising hoardings (strictly *Gucci* and *Chanel*) are entertaining a man old enough to be their grandfather over sashimi and cocktail cigarettes. Sugar Daddy won't let the designer twins pay for dinner (at least, not until later), not that they try too hard. He's already waited too long for the opportunity to flash his hideous gold watch and matching credit card.

I know it's too late for excuses and I know that I sound bitter and twisted but, personally, I've always preferred to eat in a place where I can see the food and it doesn't come served with a plume of cigarette smoke and a pungent blast of the waitresses' perfumed deodorant. Call me fussy, or jealous if you prefer, but I wouldn't even recommend this place to the cast of *East Enders* out on a payday binge and this has absolutely nothing to do with the fact that I can't stand the sight of everyone swilling imported Slavonic lagers while I'm forced to nurse an apple juice all night long.

Famous Parisian ashtrays, September 14th

By the time Sunday rolls around, the worst of the temptation is over and we're lolling about in autumnal sunshine on the banks of the Canal St Martin. The only cloud on the horizon is the trouble I'm in with Helena for smoking a packet of cigarettes over the course of a weekend which has sorely tested my resistance to the old life. I can't remember exactly when I crumbled once more at the feet of the Nicotine God, but it must have been at some point between the *Styx* and the beleaguered Yogi. I simply peeled off my low dosage junkie patch and replaced it with the tightly rolled, filter-tipped version of the same drug. I explain it away to Helena as the price I had to pay for resisting a relapse on the booze. She says the price is too high and my silence confirms that she's right about this as well.

A day in the North Atlantic, September 15th

And that's all it took for me to reawaken this morning as a reconfirmed and guilt-riddled smoker. I've brewed up a second pot of coffee and that part of my brain responsible for addictive behaviour has ordered me down into the courtyard for my favourite early morning gasper.

Another visitor is on the way over from London. Tony is an ex-colleague from the company it took me twelve years to escape and I've promised that I'll procure him a good bottle of wine and a good feed. I figure there's no harm in having one more dinner at the expense of my ex-employer, even if it means I'll have to go through another round of explanations about my not drinking. The last time Tony was here, we spent the evening sampling super-strength Belgian raspberry beer. I remember quite liking the first three bottles, but the rest is just a hazy fruit fog until the following morning when I solemnly swore off all forest fruits forever.

Before we meet, I call Ernesto, an Italian friend who at least has no interest in my inability to stop at one beer or one cigarette. Ernesto is a real writer. He writes plays which get performed, short stories which get published, and movie reviews which get read and respected. I met him on that screenwriting course at the American University in Paris, where he was looking for help transforming a fantastically morbid Italian short story into a script for film. I loved his idea, although New York Nancy, our hard-assed course leader, didn't like the ending because the unsympathetic protagonist, who's been doing a nice job of redeeming himself for all but the last few pages, fails at the last hurdle and dies a lonely and miserable death. Nance, no doubt under instruction from Spielberg himself, dutifully informed Ernesto that the ending would be completely unacceptable in California (a land where death remains an entirely optional facet of life, provided you drink enough mineral water and herbal tea) and ordered him to manufacture a nice pinky-orange Los Angeles sunset. Ernesto resisted and, giving up his Hollywood dream, turned the ending into a masterpiece of rotting human flesh.

Anyway, we're skiving off to watch an obscure Icelandic movie called *Noi Albinoi* and we've found the cheapest cinema in Paris in which to watch it – a right little fleapit located smack bang on the main crossroads at l'Odéon. I mention this only because you can hear the Parisians buzzing about on their scooters outside whenever the soundtrack falls silent. Anyway, the screen at this place is so small that you can easily imagine it has been nailed to the wall by the seven dwarves, which must be why all the subtitles are being projected onto the floor. Sadly my knowledge of Icelandic is insufficient to permit any understanding of what is being said in the opening scenes and it's a full fifteen minutes before the only other person in the theatre heaves a huge sigh and disappears to awaken the projectionist.

Not that you'd catch any sizzling dialogue even if the whole thing were dubbed into English: The action centres on a small town in the middle of the Icelandic winter (or was it their summer?). And the Noi of the title is just your run-of-the-mill, bald Icelandic teenager with bulging ice-floe eyes. He detests school and all the other inhabitants of the town, most of whom appear to be either brain dead or perpetually plastered. Either way, they spend most of their time simply gaping vacantly at a clock on the wall, trying to calculate how long they will have to wait for the onset of death. There's only one café in this town, but the owner has somehow mysteriously dredged up a beautiful daughter from somewhere in this frozen Hell and life suddenly takes on a whole new meaning for Noi (well, some meaning, anyway).

He dreams of escaping to Hawaii and, in this respect, you can't fault the guy for a minute. We're shown a little more of the town, which appears to have been hand-carved out of an off-grey iceberg. I'm freezing my nuts off just looking at the place on screen. Then Noi gets kicked out of school, meaning that the future, which wasn't looking like a million dollars in the first place, has arrived unexpectedly early. Wisely, he steals a car, buys himself a nice Italian suit and tries to persuade the girl to join him in flight. She refuses point-blank and reminds our hero that there aren't a whole lot of places to drive in the middle of the North Atlantic. Noi is soon snaffled by the police in the only car chase on ice I can ever remember seeing and then things really begin to get weird. Upon release from his igloo-cell, Noi holes up in the basement of the house he shares with his mute grandmother and the town is hit by an avalanche which wipes out the entire population with the lone exception of Noi, who is still underground at the fateful moment. And that's just about the end of the film. I'm not sure that it will have received an awful lot of financial backing from the Icelandic Tourist Promotion Board, but once Ernesto and I step back outside the cinema, dusting imaginary snow from our overcoats and blowing hard on our chapped and chilblained fingers, we agree that the film is alright by us.

As we wander across one of the bridges over the Seine, the great city of Paris is bathed in evening sunlight and I remain full of empathy for young Noi. I can imagine Helena asking, as she always does, what happens to the protagonist once the credits have rolled. I don't know. I suppose that somewhere, he and hundreds of thousands like him are still holed up under all that ice, never to be given a second chance.

Before we part, Ernesto enquires after my own abandoned script. I stare out across the river as it washes out towards the sea beneath my feet and avoid answering his question. Somehow I just don't feel like telling him about the Ferrat.

Tony is waiting for me on the steps of the opera house at Bastille and he's not in a reflective mood. In fact he's so stressed that he needs a couple of drinks before he's even prepared to contemplate dinner. In the first bar we come across I order a pint for him and a tomato juice for myself. We sit down and I ask Tony one little question about the company. Three pints later, he's still ranting and a couple of ominous purple veins are standing to attention on his temples. He has yet to ask me whether I regret leaving the company. Perhaps he fears the answer.

In vain, I attempt to steer the conversation towards Tony's favourite topic, which, sadly, happens to be Crystal Palace

Football Club. But even this fails to arrest the torrent, so I order the bill before Tony can order another pint and start marching him in the general direction of a well-known *brasserie* near the Bastille. He's still foaming at the mouth as we're seated at our table but the starchily proud waiters are polite enough not to scream 'rabies' or call in the neighbourhood vet.

By the time Tony has swallowed a glass of sangria and started in on a bottle of Muscadet, he's making enough sense for me to order something called the *plateau royal*. This is a dish piled so high with crustacea that just the sight of it would have Helena running for the hinterland. It's taken three tugboats just to get it from the kitchen onto the waiter's trolley and, splayed across a small, semi-permanent icecap, I spot lobster, crab, a family of langoustine, king prawns (pink), servile prawns (grey), mussels, scallops, clams, whelks and about two dozen Breton oysters. Fortunately Tony, who is already tucking into his half of the contents of the North Sea, is not what you'd call a waif of a lad and he's already talked himself into a formidable appetite. I don't even try to consume my share of the trawler and, long after I'm done, Tony is still shelling prawns and shovelling them onto precarious life rafts of buttered brown bread before they disappear forever on their journey into the depths of his ample belly.

'Good, isn't it?' signals Tony, as he comes up briefly for air.

'Yes, it is,' I reply. 'Tony?'

'Mmmm?'

'Is it possible to overdose on oysters?'

'Don't be ridiculous' he says, as another of the slimy ones slips easily down his saline gullet. 'Aren't you eating the whelks?'

I'm not eating the whelks. In fact I've been assiduously avoiding the unpleasant, mossy-green objects all evening. As far as I'm concerned, whelks look like garden snails with mange and possess all the consistency and taste of a nearside *Pirelli* – 'But you go ahead.'

Tony goes ahead, firing them down with the rapidity of

a semiautomatic weapon.

'Lovely things, whelks!' he manages to squeeze out at one point, before reloading once more.

'Yeah, sure they are. Look, Tony, you must come to our place for dinner next time you're over.' I hesitate for a moment, wondering whether our place is large enough to accommodate Tony's appetites. 'You haven't met Helena, have you?'

'No. You should have brought her along tonight.'

'Not a good idea that.' And I explain why.

Tony looks mildly surprised. 'Oh, so she wouldn't have liked what happened the last time I was here then... '

Dare I ask? What did he do? Swallow an entire school of sardines at a single sitting?

'What happened?'

Tony carefully assesses the lone survivor of the shipwreck in front of us. It's another whelk, but there's no escape and it goes the way of the rest of its extended family. 'I was about to tuck into a fine-looking crab when, whaddya know, out from under the shell of its dead but utterly delicious mother ran a tiny, baby crab!'

I wipe the corners of my mouth with my stiff white napkin before fixing Tony with what I hope is a steely gaze. My dining companion is busy rinsing his teeth with the last of the Muscadet and trying to catch the waiter's eye for the dessert menu. 'Tony?'

'Yeah?' he responds absentmindedly, as he picks at a troublesome piece of whelk flesh, caught between a couple of molars.

'Do me a favour, will you? If you do come to our place, don't ever tell that story to Helena, OK?'

Man down! September 16th

Of course, I can't swear it's because of the dinner, but less than twenty-four hours later I come down with a virulent stomach bug. It happens at the Gare St Lazare, where my intention is to buy a train ticket to the south of France and visit Vincent, who has secured the use of his parents' holiday apartment for a few days. There I plan to avoid any meetings with the Ferrat for a further two weeks before travelling further south and spending a couple of days in Barcelona. But my stomach begins an unpleasant armed uprising just as my number comes up at the station ticket counter, thus forcing me into a hasty decision on which train to catch. I stumble home as fast as my churning guts will allow and collapse into bed as heavily as a piece of choice rainforest teak. My temples are jumping and my lungs feel as if they're in the grip of a military dictatorship. And nothing has changed by the time Helena returns from school several hours later.

'What's the matter?'

'Sick!'

'With what?'

'Don't know.'

'What are your symptoms?'

'Stomach, head, chest.'

'Have you seen a doctor?'

'Nah!'

Such conversation is probably familiar to women around the world. When one of their number falls ill, her stride is barely interrupted. She's straight down the surgery, on to the pharmacy and a couple of prescribed medications later, she's back in the groove with barely a word of complaint. When a man falls sick, on the other hand, the storm clouds of Armageddon gather more quickly and things tend to follow a familiar pattern.

As the minor ailment enters his body, the male of the species grinds to a shuddering halt and is instantaneously overwhelmed by a sea of self-pity and the profound belief that he has landed at death's door. A brief conversation with his partner ensues, during which she seeks to establish approximate time of expiry. The male persists with a strictly monosyllabic form of communication, before his partner suggests a trip to the local GP. The male refuses point-blank, preferring to suffer without any unnecessary silence. She suspects malingering and threatens to call their GP to the house. The man insists he doesn't want any fuss, swallows two paracetamol, agrees to visit the doctor at some indeterminate point in the future and continues to make a fuss. Three malingering days later, the doctor diagnoses a non-fatal illness such as the common cold, prescribes a small selection of placebos and sends the patient packing. The male declares the dramatically large pills superfluous to requirements but his girlfriend forces them into his gullet anyway. He demands to be allowed to die in peace while she gets on with the washing up. He sleeps for twenty-four hours only to miraculously awaken in time for the big footie match. The antibiotics begin to effect recovery from the premature brush with the afterlife before the man gets out of bed as if the whole thing had never happened and refuses to finish the course of drugs. Normal service is resumed.

A taste of things to come, September 17th

As you will no doubt appreciate, I've been far too ill to make any headway on my job applications. On the other hand, my laptop is hooked up and ready to receive radio broadcasts just in time for the big *Champions League* kick-off and, as Helena prepares a simple stomach-friendly supper of boiled rice and ham, I disappear into the spare bedroom to listen to Arsenal take on the might of the Milanese.

Within a matter of weeks, this room will become the realm of my son and it remains in a fine state of unreadiness. It is still lined with Helena's half-finished pottery and the cupboards are loaded with toxic chemicals. The walls look dirty and tired, a fact that we have tried to hide behind posters and pictures which themselves hang forlorn under months of dust. At least we're about to find out whether they're to be painted pink or blue, and in her impatience to find out the sex of our child, Helena has brought forward the ultrasound appointment for the second time – a shrewd move which should cut the time spent arguing over names by 50 percent.

I swear that if such a thing were anatomically possible, Helena would have this baby tomorrow. I mean, it's not as if the ceramics are the only thing to have fallen by the wayside lately. Now only one topic of conversation holds her interest for longer than five minutes and virtually nothing else matters. I guess that's just the way women are built. Every cell in their bodies directs its full care and attention to the business of nurturing another, perfectly formed human being. I might as well be in Milan myself, for all the use I appear to be in this process, which is what I was trying to articulate from my sickbed yesterday morning when, in my semi-fevered state, I crudely described Helena as a piece of pure pregnancy. This, as you can probably imagine, did not go down at all well.

We've already exchanged serrated words over the amount of weight she's gained since Junior moved into our lives – in my view excessive, in hers perfectly normal. For the record, the total is ten kilos and counting, but I'm trying to keep my mouth shut and allow the doctor to adjudicate at next week's appointment.

As I continue to stare at the walls, Helena enters the bedroom and catches me absent-mindedly scratching my private parts.

'Are you having a little wanker?'

'What?' It takes a few seconds for my degenerating brain to catch up with her use of the English vernacular.

'Wank, Helena, the word is wank, and no, I'm not.' Then I gesticulate at her belly, 'And I'm sure neither of us should be using it when he can probably hear everything we're saying.'

Helena nods slowly before her gaze comes to rest on a single, slim folder sitting on my desk.

'How's it coming along?' she asks.

Since my last skirmish with the Ferrat, I've achieved nothing other than the opening paragraph of a letter to a former client but, after a few lines of zeal, it trailed off dramatically and tended to suggest that I was perhaps not as enthusiastic as I first thought.

My natural inclination is to banish all thoughts of work to the darker recesses of my mind, but as I sit here in Junior's bedroom, I'm finding this hard to accomplish. My guts, only recently vacated by my friends from the North Sea, now harbour a growing sense of unease about the future. I haven't worked for a year, and have barely glanced at any job ads in all that time. My CV still lies untranslated on my desk. What's wrong with me? Before I know it, my child will be asking me whether the dole cheque has arrived. They might even be his first words.

The Ferrat is expecting me to spend the week surfing the web, looking for career paths that might open up a new and exciting future, but I feel about as motivated as a geriatric goldfish in an ornamental pond. Besides, there's someone I've been neglecting lately. I weigh up the options: on the one hand, a weekend poring over the computer screen, reading about once-in-a-lifetime sales opportunities, self-starters, team players and optimal energy levels; on the other, dinner with Helena followed by a good movie.

Helena looks a bit surprised when I ask, but agrees readily enough. The only problem is that she's currently luxuriating in front of a reality show on the TV. Unusually, this particular programme doesn't concern the comings and goings of a bunch of sexually obsessed twenty-year-olds, pawing one another for the benefit of the camera crew and a few million sexually obsessed viewers. No, this is far worse: it's about a woman with a burning desire to give birth in front of a camera crew and a few million viewers, all of whom share the inexplicable desire to watch as she does so. What a crazy idea! I can't believe anyone would want to submit themselves to such a spectacle. Yet Helena, for one, is riveted.

Perhaps it's only me that doesn't want to watch as the camera closes in? I'm nervous enough about the birth without this unexpected preview, which probably explains why I'm pacing the room with half an eye on the screen. Gingerly, I sit down on the edge of the bed. I warn Helena that we'll be late for the trailers and ice cream ads, although it's becoming increasingly clear that we won't be leaving until the expectant exhibitionist has shown the world what it is that wants to emerge from between her legs.

The woman and her husband are ushered into the delivery room. The first thing I notice is that she's wearing a monumental amount of make-up for such a private function. Not half as much as her mother, however, who is hanging about in the hospital corridors with the rest of the family. As the waiting continues, they are working themselves up into a frenzy and delivering the little speeches and sound bites they've doubtless been rehearsing since one of their number got the job of delivering to the nation on prime-time TV.

Back in the delivery room, Mummy's contractions have started and she's pondering the benefits of an epidural while ensuring that her best side is facing the camera. I can't believe that I'm watching this and protest briefly to Helena about the lengths to which some people will go to get high on the drug of celebrity. Her response is perfunctory and filled with the implicit threat of violence to my person and, after a short but perfectly-timed word from an appropriate sponsor, delivery commences and Mummy begins to succumb to the pain. I notice immediately how useless her husband is. He looks like a rag doll, discarded at the side of the bed with nothing better to offer than an occasional squeeze of the hand, a couple of words murmured in the star's ear or a worrying frown at the camera.

Cut to the chickens outside the delivery room. They're utterly hysterical and pecking chunks out of one another, but at least their make-up isn't running.

By the time the baby forces its head out and starts leering into the camera lens, I'm just about ready to pass out. I glance at Helena. Her eyes are watering up nicely... Oh God! Here it comes. Squeeze, for Christ's sake. Get it over with. The thought of all that pain is bringing me to the very edge of consciousness. Get that thing out of there! What an unholy mess. Hold on, I think I'm going to be sick.

But before I can puke, the baby is propelled into the arms of the medical crew with the most appalling, primeval howl and the pent-up force of a vintage champagne cork. I jump to my feet and stare at the screen in outright disbelief. There it is. Oh my God! Why is it that opaque white colour? And why is it shivering like an enormous jelly that's been withdrawn too quickly from a darkened refrigerator? Suddenly it's in Mummy's arms, still connected by the umbilical cord, and I can't cope with this at all. I try to leave the room but my legs are no longer functioning. They tumble from beneath me like a house of cards caught in a sudden breeze, which forces me to watch as the slimy miracle nestles in its mother's clavicle and begins to cry. Helena's crying too, of course – blubbing uncontrollably into her pillow. The other Mummy looks deliriously happy, but there's no sign at all of her husband. I expect he's doing just what I'll be doing when the time comes – lying unconscious beneath the hospital bed.

I take a deep breath (my first for a good ten minutes) and the oxygen aerates a few of the thousand questions that are rattling around in my head:

1. Why?
2. Why would anyone want to put themselves through this?
3. Do I have to put myself through this?
4. Why did the baby come out so fast?
5. Do they always do that, or did they accelerate the film because the advertisers were getting impatient?
6. Are all babies that ugly?
7. How do they cut the umbilical cord?
8. What happens to the cord once it's been cut?
9. Does it get thrown in the bin?
10. Do I really have to be present at the birth?
11. Why's that then?

12. Will there be some sort of medication buffet for those who feel the need?
13. Why the fuck not?
14. Why am I such a squeamish and cowardly individual?
15. Why?
16. Why me?
17. Is it really too late to call the whole thing off?
18. Surely Helena is about to come to her senses and admit this whole thing is a monumental mistake?

But the words that continue to foam in my mouth refuse to be expelled and it's Helena who finally fills the silence: 'Are you ready then?' she asks, calmly pulling on her shoes. 'Ready?' No, I'm not ready. In fact, I don't think I'll ever approach anything close to readiness. Not now, certainly not in four months' time, not ever! Again I try to speak. No luck. My tongue is as dry as a Saharan windsock. Instead, I just stare at Helena with my lips forming a perfect 'O', as if separated by a giant, invisible gobstopper. I try sign language, but my arms flap uselessly by my sides like the wings of some flightless, primordial bird.

'Come on. I thought you wanted to go to the cinema?'

I think I'm nodding now. Either that or I must be shaking my head. Perhaps I'm doing both. All I can be sure of is that I'm frozen in front of the television screen and pointing. But Helena takes my hand, sweeps her hair behind her ears and guides me gently towards the front door.

Over pizza we speculate, for the last time, on the sex of our child. Just about everyone thinks it's a girl, including Helena. Don't ask me why, but I still think it's a boy and so does the six-time father from the Ivory Coast who delivers our pizza in his spare time. He takes one look at the shape of Helena's belly and tells us we can forget about all those girls names because we're about to have a son.

Sunday democracy, September 21st

To take her mind off tomorrow's scan, Helena has a plan – our first excursion as a family, even if Junior is still a little young to appreciate it. Today is *la journée du patrimoine* which means that, right across France, the doors of the great, the good and the occasionally corrupt are thrown wide open to all citizens of the Republic and anyone else sufficiently motivated to get out of bed and take a good look at the inner sanctums of French democracy, most of which would normally slam a heavy oak door in the face of old Joe Publique. And it's Helena's intention to visit them all. 'But we'll never get to see all of that lot' I protest, in a thinly veiled attempt to limit our excursion to a single monument (which would be bad enough), and no, it has nothing to do with the fact that Arsenal are playing United on my laptop later this afternoon.

But Helena smiles, pats the burgeoning belly and whispers that the citizen within is our passport to the front of every queue in Paris. The time has come, she declares, for this baby to begin its education and today he qualifies us all as visitors of limited mobility. I had planned on limiting my own mobility to a shuttle service between the computer and the kitchen kettle, but it's probably not a good idea if this baby emerges from the womb already more cultured than one of its parents.

'What time will we be back?' I ask, as innocently as I can.

'Around six, I guess. Why?'

'Oh, no particular reason.' But I've already done the mental arithmetic: Kick-off is 4.00 p.m. UK time. If all goes well, we'll be back in time for the whole of the second half. God alone knows why Helena thinks it's worth taking someone like me to the great bastions of French civilisation.

First stop is the *Palais de l'Elysée*, official residence of the French President since 1848. I find the presidential palace to be almost as unprepossessing as its present inhabitant. Each of its stately rooms is more ostentatious than the one before and the entire gaff is stuffed to the rafters with ornate chandeliers, fading tapestries and musty, jug-eared chairs upon which the world's politicians presumably get to plonk their plentiful posteriors. Not us plebs, though. We're herded around at a safe distance from all that gold leaf and prevented from smearing the furniture with our greasy fingerprints by a series of electrified guide ropes and guards armed with what look like cattle prods. Furthermore, I notice that the presidential carpet has been rolled up on itself just in case one of us is tempted to leave any unsightly soilings upon the very shag-pile into which the French President presumably averts his gaze when he's being harangued by the latest piece of mad, prime ministerial beef.

Much to my disappointment, we do not get to visit the presidential living quarters – I quite fancied a short stroll through the walk-in wardrobes or a quick leaf through the last piece of fiction the President's wife picked up at the airport. Sadly the doors of the presidential suite remain firmly shut and I'm unable to report whether the President is the kind of guy who leaves his underpants on the bedroom floor and hides a stack of porn under the marital bed.

Shortly before we are hustled back outside, however, I'm gazing out of the window over an expansive lawn in order to protect my eyes from some particularly gaudy fourteenth-century soft furnishings and I swear I catch sight of the old bugger himself, lurking about in the lush gardens and smoking a crafty cigarette, although it may just have been a particularly energetic garden gnome.

A Monday unlike any other, September 22nd

Despite my tendency to complain about all things French, even I have to admit that it's not only the trains that are more efficient than they are in Britain. So are the hospitals and just about every other state-funded service in this country, which is how Helena manages to upset the doctor at the maternity unit by answering a call of nature at precisely the moment we're all set to commence. The doctor opens the door of the basement chamber – which judging by her pallid skin, she inhabits on a permanent basis – and sees just the one distinctly unimpregnated male lounging in the corridor. '*Et Madame?*' she enquires, just a little icily. I don't bother to answer and settle for a series of gestures which, without overloading the doctor with detail, I hope will convey the idea that the lady in question is taking a leak. This fails to bring a smile to her face and the door is slammed perfunctorily in my face.

As she teeters idly down the corridor a full five minutes late for our allotted appointment, I notice that Helena has chosen today to sport a pair of uncomfortably high heels. I shove her through the doorframe but she remains unflustered and quite oblivious to the doctor looking at her watch and tutting repeatedly. Clearly she's unaware that Helena has never worn a watch. She'll give you the time of day alright, but be prepared for a margin of error of a couple of weeks either way. Whether or not Miss Punctuality is aware of the infuriating unimportance of timekeeping to Helena, she applies the blue jelly with all the gusto of an executioner examining the vertebrae in the neck of a particularly obnoxious princess.

Inhaling deeply, I sense that Helena is not at all nervous about the examination. Unlike me, she doesn't fear finding any abnormalities. She simply chooses to believe that the baby is strong and healthy, as if not to do so would be a sign of weakness on her part. If I'm unable to share her unbending faith, I also keep to myself any lingering fears that something may be wrong with our child. But this is the only thing that interests me once the examination begins, whereas Helena is here purely for confirmation that we'll shortly be sharing breakfast with a perfectly hale and hearty daughter.

'Sit down, please,' says the doctor to me, gesturing at a hard hospital chair.

'No thanks,' I reply. I'm far too nervous to sit and fully intend to continue hopping from one foot to the other.

All eyes are on the screen as Junior comes back into view. I'm sure it's him because I recognise those slightly alien features. I can clearly make out a head, two eyes, eyelids, nose and a small pout. So far, so good.

'What about the sex?' For a few nanoseconds, the abruptness of Helena's question reverberates around the airless cell, but the retort from the smarting doctor is not long in coming and she clearly enjoys her moment of revenge.

'Madame, the purpose of this examination is to ensure everything is in order with your baby. I'm not unduly concerned by the gender.'

You might not be matey, but then, this is the first time you've met Helena isn't it? But if I'm quietly relieved to hear of the good doctor's priorities, the mother-to-be ignores the reproach. I'm quite sure this particular fight is not over just yet. Every few seconds the screen freezes as the doctor takes another measurement and I hold my breath. Junior is being appraised from more angles than Naomi Campbell on a Milanese catwalk and I'm more desperate by the minute to know whether everything is OK, but the questions I spit at Miss Permafrost elicit nothing more than a series of grunts. Before I get an answer, she'll need to collect and process all the data. In the interim, my only hope is that she won't detect anything that causes her to arch an eyebrow or produce any unexpected clicking noises at the back of her throat.

As she continues to track the shadowy shape of my baby, I can hardly bear the suspense.

'Fingers!' she declares suddenly.

My eyes dart straight to the screen and, under my breath, I start to count as fast as I can, 'one, two, three, four... ' Then, out loud, 'What about the other hand?' But I'm forced to wait again, as Junior has chosen this moment to start sucking one of his thumbs. This is a surprise. I'd never imagined anything quite as human as thumb sucking going on inside the womb.

'A thumb!' That makes five... Six, seven, eight, nine and, yes, ten! What a relief.

I turn to Helena. She's beaming so widely that her smile is about to break open the whole room and let the sun come streaming in to the bowels of the hospital. How can she be so serene at a moment like this?

'Ah, there we are,' says the glacial one as she frames a new image upon the screen.

'There we are what?' I want to scream. Has she found something that belongs to another species altogether? If this continues much longer, Daddy is not going to be around when Junior graduates from silent, black and white movies to make his full *Technicolor* debut.

Helena pipes up, hopeful and persistent in equal measure: 'You mean the sex?'

'Yes.'

'And?'

'It's a boy.'

'A boy!' Helena looks at me quickly, but I'm too preoccupied by my search for the double helix to respond. I can only sense the surprise in her eyes as she turns back to the doctor.

'A boy? Are you sure?'

The doctor, who, let's face it, has probably played this scene on more than a few occasions, looks at Helena with only the slightest trace of malice. She points to a single slim white protuberance on the screen. 'Boy,' she repeats, much more firmly than before.

Helena looks at me again. My counting has stopped at one. I'm in a state of shock. Not because Junior has revealed himself to be a boy, but because he appears to be a rather beautiful and, more importantly, whole example of Homo sapiens. I'll get my head round the fact that I'm going to have a son in a minute or so, but right now I'm struggling with the evidence that I'm about to become the father of whoever it is lying in that bath of invisible fluid. I suppose most people would have got their heads around the enormity of this fact when Helena first got pregnant. But I didn't, not when we got the results of the blood test, not when Helena began to gain weight, nor even when she had the first scan. No! On each occasion, I felt as if I were sneaking a look at a story that belonged to another time, another place and another person altogether.

Not today, though, not as I watch his little revolutions on the screen, not when I can see so clearly his face and the mouth into which he has doggedly reinserted a tiny thumb. There is nothing at all in there that could possibly belong to anyone else. This is our baby – a baby boy, no less – and one day, soon, he's going to call me '*Papa*'.

'He's very active this morning,' says the doctor, still struggling to measure everything that needs to be measured.

'Of course he is,' I say proudly and for no particular reason.

Helena just keeps on beaming. She's looking at me again, mouthing the word 'boy' over and over again.

'What about his feet?' I ask, desperate to finish my count.

'There,' says the doctor, 'and there are his toes.'

A few moments later, the screen is snapped off and the machine starts to feed out a stuttering stream of results. 'It's a boy!' says Helena, partly because she doesn't know what else to say, but mainly because those are the only words in her head right now.

'Is everything, I mean, is it all... ' I can't get the rest of my question out, but the doctor already knows what's bothering me.

'I'll tell you in just a minute,' she says, settling at a metal desk illuminated by a single spotlight.

While she works, Helena and I stare at each other like a couple of baboons. 'It's a boy,' she says.

'I know.'

Probably because she's beginning to fear for our sanity, the doctor finishes her task quickly and tears off a single sheet of computer printout. 'All within the norms,' she declares quickly, 'except for a femur of above average length. He's going to have very long legs.'

For some reason, I burst out laughing and I'm still cackling hysterically as we emerge onto the street outside the hospital, which is bathed in brilliant Monday morning sunshine. My legs are too weak to walk all the way to the car parked a distant fifty metres up the street, so we collapse into a couple of chairs at a pavement café on the corner. Helena whips out a mobile and begins randomly dialling a few numbers. She calls her mother, she calls her father and then I believe she calls my mother with whom I may even have had some kind of conversation although I can't be too sure about that. The only thing I do know is that I'm going to have a son.

We sit and stare at our cappuccinos for a full five minutes, saying very little. A few people pass by and give us strange looks as we continue to grin and giggle. One sour-faced old biddy mutters something about 'bloody drug addicts', but I couldn't care less.

Back home, there's a lot to do: Daddy is almost ready to catch that train south to see Vincent, but first he has to prepare for a meeting with the Ferrat and make it look like he's given some serious thought to his employment situation. But as I open the laptop, I'm unable to resist the temptation and send an email to everyone I've ever known:

Le bébé called a short press conference this morning in order to reveal his half-yearly results and announce publicly that he has now struck the perfect deal between X and Y chromosomes. He has also asked me to pass on the news that he's healthy and perfectly proportioned, with a pair of exceptionally long and athletic legs.

I press send, before reluctantly pulling a lurid, pink file from the shelf. Now, what was it that I was supposed to have done for tomorrow? I glance down the list that I made more than one week ago:

1. Translate CV into French. *Not done.*
2. Rewrite list of competencies. *Not yet, no.*
3. Identify all marketing service companies in France *Certainly not.*
4. Draft letter of application to all of the above. *Are you kidding?*

I figure there's no way on earth I'm going to get that little lot done by tomorrow morning, so I might just as well do none of it and get a bollocking for good reason. I put the file away and take out a slightly shorter list which I prepared over the weekend. This one tells me what I need to pack for my week-long trip south. Vincent will be holed up near the Spanish border for a few days to escape the south London club scene and I'll hang with him before catching the train on to Barcelona where I intend to look up a few old friends in a city which was once my home. To placate Helena lest she think I'm abandoning our son before he's even born, I've promised to add a third leg to the trip, a flying visit to Toulouse, which I'll be checking out in terms of its suitability as a place to raise a family.

Helena perceives this diversion as a major triumph. So far, I've resisted all her efforts to move us out of Paris, but the other day she announced that she has decided to leave with or without me, as she can no longer bear the pollution, the noise or the aggression in the capital.

'But where would we go?' I protested through my toothpaste.

'Anywhere!'

'London?'

'If you want.'

'But I don't want. Where else?'

'Lille.'

'Lille! I'm not going there. It's in bloody Belgium!'

'OK, Toulouse.'

'Why Toulouse?'

'Because it's a nice town between the mountains and the sea and you should be able to find a job down there.'

Of course, she knew exactly what she was doing when she inserted that little geography lesson. Helena knows that I love the Mediterranean and have always wanted to live close to the Pyrenees.

'It's not far from Barcelona either, is it?'

Rhetorical question. Trap. Be careful! 'Not that far, I suppose,' I say, as cautiously as a cat burglar on some dodgy roof tiles.

'Why don't you go and have a look then?'

And before I could think of an excuse, Helena picked up a pile of schoolbooks and disappeared out of the front door.

So, this is what it's all come down to. If I don't choose the place, Helena will do it for me and the ninth *arrondissement* of Paris is automatically disqualified from consideration. I pull out the atlas: Toulouse... There it is! Smack bang in the middle of nowhere or, to put it another way, south-western France. Then I remember that Vincent comes from that area of France. I'll check it with him. I'm sure he can be relied upon to portray the place as a cross between Baghdad and West Dudley in the depths of midwinter.

Railroads, guns and a showdown, September 23rd

My train leaves the Gare de Lyon at midday, but first I have to contend with another set of awkward questions posed by the Ferrat. I pick up the pink folder and stride purposefully out onto the street although my pace slackens as soon as I catch sight of her office. She's already waiting for me and she looks a great deal more purposeful than my stride. I'm instructed to sit in the leatherette as she prolongs the agony by sending a collection of faxes.

'*Ca va?*'

'*Oui, merci.*'

'*Alors?*'

'Well, I haven't done anything, if that's what you mean.'

'You haven't done what exactly?'

'Any of the things you asked me to do.'

'None of them?'

The Ferrat gives me the sort of look she might normally reserve for a slug ill mannered enough to take up residence in her office rug. I mumble a few excuses (very busy, a bit ill, visit to the hospital) and my head sinks so far beneath her reproachful stare that I may as well join my invertebrate cousins in the carpet.

Then she tells me she's had an idea – I should find myself a job in communications. After all, she reasons, I speak a couple of languages, I know a bit about marketing and I never stop talking. Before I can protest, the Ferrat whisks me through 150 websites on her state-funded computer and suggests a few ways I might go about selling my soul and one or two other body parts to a hotchpotch of potential clients and, sure enough, I'm soon nodding and agreeing to all sorts of stuff I'm convinced I'll live to regret – if I ever manage to decipher the spidery notes I've been scrawling in a desperate attempt to avoid eye contact.

'Are you OK with all that, then?' she asks rhetorically. I continue to nod but only because I no longer know how to stop. Then the she reloads her fax machine, so I know it must be time to leave and, on my way through the door, she describes in graphic detail what she will do to me if I fail to make any progress by the next time we meet.

I settle into my seat on the *TGV* which will transport me, in no time at all, south to Montpellier and far from the threat of female violence. Briefly I review my notes. Excellent! They're utterly incomprehensible, which means I can forget all about the Ferrat and spend the next few days lounging around in the southern sunshine.

This morning Helena questioned my motives for making the trip, but I brushed off her questions and told her I know exactly what I'm doing. I'm sure that the ultrasound image of my son in my wallet will keep me strong through the potential pitfalls ahead and, anyway, the train is already thundering down the Rhône valley and it's too late to turn back now.

The journey passes without incident and dusk is falling fast as my train pulls into the station at Argelès on the Mediterranean coast. There's no sign of Vincent; in fact the place looks completely deserted and, for a second, I wonder if perhaps I've stumbled onto the set of a spaghetti western. On the approach road to the station is a grimy looking café with a single, naked bulb visible through an unwashed window pane. I take this to mean that the café is still open and that I've found the old gunslinger Vincent.

Sure enough, he's at a table inside, eating a slimy omelette, drinking a beer and smoking a *Marlboro* red. With his other hand, he's stroking an enormous, slavering St Bernard, which is inching its jaws closer and closer to the omelette. Behind the bar, the café owner watches the scene with apparent approval.

'Hello Vincent.'

Vincent gets up to greet me and offers me the hand previously reserved for the dog.

'*Bonsoir, mon ami anglais, ça va?*'

'I'm doing OK,' I say, nervously eyeing the beer, 'it's been a long trip.'

'Sit down. Have a drink,' says Vincent, as the dog rolls a bloodshot eye up towards the potential competition for the eggs.

'*Une bière?*' asks the owner.

'*Non, monsieur, un* Coca *s'il vous plait,*' I reply quickly, before attempting to lower both voice and testicles to a lower level of anxiety.

'C'est tout?'

'Oui, merci.'

For some reason, ordering the *Coke* feels like the most difficult thing I've had to do for quite some time. Maybe it's because the bar owner looks so bitterly disappointed. Before

I can change my mind, I turn back to Vincent and the St Bernard.

'You doing OK?'

'I'm good. Just taking it easy, you know, nothing wild.'

Nothing wild! How many times have I heard this particular phrase trip from his lips? It habitually precedes a night of suicidal partying and, in my case, a morning of the coldest remorse. 'Nothing wild, eh?'

'No, it's quiet here at this time of year, very quiet.'

'Good, I'm glad to hear it.'

'Yeah, most of the tourists have already gone.'

'Good.' I take a large gulp of my *Coke* and the sugar steadies my nerves a little.

'Finish your drink' says Vincent, 'we've missed the last bus, but we may still be able to find a cab.'

As it turns out, we don't find so much as a mule and end up walking the five kilometres back to the apartment, although I suspect Vincent wasn't planning on finding a taxi in the first place because he prefers to walk home along the beach while quietly smoking a joint. He doesn't bother offering the smouldering depressant to me. He knows I lost interest in that particular weed long before I put down the drink. So far so good.

The last part of our evening stroll takes us right through what remains of the bar scene on the seafront in Argelès and Vincent is right about the place being deserted. Only the pizza and kebab joints remain open and, perversely, my mood begins to lighten.

Back at the apartment, Vincent offers me the choice between the sofa and the lumpy single bed next to his. Having ascertained that he neither snores nor walks in his sleep, I go for the bed. I'm dog-tired yet unable to sleep and we fall into a conversation about the nocturnal activities of some mutual friends back in London, where nothing much appears to have changed.

'And what about you?' I ask bluntly, once his report

is complete.

'Me? Oh, I'm much calmer and taking things a lot more seriously these days.'

'Oh yeah?'

'Yep. Keeping fit, looking for a new job and going out much less than I was.'

I watch as Vincent takes off his shirt and gets into bed. He looks thinner than I remember and his movements are measured and ponderous. 'What about the parties?'

'Once a month – maybe even less than that.'

Vincent and I both know this is a gross underestimation but he doesn't want to go into too much detail with someone who has abandoned the scene. 'Good,' I say, trying to drop the subject. 'I'm glad.'

'Yes. I've told you before, it's a question of evolution. You're doing the wrong thing by trying to give up everything overnight.'

It's true that we've had this conversation before and it's also true that we disagree. 'You may be right,' I say, 'I just prefer it this way.'

'Too radical,' he says, picking up a book from his bedside table.

'Possibly. What are you reading?'

He flashes a paperback copy of *The long March to Freedom* by Nelson Mandela.

'Any good?'

'Dunno. I'm only on page 14.'

Two minutes later, the light is off and I'm out cold.

The other side of the borderline, September 26th

Vincent and I have idled away the last three days down at the beach. In the evenings, we sit at the empty beachfront cafes where I've watched him gulping beer from pint glasses and I've said little as his moods fluctuate according to when he smoked his last spliff. We do not discuss the subject of parties or intoxication again until I'm getting ready to leave:

'But it's Friday.'

'So?'

'What are you going to do in Barcelona on a Friday night?'

'What do you think?' I snort. 'I'm going to go out and have a good time'

'Aren't you worried?'

It's true that most of our wildest parties got started on a Friday night, even if they sometimes ended only when it was time to go back to work early on Monday morning. But Vincent's concern for my welfare has me on the back foot and I try to end the conversation before it gets started: 'If I can get through three nights watching you drinking and smoking, I'm sure I'll be alright in Barcelona.'

Vincent just smiles. 'Who are you going to see down there?'

'Old friends' I say, finishing my tomato juice a little more quickly than I'd intended. 'I don't know yet.'

'Well, be careful,' he says, because Vincent is fundamentally a kind person, whatever his weakness.

'Don't worry,' I say dismissively, 'I'll be fine.' And, despite the unease in my belly, I mean it too.

Before we part company, Vincent gives me a map of central Toulouse with a commentary on the town's highlights which he's annotated himself. I'd almost forgotten I was intending to go there, and stuff it hurriedly into my pocket. Then we say goodbye and wish each other luck.

A little more than two hours later, I'm stuck in a waiting room at the station at Cerbère. This town is nothing more than a giant dental cavity at the eastern end of the Pyrenees. Barely a couple of kilometres distant, on the Spanish side of the border, lies the town of Port Bou. I've been dumped here by a French train that's not on speaking terms with its brothers and sisters in Iberia. It's stinking hot, the café is closed and

I have four hours to wait for the next train.

The only thing for it is to try and make friends with a hard wooden bench on the south-bound platform. I'm in limbo-land, forced to reflect on my new life in Paris and the old one I've been chewing over with Vincent. There's bugger all to do in this clanking, cavernous ghost town except watch as the rusting goods trains are shunted to and fro across the border. There's no coffee, no newspaper and no one to talk to. I feel restless and irritable and now I've run out of cigarettes.

As lunchtime approaches, the café finally opens. I order something to drink and a sullen Frenchman tries to charge me an entire morning's takings for a single cup of insipid coffee. We snarl at each other like a couple of dusty, over-heating dogs.

By the time the antiquated Spanish train finally pulls into the station, I'm ready to kill. My mood is not improved by the Catalan lovers who join the train at Port Bou and spend the next hour enthusiastically finishing one another's sentences. I glance out of the window to see the towering *Damm* beer brewery, which warns me that we're reaching the outskirts of Barcelona. I'm feeling so edgy that I take the irrational decision not to call Helena at our appointed time and, to my surprise, I reach into my pocket for a cigarette only to find a packet of full-strength *Camel* filters. Where the hell did they come from? I haven't smoked that brand in years...

An hour or so later, I'm sitting in the *Café Zurich* at the head of the *las ramblas* in Barcelona. For years, the *Zurich* has served as the central meeting place for renegades and defectors from the wastelands of northern Europe – people drinking plenty of beer, people talking loudly of plans which go no further than the early hours of Saturday morning.People just like me.

With a growing sense of unease, I order a glass of slightly salty mineral water and perhaps this is what lulls me into a false sense of security, because my next move proves to be a big mistake. My intention had been to call an old friend who lives up amongst the peaceful pines of the Collserola forest on the western edge of the bowl which surrounds the city. But I don't. Instead I dial the number of Esteban, an old drinking buddy who lives right here in the twisted intestines of the city. He tells me to stay right where I am, because he'll be along in a minute.

The rest of the night passes in something of a haze. I remember Esteban arriving at the *Café Zurich* alright. I remember accepting the beer he proffered when we got back to his place, as well as several more taken in the bars of the old Gothic quarter. What I don't remember is what happened to my ability to say no. I lost Esteban a little later and spent the rest of the night wandering *las ramblas*, looking for ghosts and, once again, I failed to call Helena.

A lone crab, September 28th

I know my nerves will be shot once the realisation of what I've lost truly hits me but, in the meantime, I'm waiting for the hangover to kick in by swallowing some breakfast and reading the sports pages of the newspaper in the bar of an old friend. José is right where I left him all those years ago – behind the bar, stiffening coffees with anise or sweet Spanish brandy. He smiles and asks how I am. I lie and tell him I'm fine, adding that I now live in Paris and am about to become a father. As the words escape my lips, they sound as if I were describing someone else entirely. José just looks at me then carries on rinsing glasses and smiling.

I've promised Esteban that I'll come to see his band play at a blues club this evening. But, before they get started, he invites me to have a beer with him at the *Café Zurich*. I accept. Then I leave for another bar where I strike up a conversation with another lost soul from the north trying to escape his shadow. We have a couple of drinks and return to the club where Esteban has already started singing those mournful old blues numbers. I just sit there, bottle of beer in hand. The music doesn't touch me. The other people in the club don't touch me. I don't feel a thing, not even the alcohol. I don't want to be here anymore. I want to leave this place far behind. I've played with the past and it has burned me. I thought I could handle it, or maybe I didn't think about it at all, but it hardly matters now – I know that I can't. Meanwhile Esteban is singing a song about a woman lost, found, and then lost once more, but I can't quite follow the story of how it all happened. When the music stops, Esteban disappears. Someone suggests another beer in another bar and of course I agree.

We drink another beer and two shots of tequila. We talk for a while and for some reason I hear myself telling a stranger about my problems with alcohol. I don't know why, but it feels like I'm saying it for the first time. My speech is cracked with self pity and I no longer recall whether he said anything in return. Eventually he leaves to catch the last bus home and I'm alone again, in the middle of the night.

A long way from home, September 29th

Late in the morning I wake up at Esteban's place and the only thought on my mind is to leave. I want to skip Toulouse altogether and go straight back to Paris, although something inside tells me this isn't a good idea. I pack my things but there's no sign of Esteban. I leave with little more than a cursory goodbye to his girlfriend who's lying on her bed reading a cheap detective novel. Outside it's pissing with rain and I couldn't care less. I emerge from the narrow streets of the Gothic quarter and don't look back until I reach the *Café Zurich*. There I turn quickly, one last time. Behind me, I can see the two rows of flower stalls which line the damp and filthy *ramblas*, but even these vivid outcrops of colour are smudged by the steady grey rain which streams down my face and into my eyes.

When I reach the station at the Passeig de Gràcia, I eat what breakfast I can manage and buy an English newspaper in an attempt to stifle the screaming inside my skull. Once on the train, I fall asleep and don't awaken until I'm back in Cerbère some two and a half hours later. There's no connecting train for another two hours, the café is firmly bolted and the place is just as deserted as it was three days earlier. Right now I'm finding it hard to avoid the thought that this wretched hole in the mountains is some kind of antechamber between life and death. Why didn't I see it coming? On the way down, I sat here for four hours and chose to ignore all the evidence that I was headed for trouble. Now I've got to go back to Paris, where I'll be faced with a whole lot more.

If there's one thing that I'm not prepared to do, it's to hang around in this hellhole for another two hours watching the devilish goods trains shunting their rusting foul loads in and out of the sidings. It takes me almost twenty minutes to escape from the station and into the town of Cerbère itself, which is cut into the rock face at precisely the point where the Pyrenees spill down and dive headlong into the sea. But at least I manage to find a payphone and call Helena for the first time in three days. She's sick with the flu and her voice is so faint that I wonder briefly whether one of us has passed over to the other side. I ask if she'd like me to come straight home, but she says no, she has plenty of food in the house and just needs a little time to sleep it off. Helena gives me the number of a friend of hers who recently moved to Toulouse and then tells me that, at some point over my lost weekend, Cécile gave birth to a second son. Something is squirming at the back of my mind at this point, but whatever it is fails to break the surface. Helena doesn't bother me with any questions about Barcelona and I don't tell her that all I really want is to curl up in bed next to her. She doesn't even ask why I didn't call at the time we agreed. I hesitate before saying goodbye and continue to listen for a few seconds after

I hear the click when she puts down the phone.

My mood improves immeasurably once I've bought my ticket out of Cerbère. Of course I'll go to Toulouse! What better way to stop feeling sorry for myself than to start thinking about the future? An hour later, the train begins to grind its way out of the station. If ever I see this place again, it will be too soon.

The train north is empty and it's not until we've left Argelès far behind that I feel myself beginning to operate on a slightly more sophisticated fuel than pure autonomic reflex. I realise I'll soon have to face what has happened, but now's not the time.

Intensive care, September 30th

It has gone midnight when I steal into the apartment. Helena is awake but too weak to talk. She expresses zero interest in the fact that the world's fastest mechanical escalator at Montparnasse wasn't working as I passed though, nor in any of the other diversionary tactics I dreamed up on the train to divert attention from my descent into the abyss. All she wants is a hot drink of honey and lemon. Before we're both enveloped by sleep, Helena feels the little fellow having a good kick. He's been quiet all week apparently, but Helena tells me that he recognises my voice and must be pleased that I'm back. For some reason this strikes me as illogical, unlikely and probably true. It also shames me to the very core.

Paris, October 1st

Helena is off school for a couple more days before a truck pulls up in the middle of a grey morning, bearing the full load of medicines which French doctors are wont to prescribe for the most minor of ailments.

'Did you like Toulouse?' she croaks.

I look at the hope which has taken up residence in her

pale face. 'Yes,' I say, pressing her hand gently with something I hope feels like encouragement.

'What did you like about it?'

'I liked the fact you can walk in the streets and hear people talking and laughing in the apartments above. I liked the fact that when a car passes you in the street, it's the exception not the rule and I liked the pinkish-red bricks.'

Helena smiles weakly before closing her eyes once more. 'Are you going to find a job there?'

'I'm going to try.'

'Good,' she murmurs, before I leave her to fall back to sleep. I say nothing at all about Barcelona. She's suffering enough as it is.

Sitting down at my desk for the first time in ten days, I find the tattered remains of Vincent's map in my pocket. I'd forgotten the list of international companies operating in Toulouse that he'd scrawled in the margins and I start to look them up on the net. Coincidentally, the first one I try happens to be advertising a position in something called 'internal communications'. Before I even realise what I'm doing, I start crafting a letter of motivation.

Letter from inside, October 2nd

It takes me the best part of two days to write the letter, during which time Helena appears sporadically for food and a bit of human contact. But she's not getting any better and ventures out for a third visit to the doctor. She returns with another hundredweight of pills, swallows some pregnancy-friendly antibiotics and goes back into a state of suspended animation for the rest of the week.

In my letter, I've attempted to describe the qualities which make me the perfect candidate for Toulouse. Chief among these is my claim to be able to quickly synthesise large amounts of information and deliver a succinct, harmonious set of recommendations with all the panache of an ageing crooner in Vegas. All of which would be fine, were it not for the fact that my letter runs to twenty-six pages and proves precisely the opposite. I'll have to cut the damned thing down somehow. But how? Surely the HR manager will be interested in my theories linking breastfeeding to self-confidence when presenting it to middle management? I'm beginning to wonder just how much I actually want this job. The last thing I need is to be distracted by the endless internal affairs of some monolithic corporation and the last thing they need is a malfunctioning enzyme causing havoc in their corporate intestines.

I've been sleeping like a dog since I got back from the south and I'd love to claim that it's the letter that has worn me out. But my body tells me the truth, which is that I lost my way badly in Barcelona and I'm simply exhausted. It's my birthday next week – another unwelcome reminder of my mortality – and I've been having weird and disturbing dreams which only add to my general sense of foreboding. These nocturnal ravings started the night I returned and they show scant respect for order, sequence or purpose:

I'm chasing a vaporous Spanish woman into an empty house. Once I've attempted (and failed) to seduce her, she runs out of the back door and I'm alone. At least, I think I'm alone until I come across a snarling black dog. The dog is chained up, but for some reason I want to execute it anyway. Then I change my mind – there's a reason the beast must live, I think, without knowing why. Suddenly I'm on a train leaving Singapore for Bangkok. The train appears to be empty except for the ageless and taciturn Chinese man who sits opposite me, waiting and watching. I begin to feel very uncomfortable and bolt to the other end of the train where I spot an old drinking buddy who's also been trying to stay sober, only I happen to know that he's been even less successful at it than I have lately. I attempt to avoid his eye, but he's seen me already and starts chasing back through the carriages in my wake.

Whether it's all part of the same dream I can no longer be sure, but I arrive at the customs hall of an English port. My luggage is all over the shop and I'm acting very strangely. I realise that I'm very drunk and, to my horror, I find a tiny crumbling piece of cannabis in one of my pockets. I try to pull myself together and hide the dope as I approach the customs officer. Nervously, I hand him my passport and, without even looking at me, he peels the photograph from my document and sticks another, unrecognisable face in its place.

Without stopping to blink, I find myself having dinner at an expensive West End restaurant with Helena and Sir Alex Ferguson. I'm trying to ask intelligent questions about the time he spent managing Aberdeen Football Club, although it seems that Sir Alex is far more interested in seducing Helena than he is in listening to my theories about the offside trap. I come back from having a piss to find the pair of them deep in a discussion which is carnal rather than tactical. I'm furious and slap Helena's face, which swells immediately. Sir Alex isn't that bothered and calmly saunters off, presumably to start managing Manchester United. I'm left screaming at Helena and demand a divorce. Not bad, coming from someone who abandoned her within spitting distance of the altar.

The nightmarish sequence comes to a close when I get a job painting the exterior of an unknown house with some old friends, only they're more interested in playing football than they are in redecorating. Suddenly my friends are nowhere to be seen and I'm alone once more. The house, it seems, has become my responsibility and it's crumbling, peeling and rotting.

Friday night confession, October 3rd

I don't know whether the dream changes anything and I still don't know how to broach the subject, but I'll have to talk to Helena about what I did down in Barcelona. In two weeks' time, we're leaving for England to visit family and friends and, lurking in an alcove at the back of my mind, is the dark thought that, for one night, I'd like to go back to the old haunts in Brixton with Vincent.

After dinner, Helena and I fall into discussion about our arrangements for the trip. We'll be staying with Nathalie and her untamable daughters for the weekend and the idea that I can burrow my way into south London on the Friday night and leave Helena with her cousin in Turnpike Lane won't leave me alone, so I casually mention that I'd like to see Vincent.

'Do you think that's a good idea?' asks Helena, innocuously enough.

'I'll be fine,' I say, in much the same way as a man in fear for his mortal soul whistles his way through a bad neighbourhood in the dark. But the moment the words leave my mouth I know them to be untrue. I may have forgotten what happened last time I was in London, but Helena certainly hasn't.

'If you get drunk over there, I'm coming straight home to Paris.' Not that Helena intends this as blackmail, you understand; she merely has little desire to see me comatose after a night out in exotic south London. I know she's right but I'll be damned if I'm going to admit it. Instead, I take my fury into the kitchen and use it to whip up a truly lump-free béchamel sauce.

Friday evening begins and I feel that familiar longing in my belly, but it's still early and I'm about to serve up cauliflower cheese and a confession:

'Helena. I drank in Barcelona.'

She looks at me impassively. 'When?'

'It started on the Friday night.'

'I thought so.' Her gaze remains level. 'You didn't call.'

'No.'

'Who were you with?'

'Esteban at first. Later I was alone.'

'Alone?' She repeats my words, as if trying to fit a couple of pieces into the wrong jigsaw puzzle. It's not easy for her to understand the idea of drinking without company. 'Until what time?'

'I don't know. Maybe six in the morning.'

'Well, you must have met or talked to some other people?'

'Not really. I went to a club and danced a little, but mainly I was, um, just watching... '

As my voice trails off, I feel Helena's eyes trying to penetrate beneath my skin. But they don't, or maybe they can't. The truth is, this is exactly how I did a lot of my drinking – drowning in beer and staring at everyone else as they had a good time.

'Did you get drunk?'

'Yes.'

'I see. How did it make you feel?'

'Ashamed. I wanted to come straight back to Paris. But I didn't want you to see me hung over.'

'And how about now?'

'I'm still ashamed. I could try to pretend it never happened but I don't want to do that. I have to tell you what I did.'

Helena says nothing for a while. For some reason there seems to be less light in our apartment than usual.

'There's something else.'

Helena looks alarmed. I want to tell her it'll be OK, that I'm sure the worst is over, but I'm still not convinced it would be true.

'What is it?' Her eyes are retreating from me quickly now.

'You're right about London and Vincent. I know it's stupid to go down there on a Friday night. I'm not strong enough to resist a drink in those situations.'

'Don't you want to see him?'

'I'll see him for lunch.'

'Good.' She doesn't say anything else and neither do I.

Old dog, new tricks, October 8th

Helena wants to know if I'm feeling better. I nod, because I've lifted a large part of my burden just by admitting my weakness for alcohol. This morning I know there are things I cannot do and places I should never go.

Instead I spend my time struggling with such irregular French verbs as 'to choose', 'to value' and 'to die' and I find myself almost enjoying the process of learning again. I've even been back to visit Madame Ferrat and, against my better judgement, I found myself telling her about the letter of motivation. She demanded to cast a steely grey eye over the text and we went over it together, word by word. She said it wasn't too bad, if a little long, and even showed me how it might be improved. Then I told her we were thinking of moving to Toulouse. 'Good,' she said, 'it looks like we might be defining a project for you after all.'

A little later, I'm on my way to a French class which is geared towards helping me back into the workforce. It's taking place in a sixties monstrosity up in the wild outer reaches of the 18th *arrondissement*, which is not a privileged corner of Paris. The streets up here are filthy, there's graffiti everywhere, and the American tourists are conspicuous only by their absence. The local *McDonalds* appears to be fuller than it is in other parts of the city. The insistent smell of long-dead fat wafts from its fast-revolving doors along with the bland, borderless sound of R&B.

My class is a mixed bunch; mostly women from the Maghreb and the far reaches of the francophone diaspora, though there are also two students from Argentina, which I wasn't expecting. One is a fifty year-old psychologist, who has married a French woman and looks just a little bemused. The other is a heavily pregnant woman from Buenos Aires. Our teacher is an extremely tolerant woman whose name, Segolene Hauteville, is unpronounceable unless you're prepared to contort your face into a highly complicated piece of origami. She furnishes each of us with a form, with which she plans to oil a conversation about our job prospects here in France:

Please tell us about your education

It is clearly not prudent to admit to my French O level here, so I don't.

What was your job in your country of origin?

Hmmm, should I talk about my favourite job (working in a bar), the most bizarre (a stint working the bins in rural Leicestershire), or stick to the one which has sucked the last twelve years out of my life?

What training have you had in France, and have you ever worked in this country?

Much easier! In precisely eleven months in Paris, I've spent a few hours discussing cinema but I haven't worked a single day – unless you count the scribbles and coffee stains in the margins of my aborted film script!

What would you like to do in France?

I resist the temptation to write 'more of the same' or 'chilling out in cafes, staring at the finely-turned ankles of Parisian women'. Instead, I put down something about finding a job among all the other turnips in the field of marketing.

What difficulties have you encountered when looking for work in France?

Well, for starters, there's my own unwillingness. I could add stubbornness, sloth and a refusal to accept that the French do things differently from the English. And then there's that minor problem I have with intoxicating substances... I decide to tell the class I don't understand the French mentality when it comes to working – all that hierarchy and grovelling to the boss – nor why they're so obsessed with the right degree, diploma and training – surely all that's less important than good old-fashioned practical skills such as the ability to kick the sweet spot on a malfunctioning photocopier?

Demonstrating a modicum of intuition, if not psychic ability, Segolene leaves my credentials until last and asks the others to present themselves. Thus we discover that, in the middle of his sixth decade, the Argentinean psychologist had just finished his training back in Buenos Aires when he fell hopelessly in love and was forced to up sticks for Paris, which would be fine, were it not for the fact that employers in France refuse to recognise a degree awarded in another country and he'll now have to start his education all over again. The pregnant girl (who looks as if she's got more than enough on her plate without worrying about work) tells a similar story. She was ferreting away as something called a 'social communicator' in a hospital back home when one of those pesky French men crossed her path (scented heavily, no doubt, with *Dior*, *Givenchy* and petunia berries) and she, too, fell madly in love... and then heavily pregnant.

'Questions?' demands Mme Hauteville. Yeah, since you ask, I have a few: Like, what is it with the French? Why do they persist with those ridiculous accents whilst practising perfectly good English in private? And why can't they stop talking about making love and simply get on with it? I mean, can they possibly be as sexually active as they'd have us believe? And, while we're at it, is it true that there are even more shrinks in Buenos Aires than there are in New York, and what the hell is a 'social communicator' anyway?

Segolene shoots me an exasperated glance. Until now, she's done a reasonable job of disciplining her unruly charges, especially when you consider that we're in the country of revolution and Eric Cantona. But, as we get more and more excited by our wide-ranging discussion, she tries to keep our unruly verbs and adjectives under control, but we're on a roll and even she's losing her discipline. It's my turn again and I'm trying to explain what I used to do in marketing services. The social communicator wants to know how it felt, doing a job purely for the money:

'Not great,' I admit, 'That's why I quit.'

'So what are you doing now?'

'Not much! I, er, I'm writing a film script.'

'Oh, what about?'

'Um, well, me, I suppose!'

At this, my new friend the psychologist intervenes: 'Aha,' he says, 'crisis is good!'

'What crisis?' I say as belligerently as I possibly can, to cover up for the fact that his question makes me feel as if I'm having one of those dreams in which you turn up for work only to find that you've forgotten to put on your trousers.

'Sure! That's what it is, isn't it?'

I hesitate. The eyes of the United Nations are upon me now.

'Yeah,' I grunt finally and with all the grace of a stuck pig.

'What do you think?' interjects Segolene, in the interests of furthering our knowledge of the subjunctive, as well as world peace, 'Should he continue with his film script or should he return to the corporate world?'

I freeze in the silence that follows. Should it matter to me what these people think? Of course not! Why would it?

Then the psychologist says, 'He should continue to writing. Yes, definitely.'

The others nod in agreement (except Segolene, who's displeased that he's mixed his gerunds with his infinitives). But I'm beaming like a fat kid in a doughnut shop. Of course it matters to me what these people think! Why wouldn't it? I'm leaving to tell Helena all about it right now. In fact, I'm even considering moving to Argentina; they seem like such reasonable people and the therapy is so widely available!

When I get home, Helena opens the door, grins and says 'Happy birthday!'

'What?' I turn around quickly, in case I've been followed home. Nobody. In my confusion, I've quite forgotten the ageing process. Then Helena presses some cards and a package into my hands and asks whether I plan to spend the rest of the evening on the staircase. So I step inside and start opening the cards while Helena asks what I'd like to eat:

'Anything, I'm starving!'

'Greek?'

'Anything except Greek.'

She looks vaguely disappointed. God knows why: we haven't

eaten Greek once since I arrived in France. Pink fish eggs and dancing waiters just aren't my idea of a great night out. I open the parcel. It contains a furry bear and a woollen hat for our son and I think it's the nicest present I could have received.

I'm falling asleep over my grammar book when the doorbell rings. It's Isabelle, a friend of Helena's, and reluctantly I relinquish the warmth of my duvet to make conversation with someone who has turned up uninvited on my birthday. The only good news is that Isabelle speaks excellent English, which means I can forget about reflexive French verbs for the rest of the evening. I assume Isabelle will have a cup of tea and leave before dinner.

But half an hour later, she shows no sign of budging and the doorbell rings. This time, it's Helena's younger brother. Christ! We're never going to get out to dinner at this rate. Helena returns from the kitchen with some salty black olives and I wonder why she's encouraging these people to hang around when we should be trying to get rid of them.

By the time the doorbell rings once more, I'm getting pissed off in an overt and decidedly un-British fashion. I glance at Helena in a way that I hope will encourage her to get rid of whoever-it-is-this-time. But she ignores me completely and only when she opens the door does the penny finally drop. It's my Italian friend, Ernesto, and he's clutching a bottle of champagne. He steps inside and wishes me a happy birthday.

Back in the living room, everyone's laughing. The doorbell rings a few more times and, with the exception of the President, everyone I know in Paris arrives to celebrate the occasion. Even Mr Escalator is there, back from a trip to Chile, and he looks very happy. He must have sold another of his 'mince-meaters' (the enchanting slang of his colleagues for their fascinating products). He's in such a good mood that I almost don't have the heart to ask why the world's fastest moving walkway wasn't working when I passed through the Gare Montparnasse, but I eventually squeeze the question between two fat and particularly juicy Kalamata olives. 'What time were you there?' he asks. 'Was it after nine in the evening?' It was. 'Ah, that'll be because it's still officially on trial and the authorities are worried about the device heaving elderly people into the Seine at supersonic velocity. They insist upon it being manned at all times, but no one in France is willing to work the night shift.' Then he laughs and tells me to try again in the morning.

Despite my prejudices, the Greek food ordered in by Helena is delicious, as is the crispy pizza that she's been hiding in the oven all evening. I don't even mind watching our guests quaff the champagne, although my mind does dart briefly back over the Spanish border.

By the time I've seen everyone to the door, Helena is lying in a considerable heap on the bed, barely able to keep her eyes open. 'Well, did you enjoy yourself, old man?'

'I was a little disappointed.'

'Yes, I'm sorry about the Greek food'

'You promised me a *Big Mac!*'

'Next year, then.'

As she begins to drift off, I stare at the shape she makes in the bed. As usual, she has one hand cupped beneath her belly, just in case centuries of human biology suddenly require a bit of extra support and I remember something I overheard her saying earlier this evening about men having to live with a whale in the house for months. Grinning silently in the dark, I pull the quilt over both my babies and switch off the light.

Summer in the Antipodes, October 10th

The Rugby World Cup starts this weekend and, out of the blue, I receive a series of phone calls from an assortment of Celts, Kiwis and other people I barely know, asking whether I'd like to watch the opening salvos of France against Fiji in an Irish pub on Saturday morning. I try to explain to Helena how, for the six-week duration of such tournaments, this type of behaviour is considered acceptable between males and even a number of more compliant females. 'Six weeks!' she exclaims, thus forcing me to explain that the World Cup only takes place once in a blue moon. Helena quickly points out that I said the same thing about the *Tour de France*, the World Athletics Championship, the Olympics and that I'll say it again when the European Football Championships roll around next summer. I suppose I could ask whether she's ever actually lived with a man before, but I manage to resist the temptation.

Paris by open-top bus, October 11th

The pub nestles as snugly as a drunken Brit among the sex shops up on the Boulevard de Clichy, and by the time I get there, the French are already engaged in an almighty tussle with some human washing machines from the South Pacific. It's almost midday and Russell the Kiwi and Isabelle's boyfriend, Jean-Luc, are ordering their third pint of Guinness. Jean-Luc is a genuine rugby man – well over six feet tall, with the number 8 tattooed permanently between a pair of shoulders which would easily double as an emergency suspension bridge across the Seine should the need ever arise. Right now, he's getting annoyed by the midget Irish referee, the tactics of the Fijians and the fact that the French aren't producing the kind of flowing rugby he considers their birthright.

The lure of the game has brought him to the foot of Montmartre, but Jean-Luc shouldn't be here at all. Rather than downing the black stuff, he's supposed to be at a wine fair at the top of the hill, extolling the sophisticated virtues of a selection of Burgundies. Ordering a *Perrier*, I accept the predictable barrage of insults over my sexuality and parentage and chalk it all up to the awful possibility of a French defeat. Then I settle down to enjoy the rest of the game, which is quite evenly matched until the Fijians start losing their discipline. One or two fearsome punches are thrown into unshaven

Gallic features and the French extract their revenge while the toy referee's attention is elsewhere.

After the game, the players hug and the French television commentators start congratulating each other. It's lunchtime and Jean-Luc orders another pint of Guinness before remembering that he's supposed to be ruminating over Pinot Noirs rather than swilling pint after pint of Dublin's finest. Three mighty gulps later, we all stumble out of the darkened oak bar into the early autumn sunlight and I decide to accompany the unsteady troops up to the Sacré Cœur.

I can't abide Montmartre. Once upon a time, it was a village entirely separate from the Parisian sprawl. Now it attracts tourists in the same way as those adhesive nicotine-yellow strips seduce globulous bluebottles. The main square up here is the Place du Tertre and, as far as I know, you won't find a greater concentration of con artists anywhere else in the world. If you want to have your face caricatured by ruffians with mock French accents, buy a gaudy painting of the Montmartre windmills (all but one of which collapsed with dry rot at least three centuries ago) or simply sit in a café nursing a €10 café au lait, while the waiters secretly snigger over your gullibility and expect to be tipped, then this is the place to be. Presiding over the whole sorry mess, is the Basilique of the Sacré Cœur – probably the ugliest building in Paris and a massive monument to the guilt felt by the bourgeoisie towards the repressed workers of Paris who, after the French had surrendered in the Franco-Prussian war, wanted to continue sticking it to Bismarck. It's the colour of bone and, to my mind, resembles nothing so much as a human skull. I try to push my way through the swarm without opening my eyes, but this trick comes to an abrupt end when I half-squash some old woman's pet Chihuahua underfoot. She's quite indignant and her mood fails to improve when I suggest that she has no business transporting vermin around the streets of Paris. That's another thing I can't stand about this place – it's full of shivering, yapping and crapping miniature dogs which are good for absolutely nothing other than providing a bit of unspeakable, late-night solace to their museum-piece owners.

At the top of the hill, Jean-Luc strips off his French rugby shirt to reveal a T-shirt advertising a particular cave in Burgundy and everyone orders a glass of *Vosne Romanée*. Jean-Luc certainly sounds as if he knows what he's talking about. I can practically taste the stuff myself as he describes a blackberry nose and a forceful, smoked presence on the palate. I used to love this type of wine and remember how, with Jean-Luc as our guide, we once took a trip down to the Côte d'Or where a vineyard owner with a nose like a giant pickled onion was pontificating over his products in an accent so thick that, after a tad too much tasting, I convinced myself he was really from Glasgow. I bought half a case on that, my last, trip to the vineyards, although none of these bottles will be ready to drink for another decade or so. Now they lurk under my bed, waiting for my resolve to weaken.

My resolve weakening, I take leave of the boys, who look as if they are ready to settle down for another of those afternoons which only rolls around once every four years and, clearing a blue path through the hoards of elephantine tourists in baseball caps, I head back down the hill to check in on Helena.

Safe amongst the resident mix of sex workers and what remains of the Pigalle bourgeoisie, Helena's still in bed and looks bored. She tells me her feet are killing her, although I suspect the real trouble is that the Rugby World Cup has another fve and a half weeks to run. To assuage my guilt, I come up with the idea of a new pair of shoes. After all, her modest and delicate feet are carrying around a good eleven kilos more than they ever have before.

An hour later, I wish I hadn't bothered. Why can I never remember that shopping only ever makes women more disgruntled than they were before leaving home? Right now, we're in the middle of *Galeries Lafayette* and she's cursing the assistant, the shoes, the shop, the crowds and life in general.

She's perched on a green leather bench and refusing to budge, the sales assistant is in tears, and I'm thinking of calling in a UN peacekeeping force to keep them apart. 'I'll be back when the baby's born,' screams Helena, as I hustle her out of the door and toss another pair of ostrich-feather sling backs at an astonished sales girl. Why is it that these shoe designers persist with the illusion that women only ever have to walk from the restaurant table to the taxi?

The approximate distance from here to the moon, October 12th

The best part of two months has elapsed since I started work on my CV and I'm now cautiously optimistic that it'll be completed by the end of the week. At least that's what I'm trying to sell to Helena as we wander aimlessly through the Bois de Boulogne. The sunlight filters gently through the leaves as Helena does her best to understand how anyone can take so long to complete a two-page document. I attempt to distract her attention by pointing out a lone pheasant scratching away at the topsoil right in front of us. But even the rare sight of any animal in this park other than a manicured poodle fails to blow her off course. There's only one city on her mind this morning and it certainly isn't Paris. No, she wants to know when we start packing our bags for Toulouse.

Every time I move to a new city, I swear it will be the last before I bolt permanently for my own cowpat in the country. But when it comes to the crunch, I fail miserably to persuade myself to leave, unless it's for an even dirtier and more polluted metropolis. I guess I just find the idea of moving out of the city a whole lot easier to handle than genuine large, white removal vans.

Why is it so hard to abandon Paris once and for all? Why not take the plunge? It's not as if we'd be leaving much behind – just sixty-odd square metres of peeling plasterboard on a permanent building site (demolition work on the flat beneath ours started only last week). Back at home, Helena demands to know what it is that keeps me here, but I'm having trouble explaining it to myself, never mind anyone else. A call from Pierre comes to my rescue. He wants to know if everything is ready for the baby. Once again I survey our son's bedroom. 'More or less,' I say to the two-time father and hold the receiver at arm's length to stop it melting in the heat of my self-deception.

Pierre gives me a progress report on his second son, Maxime: every night he sleeps for a couple of hours before awakening for another feed and unless Cécile's left nipple is wedged tight between his gums when he does, he will spend the rest of the night wailing. He may only be a few weeks old, but Pierre assures me that his lungs are already functioning to perfection. I ask how long this nightmare will continue (although I think I refer to it as this 'state of affairs'), anticipating that it will be for no more than a couple of weeks. Pierre estimates the potential damage at around six months and I almost swallow my tongue. Six months without sleep! He assures me that I'll get used to it, but somehow this makes not the slightest dent in my apprehension, not even when he explains that there are plenty of compensations. 'Like what?' I ask, desperate for anything to cling on to, as we're now little more than three months from our own little appointment with ruin. Pierre tells me he'll send an email with an example and I go back to work on my CV. But careers past, present or future fail to hold my interest and, five minutes later, I'm relieved to see the following distraction pop into my inbox:

Clément points to the great fingernail in the sky, and asks: 'Papa, c'est la lune?'
Papa says: 'Oui, Clément, c'est la lune.'
Clément says: 'Non!'

For a good half an hour Helena and I cackle uncontrollably

over her nephew's conversation killer. It's ironic to think of how I cling to my own childish irrationality and defiance, when it's about to become my job as a 'responsible' parent to attempt to educate those very qualities out of an animal whose only desire is to thrive forever on a diet of breast milk and imagination.

9 – 6 = 3! October 13th

When Helena first became pregnant, I can distinctly remember consoling myself with the thought that nine months is a small eternity and the gestation period would last forever. Now the weeks are flying by, but I'm still not ready. I'm not even sure that I know how to get ready, other than by finding a job, which is why I'm up early this morning in front of the world's longest CV. I'd love to doze for another couple of hours but I can't because my head is already spinning like a merry-go-round full of unborn children and other faceless anxieties. The only way to stop it is to get out of bed and tune out the noise in my head.

The trouble is that all of this angst is transferring itself to my CV, along with the crazy idea that I should be elucidating every last facet of a past life which merits little more than consignment to oblivion. My CV now sprawls across so many sheets of A4 that I've pinned them to the wall, just to keep the chronology straight. I need to condense but all I seem able to do is expand and now it's about to contaminate our hallway. I've got to start hacking the damned thing back somehow. I don't want my son to open his eyes and find a list of his father's failures wallpapering the house.

At least I've got something to work towards this week, and that something comes in the streamlined form of the formidable Mme Ferrat, which is why, in the half light of dawn, I'm trying to recall exactly what it was that kept me so busy throughout all those years in marketing services. Rather than presenting my competencies as a series of unconnected and grandiose statements of dubious veracity, the Ferrat wants each of them to be imbedded in my CV. She also expects me to come up with a list of the companies for which I'd consider working and I've started on this, although progress is slow. So slow, in fact, that the only name on my list is that of a certain sports newspaper.

Down and out in Paris, October 15th

To escape being haunted by a set of malevolent spirits from my past, I catch the metro back up to the 18th *arrondissement*, where Segolene Hauteville has organised an afternoon with a careers counsellor from the ANPE. His job is to explain the intricate architecture of the French social system to an audience of bewildered immigrants, as well as to inform us about any rights we may have while unemployed. My own suspicion is that – as an Englishman who left a perfectly good job back in England and moved to France of his own free will – I'll be told that the correct answer to this is 'none'. Helena agrees with this assessment, although that's perhaps understating her reaction; she's convinced it will be a complete waste of my time and that I'd be better off sifting through the online classifieds. Maybe, but my belief is that the internet promises far less in the way of good old French melodrama.

Our session was supposed to have begun at two o'clock but, at two minutes past, I'm the only arrival and Segolene looks mildly surprised to see me. In what looks uncannily like a classroom, she's laying a folding aluminium table with grape juice and soggy biscuits, but stops what she's doing to check her watch. 'Not everyone is as punctual as the English!' she exclaims in a tone so full of scorn that I'm instantly reminded that, in France, punctuality is often interpreted as a lack of manners, if not outright moral failure. I make a mental note to remove any reference to timekeeping from my concertina of a CV, at which point the counsellor slides through the door and we're introduced. He says something to me which sounds a little like '*bonjour, comment allez-vous?*' although I can't be sure because he says it so quickly and in an accent so thick, that I'm convinced he must be hiding a thick piece of black pudding under his tongue.

The clock ticks on and a few more of my fellow immigrants amble in and take their places behind the neatly ordered row of desks. To my right, a Senegalese woman with a child strapped to her back plonks herself at a desk and slowly unwraps her son from a tight bundle of red, gold and green cloth. It's almost half past when the last of the stragglers arrives and a wizened old dame from social services steps up to the plate and asks whether we have any questions for the incomprehensible one. Difficult, I think, since none of us has the faintest idea what he wants to talk about, let alone whether we'll be able to understand him when he finally gets started. Then a young Moroccan jumps to his feet and launches into an unfettered rant about the unfairness of French employers. In a voice over which he is slowly losing control, he recounts how, although he has a *carte de séjour* (the piece of paper which legally entitles him to work in France) he has yet to find a single French boss willing to take him on as a tax-paying employee. To a man, they'd prefer him to continue working 'black' and keep most of the wages due to him in their own pockets.

At this, the sausage man awakens from his post-lunch slumber and cries, '*non, non, non, Monsieur,* you must immediately refuse and insist that he employs you on a legal basis.' To which the Moroccan quickly retorts that the minute he suggests any such thing, the employer tells him to venture forth and find employment elsewhere - if he's not prepared to agree to these terms, there are plenty of others who are. 'Irrelevant,' declares the pork-filled face of state bureaucracy, 'you must refuse as a matter of principle.' At this juncture, he receives some cautious moral support from Segolene and the dame with the wizened features, whose face has started to twitch as alarmingly as a gerbil filling its cheeks from a mountain of subsidised mustard seed. The others in the room are shrugging their collective shoulders, shaking their heads or simply glaring at the sausage as if they wish he would drop dead on the spot. The exasperated young father persists and asks how he's supposed to put food on the table for his sons if he refuses the employer's conditions. I have to give him full marks for persistence and courage in the face of state-sponsored adversity. After all, he's not entitled to claim unemployment benefit until he's been working in France (on a legal and fully declared basis, naturally) for at least twelve months.

By now, the sausage is on the verge of erupting - he didn't bring a perfectly good lunch to a premature end to have a bunch of uppity immigrants getting all self-righteous on him. No, he quite explicitly came to deliver a lecture on the right and the proper way to do things in the great French Republic, not delve into the sordid details of life on the breadline in Paris! 'Any such employers,' he informs us, in a tone clearly borrowed from Napoleon himself, 'are subject to heavy fines for such behaviour and I urge you to report them to the authorities immediately.' Finally, the man with a noticeable pot belly embarks on his lecture, which appears to have been prepared on the back of a packet of fags. I'm almost certain that it's irrelevant, not only to my needs, but to those of almost everyone in the room. As I head for the exit, he's busy drawing a nice little pie chart on the blackboard and chuntering on about some figures which prove that 60 percent of jobs in France are obtained by writing a spontaneous letter of motivation – thus circumventing the need for any assistance from the state employment agency in the first place.

Double Dutch, October 17th

'No!' says Madame Ferrat firmly.

'No?'

'This won't do at all. Not at all!'

'It won't?'

'No. For a start, it's still four pages long.'

This is true. Despite shrinking the font to a point at which even a hawk would require a magnifying glass to read it, my history still sprawls aimlessly over numerous sides of A4.

'And it's still in English.'

Also true! 'What else is wrong with it?' I ask in as insolent a tone as I can muster.

The Ferrat reaches into her hi-tech drawers and rustles out a sheaf of papers. 'Look at these.'

We spend the next half an hour poring over a number of erudite French CVs and I have to admit they are all beautifully crafted and appear to have been printed on finest Egyptian parchment. Then she returns to my own miserable effort; she handles it as if it were a soiled handkerchief, then releases it and watches as it floats down into my lap. I promise to return two weeks later with something which reads a little less like a Korean washing machine manual.

To hell with it! I've spent practically the entire week bent over my antediluvian laptop. It's Friday afternoon and the number one item on my agenda is to have some fun. Dirk and Carla are arriving on the train from Amsterdam this evening and I've promised to pick them up from the Gare du Nord, but that leaves the whole afternoon to while away in the cinema while Helena spends seven consecutive hours on her feet in a classroom, lecturing her pupils on the chocolate box of democratic delights that is the Fifth Republic.

I first met Dirk ten years ago in New York, when we were employed by the same marketing agency. I have two abiding memories of the moment he pitched up at the company offices on Lexington Avenue. The first was an appalling mustard-check jacket, which remained stuck to his shoulders for the following two years. The second was the expression on his face when he told me how he'd been forced to leave his new girlfriend behind in the Netherlands to pursue his childhood dream of living in Manhattan. I asked him why he hadn't brought her along. 'She can't get a work permit,' he'd said, with a doleful look in his eye. 'So why not marry her then?' I asked, as if it were the most obvious thing in the world. But Dirk felt it was a bit too soon to be thinking of marrying Carla.

Carla finally made it to New York two years later, shortly before I left the city, and the two of them stayed for another five years to slowly cement their relationship by roller-blading the canyons of that magnificent metropolis. Then one day Dirk took her to a restaurant at the top of a skyscraper where he planned to propose. His intention had been to suspend the moment until dessert arrived but he became so nervous that the ring box, which he'd tucked into his underpants, was getting soaked in perspiration and he found himself unable to swallow so much as a single mouthful of his starter. At the top of this particular tower, the starters were so astronomically expensive that Dirk took the sensible decision to get it all over with and enjoy the rest of his meal.

Smiling broadly, Dirk and Carla get off the *Thalys* train and the first question they ask is whether I'm finally ready to do the decent thing and marry Helena, now that she's pregnant. I think I'm being smart by avoiding the question, but these two know me too well. I have as much chance of escaping their questions as the juiciest lugworm has of avoiding the fisherman's hook.

The best man's secret, October 18th

It's my own stupid fault, of course, I know that, but I've just asked Carla what she'd like to do here in Paris and what she wants is to wander the streets of swish St Germain. 'Good,' I say without thinking, 'that way we can visit the jewellery shops and I'll find a ring for Helena.' And before I can even begin to explain that this is to make up for the lack of a birthday present, Dirk and Carla seize their opportunity: 'A diamond ring?' they intone together, as if practising for some ultra-harmonic *De Beers* advert. Hastily I explain that Helena doesn't like diamond rings and cover as much of my face as I can with a scarf.

Because they're Dutch and as blunt as a couple of rubber mallets, however, Dirk and Carla are not deterred and the inquisition restarts just as I'm trying to enjoy a cup of hot chocolate and fend off a bill for €27, which the proprietor of the café is trying to stick on my forehead:

Am I happy with Helena? Yes. Why do you ask?

Wouldn't she like to get married? Probably. I daren't ask.

Why not? Silence.

Is it true that the technical term for a child born out of wedlock is still 'bastard'? I believe so.

What is it that I'm so afraid of? I haven't a clue. Why don't you enlighten me?

By the time I reach that darker, bitter part of a hot chocolate that swills around at the bottom of the cup, I'm beginning to regret inviting these two supremely well-balanced, non-smoking and sane individuals to Paris. Don't get me wrong, I have nothing but admiration for the directness of my friends and the Dutch in general. I just don't appreciate it when aimed at me.

We visit the Place St Sulpice, which hosts the most beautiful church in the city and I point out the apartment building opposite, in which Catherine Deneuve is reputed to live. Then I buy Helena a ring, a cheap one, set with a large number of vivid, green stones so as to avoid any possible confusion, but each of these diversions brings only temporary respite from the onslaught. Eventually, I admit that I'm still thinking about marrying Helena, but just the two of us, on the quiet, down at the local *mairie* before anyone realises what's going on, especially me – I wouldn't be able to keep my mouth shut during that bit when they ask whether anyone has any objections.

Dirk quite clearly has a hidden agenda in all of this. Thanks largely to that mustard jacket, he had very few friends back when he tied the knot, which meant he was left with little choice but to make me the best man, and I believe my speech may have contained the odd reference to a unit of manhood appreciably shrunken by the cold winds that blow incessantly across the North Sea and on into Holland. Until my nerve failed me, I suspect Dirk had been preparing a very long piece of revenge that he hasn't given up hope of delivering to a wide and appreciative audience. Only when he starts making a series of uncharacteristically witty and piercing remarks that shake me all the way down to my *Adidas*, do I realise that he has every intention of broadcasting the whole damned thing this afternoon – he's just not funny or smart enough to have thought any of this stuff up on the spot.

By the time we arrive home, I'm punch drunk and hoping to hide in the bedroom, but Helena is looking perky after a six-hour rest on the bed and starts asking about dinner. Carla has bought the *Time Out* guide to eating in Paris and reels off a few reviews, which have Helena practically licking the paint off the walls. There's only one problem, which is that, of the ten bistros we call, seven are closed on a Saturday night and the other three are fully booked. Because of the European 35-hour week, all restaurants in France are now forced to close for two days a week and, as most are shut anyway on a Sunday night, the owners prefer to chase the cash that comes with the business crowd on a Monday than to cater to capricious and tight-fisted customers (like us) who wander in on a Saturday wearing nothing but their own money. We are forced, therefore, to set off in search of sustenance *sans réservation*.

Coitus interruptus, October 19th

I wake late. My guts still gurgling from the Korean beef we finally helped Dirk finish around midnight last night, I emerge from the bedroom to find him tucking into an enormous pile of croissants, which he plans to wash down with a gallon of OJ. 'Careful Dirk,' I chide, 'Helena made those plates and she won't want you licking the glaze off them. He sneers crudely and suggests an early lunch before their train leaves for Amsterdam and we round off the weekend by grazing our way across the lush, lower slopes of Montmartre. Sick of me complaining about her eating habits, Helena's just delighted as I'm forced to watch, in silence, someone who makes her own appetites look modest, and the nudging starts when, with an aperitif, Dirk consumes a bucketful of garlic olives with no regard for either their pits or his fellow passengers on the train home. Dawdling their way back home after lunch, the girls stop at a lingerie shop window to gasp over an impossibly flimsy thong composed entirely of moth wing and damask, before turning their gaze from the ephemeral undies to ask an opinion of the unusually taciturn Dirk. But he'd disappeared altogether. Eventually we found him halfway down the street, shovelling slices of pizza and *Nutella* crêpes into his gullet without pausing to swallow.

As the afternoon draws to a close, I lever Dirk back into the *Clio*, which grumbles that 1.2 litres is wholly insufficient to drag him back up the hill to the Gare du Nord, and my dear Dutch buddies get in a couple of final low blows about weddings and unemployment before staggering off in the general direction of the buffet car.

I swing the unburdened car around and, joyously, it freewheels all the way home. But somehow the departure of two of my closest friends leaves me feeling a little sad. Pondering why, the only thing I can think of is the fact that I used to be Dirk's boss. Now his career is flourishing and he's steadily building a good life for his wife and, maybe at some point in the future, a small family of extra blunt instruments.

Back home, Helena perfunctorily tries on the ring I've chosen. She doesn't like it. I didn't really expect that she would. It's too modern and the band made of metal, rather than silver (and how could I possibly have thought that silver was a metal?). Do I have the receipt? I do. I know what will happen next – it will be exchanged for another pair of earrings. I know what you're thinking... That, under the circumstances, the only ring she'll accept is one of those shiny silver numbers with a piece of chiselled and highly polished carbon wedged firmly into the deepest of settings. I haven't ruled it out as a possibility myself, even if Helena is not the type of woman to say that she likes something when she most definitely does not.

'Did you enjoy seeing Dirk and Carla?' asks Helena as we lie in bed late in the evening.

'Yes, of course,' I say. Although enjoyment is not exactly the word I'd choose to describe what those bastards put me through this weekend.

'I think Carla will be pregnant next time we see them.'

'Oh? Are they trying?'

'Sort of.'

'What do you mean 'sort of'?'

'I mean they are trying, but they panic halfway through and she makes him pull out.'

'Pull what out?'

Helena gives me that look she reserves for my more pathetic naiveties, and when that fails to register, she stares at my crotch.

I look at my crotch too, but it takes me a couple more seconds before I twig: 'I see. I wish you'd told me that earlier.'

'Why?'

'No particular reason.' I roll over and consider the damage I might have inflicted upon my friend the human pelican had I known about this a mere twenty-four hours earlier.

'Perhaps they didn't want you to know. You weren't around when Carla told me about it, and Dirk did look a bit sheepish.'

'I'll bet he did.' I get up from the bed and turn on my

computer. My email revenge is going to be very specific, very detailed and aimed at the tenderest parts of the Netherlands.

Putting the human back into Human Resources, October 21st

Before we leave for London, I've promised Helena I'll do a thorough search of all job websites and, because I mean what I say, I get out of bed and lurch straight into the little fellow's bedroom with a large mug of coffee and a false scowl intended to portray intensity of purpose. With the door closed safely behind me, the scowl disappears as soon as I begin trawling the *BBC* website for the weekend's football results, which dance across the screen until my compulsion is satiated. I make little progress beyond this point and I'm still checking the Isthmian league table (Division II, South) when it starts to get dark and I remember Helena will soon be home from school.

Hang on! What's this? Two new messages have stolen their way undetected into the mailbox of my French ISP – an address I use only for job applications. Jesus! It's from the company in Toulouse. I'd almost forgotten my application. Better open it before Helena gets back, just in case it's bad news...

Dear Sir,

Thank you for your application to join our company, which I read with no little amusement. Forgive me for coming straight to the point, but surely you do not seriously expect us to treat your application with anything other than the utmost scorn and contempt? It amazes me that anyone might have the audacity to submit such a piece of garbage to a highly trained human resource professional such as myself. You can not seriously think that I might overlook, for even one moment, the insecurities which swarm through your CV like bacteria in an overripe cheese? Nor that I might fail to see through your hilarious 'letter of motivation', which reads more like the confessions of a deranged psychopath than an attempt to convince me you might possess even one redeeming quality?

That said, I wouldn't like you to believe that your weasel-like attempts to ingratiate yourself to a consummate professional like me (whom you correctly assume to hold high and important office at this prestigious corporation) have gone entirely in vain. I took the liberty of passing on your 'application' to a few of my colleagues, and I confess that it kept most of us amused for an entire coffee break. In fact, we laughed so heartily at your attempts to cover up your descent into the abyss that my colleague Joe Snivelchops III spilt his brandy and cocoa all over the table. Luckily, your CV was at hand to mop up the mess!

I sincerely doubt that you will ever find an enterprise idiotic enough to take a risk on a man so clearly and prematurely destined for the knacker's yard, although there may be some unscrupulous employers out there willing to take advantage of your terminal crisis if provided with a sufficient quantity of used banknotes in an unmarked manila envelope.

Thus I reach that point in my letter at which it's incumbent upon me to wish you every success in your attempts to crawl your way out of the primeval swamp and back into gainful employment, or at least into a suitable institution.

On the assumption that you will never again presume to contact this company, please accept a few bogus condolences on the way your sad little life has turned out.

Cordially,

Robin J. Foreskin (B.A. Hons, 1st ° PR.Ick)

Head of Human Remains, Stiffcorp. Toulouse, France

P.S. It may interest you to know that I lunched yesterday with our company psychologist (an excellent bouillabaisse washed down with a youthful, yet perky little number from the upper Rhône valley). Over coffee and a rather complex snifter of Armagnac, I pulled your somewhat dishevelled application from my jacket pocket and shared it with my venerable colleague. His considered view is that you should submit yourself for psychiatric treatment and the maximum permissible dosage of Prozac *without delay and thus inure yourself from any further pain and humiliation.*

Of course, the venerable old sac of gonads didn't put it in quite those words, but don't you just wish that they sometimes would? In a way, it would be easier to accept than all that smug, value-added guff they habitually emit from their hairy sedentary arses.

I can't say that I'm astounded at the fact that our move to Toulouse looks like being, er, delayed, although I'm sure Helena will be disappointed. Unlike Mr Foreskin and his colleagues, she does still appear to have some misplaced faith in my abilities.

She arrives home, looking tired and wan. There's only one day left at school before the half-term holiday begins.

'Good day?' she asks.

'Well, I heard from Toulouse.'

I watch as Helena's pallid features flush with excitement. It would be cruel to let any hope linger there for too long and I shake my head quickly.

'Why not?'

'Found other candidates better than me.' Now isn't really the time to tell her about the fish soup or the company psychologist. I watch as Helena drags herself wearily towards the bedroom into which the sunlight never penetrates. I know that she's been mentally packing the suitcases which lie, gathering dust, on top of the wardrobe. How many times has she imagined our young son breathing freely and running amok in the forests and fields of the south? In truth, I'm more disappointed for her than I am for myself – I was quietly dreading spending the rest of my life wandering internal corridors laden with files that are never quite ready to close.

Helena falls asleep and I'm left to reflect on our progress as I prepare dinner. After an hour's kip, I know she'll want to discuss our next steps and I run through the options while shelling a few prawns. I enjoy Paris, although I do agree this is no city in which to bring up a child. My own view is that our son will be OK here for the first six months or so. I mean, it's not as if babies actually do anything much before they start to crawl, is it? Unless I'm mistaken, their sole purpose in life is to lie there and attract unwanted relatives the way in which leftover food attracts ants. Other than that, it's mainly about eating, puking, shitting and waking up Mummy and Daddy every time the poor sods finally nod off to sleep. As far as I can tell, it makes little difference whether these bodily functions are performed in Paris, Toulouse or on one of the moons circling the planet Jupiter.

Even I can see that the little fellow will quickly outgrow the apartment and that, like it or not, we'll have to move within a year. But to where? Toulouse looks a lot less likely than it did yesterday and I'm not prepared to go south without some sort of employment. In truth I feel no great urgency to quit our tiny apartment in the dark heart of *la ville lumière*. I throw the naked prawns into the pan bubbling on the stove and watch as they drown in the spicy red, glutinous sauce.

'What are we going to do now?' asks Helena over dinner.

'I don't know. Keep looking, I guess.'

'This child is not growing up in Paris!'

I freeze on the spot. Does she mean me, or the other one?

'No, he's not.'

'So how about London then?'

London, England. Could I possibly go back there? I've spent so long running from the place, I sometimes believe it exists only as a memory I'd prefer to blot permanently from my mind. Yet there's no doubt that my job prospects are more realistic there than they are here in France. I don't know, but I'll soon get the chance to consider it as we're leaving for London in less than forty-eight hours.

'Would you like to live in London, Helena?'

'Why not? It might be easier for you.'

Why not? I'll tell you why not! But where should I start

– the food, the weather, British Rail, or the fact that the place is awash with booze and drugs? Then there's the tabloid culture, pious, baby-smooching politicians and all those good-time estuary girls whose only desire in life is a shag and five minutes of knickerless celebrity. And how about the price of property, five quid to travel one stop on the tube, the education system and sausages made without any reference to the unfortunate animal depicted on the packaging.

'Yes, why not?' I say. 'We'll have a look while we're over there. See what you think.'

From largest to smallest – A short tour of the animal kingdom, October 23rd

By the time Helena gets back from another visit to the midwife, I'm too busy resurrecting a few cadavers from my film script to ask how it went. Quickly, we shovel clothes and a few presents into a suitcase and head for the Gare du Nord.

As we settle into our seats on the train, I realise I'm exhausted. I may not have done an honest day's work for months, but I feel like I need this holiday. I've been sleeping badly and waking before dawn no matter what time I go to bed. I've also mislaid a couple of kilos I can ill afford to lose.

'What are you worried about?' asks Helena as we pull clear of the grey, northern suburbs of Paris.

I gaze fondly at the cover of *L'Equipe* into which I was planning to dive for a couple of hours. But the train is full and there's nowhere to hide. I sigh heavily but Helena knows this trick too and repeats the question. I murmur something about going to England when I should be looking for a job in Paris. But that's not the half of it: among other things, there's the prospect of spending four days with my mother – an open invitation for her to start asking me about work, accommodation, marriage and babies – and then there's the small matter of an impending birth in the family. With another sigh, I put down the newspaper and watch Helena as she and the little fellow try to wriggle themselves into a position that will enable the pair of them to survive the journey in one piece.

'How did it go at the hospital this morning?'

'Fine. Everything's OK.'

'What happened?'

'Not much, just a check-up really.'

'Everything within the norms?'

'Yes', says Helena, with a defensive yawn of her own. She knows right off the bat where I'm going with this line of questioning and she's deflecting me by feigning fatigue. If she were at all interested in sport, it's right about now that she'd be reaching for her own copy of that great filler of time and space known as *L'Equipe.* This conversation is always the same and she can see it coming a mile off. We never approach agreement, let alone any conclusions, and, occasionally, it takes place without recourse to the spoken word. For example, Helena will arrive home from school looking knackered, go straight to the fridge and pull out an enormous half moon of Brie. Whether by chance or sheer bloody-mindedness, I can't be sure, but I'll often appear in the kitchen at the very moment she's consuming a large wedge of the edible animal fat. The darkest exchange of stares will follow. Sometimes she'll say '*Quoi?*' in a tone which borders upon the belligerent, but usually she'll just glare and challenge me to keep my big mouth shut. Obligingly, I'll tell her dinner will be ready in less than an hour, although I don't always bother. I know it's not worth it because Helena is ravenous now and when pregnant women are hungry, an hour from now might just as well be the middle of next month.

The truth of it is that Helena simply loves cheese. She also loves meat, biscuits, chocolate, and I could go on, but I'll leave you to draw up your own list of saturated fats that can be depended upon when your purpose is to gain weight. I guarantee most of them will be working their way through

Helena's arteries right now. Of course, she was eating all this before she got pregnant, but half an hour later, she'd put on her trainers and do several laps of the city to work it all off. Now that's no longer possible, because the not-so-little fellow, in collaboration with the French dairy industry, has added a full fourteen kilos to an otherwise modest frame. So now she puts in a few extra laps of the fridge instead.

About four weeks ago, she waddled off to see some medicine man at the hospital and got told she was overweight, precisely four kilos overweight. At first Helena didn't want to admit this for fear that I'd run to the vegetable shop and buy four kilos of potatoes to make a cheap point. But she needn't have worried – there was a full net of tangerines in the kitchen and I was happy to illustrate with those. I think it was at this point that Helena and I stopped communicating altogether as far as her weight is concerned. My final word on the subject was that we should be guided by the opinion of the doctor. Since then I've kept shtummer than a jilted ventriloquist's dummy. Helena's last words were that, compared with my cigarette consumption, an extra four kilos hardly represents the onset of Sodom and Gomorrah.

So you'll understand that it's with some trepidation that I come to my next question:

'What did the midwife say about your weight?'

Helena stares out of the window of the train and I follow her gaze towards a set of bulky, northern French cows which are hiding from the pissing rain under a sodden clump of bushes. Then she turns coyly back towards me:

'She wants me to visit a nutritionist.'

'Oh yeah? Why's that then?'

'She wants me to talk to him about my diet. I have an appointment when we get back from London.'

More than a little pleased with this turn of events, I sink back into my seat and don't even try to disguise the smug expression blighting my features. Best not to say anything else.

'And you want to know what?' Helena asks.

'What?'

'The nutritionist. He, well, he lives on the *Impasse de la Baleine*.'

It takes a few seconds, of course, as I thrash around in the small and balefully empty part of my brain which houses French vocabulary. Helena watches as I struggle. Finally it falls into place, the nutritionist lives on the 'cul-de-sac' of the whale.

We finally stop laughing as the *Eurostar* emerges on the other side of the Channel Tunnel. For once, the sun is shining in England as we shoot, full tilt, through the garden of England and on into London. Cousin Nathalie may be waiting for us at Waterloo, but then again, she may not – her reliability rivals that of the train service in her adopted country. As usual, the *Eurostar* slows dramatically the minute it reaches the clogged arterial tracks on the outskirts of the city and we're down to walking pace by the time we cross Brixton High Street, leaving me plenty of time to stare down the road and reflect upon all the energy, spirit and hard cash that I spent in this particular corner of London.

Nathalie is not at the station and we're left to make our own way up Turnpike Lane. Easy, I think – Northern Line as far as the Circus, the change onto the Piccadilly Line. Think again! Derailed train on the Northern Line, please use an alternative route to reach your destination and welcome to Victorian Britain.

Hours later, we've completed the long trip north to Tottenham by our alternative route of choice (a combination of the Piccadilly Line, canoe, snow shoes, hitch-hiking, and a mule). Nathalie has aged a little in the interim, but she's waiting for us at the tube station and optimistically opens the boot of her small Japanese car to welcome our suitcase. Instantly, a million different objects see their opportunity to escape the confines of her *Nissan* and make their bid for freedom. Children's toys, plastic shopping bags, surprising quantities of hi-fi equipment, wellington boots, the annual output of the British pharmaceutical industry and, inevitability, a number of wire coat hangers have all spilled out onto the road and there would appear to be no way of persuading them all back inside.

'Sorry,' says Nathalie, who tends to apologise a lot. 'Sorry 'bout that!' Her English, as you will appreciate, is quite impeccable.

Helena takes the front passenger seat while I commence battle with the two children's seats in the rear. This is Léonie and Celeste territory and you'd have to be a confirmed sugar addict and no more than six years old to feel at home here. 'Sorry about the mess,' says Nathalie, as I tear sweet wrappers and old lollipop sticks from my coat. Maybe I'll spend half my life apologising too, once my son is born.

Five minutes later, Jonah opens the door of their terraced house, his arms full of a smiling Celeste. I notice immediately how she carries the autumn fashions as gracefully as she had the spring-summer collection. Meanwhile, the dangerous one, Léonie, is lurking at the top of the staircase, planning an aerial attack.

'Hello Léonie.'

'I've got lice!'

'Congratulations. Now come here and give me a kiss.'

'No thanks.'

'Fine.'

'Léonie!' says Nathalie sternly, 'come down here and say hello.'

But Léonie doesn't understand the word 'sternly' and just lolls on the staircase, scratching her new-found friends.

'Sorry about all of this,' says Nathalie, before she tries a new tactic: 'Look Léonie, Helena's got a baby in her tummy!'

'Why?' asks Léonie, completely unmoved by this piece of news.

How come only children can get away with asking the

really interesting questions?

Léonie is only persuaded to budge when Helena hands a joint present for the girls to her sister. Less than six seconds later, Léonie is at the bottom of the stairs, she's ripped the package from Celeste's hands, her sister is in tears and the present (a dainty set of six miniature teacups and saucers) is in a lot more than 12 pieces. I watch in amazement. How quickly the whole situation has been turned upside down. And this is girls! Once we've all taken stock of the devastation, Nathalie attempts to remonstrate with her youngest daughter as Jonah takes a tearful Celeste in his arms and the human hurricane returns to the top of the staircase with some shredded wrapping paper and a little blood under her fingernails. Nathalie apologises again. It's taken the best part of half an hour to restore order.

Easing gradually into this strange new world, we sit down to an excellent Thai chicken curry, prepared by Jonah while his daughters hover around the mouth-watering platefuls of our spicy, coconut dish like two small swarms of killer bees. Eventually they're persuaded upstairs and into bed. They're tired – not as tired as the rest of us perhaps, but tired enough to fall straight into sweet, silent sleep.

In bed later that evening, I find out that Nathalie suspects she may be pregnant again. I ask Helena how her cousin feels about that. All she says is that Nathalie would prefer a boy this time. I keep it to myself, but I do wonder whether Cousin Nathalie isn't perhaps stark raving mad. Then I fall into a deep slumber and dream of lice, shattered crockery and enough babies to exhaust an economy-sized pack of nappies overnight.

A long day in London, October 24th

My plan here is to do everything differently this time. No drinking, nothing wild in Brixton with Vincent and very little in the way of communication with those elements of life in London that spell danger for my new-found abstinence. So I'm not quite sure who it is that picks up the phone and calls Vincent on the other side of the Thames the minute Nathalie and Helena have left for the swimming pool, nor why he says 'Of course I'm on for a night out. I'll meet you at Brixton tube station.'

An hour or so later, I've added three entirely new words to my script, the girls are back from the swimming pool and a strange smell permeates the dining room. At first I suspect myself and sniff at all the usual crevices – not guilty. Besides, the new, pungent intruder is distinctly artificial – a new soap perhaps? No, it's definitely some kind of a chemical and a pretty virulent one at that and, following the scent as eagerly as a bloodhound on a fresh trail, I turn from my idling laptop just in time to see Léonie and Celeste rush through the door at full pelt. The smell gets just a little bit stronger. Not far behind the girls is Nathalie.

'Sorry! Were you working? Léonie, Celeste, leave the computer alone, it's not a toy. Come here!'

'It's alright Nathalie, I'd finished anyway.'

Like two temporary restraining orders, I have an arm around each of the sisters. By now, the chemical is practically stripping the lining from of my nostrils. Then I see Nathalie rubbing at her hair with a towel. Of course, the swimming pool!

'What are they putting in the water these days? Sulphur?'

'What do you mean?'

'That smell; that's not chlorine, is it?'

Nathalie looks at me for a moment, puzzled. Then she laughs. 'Oh, that! That's not the pool – it's the girls!'

'The girls?'

'Yes, I washed their hair with a special shampoo for lice.'

I look down at the two little bundles beneath me, each safely held in her own personal headlock. Tentatively I sniff at their heads before recoiling in horror. Jesus! Now I recognise that smell. The chemical sisters are wearing matching public toilets on their heads.

'Strong, isn't it?' says Nathalie, airily. 'Sorry 'bout that. I can't wash it out for another day.'

About three seconds later, the prospective father is running away from the future and back to the past. He's underground, tunnelling fast for the West End and far, far away from invisible animals with too many legs.

Mingling with all the other tourists, I wander the book shops and stalls of Covent Garden. A milky autumn sun is warming the paved streets and the smell of freshly ground beans emanates from the coffee chains that have sprouted up all over the place like mushrooms. Very quickly, the familiar old city swarms through the rest of my senses. Throughout the years of self-imposed exile, there were always brief interludes back in London, although every time I deserted, it became harder to return. It's like getting together with an old girlfriend and expecting a terrific affair. Foolishly, one seduces the other, only for the whole thing to end in disappointment and emptiness all over again.

But while I was fading in drunken exile, England was growing up fast and, as I wander through the unrestrained laughter of Covent Garden, I notice how the mobile phone has completely eradicated the English dread of being overheard in public. I'm obliged to listen as a new generation chatters senselessly into a device which provides the perfect platform for a piece of individual showmanship, a barbed interaction or a chance to impress the girls:

'Yeah...? 'Ello mate! You awright, are yer'? Where are you now? Me? Round 'n' about. Yeah. Nah, mate. I'm on me way. Nah. Yeah. Nah, he ain't gonna make it. Too hung over, old son! Nah. Awright, mate. Yeah. Laters, then? Dog 'n' Duck? Yeah. Nah! Fuck off. Cheers mate. Yeah, right. 'Bye.'

I stop at one of the coffee shops. It's still warm enough to sit outside with a mug of foaming Guatemalan coffee in which I've invested half of my life savings and I watch as the inhabitants of new, improved formula Britain swank past my corrugated aluminium table. When these self-assured men and women of indeterminate age are not dropping consonants and lewd suggestions into a *Nokia*, they're swigging from bottles of *Diet Coke* to clear one hangover and prepare for the next. Defying the onset of winter in light, branded suits, they strut purposefully from office to pub, chewing on designer sandwiches, dreaming of winning the lottery or working up an opportunity to demonstrate on TV the personalities they've been developing in the gym. Opposite the café is another of those new model supermarkets which don't need to sell anything edible to turn a profit and where urban Britain comes to refuel on cigarettes, the tabloid press, soft drinks and hangover cures. Outside, a sign flutters in the breeze and boasts how the retailer is 'making life cheaper' every day. The New Britain talks unashamedly of little other than money, football, sex, cocaine and hangovers. Maybe the pace of change is not so evident to the resident population, but it's pretty startling to a migrant bird like me. When I return and switch on the TV, I'm expecting a bit of sponge pudding comfort and snobbery from all those Oxbridge accents on the *BBC* telling me at what time to expect the next rerun of 'Dad's Army'. But they've long since been replaced by Rafi, Tina, Toni and Darren; young metropolitan faces of indeterminate sex and origin. I've no idea what became of all the Quentins, Tarquins and Lucy-Annabelles. Maybe they all slunk off to the City to keep their heads down and make a fortune in investment banking? Meanwhile, the New England has become the most brazen nation in Europe. It wears sharp shoes, underwear as outerwear and it sprays itself with perfumes called *Hard-on*, *Compulsion*, *Voracious* or *Orgasm*.

I warm my hands on the stained china mug and allow my mind to drift back to the continent. It's possible that I'm looking through a steamed-up window onto French culture and, in reality, it's changing every bit as rapidly as England.

But I don't think so. For better or worse, the English are erasing centuries of repression in a single generation. The French may be hidebound by formality and a sense of hierarchy, they may have slaughtered their aristocracy and convinced the rest of world they invented revolution and the socialist society, but when it comes to reinventing themselves, they're left standing by events on the other side of the Channel.

So when Helena sees Nathalie's nice little two-up, two-down with a perfect little rhombus of a garden and tells me she'd quite like to move to London, it stops me dead in my tracks. Am I finally ready to move back home? I feel as if I barely know this country any longer and its aggression frightens the crap out of me.

Taking care to avoid my derailed buddy on the Northern Line, I ride south to Brixton where I settle down to wait for Vincent behind a large bottle of *St Pellegrino*. It's six o'clock on a Friday evening and the British have but one thing on their mind. I watch them make a start: 'Six pints of lager, one with blackcurrant, two with lime, three *Bacardi Breezers*, two vodka *Red Bulls* and a gin and tonic – make it a double please mate.'

Vincent arrives precisely on time, as usual, while our other friends are spectacularly late. I don't mind, as it gives me the chance to catch up with his tales of the non-stop London nightlife. It's a long night of temptation as we flit from one Brixton haunt to the next. I drink *Coca Cola* until it burns a hole in the lining of my stomach and watch the others as they attempt to obliterate all thoughts of work with beer and shots of tequila. Shortly before dawn I crawl into bed, sober and shaking with relief.

Sex, death and ice cream (or how to keep the children busy), October 25th

Very few hours later my alarm call wakes me – it feels like an ice pick chipping at my face, although it's more likely to be a few of Léonie's fingers. I may not know much about children but I do know that sleep comes to an end when they say it does, and that's just one more thing I'll have to get used to. The good news is that Nathalie has stripped the chemicals out of the hair of her daughters, so they smell a whole lot sweeter than I do this morning.

After breakfast, we begin the trip north to visit my sister, although the train only makes it about halfway up the Lea Valley before entrusting us to a replacement bus service (another phrase indispensable to the modern English language). Helena is distinctly unimpressed and her mood does not improve when our bus arrives. It looks like something that's been borrowed back from the knacker's yard. 'How far is it, exactly?' she demands as the prehistoric object farts into life. I counsel her that, when travelling in Britain, it's not distance that counts but rather patience, courage and a good supply of emergency rations. The journey around the rape fields and roadworks on the border between Essex and Hertfordshire is a nightmare. The bus was clearly assembled before the invention of shock absorbers and every time we hit a bump or change in the road surface, Helena feels the full force of the blow in her ripening belly. I try to find her and the little fellow a sitting position which, if not exactly comfortable, at least gives them a shot at surviving their first experience of the B6342. She may be in agony, but at least she's forgotten about moving to England.

My sister is already aware of our dilemma – this part of the track will be closed for the next six months – and she's graciously agreed to pick us up in (or should that be rescue us from) Harlow. She, David and Lily are already waiting when the bus lurches to a halt in front of the station.

'Hello David.'

'Hello, um, Uncle, can I just ask...?'

'Yes, David?'

'Have you heard the new *Black Eyed Peas* CD?'

'No, David, but I've a feeling I soon will.'

'Why do you say that, Uncle?'

'Oh, no particular reason, David.'

I'm not sure whether I find it easier to cope with the brutality of Léonie or the way in which David whittles away at your patience with a relentless stream of quiz-show questions, all of which happen to be on his specialist subject. But until designer children become available at your local hypermarket, I guess I'll just have to take pot luck along with everyone else. The only respite comes in the form of the latest *James Bond* movie, which David watches on DVD every other day and to another screening of which we are all invited after lunch.

Ten minutes, thirty deaths and a couple of shags into the film, Helena decides she's had enough and leaves the room. She prefers not to risk this type of 'entertainment' penetrating the womb and upsetting her son. Shortly afterwards, I catch my sister slipping on her coat while David isn't watching. She's off to buy dinner at *Tesco* and I take the opportunity to bail out as well. I ask her what she thinks of David watching this kind of film and she looks at me wearily. I guess she's just grateful for a few minutes' respite from David's Q&A sessions and I can understand that. She also reminds me that there are worse things than bad *Bond* movies, all of them freely available on TV or the net.

As we cruise the aisles of the supermarket, looking for an unlikely combination of root vegetables and ice cream, I'm left to reflect that bringing up children is about more than nursing a child through the first few weeks of sleeplessness and setting in motion the process of two-way communication. The real trouble begins when they start exercising a will that runs in direct opposition to that of their parents, something already apparent in David, who is steadily wresting control of all family entertainment with the fervour of a pockmarked, post-commie *Bond* villain.

I'm beginning to feel the effects of the late night in Brixton when my sister finds me musing over the loss of childhood innocence next to a pile of overripe avocados.

'You look worried,' she says.

'Oh?' I say, while absentmindedly admiring the perfection of a genetically modified carrot.

'What's on your mind?'

'Nothing. Just bringing up kids, I suppose.'

My sister emits a low, derisory snort. 'Don't worry about that,' she says, 'just enjoy your last couple of months of freedom. For the next eighteen years, you won't have time to worry about anything beyond basic survival.'

'Is it really... ' My question tapers off into the white light of the supermarket.

'Really what? As bad as they say? It has its moments,' she says, before snatching the carrot from my grasp and wheeling her trolley towards an almighty row of clinking and grinding tills. Then she stops and looks back to find me still rooted to the spot.

'Come on,' she says, 'there'll be trouble if dinner's not ready by the time Bond's finished bonking Halle Berry for the tenth time since Saturday.'

Over dinner, my sister is the first to pose the question everyone else will ask on our brief stay in England. No, not the one about who is going to win the Rugby World Cup – the one about the baby's name. I was under the impression that this had already been decided and that we weren't going to discuss it with anyone. But it turns out I've got this quite wrong, because Helena is now reeling off a host of names to all at the dinner table plus a shoal of tropical fish, pressing their noses against the glass of their murky aquarium in anticipation. From what I can gather, it seems *we* were thinking of Marc and now *we've* decided against it. This is the first I've heard of it and question Helena on the spot. 'Too short,' is all she will say, before she runs down a list of other possibilities to check out what my sister and the fish think. I notice she has seen fit to reinclude a number of names which I thought had been permanently ruled out. Wrong again! As far as Helena's concerned, the only rule is that the name has to work in both English and French, which does at least disqualify Nigel, Bartholomew and Rupert.

Man and the Age of Reason, October 26th

The place is now empty of all nieces, nephews and *Bond* girls. They've all departed to catch an early charter flight from Gatwick, leaving Helena and I to rattle around in their large house and finish the washing up. Over breakfast, I turn on the rugby, only to discover that England are losing to an atoll in the South Pacific called Samoa. Helena has never heard of Samoa and wants to know how it's possible that the entire male population of this tiny island is beating a team from overcrowded England. I sigh heavily and decide against an explanation for two reasons: firstly, Helena, along with most other women I know, has about as much interest in sport as I do in leg waxing. Secondly, I fear she will start drawing all sorts of unwelcome parallels between the fate of the English rugby team and that of the father of her child. You can imagine the sort of thing: how both possess all the requisite parts to do the job properly yet somehow contrive to turn triumph into disaster. Besides, I'm still hoping to reverse the trend and produce the goods when they're most needed.

I switch off the central heating and the TV and we head back to the station. It's a beautifully sunny day as we climb aboard the pony and trap bound for London. I don't think Helena had anticipated quite such an authentic demonstration of life in nineteenth-century Britain and I watch her wince as the lead horse crunches into first gear. It's going to take something pretty special to detract her attention from the pain and I suspect the rugby will not do the trick. So I launch into an ill-advised monologue about sex, pregnancy and an assortment of other topics about which I know absolutely nothing.

This particular conversation has been a long time coming

and not even my residual shame over the cancellation of our marriage is enough to stop me from saying that which I have no right to say. Despite my claim to find heavily pregnant women sexy and attractive (well, Demi Moore on the cover of *Vanity Fair* anyway), our love life is not what it was since Helena fell pregnant and this has not gone unnoticed in certain quarters. Women do not lose their sexual appetites or suddenly come over all bashful because the unborn are watching and the closer we come to the birth, the more I'm feeling the pressure. To my embarrassment, this seems to have manifested itself as a general numbness in that part of the male anatomy which is usually the last to be afflicted by any such insensitivities.

Our coach hits a large meteor crater on the B6342, but Helena doesn't even blink. She can't believe that I'm criticising her for putting on weight during gestation. Am I criticising her? Damned right, I am! The minute her pregnancy was confirmed, she began to eat as if her life depended upon it. Sure, I've heard all her reassurances that she'll lose twenty kilos and more the minute our son is born and I'm well aware that my attitude is making her angry, but as the bus growls into somewhere called Broxbourne and we rejoin the train, I refuse to back down.

The British Grand Prix, October 27th

So she knows how I feel and I know how she feels. We'll never agree, but at least the conversation has cleared some of the hot, polluted air between us before we leave for the house that my mother shares with an ageing but ferocious cat named, somewhat misleadingly, after a common garden herb. Helena points out that the *GNER* train bound for the north looks like a French *TGV*. Sure enough, there is some outward resemblance, but the illusion is soon shattered when the train is badly frightened by a small stream the track is forced to traverse. It judders to an abrupt halt, leaving us plenty of time to gaze lazily out of the window and count the stickleback idling in the water.

When we arrive, my mother is standing in the station car park, looking at her watch. 'You're late,' she says, in a tone which leaves me in no doubt that she holds me personally responsible for the timetabling of all trains in the country. 'Yeah, sorry about that,' I say, unsure whether this is a habit I've caught from Nathalie or just me slipping automatically into the role of chastened son to my mother's top dog. But there's no time to ponder family dynamics right now, as she impatiently revs the engine in her determination to make up for the time unnecessarily squandered by the crumbling rail network.

As we tear up the twenty miles between the train station and the village in the vale, there's just enough time for me to regret telling Helena that my mother suffers from glaucoma and, as the G-forces momentarily relent, I turn and catch sight of her face – Helena's expression lies somewhere between alarm and outright terror; she's clutching her belly and watching the countryside disappear behind us faster than a piece of government legislation protecting the green belt. I say nothing, as I know that my mother regards her driving as 'sensible'. Damn that word – it nearly strangled my childhood and now it returns to me at the same velocity as the bugs being splattered against the windscreen.

We pull into the drive in front of my mother's house and dinner is on the table fifteen minutes later. 'We have to be quick,' she explains, 'I'm hosting a group discussion for some people from the local church this evening.' For a single, mad moment, the thought enters my head that I could join the group and leave Helena to sleep off her near-death experience in the back of a *Mazda*. Then the doorbell rings and the first of the group arrives. The reedy woman who steps inside could only have been born in England, and I decide on the spot that I'd be better off retiring upstairs with Helena and a good book. Her skirt (below the knee) is of the coarsest tweed, her shoes chestnut brown, highly polished and undeniably sensible. Her white shirt is starched and buttoned all the way up to the lower jaw and she moves with the flexibility of a prototype robot. Her manner of speaking, however, suggests that far beneath all this surface control lies a deeply ingrained hysteria. Helena has probably never seen such a creature before and, once we are safely upstairs, she asks me whether I think the poor woman has even heard of the female orgasm. 'Probably not,' I answer, 'although I'm sure she serves up an excellent high tea of scones and homemade strawberry jam.'

Domesticated animals and leafless trees, October 31st

In the morning we pay a visit to the windblown cemetery just outside the village, where my father is buried. He lies underneath a rough-hewn granite headstone on the windswept escarpment which borders the vale to the south. My mother has planted a miniature rose bush on his grave and, with winter closing in, there are a number of dead rose heads on the bush which I carefully pick off with chilly fingers. I look up to see a tear rolling down Helena's cheek. In silence, we reflect upon the fact that he will never see his grandson.

Helena's English lesson is almost over. My mother drives us out of the vale and back to the station. We have one more visit to pay before returning to France and making preparations for the birth.

My old boss at the marketing agency has invited us to his house in the Hertfordshire commuter belt. I worked with this man for twelve years and across three continents and he looked more than a little bewildered when I walked out of the door to concentrate fully on a crash I could no longer postpone. We'd enjoyed one another's company over beers and single malt whisky on many an evening and I came to know his family well. He and his wife have done just about everything the opposite way round from me: they were childhood sweethearts, married at university, and began their working lives in London together. She soon gave birth to a son, and then another. Occasionally I played football with their children, although the thought that I should be playing with my own sons never occurred to me.

This is the man who'd first offered me the opportunity at the marketing services company, even if he'd done his best to give me a hard time when I pitched up for the interview. I was already thirty and just back from a five-year holiday in the Spanish sunshine. It was the second interview and my idle prattle was taking me in the right direction until this straight-talking man leaned back into his chair and pinned me to the wall with a single thrust of well-honed steel: 'So tell me,' he said, as he examined the sole of his shoe for any vestiges of canine excrement, 'what's it like to be so old and to have achieved so little?' I can't remember what I said in response. What could I say? It was more of an observation than a question and the bastard had seen right through me.

As the train pulls into Kings Cross terminus, I tell Helena to take a close look at what our lives might have become had I not quit purely because no one was prepared to fire me. My old boss now lives in a listed cottage deep in a forest of ancient oak, while most of our lives are neatly contained by the two heavy suitcases I lug off the train for the short walk up the road to Euston station.

On the platform, his handshake is firm and his gaze steady. 'How's that midlife crisis coming along?' he says. 'Will it all end in suicide, or a tattoo on the arse and a nice little *Porsche*?'

I attempt a quick smile but it probably comes across as more of a grimace.

'Never mind,' he says, proffering a hand, 'let's have one of those bags.'

He may not be the most demonstrative of men, but his support in my darkest hours was unstinting and, as further evidence of his good nature, he takes Helena's arm with his free hand and helps her to board the train. As we settle into the mock-velour seats, my attention is drawn to a pair of large silver cufflinks which adorn his pinstriped shirt. He sees me staring and makes a half-hearted attempt to shuffle them under the sleeve of his jacket. I say nothing, not because I'm above mocking my old boss but because I feel guilty about modelling my film script villain on some of the more ruthless aspects of his character.

As the train pulls out of the station, I quiz him closely about the company I left exactly a year ago. He updates me with a few anecdotes about the colleagues and friends we've made around the world, before launching into a description of a number of ongoing structural changes at the company. It takes a little while before I notice him using the personal pronoun to describe the implementation of these initiatives and when I question him further, he clears his throat briefly before informing me that I am sharing the commute with the newly appointed global CEO.

The headache I've been assiduously developing on the train worsens as soon as I contemplate the luxurious stability he's constructed for the family at home. Their kitchen alone must be twice the size of our apartment back in Pigalle. Warming the whole of the ground floor, an *Aga* burns in the heart of the room and my misery only increases when a pan full of sizzling scallops is pulled from the hob and his wife drizzles them in a sauce of lime and chillies. They're so good that I ungraciously demand the recipe. I'm seriously lamenting this diversion to the land of what might have been and, by the time a sticky toffee pudding marches out of the *Aga* my head is throbbing with regret. All I want to do is to run back to Paris and hide under the duvet.

Somewhere in the outer solar system, 1970

In a cold sweat and full of fear, I'm awakened by a nightmare. I lie in the dark for a few moments and try to get my bearings. As my pulse begins to slow, the sinister vision gradually fades and I remember the frequent bouts of nocturnal anxiety I suffered as a child. Growing up, I was mortally afraid of the horrors that darkness would bring and, every night, I would read by the light from the staircase to delay the inevitable for as long as possible. But as soon as I put down my book and closed my eyes, that same awful vision would reveal itself, as if a malevolent spirit were projecting a black and deeply disturbing film onto the back of my eyelids:

I'm in space, unattached and in some kind of orbit above the earth's atmosphere. It's not particularly cold and I'm unaware of my body as it moves slowly through its trajectory; the surface of the planet far below. Without the assistance of gravity, I'm unable to control my drifting, which only adds to my terror as I float through the indigo silence. How did I come to be here in the first place? Am I alive, or already dead? The questions reverberate through me until I'm overwhelmed by a single thought: soon not a trace of me will remain – not one nerve, sinew or thought. I will cease to exist, even as a memory in my own family. My words will vaporise, my skin will shrivel and my bones will crumble away into nothingness...

I kept this nightmarish vision to myself. If it recurred during the day, which it often did, although without the same intensity of fearful awe, I would hurriedly dismiss it and turn my mind to such practicalities as cheating my way through mathematics at school. After all, there was nothing specific to be afraid of... unless you count death, of course – the granddaddy of all fears.

The long road back, November 1st

Unable to sleep, I join my former boss's sons in front of the TV for a quick update on the rugby, but even a dose of Saturday morning sport fails to stir me from my torpor. I notice how fast the boys are growing – their limbs are being pulled in every direction, their voices have broken and the shape of their faces is stretching into line with their nascent personalities.

A couple of hours later, I'm staring out of the window of the train as it re-emerges to torrential rain on the French side of the Channel. I've been dozing over the sports pages of *The Independent*, not because I'm tired but because I don't want to discuss my self-loathing with Helena. Now, coming back to full consciousness, I feel as if every mistake I've ever made has finally caught up with me here on the colourless fields of northern France. I reflect that this is the last day of Helena's second trimester and watch as a large orange sun sinks fast behind a veil of heavy grey cloud.

THE THIRD TRIMESTER

Paris, November 3rd

I begin the seventh month of pregnancy with a head cold and both feet firmly in the mud of the past. I pull the covers back over my head. Time has finally run out on me and I feel as if the last twelve months have been entirely consumed by my struggle with a thousand forms of self-defeating behaviour. Now I've got to go back to work with a full set of unrealised dreams. Is this all I've been fighting for these past months?

Helena brings me back to reality by pointing at a couple of appointments marked in red on our calendar: I'm due to see Mme Ferrat; and she's off to the nutritionist. Only Helena doesn't want to visit the nutritionist and I can't face the thought of a session with my feline counsellor. Since I last sat in front of that stainless steel expression of hers, I've done bugger all about my CV other than take it on a tour of the British Isles and I'm beginning to suspect that Mme Ferrat is getting frustrated with my lack of progress.

'I'm not going,' says Helena, her face a picture of the purest defiance.

'Oh, why not?' I venture, with a quick look at her belly.

'What's the point? I haven't done what he asked me to do?'

Sounds familiar. 'Which is what?'

'Prepare a list of what I eat in an average week.'

'I can help you with that. Come on, we'll do it now.' Anything to avoid sitting down with my own problems.

Helena looks less than enthusiastic as I draw up a list which I divide into four columns – one for each regular meal of the day, and another entitled *grignotage*, the delightful piece of onomatopoeia which serves as the French word for snacking. Helena circles the table, glaring over my shoulder at something she'd rather not allow into existence.

'How often do you eat chocolate biscuits?'

'I never eat chocolate biscuits!'

I stare at her incredulously. 'What?'

'I don't eat chocolate biscuits.'

This is not unlike me telling the Ferrat that I want a job and I'm trying my damnedest to find one. For the sweetest of moments, I allow myself to enjoy the pleasure of having a partner in denial. 'Let's say five days a week then, shall we?'

'Three,' says Helena.

'Four minimum, and I won't put down any quantities, OK?'

Silence. I fill in the relevant space on my list. 'Cake?'

'Never!'

'Three times a week?'

'Twice.'

'What about snacks at school?'

'No. Haven't got the time.'

'OK, only at home then.'

Half an hour later, once we've quibbled long and hard over every single one of the 500 varieties of French cheese, I hand the finished product to Helena. She then proceeds to haggle it down to something which looks reasonable, and might even be a nice idea, but bares very little relation to the truth. Never mind, the important thing is that she goes and hears the guy out. Then I go back to that other work of fiction, my CV.

Helena arrives home with a brand new list that's been sketched out by the nutritionist. It bears no resemblance to my portrait of her eating habits and words such as 'chocolate' and 'cake' are conspicuous only by their absence. The word cheese does make an appearance, but only when preceded by such unfamiliar phrases as 'thin slice of' or 'reduced fat'. Anyway, it matters little, as I'll never see the list again although every time I open the kitchen cupboard, a swarm of chocolate fingers leaps to the floor in an ill-fated attempt to escape the jaws of woman who never eats chocolate or cake.

The telephone rings. It's Dirk. He thinks he may have found the perfect job for me if only I'd stop protesting long enough to listen to what it entails. The company concerned is one of his clients based in Holland, although Dirk thinks I'd be able to do the job from Paris, London or even from the back of a rickshaw in China, since it involves a lot of travel. He instructs me to email my CV and my hopes rise a little until he tells me the name of the client. The product they want me to sell is a hoppy little beverage known as beer and, as my end of the line goes silent, Dirk wants to know whether that's going to be a problem. The job doesn't require me to drink the stuff, he explains, just to help push it to anyone, anywhere, with a bit of disposable income and a desire to change their perception of reality. I say I think it'll probably be OK and put down the phone.

By the time Helena asks me whether it's a good idea to work for a beer company, I've already prepared my answer. I think it'll be just fine, because I've just made the decision to start drinking again. Not much, mind you, just a couple of glasses of wine with dinner like everyone else.

Helena wants to know whether this has anything to do with the fact that I've been in a foul mood since our trip to London, and I reassure her that the two are quite unrelated. She looks at me hopefully and confesses that it would be nice if I could manage an occasional glass, although she appears to have her doubts. Not me – I'm already convinced. After all, I'm about to have a child in my life – something that will be even more important than me. I'm about to grow up, so of course I'll be able to restrain myself over cocktails and stick to a single glass of beer at even the happiest of hours. In my own effortless logic, therefore, it will not be a problem to get myself employed by a beer company.

All things considered, it's quite a speech and I round it off by telling Helena I'll be putting it all to the test later this week when my shellfish friend Tony arrives back in Paris. We've arranged to meet at a pub called the *Frog 'n' Rosbif*, where I shall enjoy two quiet beers and a civil conversation. I don't doubt my ability to stop at two and thus reinvent myself, overnight, as model of temperance.

The beast, November 6th

In fact, I don't quite make it all the way to the weekend before my resolve is put to the test. Tonight one of my favourite DJs is in Paris to play the *Styx*. After dinner, I put on one of his CDs, just to get in the mood. As the bass line hums through my belly, I feel that familiar buzz of anticipation, which I mistakenly put down to the music. Then I call a friend of Vincent's; someone I last saw slumped across a sofa somewhere in south-east London after an all-night party. We arrange to meet at the *Styx* and a couple of hours later, as Helena retires to bed, I slip silently through the front door and out into the night.

It's still early and I walk to the club which is no more than twenty minutes from our apartment. I decide to take the first of my two beers before entering the club. This is an excellent idea because it will be less expensive in a pub and it will soothe my jumping nerves. Makes sense, right? I stroll up and down the broad, damp boulevard which is home to the *Styx* and study the bars. My head is full of thoughts of the fuzzy conviviality I associate with such places the world over – that early evening laughter, the metallic tang as the magic liquid hits the back of the throat. Yet, as I peer through the windows of these neon-lit watering holes, they look neither warm nor welcoming. They're littered with shabby, unaccompanied middle-aged men, standing as if mesmerised at the bar and staring at rows of green bottles or filling in tickets for a lottery they'll never win. I walk up and down the street for a few minutes in the hope of stumbling upon a bar that will provide me with what memory promises. But I can't find even a facsimile and I'm forced to opt for a seedy joint directly opposite the *Styx*. I order a glass of German pilsner and leave the barman to pour it while I make for the toilets. As I reach the top of the stairs, a huge, unseen Alsatian springs to life and bares a full set of distinctly non-vegetarian teeth. Luckily the beast is chained to the floor, but I jump out of my shoes with shock all the same. The possibility that my rendezvous with this satanic beast may not be a coincidence doesn't even occur to me. Back at the bar, I sip at the first beer I've touched in quite a while. It tastes OK. Not great, just OK. Once I've emptied the glass, I replace it on the bar, pay my bill and leave. I feel no immediate desire or craving for another.

I'm one of the first to arrive at the *Styx* and the DJ is already playing a seductive mix of funk, house and electronic samba. I walk straight to the bar and order my second glass of beer. Sure enough, it costs me twice as much as the first, but that's OK since it'll be my last. I allow the sounds of Brazil, Chicago and New York to wash over me as the beer settles into my senses as easily as an aching foot reaches for the comfort of an old slipper. By the time Vincent's friend arrives, I've finished my beer. He apologises for being late and says he's going to the bar. He asks whether I'd like a drink. Well, yes, I would. I'd definitely like another beer, please.

Halfway through the evening I switch from draught something-or-other to bottles of *Kronenbourg 1664*. To be honest, I can't tell the difference in terms of the taste; I just prefer the way the bottle looks. I spend the rest of the night on the edge of the dance floor, watching and not daring to enter the fray.

The chemistry experiment, November 7th

I leave the *Styx* at four in the morning without feeling particularly drunk. I walk home for a bit of fresh air and

Helena fails to wake up as I slip into the bed beside her. When she gets up for work, I stir, but sleep on for a further two hours. When I do get out of bed, it's in the familiar, thick fog of a hangover. I blame it all on a lack of sleep and the fact that it's been weeks since I last had a drink. After a restorative brunch of bacon and eggs, I sit down and work on my script a little. Late in the afternoon, I leave home to meet up with Tony and I'm feeling a little better. Vincent is also in Paris this weekend, so I call and ask him to join us later in the evening. I do not question why I was unable to stick to my two-beer plan.

At the *Frog 'n' Rosbif*, I settle down with a newspaper and a large glass of *Pepsi*, which quickly kills the remains of my hangover. I know that when he arrives, Tony's first pint will disappear on its way from tap to table. The second I may glimpse briefly, but I figure I'll wait until he's calming down over a third before getting started myself. Meantime, my brain continues to operate quite independently of reason and years of experience. It tells me that Tony is a good, responsible father of two teenage daughters. Sure, he likes a beer, but he's not an alcoholic. He drinks when he has a reason to drink – when Crystal Palace lose a football match, for example (that way he can drink twice a week) – and he shows no sign of suddenly quitting a job, bolting to a foreign city and attempting to sell lamentable film scripts to Hollywood. He's a stable, practical man who enjoys an occasional beer, just like me.

Tony arrives half an hour late which gives me plenty of time to study the menu at the pub. Four different kinds of beer are brewed on the premises and before Tony has even removed his jacket, I hear myself suggesting a jug of *Inseine*. At no point does this strike me as anything other than entirely rational behaviour. Not even the name of the beer gives me a clue. Unlike the fizzy lager at the *Styx*, the ale actually tastes good. We fall into an easy conversation and it takes around half an hour to work our way to the bottom of the jug. Tony looks at his watch. We have a good couple of hours before he leaves for a flight back to London and his two daughters. When Tony suggests the *Dark de Triomphe* might be worth a try, we're right in the middle of a three-pronged conversation about the canyons of Arizona, England's chances of lifting the Webb Ellis trophy and the clarinet lessons of his eldest daughter. The realisation that I'm about to exceed my self-imposed two-pint limit for the second day in a row will not arrive until tomorrow morning.

By the time Vincent joins us, we've finished the second jug and commenced a third. We're back on the *Inseine* and I'm feeling pleasantly intoxicated. Just as it always has, the beer has released me from the confines of an awkward personality and transformed me into someone with opinions, self-esteem, purpose and a set of convictions (although I'll have misplaced all of these long before dawn).

Tony leaves. I polish off the jug. Vincent sits over his first pint of lager. I do most of the talking and he listens to a stream of my inconsequent thoughts. At eight o'clock in the evening, we leave the bar. Nicely warmed up from a reasonable two pints, Vincent's off to a party. I want to go with him before I remember dinner and Helena. From a phone box, I call home. She's on the line, so I leave a message. Outside the air is cool and the roads are busy. People are rushing home to prepare for the weekend. The tail lights of the traffic begin to blur in the inky black streets of Paris. I realise just how drunk I am. On the way home I look at my watch and wonder whether I have time for a last drink, on my own, in the bar directly opposite the metro exit. I've no idea how this thought worked its way into my head.

Helena and I eat the sausage casserole I'd prepared earlier in the afternoon. As far as I can tell, it doesn't taste of anything much. I drink a lot of water. We don't talk much over dinner although I do a bit of grinning, a lot of leering and then some washing up. Soon afterwards, I fall into bed unconsciousness.

I'm lying awake in bed. I don't know what time it is, but it must be very early. My head doesn't hurt, so I must still be drunk. There are three thoughts in my head and they're chasing each other around my skull like gerbils in an overcrowded cage. I allow them to continue for a few minutes before they begin to drive me mad. I get out of bed and stumble to the bathroom. I'm aware that someone is watching me from the mirror although I manage to avoid his eye. Then I go back to bed where sleep continues to elude me and the same thoughts haunt me like three lost souls in a state of eternal agitation: terror, bewilderment and despair – we are old friends.

I finally fall asleep again as the day starts to dawn cold and grey. An hour or so later Helena brings me a cup of tea and the news that the first of the Rugby World Cup quarter-finals is about to begin. Without drawing the curtains, I switch on the TV and begin watching listlessly. As the colours of their respective team jerseys start to merge into one, I'm barely able to distinguish where this game ends and the next begins.

I emerge for lunch and say little. 'You were drunk last night, weren't you?' says Helena. I nod. My hangover starts to kick in after lunch and the questions start to form in my mind like storm clouds gathering over the North Atlantic. Why had I not stopped after two pints? Why had it not even occurred to me? Is it worth continuing the attempt to control my drinking, or is the answer already obvious?

As Helena tries to catch up on the sleep which I disturbed last night, I commence work on the baby's room with a heavy heart. One by one I stow away plastic bottles full of chemicals as well as Helena's unfinished plates, bowls and goblets. Halfway through the afternoon, Vincent calls. He wants to know if I feel like a drink later this evening. I tell him I don't, and suggest that we meet in the morning to watch some more rugby. Then I go back to work, packing and sealing the cardboard boxes with heavy-duty tape. In the early evening Helena and I eat dinner together. Soon afterwards I collapse into bed and commence my search for some vermin-free sleep.

A decision, November 9th

This morning I do catch my eye in the bathroom mirror. I admit that we need to talk, but now's not the time. I've promised Mr Escalator I'll pitch up at his place to watch the French take on Ireland and, on the way there, I score a few croissants for breakfast. Young Agathe swings open the front door and joins us as we settle down for the *Marseillaise*. As the French punt the first ball deep into enemy territory, I notice how, now he has a daughter in his life, the Escalator is forced to do everything with one hand because the other one is constantly required to steer Agathe away from the prohibited objects to which she appears to be magnetically attracted. Bet that's difficult with a hangover, I observe silently, as the Irish are squeezed backwards under the pressure of another sustained French attack.

By the time Helena joins us, it's as good as over. If all goes to plan, *les bleus* will be meeting the English in one of the semi-finals next weekend. With Agathe snuggled safely at her mothers' breast, Helena and Inès start cooing over the baby and fall into a fascinating discussion about the molecular structure of panty liners, leaving me and the Escalator free to concentrate on Celtic attempts to salvage a bit of pride.

After the game, I put in a quick call to Vincent and we arrange to watch the England game at a nearby pub. Vincent orders a beer and I order coffee as we settle down to watch a plucky Welsh team take on the fearsomely unshaven English pack. Logic and forward momentum eventually overcome pride and gallantry, which means it must be time for me to go home and confess to Helena.

'It's over,' I say, slumping heavily into the sofa.

'What, the rugby?' asks Helena optimistically.

'No, not that. Not yet.'

'What, then?'

'The experiment.' I'm staring at a blank spot straight in front of me and having a great deal of trouble getting a few simple words out of my mouth.

'Have you been drinking again?'

'Not a drop. That's the point.'

'But the others must have been drinking while the game was on?'

'Yes, they were... ' I stop and swallow hard, turning to face Helena. 'But I'm not like the others.'

'What do you mean?'

'I can't just pick up one drink and then walk away from it.'

'Why not?'

'Because I'll always want another one.' Helena follows my gaze back to the vacant spot on the wall.

'It's over. I knew it as soon as I woke up this morning. I can't enjoy it if I try to control it.'

'So now you want to stop altogether?'

'No, but I don't have a choice.'

'Not even a glass of wine?'

'Not one.'

'Not even on special occasions?'

'Never.'

I review the emotions racing across Helena's face – sadness and fear, mixed with a little hope. I suspect her expression broadly mirrors my own.

After my capitulation, sitting here staring at a future without the transitory pleasures of the odd skinful, I was expecting to feel sorry for myself. But this proves not to be the case and a strange sense of relief descends upon me. I suppose it's because I've chosen not to continue my battle with alcohol or, to put it another way, the battle against myself.

'Who won, then?' asks Helena after a lingering silence.

For a moment, I'm thrown completely by her question. 'I don't know. Nobody, I guess.'

'The rugby, you fool!' Helena throws back her head and

starts hooting with laughter. God only knows what she can find to laugh about: First she shacks up with a man who's asked her to marry him. Then he reneges on the deal and admits to a drinking problem, but not before he's got her pregnant. And all she can do is laugh. What on earth is wrong with the girl?

Paris, November 11th

How long have I known, but refused to admit, that my drinking is out of control? A long time, I suppose, but my first line of defence was always to surround myself with people who drink as much if not more than I do. Now I realise that it has nothing to do with quantity and everything to do with the fact that I was drinking to escape reality, and this is what I've got to start dealing with this morning. I feel like a child crossing the border between two countries for the first time, expecting an immediate and dramatic change in landscape to go with the change of colours on the map. But the truth of it is, you're far more likely to find a local dispute between two farmers about where to draw the line in a field full of turnips.

Helena leaves for school, her stomach hardened by a series of intermittent contractions. I visit the *boulangerie* for a loaf of bread and shy away from the blonde with flour on her hands. Next I brew up a pot of coffee and eat exactly the same breakfast I did yesterday and the day before that, before settling down to check email. I have no messages from Hollywood producers aware of my decision and clamouring to read my script, nothing from the Archangel Gabriel to tell me I'm on the right track and nothing from Satan to tell me I'm not.

I shut down my favourite sports website and open up a few that are dedicated to finding gainful employment. Then I enlist the help of Isabelle to translate my CV into French. The Ferrat is waiting for me and I'm desperate to demonstrate at least a little progress by the time our next appointment rolls around, and preferably progress in French.

I find a couple of ads which are harder to ignore than usual. The first concerns a position in the marketing department of an American computer peripherals giant. It's well paid, based in Paris and exactly the kind of thing I swore I'd never do again. I print off the ad. The second is looking for a sports journalist whose mother tongue is English. Other than the tongue and a life spent buried under sporting statistics and superlatives, I have no qualifications for the job whatsoever, but I print that one off too and start drafting two letters of motivation. The first claims I'm desperate for a return to marketing services, the second that I'm desperate to escape. I guess the truth lies somewhere between the two.

Marketing men and women, November 12th

The week passes quickly and Isabelle rings every day with questions about my epic CV.

'What's a business plan?'

'It's an imaginary set of figures presented each autumn to your boss in the hope that the number of zeros will loosely correspond to the amount of profit needed to ensure something called 'full shareholder value' and thus guarantee senior management a very fat bonus. It requires the support of an article from the *Financial Times* on the state of the economy, which you probably haven't read, and which will need to be copy-pasted into the document.'

'What?' I appear to have confused, rather than clarified, matters for young Isabelle, who is unfamiliar with the machinations of bottom-line accountancy.

'Sorry,' she says, 'Can you say that a little more slowly?'

'It doesn't matter Isabelle, just leave it in English and surround it with inverted commas.' Her relief is audible.

'What's a focus group discussion?

Ah, the focus group discussion – the one part of my earlier life that I really enjoyed. For those of you who are not familiar with the way in which companies and governments run their daily business once they run out of ideas, please let me explain. The action takes place on either side of a one-way mirror through which the marketing men or government technocrats are watching a table full of consumers (otherwise known as people or human beings). They've been invited to discuss their reactions to a new type of roasted fish finger or the proposed plan to further erode their civil liberties. On one side of the mirror, the put-upon citizen is given a hard time by someone in the pay of the client (like me), whose job it is to expose the process she goes through when choosing between two different brands of fish finger at her local supermarket. For example, 'If eight-year-old Johnny enjoys his reconstituted fish nuggets at both lunch and dinner, why is that you mummies doesn't yield to the pressure and start feeding him the tasteless little yellow pellets with a bit of extra sugar at breakfast time?' As far as the man hiding behind the mirror is concerned, the idea is to find some kind of hook upon which the boys at the ad agency can hang a new tagline and a bit of their dirty washing: *New recipe Turd 'n' Dye fish balls – in a convenient new formula which requires no processing by any part of your intestines!*

On the other side of the mirror, the marketing man is munching his way through a lifetime's supply of peanut *M&Ms* and cursing the wretched housewife for her futile resistance to his plan to eliminate unprofitable green vegetables from the diet of all schoolchildren. He's convinced himself that his product is the *Rolls Royce* of fish fingers and the reason he believes this is because he's spent the last five years of his life sending out messages to precisely that effect. So he can't understand why one of the women on the other side of the mirror is poisoning her peers with her unwanted use of initiative and questioning the lexicon of E-numbers his design people have so cleverly hidden on the back of the pack. That's the problem with real housewives, you see: their heads are so full of bringing up children, shopping, cleaning and generally making ends meet, that they never find the time to sit down and fully appreciate the genius of the advertising industry.

'I'm not sure what you call them in French, Isabelle. Just put 'studies of consumer psychology and motivation', or something like that.'

'I still don't understand what it is that you do,' says Isabelle, once I tell her we've finished.

'Don't worry about that,' I reply. 'You're not supposed to.'

If I'm honest, I'd rather be paid to watch and write about sport, or the other great male obsessions, than help ruin the health of future generations of children by flogging them reconstituted fish droppings or snacks which search endlessly for the perfect combination of salt and sugar. On the other hand, the little fellow may prefer to have his fish fingers on the table in front of him, rather than hearing about them from his friends at school and starving to death while Daddy wages his pointless war against a tidal wave of consumerism. So I finish both letters and it takes me the rest of the week.

The invention of road signs, November 13th

It's autumn in the Bois de Boulogne, and the paths which criss-cross this patch of fading brown and green are strewn with rotting vegetation. The mass of featureless corporate towers at La Défense is already visible through the trees which are hurriedly making their preparations for winter. Beneath me the ground is soft and I can smell the mud as it's stirred up by the knobbly tyres revolving beneath me. There's an agreeable smell in the air, which I can't quite place but, for some reason, it encourages me to crank up the speed of my bike.

Out in the fresh air, my plan had been to think through my employment situation and decide whether to continue my pursuit of the past or wait for the green shoots of spring and a better idea. But, as I leave behind the limits of the city, the sense of release is so intense that any such thoughts evaporate through the aerodynamic holes in my helmet and leave me free to concentrate on negotiating the half-hidden tree stumps under the leaf fall. There's that smell again. I search the remains of my memory but still it escapes me.

I follow a stream, which cuts its way through a flat, and no doubt incredibly valuable, piece of Parisian real estate. There's no wind at all today and the surface of the water is as unruffled as a politician in possession of a perfect alibi. I watch my surroundings fly past in the reflective meniscus of the stream alongside. I can see tiny birds flitting from branch to branch and can almost hear the sigh of the heavy beech and oak trees as they unburden themselves of a few more skeletal leaves.

Eventually I emerge from the wooded area onto the fringes of the expansive racecourse at Longchamps. The last time I was here, the place was throbbing with the excitement generated by Europe's richest horserace, *le Prix de l'Arc de Triomphe*. I can't tell you who won – I was watching from the wrong side of the fence as the leaders tore past and all those electric silks were sucked back into the vortex of raincoats, betting slips and desperate men pissing their pants in the main grandstand.

But today Longchamps is silent and I'm thinking how, as a kid, I just about lived on my bicycle. I remember the Italian ten-speed racer bought for me out of the blue by my parsimonious father. It must have cost him more than he could really afford, but for a while I had the best bike in town. Then I remember all that other stuff I did as a kid, like stealing sweets when I thought the shopkeeper wasn't watching, playing football in the mud with my friends, or sneaking downstairs to watch a film late at night in the hope of glimpsing a breast exposed by some careless actress. Only alone, on the cycle tracks of my home town, did I truly feel whole. On how many occasions did I race home against the best that professional cycling had to offer? Sometimes they would beat me home for tea, but when it really mattered, they never quite had the legs. With the front gate in sight, I'd push hard on the pedals and put in a finish of such devastation that many of the all-time greats were left gasping in my wake. My progress is statelier today but I've finally realised what that smell is – a mixture of damp bark, decaying leaves and muddy knees – the smell of my youth.

Childhood was not a place I ever really wanted to leave. From an early age, I was determined to keep the whole business of growing up at a safe distance. While others were honing their life skills by rebelling, fighting, arguing, tasting both victory and defeat and generally meeting life on its own terms, I did all in my power to avoid it altogether. At the age of sixteen, I finally found the ally I needed for the war I planned to wage on the world – the one I'd been waiting for all along – alcohol. Here was an invisible, magical substance that evened out my mood swings, gave me a confidence I had not earned and permitted me to talk to those mysterious and beautiful creatures called women.

It was there for me whenever I called for help. In whatever form it took, this mildly poisonous compound always furnished me with what I needed, whether it was a bit of courage or a modicum of professional success. But I also moved country every three or four years and my relationships lasted only as long as it took for my girlfriend of the day to see through the veneer behind which I hid the deeply shamed child inside.

While others would nurse a medicinal morning pint, I'd lay off for a day or so, and it was this ability to stop temporarily which became my excuse and enabled me to draw an imaginary line between myself and the unshaven man with the jitters and no awareness of the way he's perceived by the rest of the world.

Barely five days before I locked myself behind my mother's bathroom door with Helena and that pregnancy testing kit, I'd boarded a train for London, where Helena was to join me at the weekend. When I arrived in London on the

Wednesday evening, Vincent's birthday party was already underway and it continued, in a blur of booze and stimulants, with very little in the way of food or other unwanted interruptions, until I awoke on the floor at Cousin Nathalie's four days later. I have almost no memory of what I'd said or to whom I'd said it. The only certainty is that I'd come out of a blackout as Jonah was driving me home and I spent half the night bending his ear with a flurry of slurred and unconnected words which dropped unchecked from my wine-stained lips.

Helena's face, as she peered down at my limp and broken body the next morning remains unforgettable. She wore an expression of disgust, fear and disbelief and, reflected in her pupils, I saw a rough sketch of what I'd become. I instantly knew it was time to end the only relationship to which I'd ever been true, but which now threatened destruction. But I didn't know where to start? Part of the answer would come later that day. I wouldn't know it for another few hours, but Helena was already pregnant.

Why ears are of more use than eyes in the dark, November 14th

Helena and I share a dinner of calf's liver and spinach, a dish rich in blood and iron, and perhaps this is what prompts my dream: I'm in a hospital corridor as Helena gives birth in the delivery room. I should be in there with her but for some reason I'm unable to persuade my legs across the threshold. They are as heavy and inflexible as two pieces of Victorian lead piping. By the time I do get into theatre, the birth is over and my son is already sitting up in bed beside Helena. He has a very large and beautiful head and I'm listening to him as he talks. Talks? Yes, he's quite calmly and rationally stringing together entire sentences and addressing them to me. I don't understand how this can have happened, but it fills me with a sense of sadness and loss. How is it possible that I've already missed part of my son's life and become an absent father?

I wake up and immediately put my hands on Helena's belly.

'What are you doing?' she asks, unused to me making unprompted contact with our son.

'I don't know... I had a dream.'

'About him?'

'Yes. Is he awake?'

'He always wakes up when he hears your voice.'

Instinctively I withdraw my hands from Helena's belly.

'Yes. Put your hands back. You should be able to feel him kicking.'

Sure enough, I can feel a full series of hard wallops under the surface of the skin.

'He hears everything we're saying, you know.'

I give Helena the same look that Pythagoras must have got when he first conjectured the earth wasn't flat. 'You really think so?'

'I know so.'

'How's that then?'

'Some of the women who've already given birth at the hospital bring their babies to prenatal chanting. The minute the babies hear the singing, they start to smile.'

I give Helena that look again.

'It's true. Come and see for yourself.'

'To prenatal chanting?' I ask, as if I had a particularly sharp fish bone stuck in my throat.

'Some of the other fathers are there.'

'They are?' I allow my fingers to fall from Helena's belly and think of everything else he may have heard, lying there, ear cocked in the womb.

Injury time in the Hundred Years War, November 15th

I'm slow to gather speed as I hop back and forth between the usual tasks – making coffee, email, the fruitless search for unexplained cheques in the post-box, the daily list of 'to do' items which will never get done, and the long periods of solitude. Helena's frustration at the way I spend my days is growing and she explains it in clear, uncomplicated language – she'd like me to sort out the future, but not at the expense of the here and now. I may be physically present at mealtimes but I'm not exactly effusive and certainly not good company. When I do talk, it tends to be about the past or some hazy, promised land in an ill-defined future or the imminent match between England and France.

We'll be watching the game in Caen, although Helena's parents don't know it yet. Hopefully the interest in their daughter's pregnancy will mean they fail to notice me spending hours on the sofa screaming at the TV. As I prepare a bag for the weekend, I resist the temptation to pack all my isolationist paraphernalia – laptops, literature on addiction, and full colour pull-outs from *L'Equipe*. Besides, Helena and I need to talk – about what I've no idea, as she hasn't told me yet. But I'd better watch my language, just in case you-know-who is tuned in.

In Caen, I try to turn my mind from the game and to focus on Helena, my son and his grandparents. After dinner, as we idle beside a log fire, someone proposes a game of *Scrabble* and I foolishly agree to play. But because my French vocabulary extends about as far as a family of frogs with their feet tied together, I'm to be allowed to make use of an enormous French dictionary. Not that I expect this to help me in any extravagant fashion.

I pull seven letters from the bag and two of them are the letter 's'. The rest are a series of consonants from which I couldn't compose a word in Serbo-Croat, never mind French. For the first couple of rounds, I'm content to tack an 's' on to the end of words composed by other players. But, by the fourth or fifth round, it's getting embarrassing and I still have a 'j', a 'z' and a couple of other letters that I didn't even know were legal tender in France. The only French word I know containing a 'z' is Charles Aznavour and not that there's much hope of getting that little lot down on the triple letter, even if my opponents did take pity on me and accept a proper name. I find a small hole in which to insert the 'j' next to an 'e'. Terrific stuff! One year in Paris and my vocabulary extends no further than a simple personal pronoun. My effort draws a little sympathetic applause from the other players but I want to crawl into a darkened hole, because I happen to be a highly competitive bastard who always wants to win, whether at *Scrabble*, conkers or polishing shoes.

Mercifully, Helena's father puts me out of my misery when he lays down a quadruple-counting, sixteen-syllable snorter that ends on a triple letter and pulverises everyone else into the dust. I'm left with my 'z' and a large number of other high-scoring letters which are duly deducted from my meagre score. The final result:

Helena's father (representing France): 16½ million points
Helena (France): 137
Helena's mother (France): 126
Me (United Kingdom): minus 52

After a trouncing of such proportions, I'm smarting and run straight upstairs to bed in the hope that, tomorrow morning, fifteen Englishmen will extract revenge against the entire French nation on my behalf.

A slippery surface in Sydney, November 16th

I'm up early and I'm very nervous. Helena's father is already at the breakfast table. He mentions neither the rugby nor last night's *Scrabble* (in his place, I'd be boasting well into the next millennium) and, for some strange reason, he wants to start a conversation about sweaters.

'Do you like that sweater?' he asks me.

I've got half an eye and all of my attention fixed on a

copy of this morning's edition of *L'Equipe* and jump to the conclusion that Helena's father is talking about the rugby jersey, as modelled by the French fly-half on the cover of the newspaper.

'Apparently it's more aerodynamic and prevents you being tackled too easily,' I say.

'What?'

After last night, I've lost any remaining confidence in my ability to converse in a foreign language. I'm sure that I've used the right word for 'tackle' (the bone-crunchingly descriptive verb '*plaquer*') because all I've been doing for the past few weeks is listening as the French commentators describe Fijians, Samoans and Romanians getting splattered over the arenas of the Antipodes. Maybe the problem is my pronunciation of the word 'aerodynamic'? So, while Helena's father dips a croissant into his coffee, I repeat the word in an accent worthy of Peter Sellers: '*a–e–e–e–e–r–o–o–d–y–n–a–m–i–q–u–e–e–e!*'

I wish I'd thought of that one at the *Scrabble* board and, to add to the effect, I make like an aeroplane with my outstretched arms. Helena's father quietly puts down what remains of his breakfast. He stares at me thoughtfully for a couple of moments (or perhaps for as long as he can bear), but says nothing. At this point, Helena appears in the doorway, looking decidedly unaerodynamic. She's wearing the new sweater that her mother bought for her yesterday in the Saturday crowds of Caen.

Suddenly it all falls into place. I stare at Helena's sweater and start to gibber just as Helena's father registers the cover of *L'Equipe*. Without saying another word, he picks up his raincoat and heads to the market for fresh fruit and vegetables.

'Wait a minute!' I cry. 'You mean *that* sweater... ' But he's already gone and is now no doubt mightily relieved that I never got round to marrying his daughter.

'What's wrong with my sweater?' asks Helena.

The broadcast from Sydney kicks off with the French

commentator telling a joke he has prepared especially for the occasion: 'What's the difference between the English and the French?' he asks a colleague back in Paris. I can think of a million ways to answer this before breakfast, but please do enlighten us... 'The French are arrogant and they know it, while the English are arrogant and they don't'. Cue general snuffles of amusement via satellite as we settle down for kick-off. Helena watches as the game kicks off. Forgetting entirely that there are now three, rather than two of us watching this game, I curse loudly, pace the room unnecessarily and, as the French take the lead, start to trash the sofa. Helena's father comes back from the market and wants to know if everything is alright. Out of the corner of my eye, I glimpse something resembling pity on his face as he contemplates the scene, but then he's off again to polish the apples and pears he's bagged down at the market. Meantime, back in Sydney, it's suddenly started to pour with rain which is a godsend for the English (for obvious reasons) and terrible news for the French.

Sure enough, the English gradually mud wrestle their way into the lead and, by the time it's all over, the French commentators are not quite as perky as they were before kick off. Their gloomy post-mortem focuses on the inclement weather patterns of the southern hemisphere. 'It's not fair,' one of them whines, 'the ball was as slippery as an eel and we couldn't play our natural game.' Oh, what's that then? Beach bloody volleyball? Well tough luck, my little froglet, this is rugby and sometimes it gets played in the rain, especially, I feel obliged to admit, in that murky little kingdom which lies between Cornwall and Carlisle. While the English players are gracious in victory and walk off the pitch without any undue celebration, I spend three hours high-strutting it around the living room and struggle to resist an urge to get straight on the phone to the Escalator.

By the time I've calmed down, lunch is on the table. Helena's father has scored some spectacular oysters, which are to be washed down with a shallot and vinegar sauce and a bottle of Alsace. In my excitement, I glance at the bottle and reach for its scrawny French neck before, with a grimace, I remember all over again.

For the rest of the day I try to behave like one of the more highly evolved apes and support my efforts by trying to avoid further grammatical errors or lengthy outbreaks of crude gesticulation. In the afternoon, we jump into the car and drive to the beach. The skies are clear and I look out to sea, where I half expect to see England celebrating on the far side of waters the colour of dulled gun metal. The last time I was here it was with David and Lily and I can picture them now, buried up to their necks in the sand in the belief that the summer would never come to end. But now a biting wind is whipping across the beach and we pull our woollen scarves tight around our ears.

Keen to avoid any further rounds of *Scrabble,* I ask Helena to help me translate my letters of motivation while her parents liberate the rest of their living room from the sweat, mud and tears left by the passage of the rugby.

'Helena, How do you say, 'I'm perfectly fluent in French'?'

'You mean in English?'

'No, I know how to say it in English. How do I say it in French?'

'Why do you want to say that you're fluent in English, in French?'

'I don't. I want to say fluent in French, in French.'

'Are you?'

'No'

'Why do you need to say it then?'

'Because I'm trying to get a job and that's what I'm expected to say'

'Isn't it better to tell the truth?'

'In a letter of motivation? Are you mad? If I tell them the truth, I'll be locked up for so long that our son won't recognise his father in anything other than Her Majesty's standard issue.'

'Well, if you're sure... '

Slowly we work our way through my all-purpose, self-adjusting letter of motivation and Helena dutifully translates the assortment of lies that I've included in it. These include an explanation of my unemployment that references unspecified personal projects and study at one of the more 'esteemed Parisian educational establishments', which, hopefully, sounds like a year spent in the library of the Sorbonne and not that evening film course at the Star Spangled University of McBush (for which the only entry requirements were a cheque for several hundred Euros and bugger all else to do on a Tuesday evening). Then I seal the letters in an envelope with my CV and slam dunk the whole lot into a bright yellow letter box in Caen.

The effects of pregnancy on the human intellect, November 17th

I'll admit to feeling vaguely disappointed that there's no letter waiting on the doorstep when we get home, although I'm in no way prepared to connect this with the quality of my application. Maybe that post box was a fire hydrant, after all? Anyway, there's no time to reflect upon any of this as another job opportunity announces itself almost immediately.

It comes from a man I've never heard of, let alone met, who wants to discuss with me what he insists upon describing as 'a fantastic opportunity'. He tries explaining it over the phone but I catch only a few disconnected words: '*innovative front-end methodologies*', '*rock-hard software solutions*', '*envisioneering mindsets*', and '*ongoing HR support*'. I think he also mentions the French equivalent of 'a piece of piss' although I wouldn't swear to that. None of these words mean anything to me in isolation, let alone when all strung together within the uncomfortably narrow confines of a single telephone call. But when I discover that these duties are to be performed in Toulouse, I hear myself agreeing to meet the mystery man just as soon as I can.

Almost before I've put down the phone, Dirk is on the

line from Holland. He wants me to know that Carla is pregnant and before I can finish offering my services as a midwife, I suddenly realise what he's trying to tell me.

Carla is two and a half months gone and, in his finest guttural Dutch, Dirk is just a little overexcited about the whole thing. He knows that it's way too soon to be telling anybody and, in particular, he's been instructed not to tell me, but as it appears to have slipped out, he makes me promise I won't tell Helena (who, as you will remember, guessed that this news would not be long in arriving). Naturally I promise not to breathe a word to anyone.

'I'm to-tally excited,' Dirk repeats for sixth time since I picked up the phone all of thirty seconds ago. But I have a number of things to do this morning other than measure Dirk's incredible shrinking vocabulary, so I repeat my congratulations and tell him I'll be back in touch soon about the job.

'Dat's to-tally great,' burbles the Dutchman, 'and please say hello to Helena.'

'I will, Dirk, I will.'

At this precise moment, Helena enters the room. 'Who was that?'

'Dirk.'

'How is he?'

'He's totally... He's good. And Carla's pregnant!' Shit! The secret's out already.

'Pregnant? I knew it!' Helena performs a quick piece of mental arithmetic. 'It must have happened when they were here in Paris!'

'I guess. Look, Helena, she's only two and half months gone and we're not supposed to know. Please don't say anything to anyone.'

'Of course I won't!' says the woman who broadcast our own news across the globe while I was still enjoying a post-coital cigarette.

'And how does Dirk feel about it?'

'He's... I think you should ask him yourself.'

Helena purrs back out of the room and I'm left to compare Dirk's reaction to the news with my own all those months ago. Suddenly I feel like calling him back and telling him to be careful what he says because the baby is already listening. Then I think better of it. After all, he might want to know why the prospect of big-eared babies fills me with fear and anyway, I like to think my attitude has improved since we found out that Helena was pregnant (even if my behaviour has not).

'Cheri!' My daydreaming is interrupted by the call from Helena's operational headquarters, formerly known as our bedroom.

'Yes?'

'What are you doing?'

'Working.'

'Come and look at this!'

I open the bedroom door onto a familiar scene – Helena is stretched out on the bed with her sweater rolled up to her breasts, revealing a couple of hectares of skin pulled taught across her spherical belly. I can't believe there are another two months to go (leaving plenty of time for the fearless father to turn back into a rabbit pissing its hind legs with fear).

Helena places my palm against a stomach that's being stretched to breaking point by another contraction.

'I can't move.'

'Why don't you call the hospital?'

'I did. They said it's normal.'

'What's normal – that your body is trying to expel him ahead of schedule?

'I just have to stay horizontal.'

'Well, that shouldn't be too arduous for you, should it now?

'Yes, but I'd like a cup of tea.'

'I see.'

'And I was wondering if there were any of those biscuits left?'

'I expect most of them fled the country when they read

the nutritionist's list, but I'll have a look.'

As the kettle boils in the kitchen, I ponder the onset of Helena's contractions, as well as the improbable geometry of her belly. It seems to me there are but two possibilities here – either the hospital has got her dates completely wrong or she's been seriously overdoing the chocolate digestives.

If there's one thing I'm looking forward to more than the Rugby Cup final, it's the end of Helena's pregnancy and not only because I'm hoping it will put an end to all the washing up and other household tasks that need to be performed vertically and therefore by me. No, it goes so much further than that. As the pregnancy progresses, the focus of our lives has narrowed to such an extent that it now covers an area no wider than Helena's expanding belly. It's almost as if, at the precise moment X met Y, she lost interest in all activities other than her internal plumbing and formal high tea. First her ceramics studio fell into disuse and then she ditched most of her non-pregnant friends. Not long after that, shopping fell by the wayside (unless we were in the immediate vicinity of a toy shop or an outlet of *Gap for the As Yet Unborn*). Next to go was the cinema, something she used to adore. Now even my suggestion that we pick up an old black and white favourite from the video shop is met with a disinterested shrug of the shoulders. Our conversation, which once ranged freely from the metaphysical and miraculous to the astoundingly trivial, has narrowed to precisely one subject. OK, so there are plenty of variations on the theme – his name, the colour of his eyes, whether he'll support England or France, become an atomic scientist, invent a new style of jazz trumpet or content himself with a career as a chartered accountant – but in the end, it all boils down to the one subject.

Of course, I've yet to say any such thing to Helena. What's the point? It would be tantamount to suggesting that he's anything less than the epicentre of the known universe. Perhaps it's just hormonal. (And what the hell are these hormones anyway? Amino acids? Talkative little pieces of protein and peptide, or merely a string of bad jokes that take nine months to fade from the memory?) I've no idea, but I do know that our son, not satisfied with occupying virtually the whole of her body, has now infiltrated her brain and is beginning to distort her memory. Even when he does leave his starter home and takes up residence in the physical world of reality TV and bite-size *Twix* bars, Helena won't be delivered back to me as automatically as a piece of registered mail. Oh no, I have no such illusions. What has been, up until now, a lump in the belly, a suggestion, an unseen and almost abstract presence, is about to come howling into existence and demand not only the rapt and undivided attention of his mother, but also that of the unruly collection of ribosomes and other genetic material which goes by the name of '*Papa*'.

All of which reminds me that if I'm serious about my progression from swamp animal to employable parent, then I'd better get back to work. I have a job interview on Friday and I've done precisely nothing to prepare for it other than search for a clean shirt. Nobody wears a tie to an interview any more, do they?

Trains, boats and a German car, November 21st

I set off in plenty of time for my appointment, which is just as well, because the metro isn't working and only thing running south today is a large colony of rats. This leaves me freezing my nuts off at some unfinished bus shelter in the south of Paris, where I'm trying to decipher an upside-down map of bus routes for what looks like another city altogether and I'm already fashionably late for my appointment at an agency that's in direct competition with my previous employer (i.e. one about which I've been making snide remarks for over a decade).

Fifteen minutes later, my bus dumps me at an industrial

wasteland on the lower reaches of the Seine and I'm forced to swim the remaining three miles. But I needn't have worried about being late because there's plenty of time to remember that the French invented not turning up on time as I sit in the waiting room and sip tepid mineral water from a giant upside-down bottle. Waiting for the boss, I study what I've been missing this past year, as gaunt employees hurry past under enormous weights of paper. Two minutes later they're hurrying back in the opposite direction, bearing what looks suspiciously like the same load. The phone hasn't stopped ringing since I arrived, but nobody seems concerned enough to answer it. The place smells of stale, recycled air and everyone here wears a pained expression, conveying equal measures of martyrdom, necessity and disgust.

Just as I'm on the verge of getting to my feet and making a run for the exit, the boss arrives to greet me. He's wearing a suit but no tie and I loosen mine surreptitiously as he ushers me back towards the lift. 'Would you prefer to speak in English or French?' he asks. Recklessly, I tell him it's all the same to me and sure enough, the little bastard chooses French. This is a huge strategic error on my part and the job is probably lost before we're even back on the ground floor. Nonetheless, he's polite enough to take me for a ride in an enormous white Mercedes and then for lunch on an old barge on the river.

I hate interviews, especially interviews that start in cars. Before the first question has even been asked, you have to decide whether it's appropriate to wear your seat belt. If you do put the damned thing on, you can be as sure as hell that it will be interpreted it as a lack of confidence in the boss's driving. If you don't, chances are he'll detect an overly cavalier attitude or a lazy mind. In the end, I decide not to wear it, on the grounds that I need to demonstrate utter fearlessness as one of my myriad qualities. But as soon as the *Mercedes* reaches 100 kph in a steaming, narrow side street packed with bikes and delivery vans, I start fumbling for the buckle.

Bad move, I reflect, as the interview has not even begun in earnest and I'm already exuding indecisiveness from every pore in my body (as well as an acrid reminder that I forgot to coat myself in deodorant this morning).

Our chat is as idle as chat can be when you're travelling faster than *Concorde* in a busy street with priority from the right. Miraculously, we arrive at the restaurant in no more than just the two pieces and I still appear to be in with a chance of a) keeping most of my breakfast where it belongs, b) being present for the birth of my son, and c) getting a job cleaning the office toilets. The restaurant is full of businessmen paying for their lunches with other people's money and the tablecloths are so white that you feel obliged to tip the waiter just for showing you to your seat.

'Wine?' asks the boy racer as he forces the menu into my increasingly sweaty paws. Shit! What do I tell him? That if I take as much as a glass, I won't make it home in time for Christmas? But a diminished voice inside tells me not to panic and says,

'Not for me, thanks. I'll have some water. But you go ahead'.

I begin to relax somewhere between a carpaccio of cod starter and an unwisely chosen rack of lamb (getting your knife between all these ribs may exhibit attention to detail alright, but the jus in which it's been cooked doesn't look great on my off-white shirt). Fortunately, it turns out that the man spent four years working in London, so he's only too happy to switch into English over dessert and the really difficult questions. Then he explains that he's only just joined the company himself and he's interested to know what I'd do in his shoes (no idea – drive a little more slowly perhaps?). Then he wants to know what I see as the major challenges facing the marketing sector. Well, there's my little film script for starters – that should blow the lid off the whole industry.

After a rather stunning chocolate cake which the waiter

drowns in a raspberry coulis, he confesses that he doesn't actually have a job to offer me, although he'd like us to stay in touch. Untruthfully, I say that's fine by me and the conversation drifts back to last weekend's rugby match. Since there seems little immediate chance of employment, I decide it's safe to gloat a little and look forward to tomorrow's final. He takes this in reasonable cheer and picks up the bill. Two hours later, he's had a break from his problems at the office and we've both had a good lunch. I may still be unemployed, but the obsequious waiter seems happy with his tip and only the tablecloth seems to have come out of the deal any the worse. I'm offered a lift to the station, but decide this would be pushing my luck just a little too far. God knows whether he made it back to the office – I've heard nothing from him since.

On the way home, I realise that I'm relieved that I won't have to contend with an offer. But why? Because I never want to go back to that world, or because I'm too busy creating my own? There's still the interview with that guy from Toulouse, although God alone knows what that's all about. At least it has nothing to do with marketing and, if nothing else, it will give me a bit more interview practice and my suit another airing. But before I start thinking about any of this too deeply, I remember the copy of *L'Equipe*, which is rattling around in an otherwise empty briefcase and spend the rest of the journey completing my analysis of the big game.

Life by satellite, World Cup final day

I'm watching the game at Russell's place, although I'm surprised he didn't throw his TV into the Seine when the All Blacks got knocked out of the tournament. But when I called to commiserate after the semi finals, the wounds were already healing and he offered to cook up a fried breakfast for the final.

I don't know Russell so well, although I do feel a certain

kinship with him. Like me, he came to Paris to live with a French woman and, like me, I don't think he knew what he was letting himself in for. We both arrived here with inane grins and French vocabularies that stretched no further than *je t'aime*. Now he's about to get married and, unlike me, he has yet to show any signs of backing out.

I pitch up at Russell's place with a sacrificial baguette and the expression of a small insecure boy who's about to be caned by a bullying headmaster.

'Confident?' he asks.

'No.'

'Why not? England are the favourites.'

I could tell him why not, of course, but I don't feel like spending the morning reliving decades of abject national failure at major sporting events. 'So was Goliath,' I say moodily, 'and look what happened to him.'

'Confident?' This time it's Ophélie, Russell's future wife and every inch the cool Parisian sophisticate. It's still early in the morning and she emerges from the bathroom wrapped a white towelling bathrobe, although I don't find it too hard to picture her stepping straight off the pages of *Vogue*.

'No.'

'Oh, why not?' Her smile is relaxed and urbane.

'I'm just hopeful, that's all.'

Ophélie looks at me with a hint of concern, wondering why on earth a grown man might look so worried about a rugby match. I saw that same look not twenty minutes ago when I kissed Helena goodbye with an expression that suggested I was heading for the trenches in 1914.

You'd have to be a vestal virgin, a Benedictine monk or a French rugby player not to know how the game ends, or quite possibly all three. I'm still glued to the sofa and watch in silence as the English begin their celebrations. I feel no exhilaration and I'm tired. In fact, I'm exhausted. I think briefly about the thousands of hours I've misspent watching sport on television. String them all together and it probably amounts to several years. Another mind-numbing addiction to add to the list.

When I get home, Helena opens the door, takes one look at my face and assumes that England have lost. I try to explain, but the words refuse to form properly in my mouth and adhere to my lips as spittle and foam. I stumble into our bedroom, lie down and fall asleep.

When I wake up the world hasn't changed. I'm still unemployed and Helena is still pregnant. It's late on Saturday afternoon, normally about the time that I'd switch on the *BBC World Service* and listen to the football results. But not today. Rather than fuelling my life-long interest in sport, the victory has had the opposite effect. I couldn't care less and pick up a book. I stop reading only when my eyes close once more.

A drug called work, November 24th

In my dream, I'm starting work again. Someone with a blank where there should be a face shows me to a massive mahogany desk in an open-plan office. The company bears the same name as the organisation I used to work for, although the building is unfamiliar and I don't recognise any of the people here. I'm determined to work hard and settle down behind my desk to make a start, secure in the knowledge that I won't let a second opportunity slip away. Then I sense, rather than see, another employee arriving late. I glance up with the intention of introducing myself before getting to grips with the two hefty volumes of data, under the weight of which the old wooden desk is groaning. It's Vincent. He's grinning widely and sweating only slightly. He offers to show me around the premises and, reluctantly, I follow him out of the building. Out by the car park, he shows me a huge piece of manufacturing plant. It looks like a recycling machine and some of the employees are climbing inside it.

'Get in,' says Vincent.

'No.'

'Come on, you'll enjoy it.'

'What is it?'

'Don't worry about that, just get in!'

'Look Vincent, I came here to work. I don't want any of this.'

'Suit yourself,' says Vincent, inserting a liquid capsule into the front of the machine. Then he clambers into a huge open valve at the front of the plant as I watch from below. Soon I see Vincent floating through the transparent piping of the machine, as if suspended in some unctuous fluid or floating weightlessly in space. He's smiling and is quite clearly high – the liquid must have some sort of psychoactive properties. I watch for what feels like an hour, feeling less and less comfortable, before Vincent pops out at the other end of the machine. He grins and his eyeballs resettle into their sockets. 'You sure you don't want to try?'

Life, death and all the little bits in between, November 25th

Back on planet earth, I'm jolted awake by Helena. The frequency of her contractions is increasing and I place a hand to her stomach which is as hard a school trigonometry exercise. After breakfast, she calls the hospital and they instruct her to come in for an examination. I'm feeling heavy and more than a little jumpy, and I don't know whether it's down to the dream, the contractions, the thought of the past or fear of the future. After lunch, I go for a bike ride, but it's too soon after eating and my legs feel heavy and my chest is tight. I can't find any kind of a rhythm and return home feeling dead beat rather than relaxed.

Before we can leave for the hospital, we are forced to wait for Helena's brother to return the car he borrowed for the morning. He's late and Helena is getting annoyed, which only serves to worsen her contractions and heighten her anxiety. We call little brother, who's still eating lunch in a brasserie on the other side of Paris. Helena shoots off something which doesn't sound a lot like sisterly love and snaps shut her mobile. I doubt that little brother will be enjoying a leisurely coffee with his dessert. We call the hospital again and they want to know why we've waited so long. If you're having contractions, matron explains, you should be making your way to the hospital without stopping for so much as a pee. This winds Helena even tighter and my attempts to calm her down are becoming more and more futile.

Half an hour later, little brother finally pulls to a halt outside our apartment building. I slide silently into the drivers' seat and he gets another earful from big sis. It's late afternoon, the Parisians are beginning to seep home from a weekend in the country and the traffic is as dense as a public school pudding. Inside the underpowered *Clio*, the windows are steaming up quickly as the three of us exhale apprehension and a smattering of expletives. As we jump through the potholes of the Boulevard Rochechouart, the filthy artery which leads the way out of Pigalle, we are rudely interrupted by every set of traffic lights in north-eastern Paris. It takes a full hour before we jerk to a halt outside the hospital in Belleville. If the real thing proves to be as complicated as this trial run, our son is more likely to be born in an upholstered sardine can than in the comfort of his own hospital linens. Helena is whisked through the door marked 'births' and on into the nerve centre of the maternity unit and it dawns on me that I may be seeing the little fellow a little earlier than planned. I remember his unfinished bedroom and shudder violently. I really don't want to meet him just yet. It's too soon. I want him to stay right where he is for at least another two months and, right there under the gaze of all those pastel-coloured nurses, I solemnly swear never to complain about the complications of pregnancy again.

My mind races back to another day, just two short years ago, which ended in almost identical circumstances at a hospital in Barcelona. I'd flown in from London to visit my friend and old drinking buddy, Josep. He was lying in hospital, seriously ill with cancer, although I hadn't realised how ill until I arrived. I went straight to the small apartment that Pierre and Cécile were renting not far from the old port. Pierre was in Paris looking for a job and a house, leaving Cécile alone and heavily pregnant with Clément. That morning, we shared a leisurely breakfast and chatted for a while. I hadn't even unpacked my bag when a call came through from Josep's sister who told me that things had taken a turn for the worse. I left for the hospital immediately and she intercepted me on the ward with more news: Josep was not expected to live for more than a few more days. I heard the words, but struggled to make sense of them. The last I'd heard, a combination of radio and chemotherapy had sent his cancer into remission. Now the silent rogue cells were burning their way through an artery in his neck and the doctors said there was nothing more they could do.

I looked into the face of Josep's sister. It was as bleak as an exposed mountain peak in a snowstorm. Josep himself was lying motionless on a metal bed, although he still wore that familiar insolent grin which I remembered from so many nights spent laughing and squandering our youth in the bars of Barcelona. He was unable to speak, so I gave him a pen and a piece of paper, upon which he wrote me a couple of questions. Had I come to Barcelona on holiday? I nodded a yes. And how long would I be staying? At least a couple of weeks, I told him. Josep smiled and closed his eyes. Then, as dusk fell, the little that remained of his short life ebbed pointlessly from his veins.

There was nothing more to be said or done at the hospital. I took a taxi back to Cécile's. She had only met Josep on a couple of occasions, but she was shocked by the news. Like everyone who knew him, she'd fallen for his easy charm and a nature that was as tender as a slice of the finest Iberian ham. Then she pointed at her belly and told me she was in pain. I suggested she call the gynaecologist and he told her to go straight to the hospital. Mutely, I hailed a cab and slid onto the back seat beside her. She said there was no need to accompany her but, on such a night, where else could I have possibly gone?

We ended up on a deserted maternity ward at half past midnight. Cécile was wired up for tests while I sat in the empty bleached corridors and waited. The premature contractions were pulsing hard through her body and it took the nurses half the night to get them under control. This gave me all the time in the world to reflect on birth, death and the brief interlude which lies in between.

Now, with my fingers wrapped around a polystyrene cup from the hospital vending machine, I remember my friend Josep and the three laughing, little boys that he left behind. He and I had many things in common and we shared a number of bad habits. Now he's gone and, as I wait for news of Helena and my son, I fail to comprehend why he was never given the second chance that has mysteriously befallen me.

A short time later, I'm called into the room in which Helena is being examined. Just as Cécile had been before her, she's wired to a machine, which is attempting to make sense of the commotion going on inside her body. The midwife pulls her face into an expression which aims for something between maternal and remonstrative before telling Helena that she's got to start taking it easy. She's to get into a horizontal position and stay there for as long as it takes. Helena and the midwife both look at me to ensure that the implications of this have fully penetrated where they were intended all along. OK, I get the picture. From here on in, I'm the one doing the hoovering.

The Devil goes phishing, November 26th

Once I've finished rinsing the dishes, I'm off for a peek into a future without marketing services. The only thing I know about the prospective job in Toulouse is that Helena thinks that I should accept it immediately. She also thinks we should throw all of our stuff into the back of a lorry this afternoon, drive 1,000 kilometres south, find a house, redecorate it, have a spot of supper and all live happily ever after. I, on the other hand, prefer to listen to what the job is all about, have a long think about whether I can see myself doing it for a few years, discuss it with everyone I know, sit on the decision for a couple of decades, change my mind a hundred times and finally do nothing.

The job is for large French IT consultancy. The company has sold a very expensive piece of software to a major industrial concern in Toulouse and now they're looking for people to support the system when it starts crashing. I ask the man who has come all the way from Toulouse and put a cup of coffee in front of me whether he's actually read my CV. I feel so sorry for him that I hesitate to take a first sip from my cup. It's probably too late to get his ticket refunded, but maybe he can get some money back on my double espresso.

He tells me not to worry too much about the details and explains that I'll be given all the training I need and as much support as Dolly Parton at a toga party. Then he tells me that he was interested in interviewing me because my CV claims I can converse in three European languages. At this, I reach for my cup and take a sip of the coffee.

'How long would the training last?'

'Six weeks.'

'And that would give me enough time to learn all I need to know?'

'More than enough.'

'But I'm the man who thought *Microsoft Word* was a very small lead pencil?'

'No problem. All you have to do is sit by the phone and take the calls as they come in. Anything you can't handle goes straight through to a technical support centre in Lower Saxony.'

I avoid asking the obvious question, because I'm beginning

to think that there may be something in this idea after all.

'So, if I understand this correctly, I'm sitting by the phone waiting for it to ring, taking the call and listening to a problem that I can't solve, before telling the user that I haven't a clue but I know someone in Germany that probably does and that's fine so long as I do it nice and politely and in the language of his choosing.'

The guy from Toulouse just laughs. 'I'm sure you'll be of more use to us than that!'

I'm not so sure but I press on regardless. 'What do I do when the phone isn't ringing?' I ask, my devious skull suddenly full of finished film scripts and dramatic award ceremonies.

My man just shrugs of the shoulders, grins and takes a long slurp of coffee.

'I see. And what about the pay?'

The pay isn't great, as it goes, and the job is only guaranteed for six months. After that, I may get renewed for a further six, but I already know what Helena is going to say, which is that this is our chance to get a foot in the door of the big south-west, and I can start looking for another job as soon as I get there. In short, this is our big chance to escape the turd-lined pavements of Paris.

The man from Toulouse says he'll send me a letter detailing the offer, but then he'll need a really fast decision. A simple yes or no is all that's required and if he thinks I'm capable of that, then my CV must be a real masterpiece of subterfuge and deception.

After all that caffeine and my first sniff at employment in quite a while, I don't bother catching the metro – I simply jump into the sky and wing it home over the slate grey rooftops of Paris. Before pushing open the front door, I take a deep breath and a couple of minutes to calm down. After all, I know what's coming next.

'How'd it go?' asks Helena.

'Good.'

'What's the job?'

'A bit of reading, lots of writing, and diverting a few phone calls.'

Helena gives me an odd look, but I don't go into any detail. She's the only person alive who knows less about computers than I do. 'When does it start?'

'That's the problem. He wants me to start in two weeks time.'

'Why's that a problem?' asks Helena, as she starts throwing things into a suitcase.

'Well, it's not the kind of job I'd imagined myself doing and it means moving our lives to Toulouse less than two months before the baby is born when you are supposed to be horizontal. That's why.'

But this only prompts the spiel I've been waiting for – the one about big opportunities and the southern lifestyle, about gardens and houses, mountains, freedom and children growing up among gambolling lambs. She's not putting the pressure on, or anything as unsubtle as that; she's just letting me know that it's a very close call between utopia and the pet litter tray of Paris and she may just have a slight preference in favour of moving tonight. Then she goes back to her packing, leaving me alone, head in hands on the sofa.

I can see why Helena wants to do it, of course. We've both seen all those babies being shunted around Paris in prams, and the monoxide-yellow, hollowed-out faces of their mothers as they try desperately to avoid being knocked flying by a fast flowing stream of scooters, taxis and French pedestrians in oddly-shaped designer spectacles. Every night, Helena dreams of a house with real grass in the garden and enough room to be able to turn around without tucking her elbows into her midriff; she dreams of living somewhere that you don't have to drive forty-five kilometres just to find out whether the sun is shining, and worse still, she probably remembers me telling her that I want all these things too!

But before I can reflect any further, deep in the bowels of

the earth, the fallen angel responsible for all terrestrial marketing gets an email informing him that I'm thinking of bolting for freedom. He opens up his address book and gets on the phone faster than a stockbroker onto an insider deal.

First up is Dirk. He wants to know whether I've heard from the beer company. I tell him that they continue to bombard me with their communication but, so far, I've had no personalised messages. Dirk ignores this remark and tells me to talk to one of his colleagues in the Netherlands, because he thinks he has something that may be of interest to me. Before the phone has a chance to cool off, another old colleague calls from England. She wants to know whether I'm interested in running a small agency in the suburbs of London, but I'm forced to put her on hold because there's a man called Henry on the other line who needs to know whether I'm interested in a bit of freelance research work in Slovenia. Who the fuck is Henry, and how did he get my number? And where was he six months ago, when I was looking for precisely this kind of work? Then I'm back on the line with London – if I don't fancy the suburbs, there's always the office in Casablanca. Next it's the turn of Dirk's colleague who says I can have sole responsibility for a major international account, if only I'll sign my own death warrant and return to the fold. For all he cares, I can run the account from Toulouse or the middle of the Mojave Desert. I tell him I'll need to check the idea out with my old boss before we can make any progress on this one, but my old boss doesn't bother waiting for me to call because as soon as I've put down the phone, I discover he's left a message on the answerphone – have I ever fancied working in Switzerland and would I please call him back at the first available opportunity?

I take the phone off the hook. After all, I've yet to hear from the pharmaceutical company that wants to sell used needles to Swaziland, the tobacco company which is targeting the under-twelves in Myanmar or anybody in the arms industry, and I don't want to tempt fate by staying on the line. Instead, I go find Helena, which isn't too difficult as she's not on the sofa or the phone, so she must be in bed.

'You've been busy. What's going on?'

'Jobs.'

'What kind of jobs?'

'All kinds?'

'Where?'

'Wherever you want!' This is not making sense and Helena is getting impatient, so I try to keep it simple.

'Where do you want to live?'

'Toulouse!'

'What about Switzerland?'

'No.'

'Amsterdam?'

'No'

'Casablanca?'

Helena pauses for a moment as I watch my questions crossing her brow like overburdened camels on a trek through the desert. She shakes her head. 'Not really.'

'Me neither. How about London?'

'Maybe.'

'Paris?' It's a trick question, of course, but Helena's seen it coming a mile off and shakes her head more vigorously than a supermodel on a hairspray shoot.

'I see. Well, let's wait and see what happens tomorrow. I'm going shopping.'

Down at the fish shop, I start looking for answers. Should we have cod tonight, or does the haddock look fresher? Is sardine fishing sustainable? Do they still use antibiotics when farming salmon? The sea bass looks good... Is it inevitable that I'll end up back in marketing services? I wish I could share Helena's certainty. Ah well, tomorrow is my last appointment with the Ferrat and she's proposing to weigh up everything we've discussed over the last few weeks before deciding how to focus my feeble efforts to return to the workplace. I hope she's got some ideas, because I haven't a clue. Not even Helena can help me with a decision over the fish, however, so I plump for smoked haddock and, as I make my way home, try to recall the recipe for kedgeree.

Late night cravings, November 27th

Helena's contractions show no sign of relenting and the doctor has switched her medication. She's not getting much sleep at night, either. Every time she dozes off the chef in the restaurant below drops a plate or a few dark, Scandinavian curses and she's wide awake all over again, moaning and clutching her stomach. I quite enjoy the simple clatter of plates, but pregnancy has heightened Helena's sensitivity, not only to noise, but also to smell and to taste. She can hear the rollmop herring as they chat to one another excitedly about the afterlife, she hears every order that's whispered to the pig-tailed waitresses and if that girl in steel-capped stilettos totters drunkenly to the toilets beneath our bedroom one more time, I swear Helena will kill her before the moon rises.

Why breakfast is crucial to a good start in life, November 28th

At the table, I'm reading the back of a packet of *Weetabix*. Thanks to modern marketing, it's no longer possible to eat breakfast in peace and today I'm obliged to share my time and space with a bunch of unlikely characters airbrushed into existence by an unscrupulous advertising agency. That's how I came to be sharing breakfast with Valerie and Amandine, both of whom are just bursting to tell me their *Weetabix* stories.

According to the back of the packet, Valerie is thirty-five and eats three *Weetabix* a day with semi-skimmed milk. What they don't tell us is whether she eats anything else because she's as thin as a rake and looks a lot like Cindy Crawford.

I know this because there's a picture of her leaping around at a swimming pool as acrobatically as a dolphin in a pink bikini. There's no way Valerie is thirty-five. I doubt she's even seen twenty, but that's the nice thing about advertising – there's such a big, fat margin of error when it comes to telling the truth.

Then there's Amandine, who is the most literate, well-mannered and persuasive nine-year-old with whom it has ever been my pleasure to indulge in a little early morning banter. Amandine assures me that she's growing up quickly and expending so much energy by listening as intently as she possibly can to her teachers at school that she doesn't know how she could manage without forcing at least seven of the tasteless wheat biscuits down her gullet every morning (with the aid of a bit of hot milk, apparently). Her advice to me is that, if I'm having trouble making decisions then I'm probably not eating the recommended daily amounts of niacin, thiacin and vitamin *Jaguar XJ12*.

The Ferrat, on the other hand, is very much the decisive type. I wonder what she eats for breakfast? I must remember to ask her later this morning, once she has gazed into the tea leaves and told me what the future holds. I check in on Helena. She and our son are finally sleeping, so I leave a glass of orange juice by the bed and a written reminder not to skimp on the *Weetabix*.

I'm expecting this morning's meeting to comprise an all-round assessment of my strengths and weaknesses, along with a series of sure-fire recommendations in terms of my future career path and perhaps the added bonus of a job running a large part of south-western France. So I pitch up on the Ferrat's doorstep in bullish mood, desperate for an alternative to a life back in chains at *Satan, Hellfire and McProfit*. This, after all, is why I agreed to all this counselling in the first place.

As I take my place, for the last time, in the black leatherette opposite Mme Ferrat, she's already filling in a form which is nothing more than a pale rehash of all we have discussed over the past couple of months. She thinks that my chances of a return to gainful employment are excellent, provided I agree to eat an extra large slice of humble pie, keep all my opinions to myself and go straight back to marketing with the sick note she'll help forge.

She gives me a copy of the form as we say our fond farewells. I throw it into the first rubbish bin I come across, not because I consider our conversations to have been a waste of time (I don't), nor even because I'm beginning to understand that my ailing film script is the only excuse that remains between me and a job back in marketing. No, I throw it into the bin simply because I refuse to accept the inevitable conclusion she has recorded in her tidy, black handwriting.

Why is it that I've yet to come to my senses? What's wrong with a job in marketing? Who cares how you earn the money? Why can't I aspire to an Italian suit, a modest German motor and dinner at the latest sushi bar like everyone else? I used to want those things, didn't I? So what happened? What is it that's given me the taste for endless freedom and irresponsibility and why can't I wash it out of my mouth with a cupful of a peppermint mouthwash just like they do on the TV? What matters now, surely, is the health and happiness of my family – is it such a problem for me to shut up and accept that it's time to turn provider?

I don't know, but the eighth month of pregnancy is almost upon us and if I don't come up with some answers soon, all decisions are liable to be taken out of my hands. As I walk home, the air is so cold I can see the confusion in my head as it's expelled as plumes of hot, directionless steam. I fear my son asking me why he doesn't have any shoes, and me explaining how I once made a few bad decisions but telling him not to worry, because the skin on the soles of his feet will soon toughen up.

What I want to be (when I grow up), November 29th

I've told the guy from Toulouse that I'll give him a decision on Monday morning. And I've said the same thing to my old boss about the job in Switzerland. Sounds easy enough, doesn't it? Almost as if I'll spend the entire weekend lost in serious thought – weighing up the pros and cons – before the answer appears in a blinding flash of the obvious, or gets announced on *Larry King Live*. Where did I mislay the machinery necessary to make these infernal decisions? Why is there no satisfying click when I hit upon the right answer? Why am I sitting here frozen with indecision? My sole intention is to reach a logically deduced conclusion and that can't be so difficult, can it?

No. So why not calm down and draw up a list of the pros and cons for Toulouse and Switzerland?

What, like this?

That's it, nice one!

I wonder who Arsenal are playing today?

Shut up and concentrate!

Switzerland is a pretty boring place, isn't it?

So they say! Is that a con, then?

Beautiful mountains though, which must be a pro.

When are you going to find the time to visit the mountains?

Right! I'm going to be working my arse off all day, weekends too – another definite con.

But think of the money!

Money's not everything though, is it?

No, but it helps. Kids need a new pair of shoes at least every three days.

So where does that leave us?

No idea.

Wonder how that cake Helena's baking is coming along?

Sure smells good.

Hope it's apple and yoghurt cake – that's my absolute favourite!

Mine too!

Half an hour later, my list is almost finished but it doesn't look like it will be spitting out the answer any time soon. What's more, *it is* apple and yoghurt cake and, after all that marshalling of disorderly thought, surely I've earned a bit of a break? I show Helena the list. Ungraciously, she wants to know what I'm going to do with it next.

'Why, make a decision of course!' I reply.

'Go on then,' she goads.

At what point do other people decide what they want to do with their lives? My childhood daydreams were probably the same as yours. First, I was going to become a pilot, then a footballer, the President of *Ferrari*, the first man to tunnel right through to Mongolia, before I hit upon the idea, right in the middle of a mathematics exam, that the only possible course was to become a male escort. I was still a virgin, you see, and really had no idea how else I was ever going to get near the breast of a woman. The only problem was the shame I felt over my body. If I couldn't bear to look at myself in the mirror, how on earth was I going to stand naked in front of a wealthy, sex-mad, middle-aged woman?

Why the French never take milk with their tea, November 30th

We've been invited to tea by the Escalators and I still haven't made the decision. It's been pouring with rain all day and it's not going to let up just because we want to make the short walk round the block and on into the centrally heated paradise inhabited by Agathe and her family. Helena no longer has the strength to support a flimsy umbrella above her head, so the task of protecting her falls to me. By the time we arrive, she's completely beat and I'm as wet as a monkey that's fallen headlong from the rainforest canopy into the Amazon River.

As we settle into their luxurious sofa, Agathe's in the bath and Mr Escalator is building a log fire and stabbing a few twigs in a desperate attempt to avoid any conversation about the rugby. To stave off the inevitable, he's busy telling me some cock-and-bull story about his application for a new job selling driverless metro trains. What a load of old hogwash! This man was born to sell moving walkways, trust me. Bright-eyed and nappy-tailed, Agathe emerges from the bathroom. Helena perks up a little as she takes the terry cotton bundle in her arms but she's too tired to support her for long and young Agathe suffers the extreme misfortune of being passed to me. This obliges me to consider all that weight Helena has been carrying around and why that might render her incapable of lifting anything heavier than a cup of tea. And that's when the thought pops into my head – there's no way I can go to Toulouse. Not now. The job down there starts in less than a week and Helena can't travel. How can I possibly leave her to fend for herself in this condition? It's really quite simple and I'm going to have to turn down the job for the most practical of reasons.

As I continue to gaze psychotically into the embers of the fire, Agathe reminds the neighbourhood that it's feeding time. How can something so small generate such a tremendous noise? Her lungs can only be the size of two uninflated party balloons, but the sound isn't unlike that of a luxury cruise ship docking in northern Paris after months on the high seas. Inès checks her watch, plucks Agathe from my shoulder and inserts a bottle into the miniature foghorn.

Pregnancy and other infectious diseases, December 1st

On the way home last night, I explained to Helena why I've decided to turn down our chance to go south. She was disappointed, but simply too tired to put up much in the way of resistance. I told her there'll be other opportunities and I can only pray this is true. This morning I confirmed my decision to that trusting soul from Toulouse and now I'm heading straight into a meeting about the job in Switzerland.

In a café down the street, I find a woman of steel and bitumen who works for one of the Swiss company's marketing suppliers. She has time for precisely one coffee and two pastries, but no pleasantries at all. It's straight down to business as she briefs me on my potential role in the expansion of what is already a mighty empire. But, as she stokes her engine by swallowing a few more lumps of coal, the only thing I can think of is warming my hands over a telephone hotline down in Toulouse. I can't get it out of my head that I've made a horrible mistake. Occasionally I manage to tune into what the locomotive is saying, but I'm not making much of an effort to do anything other than say what I suspect she wants to hear.

'So, as you can see, it's a huge job,' she's saying, 'a real opportunity to shape the way a global giant is developing for the future.'

'Of course.'

'It's a very political role, of course, as every country – or vertical if you prefer – has its own agenda, which more often than not conflicts with the horizontal – the product lines.

'Horizontal, yes, and vertical, naturally.'

'Your job will be to help mesh a lot of conflicting interests.'

'To mess what?'

'And you'll be spending a lot of time on planes.'

'Air miles. Great!'

'It's a golden opportunity.'

'Once-in-a-lifetime'

'To construct some of the biggest brand architecture in the world.'

'Armchairs and skyscrapers.'

'And persuading people all over the globe that, while they might have a choice, there's really just the one way to go.'

'Right, um, no choice at all.'

'Good,' says the steely one, before casually brushing back her sleeve for a crafty glance at her pearly timepiece. 'Here's what happens next: I'll send your CV to the head marketing honcho – you do have a CV, don't you?'

'Sure. I, er, rushed one off the other day!'

'Good, email it to me before breakfast tomorrow and I'll send it to the Swiss office with a note of recommendation. That way, we'll try to get you some face time with the man himself. Sound good?'

Before I can even thank the woman, let alone polish her shoes, she's already out of the door leaving me with a strange, queasy sensation in the pit of my stomach.

I spring on Helena as soon as she's back from her latest trip to the hospital, giving her just enough time to swallow a couple of anti-contraction pills and no time at all to tell me what the doctors have said.

'I've just had the preliminary interview for Switzerland.'

'How'd it go?'

'Good, I think.'

'So why do you look like you've been bitten by a rabid dog?'

'Foaming at the mouth a little, am I?'

'You are. Sit down and tell me all about it.'

But our conversation is constantly interrupted by the sound of tiles, porcelain, and perhaps even bones being broken in the flat beneath ours – the landlord has apparently decided that he will double his income by breaking the place apart and starting all over again. Over the din, Helena runs through her list of prerequisites for my return to work and I provide the appropriate, monosyllabic answers.

'Will you have any time to continue the screenplay?'

'No.'

'Will we be able to live in France?'

'No.'

'Will be you doing a lot of travelling'

'Yes.'

'You aren't seriously considering this position, are you?'

'Yes.'

'Yes, you are considering it, or yes, I'm right, and you're

not considering it.'

Beneath our feet, the workers are drilling deep into the underworld and the sound and sensation are identical to the business end of a bit of root canal work when the dentist reaches your jaw bone.

'Yes, I'm considering it.'

'I see.'

Helena looks shattered and just about ready to drop. Her eyes are dark and hooded. Her very presence here in the kitchen is an act that defies medical science. Finally I remember that I need to ask how it went at the hospital.

To prevent further contractions, Helena's been given a medication that started out life as a gerbil tranquilliser. The problem has been caused, in part, by her concern over the birth; not that Helena appears to spend inordinate amounts of time fretting over the intense pain to come. If I were a woman, the thought of twelve hours of agony would be the only contraceptive measure I'd ever require. In fact, if the future of the entire human race depended on the willingness of the male to bring a pregnancy to term, I can safely say that the species would, by now, exist only as a set of fossilised remains buried deep under centuries of sand and mosquitoes. Women do get a little help from their hormones when they need it most, but what are they thinking before they get pregnant, when, presumably, they're still in full possession of their senses?

Over a dinner of grilled merguez sausage and baked potatoes, we fall into a discussion of Carla's pregnancy and Helena proves, beyond all reasonable doubt, that men and women are fundamentally different creatures. I can't understand how it is that Carla can have fallen pregnant so soon after she swore she was not ready to have children. Of course, I do understand how it happened in the carnal sense, but the way Dirk told it, the baby-producing side effects of a bit of a bonking were the last thing on her mind. She was still thinking careers, waiting 'until the time was right – maybe in a few years' time', that sort of thing.

At this Helena smiles enigmatically. 'Ah yes,' she says, 'but when they were here, I had a little word with Carla.'

'What do you mean, "had a word with her?"'

'I planted the seed in her mind.'

'What seed?' I don't like the direction this conversation is headed one bit...

'I'm not going to tell you.'

'Hang on a minute! Are you telling me that something you said to Carla has caused her to go straight home to Amsterdam, throw the condoms into a canal, forget her career and start behaving like a *Viagra*-fuelled bunny?'

'I wouldn't put it quite like that.'

'But that's the basic idea?'

'Yes.'

'Right. Now you have to tell me exactly what you said.'

'Why?'

'Because I need to know, right now, how this... this seed is passed from one woman to another. That way I can send a group email to every male on the planet and warn them.'

'I'm saying nothing!'

'Come on, Helena!'

She looks hard at me for a couple of seconds before fingering her belly.

'Don't worry, you're still pregnant. You can tell me now. How did you do it?'

'Well, when I asked her, she told me she wasn't ready.'

'Right. That's what she always told me. And Dirk.'

'Well, I simply told her that she might never be ready. She might end up waiting her whole life for the right time and the desire to make a baby.'

'What do you mean?'

'With a very few women, *l'envie* – the desire – never comes. With others, it comes too late or when the circumstances are really not right, or you're with the wrong man. I told her that I could have spent years waiting for the moment when you were right and I was right, but I wasn't prepared to do that. I took the view we were both in good health and there would never be a better time, or a right time, to put our trust in life and let it lead us where it wanted.

I stare at Helena for a moment. 'That's it?'

'That's it!'

I don't bother to ask Helena who it was that whispered this little secret into her ear. It doesn't really matter anymore.

'You never told me,' is the only half-hearted protest I can utter.

'No, of course I didn't. Men are never ready.'

Well, I'll be damned! There may be all that pretence at sensible, rational discussion, about timing and planning and all that other good stuff, but when it comes right down to it, it's just one woman whispering the secret seed into the ear of her sister.

Later Helena confesses that she's already had the same little conversation with her friend Isabelle, which means that, not so long ago, Isabelle entered this house unencumbered by even the thought of a sprog. No doubt she and Jean-Luc had once discussed it over a few drinks as something they may well consider, one of these days, before resolving to dedicate themselves, for another few decades, to the delights of Parisian theatre, cinema, bars and restaurants. I can still picture Jean-Luc the last time he was here, inhaling deeply the fumes of an aromatic red Burgundy: we're talking football and there isn't a nappy on the horizon. As I turn my head, I can still see Helena and Isabelle, deep in conversation on the sofa opposite. Soon our guests will be picking up their coats to leave for the night and Jean-Luc will exit with nothing more than the memory of an agreeable evening. Isabelle, on the other hand, will be leaving with just one tiny, additional thought that wasn't there when she walked through the door – a minuscule seed, planted in her head by Helena and ready to germinate should it receive so much as a single droplet of nourishing rain.

Why pregnant women require a little additional support, December 2nd

The reality of what's happening to Helena's body and what I shall be forced to witness, is about to come that much closer to home. She's filled my diary with a host of most unwelcome appointments and I'm still hiding behind my desk before we leave for the hospital to watch a film about childbirth, to learn how to deal with her contractions and, worst of all, endure an illustrated lecture on the pain she'll experience during the birth. There's no way out, believe me I've tried, but every expectant father in Paris will be there and my protests have all been in vain. As if that were not bad enough, we also have the last ultrasound appointment next week – a final trailer for the full-length feature film, 'The Revenge of the Little Fellow' – before he finally lands, screaming and naked, to wreak havoc in the midst of our unprepared lives.

Helena left a little something on my desk last night. It's an article ripped from this week's *Elle* Magazine about the way in which children interrupt the sexual relationship between their parents. Two cartoon drawings adorn the article (and naturally my attention is immediately drawn to the pictures, rather than the acreage of tiny French text which surrounds them). The first shows a man trying to get his arms around his wife and failing because her pregnancy protrudes between them and ensures they're always separated by a good three kilometres. The second depicts a couple separated in the parental bed by three smiling, space-hogging children. The implications are clear and so is Helena's frustration at our own sex life. The argument started again this morning when I was hanging out the washing. She saw the look on my face as I came across a pair of her cavernous maternity knickers in the laundry basket. She snatched them from my hand with a comment that there was no need for me to start pulling faces because she'd be throwing them into the bin soon enough.

To have been caught red-handed in this way makes me feel like a major arsehole. Do I expect her to be wearing a thong on the day I drive her to the hospital to give birth? I know it's unreasonable, especially when you consider that she's not the tallest of women in the first place. This means our son cannot stretch his burgeoning limbs vertically and Helena is left with no choice but to expand horizontally. Now she looks like one of those bulbous toys with such a low centre of gravity that you can't push them over – a bit like Diego Maradona, but without the stubble or the cocaine.

She's also starting to get seriously sensitive about her weight. I'm trying not to say anything about it and have almost completely refrained from referring to her underwear as 'industrial'. More often than not, it's Helena herself who starts the weight gain conversation, (even if I invariably get the blame for bringing it up). She's put on over seventeen kilograms since conception, of which the little fellow accounts for no more than two and a half. Even if you add a bit extra for all the fluids, the placenta and the extra underwear, that still leaves quite a few kilos for which there is no obvious explanation.

Of course, last night didn't help matters much when Helena caught me looking wistfully through a photo album of the summer holiday we shared in Corsica little more than a year ago, when all she wore for the entire two weeks was a slinky black swimming costume. Anyway, Helena thought half an hour was an excessive amount of time to be dwelling on one particular shot and finally she snapped:

'I'll get my figure back, you know.'

Like an idiot, I pretended not to understand the connection between what she was saying and a picture of her topless on the beach near Ajaccio.

'Eh?'

'You know what I'm talking about.'

'Oh, you mean this,' I say, waving a hand far too casually

at the offending shot.

'All women do it, you know.'

'What's that?'

'Gain weight during pregnancy.'

At this point I really wanted to ask whether they all gained seventeen kilos, but I stopped myself just in time. Nor did I mention exercise or chocolate biscuits. Not once. Instead I tried to interject a little light-heartedness into the conversation.

'And do all their boyfriends take a mistress for the duration?'

But this proved to be another horrible, tactical error and she gave me the kind of look that castrates at sixty paces. 'Husbands!' she said, finally.

'What?'

'I said 'husbands'. Boyfriends don't have mistresses. That's what you call screwing around.'

And with that she was gone, leaving me to marvel at the improvement in her use of the English language.

Customer service and other French sausages, December 4th

The daily grind continues unabated: shopping, cooking, washing-up and looking for jobs. The only relief comes when I sit down to erase a few more passages of my ailing film script. The medication appears to have eased Helena's contractions, but she's getting more and more pissed off about the racket from the apartment below which starts at 8.30 sharp in the morning. The site foreman has a voice like Tweetie-Pie in the cartoons. Every time he opens his mouth to speak, it tinkles up through our floorboards like a thin plate of glass shattering. This cocktail of inactivity, noise and an excitable set of hormones is driving Helena to extreme levels of irritation and some increasingly bizarre decisions, the latest of which is her unilateral refusal to pay the rent on the grounds that the building is turning into an industrial wasteland. The fact that the agency will no longer take her calls only fans the flames of her anger. Every time she calls to complain, she gets no further than the secretary, a hapless French skivvy who tells her that the person responsible is in a meeting. It doesn't help when Helena points out that the woman cannot possibly have been in a meeting all day, every day for the past three weeks. The truth, which Helena refuses to countenance, is that the agent deems it beneath her to talk to the tenants for whom she's responsible. If you're late with the rent, you'll receive a snooty letter, alright, followed by a fine, but actually conversing with these people is simply out of the question.

It's not the first time I've come across this problem in France. When there's a problem of this nature and you ask for a bit of old-fashioned combat with someone in a position of authority, the request is invariably denied. The 'service provider' will simply demand that you detail your complaint in a letter and then keep you waiting the rest of your natural life for a reply. My first brush with the great, multilayered bureaucracies of France occurred after I'd taken a conversation class at a well-reputed language school. Our teacher was a woman of about 135 years old, whose brain and sensibilities had ground to an abrupt halt in the mid-1960's. The only subject she deemed worthy of discussion was that of the ongoing war between the sexes and, despite her initial assertion that the students would get to do 80 percent of the talking, in reality she was the only one who got to voice an opinion on her pet subject. We students were never given the opportunity to exercise so much as a single word from our hamstrung vocabularies. The old trout would just rattle on about the evils of men and their dicks for as long as any of us were prepared to remain awake. After a couple of weeks of this, I could no longer allow myself to pay good money to listen to her one-sided story. Fizzing into the administrative office like an erratic home-made missile, I demanded an interview with the Controller of Teaching.

'Impossible,' declared his secretary, 'he's far too busy.'

'Hang on a minute, I haven't even asked for an appointment yet.'

'He's in a meeting.'

'What, for the rest of the month?'

'Certainly!'

'Fine, I'll wait.'

'No. You'll have to write a letter.'

'OK, give me a piece of paper and I'll do it now.'

I could tell from the look on the secretary's face that my demonstration of all that's considered undesirable about us Anglo-Saxons in France wasn't exactly appreciated. But, reluctantly, she handed me a sheet of paper and a biro. Several minutes later, after I had deliberately misspelled every French verb at my command, I handed back the poisonous quill and asked if I might be allowed to deliver the letter personally to the President of the Republic, whose office was right next door to her own.

Cue more Gallic grimacing: 'Of course not! I'm his secretary. He will speak only to me.'

'But I promise I'll try not to frighten him. I just want to explain why I've written the letter.'

'Such a thing is quite impossible.'

'But surely he'll be interested to hear why I'm demanding a refund? After all, it directly concerns the quality of the teaching, for which, unless I'm mistaken, he has ultimate responsibility.'

Apparently not. She snatched the letter and marched into the adjoining office. But she also made the mistake of leaving it slightly ajar, allowing me to poke my unwanted snout into the crack. Only a quick glance, you understand, but long enough to ascertain that the old bugger was not in a meeting at all. Sure enough, he was enjoying a milky coffee and perusing the newspaper with his cheesy French feet up on the desk. I withdrew quickly and waited for the secretary to return, grateful for the only real insight into French cultural life that the school had to offer.

'He's still in a meeting,' she said, 'but I've delivered your letter personally and he's assured me he will reply in due course.'

I contented myself with a quick grin at the secretary. After all, it's not her fault that officialdom in France makes the old Soviet Politburo look like a naked rave in a muddy field.

The limbic system of the mammal, December 5th

I've decided to pay another visit to the cinema and I'm going alone, so I don't have to worry about what anyone thinks of my choice of film. If I feel like it, I can watch Arnold Schwarzenegger in *Snow White and the Seven Dwarves* and nobody ever need know. As I get stuck into a hundredweight of buttered popcorn, a sprinkling of other loners settle down in the dark of the cinema like isolated snowflakes. I've no idea why they're all here. We all have our own reasons, I suppose – our histories, successes, failures and a death to face – but whatever the truth of it, this afternoon we've all chosen to expose ourselves to one of those raw and sentimental epics in which British film-makers seem to specialise.

It's getting dark as we spill back out onto the street after the film. We're all still maintaining our distance and pretending not to notice one another's tear-stained faces. Not so long ago, if I'd been asked to sum up this film in a single word, I would no doubt have plumped for 'fake' and, had you been foolish enough to ask, I'd have told you I hated everything about it – the acting, the director, the story, the scenery, the emotions, the soundtrack, and the stupid popcorn too. What I would never have told you, however, is that I hated myself even more, because in the end, the only fake proved to be me.

As I walk home from the cinema, many conflicting emotions course through my veins – regret at the passing of years, jealousy over a bunch of characters in a film and envy over their creator, fear over the impending birth and so many others, the origins of which I cannot even begin to trace – waves of anger, hatred, joy and loss. Though some of these have doubtless been planted in my mind by the film, others arise as naturally as tears, laughter and a host of other endorphins. A few months ago I'd have walked straight into the nearest bar and throttled these feelings the moment they showed the temerity to reach for the surface. But tonight, in the crowded streets around l'Opéra, I do not try to deny them their rightful place in the maelstrom of human life.

The true dangers of carbon monoxide, December 6th

I've taken to spending Saturday mornings with a group of non-drinking friends. Together we share the same pleasure in making an early start to that part of the weekend which, for years, had gone missing from our lives. In the past, Saturday mornings were reserved for hangovers, haircuts and bouts of self-loathing which often endured long into the weekend. But today I'm up early, walking alongside the banks of the Seine and enjoying the sunlight as it reflects sharply off the slate-grey roofs and cream-coloured paintwork of the Hausmannian architecture. It feels good to be awake, alive and, for once, to be living in the present.

I jump onto the number 63 bus to trace my way home. Automatically, I begin scanning the faces of my fellow passengers. Why are other people a source of such endless fascination to me? Why do I feel this compulsion to speculate on what lies behind the mask of their features? Back in the corporate world, I'd barely be listening when a client attempted to convince both me and himself that his latest widget or line extension had been developed out of a genuine concern for mankind when we both knew it was little more than a naked attempt to improve the bottom line for a small number of cash-rich corporate shareholders. Of course, I did my best to insert some vigorous head nodding at those moments when a little reassurance seemed most urgent, but what interested me more than the product he was looking to foist upon the maximum number of lower primates was the personality and the character he was trying to hide beneath his button-down collar. After all, what could possibly motivate anyone to devote a lifetime to promoting a strawberry cheesecake flavoured underarm deodorant? Surely I'd find a clue in their voice, their body language or a few careless details from their personal life or past? Most of the time, it would turn out to be nothing more than a desire for security, or the basic need to provide for the family and, despite my resistance, I can feel that instinct growing stronger in me every day.

The bus pants a little more heavily as we reach the foot of the climb up into Pigalle, leaving a plume of leaden grey exhaust in its wake. Sod it! There's nothing for it. I'll have to go back to my job and forget all about the film script. It was only ever a dream. This time I'll listen to my clients and take an interest in their sensational claims and petty deceptions and I promise I won't look beyond the rubberised sheaths which they slip over their souls before work every morning before work to protect themselves from the ugliness and sheer brutality of marketing. I won't even ask myself how long they've had that nervous tic. No, I'll keep my mouth shut and I'll familiarise myself with whatever it is that they want me to love and help sell: rubber tyres, condoms, washing powder, mobile phones, *Botox* injections, ice cream, hamburgers, slimming aids, credit cards, consolidated debt, newspapers, a new financial service, erection pills, cigarettes and beer. Did I say beer? Well, sorry, I'm going to draw the line there and, while we're at it, let's rule out cigarettes too. Just because I've failed to kick the nicotine addiction doesn't mean that I want the deaths of a few million teenagers on my conscience. I'll just have to be careful about my limits. Who knows, I might even find out what they are before I'm swept over the cliff by a torrent of fast moving goods and back into the dark, polluted tides of consumerism.

By the time my bus dumps me on the filthy pavements

of Pigalle, farts and moves off again, I've convinced myself that it's all over before I've even got started. I've had my chance to pursue a few dreams and my output comprises nothing more than the incredible shrinking film script. I try to console myself with the thought that I can keep up the script as a hobby or maybe write a couple of personalised children's stories for my son. That's probably more my level anyhow – a tiny and captive audience between the ages of one and eight, with a vested interest in holding the attention of its father.

As I approach the apartment, my early afternoon light-heartedness is slipping away faster than a mobile telephone company's introductory offer and, in my head, I'm already rehearsing for interview. How do I disguise the obvious cracks in my CV? Or do I just come clean, admit to some sort of nervous breakdown and concede that I'd be delighted to lick the toilet floor clean? Yeah, right. I can just see the looks on their faces. After all, this is marketing. The last thing they want to hear is the truth about my personal life. Fuck it! I'll tell them I've been studying the effect of fossil fuel waste on the mating habits of the lesser leatherback turtle off the southern shores of Antarctica and watch as their eyes start to glaze over.

My resignation from the creative life has imbued my features with all the qualities of an approaching storm – one that's about to be unleashed on Helena – who else? As I turn the key in the lock, I hear voices in the living room. Damn it, Helena's parents! My back catalogue of resentments will have to wait and, after the full round of kissing, hand-shaking, and *comment allez-vous*, I'm promptly dispatched to the *boulangerie* to buy something for tea. I return with a bagful of cream cakes and, fortunately for all concerned, the sugar mollifies the desperate child whose sole desire is to rampage through the apartment.

But it proves to be a brief stay of execution for the tantrum that's determined to have its day. I've slept too long and too hard and the earth is giving way beneath my feet as I get out of bed. Sullenly, I lock myself away in our spare bedroom to write emails and spend a few hours following irrelevant football matches on the internet. As the weak December light grows ever dimmer, Helena interrupts my gloom with a cup of coffee and an attempt at polite conversation. But the most I can manage by way of response is a series of primitive grunts. Then she reminds me that we're expecting company for tea.

'Who?' I thunder.

'Jean-Luc and Isabelle, remember?'

'No. Why are they coming?'

'Because they're our friends and they want to know how we're getting along.'

'How long are they staying?' I demand in a tone of voice which suggests that Helena has invited a family of particularly venomous snakes to spend their summer holidays on our sofa.

'I don't know. As long as they like, which won't be very long once they catch sight of your face. I thought you were going out anyway?'

'I'm going to a party in a little while,' I say.

'Well, I'm going to bake a cake. Perhaps you could give me a hand with the table?

'I'm busy. I'll be out in a minute.'

Helena takes a wearied look at the web page open on my computer. Fortunately, she has no idea that she's looking at the football results from the Slovakian Amateur leagues.

'OK, thanks.'

All of which only makes it worse, of course. I mean, if she just told me to grow up and get a life, then maybe I wouldn't behave in this way. Instead I return to my obsessions and continue to glower at our totally innocent house plants.

When Jean-Luc and Isabelle do arrive, I find myself in the

midst of drafting a long letter to an uncle with whom I have not spoken, let alone corresponded, for the best part of twenty-five years. I'm not sure whether he'll be the slightest bit interested in any of my activities after all this time, but it's been a good hour since the final whistle in Bratislava and I just don't feel up to anything else. Maybe I'll grow out of throwing tantrums at about the same time as my child. Sometimes I wonder whether it's not a twin brother I'm expecting, rather than a son.

As I board the metro, everyone moves immediately to the opposite end of the carriage. I'm going to have to do something about my mood if I'm to avoid infecting the other guests with the emotional equivalent of the Black Death. But I've never felt less like a party and, as if things weren't bad enough already, I'm sure everyone will be quaffing champagne. In my current frame of mind, this spells danger to my abstinence, so I get off the metro two stops early in an attempt to walk myself into a better mood.

At the party I fall into a conversation with a girl from England who everybody else seems to be avoiding and together we embark on one of those conversations in which the English specialise: complaining about the weather and the irrationality of the French, before moving on to question the sexuality of certain members of the Royal Family. After half an hour or so of this, I figure I'm entitled to ask her what she does for a living and it turns out that she manages to combine a book-keeping job with a bit of reflexology (a bizarre combination, in my view and a bit like combining mass murder with a spot of charity work), but at least she has found her own way of navigating through a paradoxical world that teeters endlessly between *Disneyland* and self-destruction. After a nanosecond's hesitation, I decide to unleash my own dilemma upon her: I explain that, for the last twelve months, I've been vacillating between a return to outright capitalism and spending what remains of my money on a rusty white van and a mud hut in the south. 'Go for it,' she says without pausing for breath.

'Leave marketing and go south immediately. Don't even think about it. You can make it work, and you'll never regret it.'

Insulating baby – why two coats are always better than one, December 10th

Why do I persist with this damned film script and how can I even begin to think of a decent ending when in the blackest of moods? If this is all sobriety has to offer, wouldn't I feel better off taking a few slugs of Scotch straight from the bottle? I don't know but I've asked Helena to give me a bit of space while I figure the whole thing out.

The phone rings. It's Helena. She's down at the local bric-a-brac market and has apparently found a wardrobe for the little fellow's bedroom. I had no idea we were looking for such a thing, but Helena wants to know why I'm not already down there to size it up. I remain icily silent on the end of the line. Helena loves these markets, in which a bunch of unlicensed conmen will try to sell you whatever decent folk have thrown into a skip by cover of night. Personally I get about as much of a thrill out of them as I would a cold bath in the middle of the Siberian tundra, but I already know that her question offers me no choice and, to let her know what I think of the whole idea, I replace the receiver as if I were crushing an extended family of cockroaches. No point in telling Helena that a part of me is relieved to abandon my idiotically one-dimensional characters to stew in their own juices for a while.

I find her standing in the middle of the street staring lovingly at a large object that, frankly, looks as if it would be doing well to attract the interest of a family of starving wood-worm.

'What do you think?' she says hopefully.

'How much is it?'

'Never mind that, I just want to know what you think.'

What I think is that I don't want to be here, freezing my

nuts off, looking an old, beat-up wardrobe. I want to be left alone, in the warm, mulling over the unpleasant death I'm planning for my vaguely fictitious film script villain.

'From the colour of it, you would think it belonged to the Third Reich,' is all I can manage by way of response.

'Don't worry, I'm going to repaint it.'

'How much is it, then?'

'€250'

'What! Even though we have to repair it, paint it and presumably cart it home?'

'No. They'll deliver it.'

'I'll bet they will. If they don't, I imagine they'll be arrested for littering the street.'

'What?'

'Never mind.'

'So, what do you think?'

'Other than the fact that it's bloody expensive, you really don't want to know what I think.'

'Good, we'll buy it then.'

'Helena, I don't know why you brought me out here in the first place. You knew you were going to buy the damned thing and I was trying to work.'

Helena gives me a look which conveys instantaneously her conviction that I'm not taking sufficient interest in my own son's welfare and I know that I'm beaten. I also know that there's no way she'll be painting this dilapidated object. That task has already fallen to me.

'Good. Now, can we go home?'

'No. You have to pay first.'

It takes me an inordinately long time to peel the requisite number of banknotes from my wallet.

'Come on,' says Helena, 'we're due at the hospital.'

I've given up all hope of doing any more work on the script today and I'm reduced to stomping around the apartment in an attempt to attract some unwarranted attention to myself. But I'm forced to abandon my sulk when I hear

Helena yelping like a dozen newborn puppies in the kitchen, where I find her doubled over the kitchen sink, surrounded by a mysterious pink liquid that's dripping steadily onto the floor. I'm sufficiently concerned to drop almost all of my imaginary grievances.

'What's happened?'

She points at the kettle and then at a sodden teabag which lies at her feet. Somehow she has contrived to pour a cup of boiling hot raspberry tea all over her belly.

'Are you alright? Let's have a look at it.' I'm feeling guilty now.

Helena makes her way gingerly through the apartment and into the bedroom where she uncovers her belly. There is a nasty scald mark, at what must be about eye level for the baby.

'You think he's alright?' she asks.

'I guess so. He's well protected in there, isn't he?'

'I don't know, but he must have felt it.'

'Unlikely. He's not right under the surface, is he?'

'I don't know.'

In truth, neither do I. I haven't picked up our copy of *Future Maman* for months. All I know is that, even if he were born today, he'd stand a good chance of making it. But I know nothing of how he's nourished, what he breathes, how much of the outside world he perceives, or whether he has appreciated his first cup of tea.

As silence descends upon the house once more, I tiptoe back to my laptop and check to see whether anyone has registered the fact that I'm just about cooked as far as my script is concerned and ready to accept a job in the real world. Opening my email inbox, I'm offered low interest credit, the opportunity to chat cheaply to the girl of my choice and a flashing banner ad alerting me to the possibility of a $20,000 jackpot. I've heard nothing from the Swiss and as far as job offers are concerned, I might just as well be six feet under.

Three minutes later, a pale spectral figure appears at the door, wielding a can of paint and an undersized brush. It turns out to be Helena, who has a notion that she'd like to paint the remains of the wardrobe. This doesn't immediately strike me as the best idea she's ever had:

'You mean that thing?' I say, nodding at the unruly pile of rotten planks standing shamefacedly in the far corner of the room.

'Yes,' she says quietly. It looks more likely that she'll lapse into unconsciousness than decorate something which stands a good foot taller than she does.

'I don't think so. I think you're going back to bed.'

'But... '

'You've got a big day at the hospital tomorrow.'

'I know, but... '

'And I don't know about you, but I don't want to see our son coughing to death as a result of inhaling toxic paint fumes before he's even born, do you?'

'I thought just a first coat.'

'Give me the brush.' I make a grab for the paint pot but Helena is stubborn and doesn't let go easily. 'Toxic fumes, Helena; gimme the paint!'

'But I have to get the room ready.'

'Delicate little pink lungs, Helena!'

Finally the little ghost turns on its heels and disappears.

The salad bar (eat all you want), December 11th

Our first appointment of the day at the maternity hospital is to watch a film about childbirth. I'm looking forward to this about as much as the woodworm are looking forward to their second coat of paint. I ease Helena into the *Clio* and she assures me that, among the current batch of expectant mothers, she's the only one not habitually accompanied to the hospital by a suitably acquiescent partner. My defence – that there's little point in me attending prenatal chanting if I don't know the words – is as flimsy as it is irrelevant. I know I have to be there, but that doesn't mean that I have to look forward to it, now does it? My mind races back to that disconcerting TV birth. That was shocking enough, even after it was all trimmed and tarted up for TV, but this is going to be far, far worse. It's a hospital production and I've a horrible suspicion they won't have bothered the censorship board with this video nasty.

Down in the basement of the hospital, I arm myself with a cup of machine-made coffee and slip into the mask of bravery. We're shown into a room containing a television set, a bunch of brightly-coloured floor mats, five pregnant women, one midwife and not a single father (unless you count me). I've been duped and immediately shoot an alarmed glance at Helena but the midwife has already arm-wrestled me onto the mats and tells me to make myself at home. All the pregnant women ignore me completely as the black-belted one introduces the film.

She tells us we're about to watch a video showing five very different births. Five! Nobody said anything about five. I'm not sure I can manage one without a large dose of horse tranquilliser. What am I doing here? I send Helena a psychic email explaining that I'm going to make a run for it and she catches the look of wild panic in my eyes, but I can tell by the way she's flaring her nostrils that I'm to stay put and shut up.

'One of these births may well be how it turns out for you,' declares the midwife. 'We're going to see a normal birth without anaesthesia, one with an epidural, a birth by caesarean section, another using forceps, and finally a birth with a number of complications. Any questions?' The room falls silent and the only sound is that of my heart attempting to beat its way out of my chest.

There are a number of questions running around my head, but the main one concerns whether I can leave after we've seen the normal birth as there's a 60 percent chance that this is what Helena will have to endure. But I'm way too ashamed to ask and it wouldn't get me any closer to the exit anyway, so all I can do now is to lie back on these uncomfortable mats, swallow my fear and allow you to share the experience.

The film opens with a bit of piano music and a few tasteful shots of the hospital with nurses smiling and walking down corridors just like they do on *ER*. But just at the point when I start looking for some kind of plot line, the director suddenly introduces us to a woman up in the stirrups, breathing about as easily as a pack of greedy monitor lizards. Where's the scene-setting, the part which establishes the main characters? There's no plot to this whatsoever and all attempts at decorum have gone by the board – it's just another remake of *The Exorcist*.

The camera has been placed squarely in what might politely be called the 'line of fire' and the only thing to be grateful for now is the fact that we're not subjected to the entire twelve hours of labour. As I reopen my eyes the midwife has managed to get her fingers between the poor mother's legs without spoiling any of the camera angles and, before you know it, she's squeezing out the head of a small squashed reptile – sorry, did I say reptile? What I meant was small squashed human being. By the time the baby is placed on her mother's breast, I register the fact that Helena is sobbing and about to pass into a catatonic stupor.

I look back at the screen when I hear the tinkling piano music again. Next up is the labour with epidural and, mechanically speaking, it works in much the same way: woman breathes very hard, gets shouted at by midwife who eventually moves downstream and eases gloved hands into mother's slippery bits. Baby's head appears, midwife does a bit of yanking on the cranium, twists the shoulders, corkscrews the body out of the woman and Helena promptly bursts into tears. Yet the most remarkable thing about this birth is the fact that the mother looks as if she's sitting on a bench at the railway station, train spotting. Obviously she's not wearing an anorak or anything. In fact she's stark naked, but throughout the birth she wears an expression that suggests she's seen all these trains before. She's completely uninvolved in all that sucking, gurgling and gouging going on between her legs and, frankly, I find this even more disturbing than the agonies suffered by mother number one.

The third birth is the caesarean section and I really don't want to see this. Isn't that precisely the point of a caesarean – that nobody has to watch because the mother's asleep anyway? Only she's not, as it happens: mother, father and, if you're lucky, the surgeon, are all wide-awake throughout the procedure. I realise this when a curtain is drawn between the upper and lower halves of the mother's body and, as the fun begins, the camera remains trained on the mother's face, although I'm not sure why, as most of the action is taking place south of the curtain. At the crucial moment, however, the lens swings round and we're forced to watch the baby as it's hauled out of a belly that looks nothing like a human belly, but everything like a trap door made of pale, human flesh.

Other than the choice of exit route, the most obvious difference between a 'normal' birth and a caesarean section is that the baby is not required to undergo the trauma of being forced upside-down through a live piece of piping that's at least two sizes too small. This is why, in natural childbirth, he or she emerges red-faced, screaming and clearly petrified at the thought of leaving a place that, for the last nine months, has been a pretty snug little hidey-hole. But the caesarean baby in this video isn't even awake when plucked from that white, interior world and it certainly doesn't look like it was expecting an eviction order. Upon arrival, the baby resembles nothing so much as a creature from another world which, after all, is precisely what it is. The whole thing leaves me as shocked as someone who has gone fishing for sea trout, got a bite and, to his horror, hauled up a translucent ghost-fish that belongs at a depth of 2,000 metres.

Mother number four is also having a bit of trouble. First, she doesn't speak any French and can't understand the exhortations of the midwife when asked to push harder. Then we learn that she's already been labouring like this for four hours, so maybe it's not that she can't understand the midwife, but rather that she wishes the bitch would just go to hell. Anyway, the midwife arrives at the conclusion that this baby clearly isn't coming out of its own accord, so she reaches for what appear to be a couple of outsized salad spoons. How can she take lunch at a moment like this? But no, these are the forceps and gently they're inserted into the sides of the vagina to help ease out the baby's head. This does not appear to add greatly to the mother's suffering and once a little vinaigrette is added to the proceedings, the head is out, the shoulders twisted around and it's practically all over before the baby is served up onto Mummy's shoulder as easily as a salade niçoise.

I can't help but feel pleased for the mother this time. Despite her exhaustion, she manages a huge smile of delight and you can almost touch her elation. It all looked really natural which I guess is why Helena has now recovered from the shock of the caesarean and is in floods of tears once more.

More piano music. Here comes number five. The thought crosses my mind that this isn't nearly as bad as I'd feared. Am I actually enjoying it? Well no, but at least I'm still conscious. Hang on, something's different here... Who's that guy? Yeah, him, the psychopath wearing the glasses? Why, of course! It's the father. But why is he the first we've seen all afternoon? I thought the father was always present at the birth in these enlightened times? Maybe that's the reason these particular births have been chosen? They're the only ones in which the father is not conspicuously passing out in front of the cameras or doing something even worse like attempting to chat up the midwife, tuning in to the footie on a hospital monitor or telling crude and poorly-timed jokes. I glance at Helena to make sure she's registered the fact that, compared to this guy, I'm an absolute dream. But her attention is riveted to the screen and the not-too-distant future.

While she's being strapped to the bed, number five is telling us precisely how much tai chi and reflexology she's been doing in preparation for this very day. Apparently her husband has been in attendance at all the preparatory classes. The smug little bastard! We'll see what happens when the real action starts.

Cut to the end of the contractions and guess what? I'm afraid that, despite the essential oils burning in the background and the henna symbol Daddy has tried to tattoo between a pair of eyes which are way too close together, Mummy's in a bit of trouble and a whole lot of pain. Zen Man approaches the bedside and whispers a few words of encouragement in her ear – he tells her to relax, to breathe deeply and remember all they have practised together on the bean bags back home. But Mummy's serenity snaps as abruptly as a brittle twig thrown onto a roaring fire. In a startling display of spittle and four-letter words, hubbykins is invited to fuck off and die and his participation in the once-in-a-lifetime event is brought to an abrupt end. So much for birth as spiritual initiation. Secretly I reflect that this couldn't have happened to a nicer guy, but then again, I'd better be careful – I don't have a great track record myself and Helena has already warned me that if she's in great pain, she's liable to explode and demand my expulsion from the room. Meantime, a soft focus close-up shows the Zen Man looking as doleful as a puppy that's pissed on a new carpet, because his partner has reneged on their watertight agreement and spoiled their child's only shot at a perfect, harmonious birth.

It all ends well enough, though, and I'm able to watch without squirming as the baby unfolds like a rose in time-lapse photography. I'm almost ready to concede that childbirth is a beautiful and moving experience. But I still beg to differ from all those ageing aunties, who will insist that all babies are beautiful. They're not. They may improve with age but, believe me, they're all born as revoltingly ugly as any other piece of amphibian roadkill.

At the end of the film, the hospital *chef de service* is interviewed by the production team. This was an extremely bad idea. Just when I was getting a bit of confidence in the whole idea, we're suddenly presented with this bizarre figure, who looks exactly like a hard-boiled egg or, from certain angles, not unlike Salvador Dali upside down.

From the hospital cinema it's but a short step across the hall for our final private viewing. Courtesy of the ultrasound, we are to be treated to one last, sneak preview before the little fellow is unleashed upon the world. For once, I'm the calmer of the two as the jelly hits the belly and it's Helena's turn to get nervous. She tries to explain how our half-English son has already tried to drink his first cup of tea and demonstrates the results to the doctor who concedes that this was an unwise experiment but confirms that he's so well insulated we have nothing to worry about.

Then the search for our son begins again. 'There he is,' she declares and, sure enough, we find him reclining in his subcutaneous bubble bath, gurgling and waving his arms around vigorously enough to land a light aircraft. All of his facial features are now quite clearly visible. I can see the shape of his forehead, the gentle slope of the nose, and a tiny pair of lips which appear to be forming a few early words. He looks pretty happy and is obviously unaware of the five possible traumas to come. Looking anxiously for any sign that there might be something wrong with the only thing that truly matters in her life right now, Helena scans the screen, then my face and finally the implacable features of the doctor. But I'm calm, the doctor is calm and you can almost feel Helena relax as she exhales for the first time since breakfast.

'Is it still a boy?' she asks somewhat bizarrely as the doctor twists the joystick away from his face. The doctor says he has not mutated into a she since our last visit and starts taking a series of measurements.

'Hmm,' she murmurs, 'large head, long legs, long arms. He's going to be a tall one, a bit like his father.'

Helena looks at me approvingly: 'Yes, you were a big baby too, weren't you?'

'I am? I mean, er, yes, I was.'

'He's in the 95th percentile on all measurements,' adds the doctor, as Helena beams with pride and I demand an explanation.

Our chit-chat is brought to an abrupt end when the underground chamber is filled with the amplified thunder of a tiny heartbeat. As his perfectly regular pulse etches its luminous green way across the screen, I reflect upon the true wonder of this evidence of a life. Despite the usual boyhood obsessions with the irresistible slope of the breast, it took me a long time to discover how babies were really made. Even when I did (thanks to some rudimentary diagrams and whatever lewd scribbling were available on the walls of the toilets), I remained unwilling to apply this theoretical knowledge until well into my fourth decade. In the interim, I was more than content to concentrate on those bells and whistles which make the act of procreation such a pleasurable one. But the few, mechanical facts at my disposition are hopelessly inadequate when it comes to explaining how such an act can produce the highly coordinated cells, all flying in formation, with which I'm confronted today.

I know little of the tiny building blocks of life – of their division and multiplication – still less of the chromosomes or that final twist of DNA. Yet, for the most fleeting of moments, it all seems so unimportant, as if it were really no explanation at all for the fact that Helena's belly, which not so long ago housed nothing more exotic than a selection of the finest cheeses in France, is now fit to burst with something infinitely more wondrous – a complete collection of limbs, nerves and sinew, all dancing around to the steady beat of another unique human heart. He can already hear, soon he will talk and develop thoughts and a will of his own. I'm told that Helena and I have created this life and I suppose it must be true that we set these events in motion. But since we lit the blue touch paper, all we've done is step back and allow the raging miracle to burst into being.

We'll soon be needed again, of course, but right now

something else is doing its work and to be honest I haven't a clue what that something is – human biology, evolution, or maybe even a God. Perhaps the most beautiful thing of all is that there's really no need to for me to understand any of this. I'm free to accept it all as some inexplicable gift.

My reverie is broken as the ultrasound is snapped off. That's it now! The medical profession has done its part. It has peeked, poked, monitored, measured and printed off the results. It has even attempted to reassure, although in my case that's beyond the limit of its abilities. Doctors love to convey a semblance of control but, despite all that sophisticated mechanical wizardry, they have even less influence over the process of creation than Helena and I. Now there is really no more any of us can do, except wait. As we leave the hospital, the doctor slips me another photograph of our son and I cram it into my wallet. Every half an hour or so for the rest of the day, I take it out for a quick look.

Sensing that the ultrasound has cleared the clouds that have been gathering in my head for the past few days, Helena seizes her opportunity to raise, once again, the subject that's been occupying inordinate amounts of her time:

'Don't you think it's about time we agreed on a name?'

I know what this means: it's about time I agreed with Helena's own choice of name. I help her into the passenger seat which gives me a few valuable seconds to walk round to the other side of the car and consider my strategy. 'I thought we'd already agreed?' I say, snapping shut my safety belt.

'Really?'

'Yes, on that name that works in both French and English.'

'Yes!' cries Helena excitedly.

'We both like it, right?'

'You do? I mean, yes, we do!'

'We do.' I ease the car out into an orderly flow of rush hour traffic.

'So?'

'So, Thomas it is then!'

I choose this moment to study the action in the rear-view mirror, although I soon feel Helena's glare burning its way into my temple.

'You know very well it will not be Thomas.'

'It won't?'

'It won't!' Then Helena reminds me of that other, rather old-fashioned name of which she still hopes to persuade me.

It's 99 percent certain she'll succeed, of course. I'm just enjoying resisting the inevitable for as long as I can. Where's the harm in that? Anyway, it's not so much the name and more her tactics that I'm resisting. She's spent months poring over the complete list of boy's names and, several weeks ago, she produced the final edition of her shortlist. Only it wasn't that short. It took more than three days just to read the thing before I rejected every single name on it. I rejected Elliot (which sounds too plummy and back-of-the throat), I rejected Ethan (too pagan and ritualistic) and I rejected Ruben (too Lower East Side). In fact, I rejected everything from Antonin (which I couldn't pronounce without swallowing the tip of my nose) to Zebedee (what do you expect? He's hardly going to thank me for naming him after a spotty French puppet with a ludicrous moustache, now is he?).

Purely out of retaliation, Helena proceeded to reject all of my own choices and the game has continued for weeks, which is why he will remain 'the little fellow' for as long as I can get away with it.

'So what about it then?' asks an exasperated Helena as I pull the *Clio* into a parking space barely six kilometres from our apartment.

'What about what?'

'You know what!'

'You mean the name you love and the one for which he'll be taunted across the playgrounds of Europe?'

'Yes, that one!'

'Well, in the event that neither of us can think of anything better, I suppose I can be persuaded to consider it, although most babies are named at the last minute, you know. That's how Agathe ended up as Agathe, remember?'

'No. Agathe ended up as Agathe because her parents thought she was a boy and they didn't get any further than the girls names beginning with A before she had to be registered at the town hall.'

This may be true, but I haven't forgotten that Helena will still be in hospital when the time to register the name finally arrives.

The truth about male hormones, December 12th

I've been awake since 4.30 this morning and even in here, buried deep under a quilt of pterodactyl down, it's freezing cold. Helena, sleeping noiselessly next to me, doesn't feel it, as her own central heating system was completely overhauled eight months ago.

Why am I awake at this hour? I suppose it could have something to do with the questions and emotions that are bombarding me like a legion of vengeful soldier ants. There's no sense or logic to their angle of approach. Why have I still not bought a radiator for the little fellow's bedroom? What will happen if I fail to find a job? Have we got anything to eat in the house? What time does the *boulangerie* open? Eventually I can stand it no longer and to shut down the racket in my head, I force myself into the kitchen to make a cup of tea. By the time Helena joins me, I've had breakfast, showered, finished painting the wardrobe, checked my emails and I'm about to depart for the supermarket to sift through all that packaging in the hope of finding some food.

A little later this morning, we're due back at the hospital, this time to talk about dealing with the onset of contractions. I probably have enough experience to give the lecture myself by now and I'm sure Helena feels the same way. She looks strained – as if she's had quite enough of this pregnancy lark. I know how she feels. Nine months is an eternity and I'm not the one with an extraneous child tucked into my pants. As I sift through a basketful of fruit and veggies, it occurs to me that the mother of three or more children spends a significant part of her life bloated, short of breath and emotionally exhausted.

Helena attempts to manoeuvre her way into our cramped little kitchen. It's like watching a pilot trying to land a jumbo jet onto a thin strip of land between a mountain range and the coast. Every movement has become an effort for her and some, like picking up a bar of soap that slips from her grasp, are no longer possible. I ask how she feels.

'I'm fine,' she says, 'I slept well.'

'No,' I say. 'How does it feel to be pregnant?'

'Huh?'

'Does it feel any different?'

Helena looks pointedly at her overflowing belly, then at me. 'Have a guess.'

'No, not physically. I mean how does it feel in your head?'

'No different.'

'But what about your moods?'

'What moods?'

Careful! I can already hear the quicksands sucking at my ankles. 'I just wondered if you feel more, um, sensitive than usual.'

'Sensitive?'

'Yeah, more emotional maybe.'

'What do you mean?'

What do I mean? I'll tell you what I mean! I mean her propensity to burst into tears the minute the restaurant below opens its doors for dinner. I mean how come she's ecstatically happy one minute, only to descend into the foulest of tempers the next? I mean a sense of humour that has gone walkabout and I mean the fact that I can't seem to do anything right.

Even a throwaway comment is likely to be reinterpreted by the massed battalions of Helena's hormones as the deepest of personal insults. *That's* what I mean although that's not quite how I'm going to phrase it:

'Oh, I don't know, just that you get upset more easily these days, that's all.'

'No I don't!'

'You do!' And here we go again.

'What about *your* moods then?' She's changing tack and as usual I'm the last to notice that the winds have changed.

'What moods?'

'I never know what kind of a mood you're going to be in these days.'

'What are you talking about?'

'I'm talking about two days ago, when I asked you to help me with the wardrobe and you sulked for the rest of the day.'

'I did not!'

'Yes you did.'

She's right. I did and I know I did. And she's right about my moods. But knowing it and admitting it aren't quite the same thing, are they?

'What's the matter with you anyway?'

I don't want to have this discussion. Not now. Not ever.

'Sit down!' says Helena sternly and something about her manner convinces me to do as I'm told (though it could be the irons she's snapped around my legs).

'Why don't you talk to me?'

'About what?'

'Well, why don't we start with your anger?'

'I'm not angry!'

Helena waits for a moment. 'Why are you angry?'

'I don't know.'

'Yes, you do. Tell me.'

I sit there in silence, arms crossed firmly over my chest. I know that I can't win, that I'm going to have to tell her. I feel about thirteen years old.

It turns out that I'm angry about a great many things: I'm angry that I was awake and unable to sleep at 4.30 this morning, I'm angry about the fact that it's bitingly cold in the apartment, I'm angry about painting the wardrobe and doing all the washing up, angry that I can't find a job, furious that I can't speak French, incensed that Helena is pregnant and livid because I'm sure I won't make a good father. I'm angry with France and the French, angry with England and me being English, I'm angry with Helena, angry with the restaurant, the neighbours, the street, the city and the rest of the fucking planet. Most of all, I'm mad as hell that I can't go straight to the pub and drink until I'm so pissed that I can't remember what I'm angry about in the first place.

When I'm through, we just sit in silence in our dark little apartment and Helena is the first to speak. She tells me that when our son is born the world will suddenly look a whole lot different, that I'll stop being angry with everything and everybody because my life will be changed by the fact that I'll have to look after someone else. She says there'll be no more time to waste on regret and pointless conversations which take place in my head before dawn.

I don't know whether this is true, but even the prospect of it makes me feel a little bit better, so I set off to buy something I hope will keep the entire family warm through the winter. Half an hour later, I'm back with a oil-filled radiator, although carrying the thing home has damned near killed me. At home I find Helena hanging out a couple of acres of pregnancy underwear and I watch as she tries to shuffle it out of sight before I can give it a dirty look.

'They've found him,' she says.

'Found who?'

'Saddam Hussein!'

'Who found him?'

'The Americans.'

'Oh!' Helena extracts another pair of billowing white

knickers from the tangled mess in the laundry basket.

'He wasn't hiding in a pair of those, was he?'

It takes a few seconds to sink in and she looks at me before she looks at the knickers.

'After all, there's room for half the elite Republican Guard in there.' I'm taking a risk on several fronts here – a risk with the pride of French women, a risk our conversation earlier this morning hasn't completely cleared the air and not least the risk that several kilos of damp underwear will be thrown in my face. It could go either way, but when the hint of a smile darts across her face and she turns her back to hide the evidence, I know I've got away with it.

After the mental exertions of conversation, I'm overtaken by the desire to do something physical and to inhale the fresh air as deeply as I possibly can. Since this is something that's not easily achieved within the confines of Pigalle, I race downstairs, jump onto my bike and begin dodging my way through the northern boulevards of the frigid stone city. I feel strangely liberated as I pass the Eiffel Tower which appears to have been truncated at the midriff by the damp grey clouds which are being whipped low over the Paris skyline. Occasionally the sun peeps its head out only to retire for another few minutes' more kip. In no time at all I'm entering the calm of the Bois de Boulogne. The place is almost deserted, the trees have been completely shorn of their summer finery and very few leaves remain on the ground. To assist the rapid decomposition of the vegetation, a sudden rain shower sweeps through the Bois.

I follow a favourite track in a westerly direction – one which takes me as far as possible from any sign of humanity. It's a few degrees warmer in the woods than it is back on the naked, shivering streets of the city. At first, the ground is packed hard beneath my tyres and it feels as if I'm floating just above the surface of the earth. Then my wheels sink into muddy patch, slowing my progress and sucking me that little bit closer to the earth's core. Through it all, a steady heartbeat carries me on to the next post. Occasionally I encounter other people, out forging their own paths through the early winter afternoon. Some walk alone or with a dog, others alongside a husband, wife, or lover. Some walk in silence, eyes to the front, others are engaged in gentle conversation and pause when their discourse reaches a natural lull, only to move on again once agreement is reached. Then there are those locked in a steady embrace and for whom the world has come to a temporary stop. They hear only the sound of one another's breathing. They're complete today, in their own little world, and barely notice the seasons shifting around them or the coming of the dew as it settles in their hair.

As I reach home, the adrenalin in my body adds a sensation of mild elation to the tiredness. I put the finishing touches to the wardrobe and we eat a simple dinner of curried vegetables and rice. The winter solstice is approaching fast but today has proved longer than any other in my life. Now I'm craving rest.

The anatomy lesson, December 13th

'Come on Helena. We're going to be late for the hospital.'

'Won't be a minute.' She's back in the study as it continues its unstoppable conversion into a baby's bedroom.

'Come and have a look.'

Inside the wardrobe, she has arranged all the baby's clothes. His first stuffed toy is in there too, a small bear with less than a month and a half to wait before its permanent playmate arrives.

As usual we're the last to arrive at the hospital. The midwife and four overripe mothers are already sprawled across the floor mats. Once again, I'm the only father. The others can't all be working, surely?

The midwife launches straight into her spiel. She asks whether we know how the baby is positioned in the womb.

Then she asks for a volunteer to draw our ideas on the blackboard. Helena snatches the chalk before anyone shows the temerity to draw anything other than *her* baby. First she sketches an enormous belly, then a baby upside down in the womb which she surrounds in blue chalk to represent the amniotic fluid. I notice that Helena builds a nice buffer between the womb and the skin on the outside of the belly. Whether she does this because she's still worried about the spilt tea or she's just leaving room for some Roquefort cheese, I'm not entirely sure but once again it strikes me as odd that babies spend so much of their time inverted like this, before plunging out to join the rest of us right-way-up bipeds.

The midwife asks whether the rest of us agree with Helena's sketch, although she does it in such a tone that you know the answer already. But none of us is any the wiser, so she has to get off her nice plump floor cushion and finish the job herself. Immediately she erases Helena's buffer zone and demonstrates how the little fellow's legs really are just below the surface. So, I wasn't imagining it when I saw him wiping his feet on the inside of Helena's belly. Then the midwife picks up a life size model of a baby and a model of a detached pelvis, which just happens to be lying around on the floor, and proceeds to demonstrate the probable exit route that the little fellow will be taking next month.When she asks whether we think this will hurt, I find that my French isn't good enough to express my suspicion that it will be nothing short of excruciating.

We're told not to hesitate once the contractions start and to get down to the hospital as soon as we possibly can, without calling an ambulance and preferably without crashing the car. It may even be better to catch a cab, she suggests, but don't say anything to the driver – he may be less interested than we think and definitely won't appreciate any placenta on his upholstery.

Sports personality of the year, December 14th

Our focus on the birth has been so complete that even the intense burst of advertising activity heralding the onset of Christmas has failed to penetrate my consciousness. But only now, a dozen or so posting days from the most important event on the retail calendar, I remember that we'll be spending Christmas in Caen with Helena's family, which means it must be time I went shopping.

Somewhat illogically for an unemployed person, I've chosen a Saturday morning to get started and the whole of suburban Paris has already passed through the revolving doors of the *Galeries Lafayette* before me, although most of the sales staff appear to have taken the morning off. Outside it's pissing with rain so the department store is also stuffed to the rafters with old ladies armed with umbrellas. One wrong move in here (men's ties and socks) and a member of the blue rinse brigade is likely to impale me against the large and highly decorative tree which is the central feature of the store's Christmas campaign. Propelled forward by the immutable laws of perpetual motion and carried up five sets of escalators without getting close enough to even spit at the wares, I'm sworn at, stabbed three times in the leg, insulted by a security guard and almost get my wallet filched. But I know when I'm beaten and leave the seething masses to return home shorn of all dignity and with nothing more to show for my excursion than a packet of charity Christmas cards.

Meanwhile, Helena has been reassured by the hospital that her intermittent contractions are par for the course, so she's decided that we're capable of entertaining this evening. I have my doubts, especially when she abandons me in the kitchen two hours before our guests arrive with a dozen half-stuffed courgettes. We stare at each other for a while, but the vegetables remain stubbornly mute and clearly have no intention of telling me how I'm expected to fill them with mincemeat.

Paris, December 16th

I made the decision not to accompany Helena on yet another trip to the hospital earlier this morning, as the topic of the day, once again, was pain. She returns with the news that in this, the thirty seventh week of pregnancy, the little fellow is now fully formed and ready to go. All he's doing now, according to the medical profession, is waiting to catch a ride on the right wave. Why do they insist upon providing you with such useless information?

'Any news? asks Helena.

'Not much, just these.' I show her a couple of job descriptions

'Are these marketing jobs?' she asks, as her eyes jump to the salary at the bottom of the page.

'Yes.'

'I thought you didn't want to do that any more.'

'I don't, but I'm thinking of the baby.'

Helena leaves the room before I can explain that I'm too scared to turn my back on what I know best. Like an unwelcome alien which has beamed itself aboard *The Starship Enterprise*, the horrible idea is now fully formed in my head. I've decided to return to marketing services. Gyrating eternally in the particle accelerator of capitalism may not make me happy, but at least it will fill his belly.

The phone rings. Someone says hello. At first I think it's Helena's father and I ask him what he'd like for Christmas. There's quite a lot of silence on the other end of the line before I realise that it's not Helena's father at all, but an old colleague from the UK. He tells me about a job that's going in London and wants to know if I'm interested. I don't know what to say so I ask for a bit to time to think about it. Then I apologise about the Christmas present and promise to send him a card instead.

Christmas wrapping, December 18th

Over my shoulder, the dark angel of marketing is whispering persuasively that I'll be able to return to the world of loud ties and shiny suits without sinking into depression or a bottomless keg of beer. But how should I approch the possibility of a move to London with Helena? I'll need to emphasise the positive aspects from her point of view. But what on earth are they likely to be? The money? No. The football highlights on a Saturday night? Hardly. The fact that London offers more green space than Paris? Maybe, but it's also twice as expensive and we won't be able to afford a house with a garden until I'm on the payroll of Lucifer himself. No, there must be something else... Why, of course, Cousin Nathalie! I'm sure Helena would like to be close to her favourite cousin and watch our son growing up alongside Léonie and Celeste. It's got to be worth a try. But hang on a minute, why am I trying to convince Helena when I'm far from convinced myself? Sod it! I need a break from all this self-torture. I'm back off to the shops. Maybe if I sit at Santa's knee long enough, he'll come up with the answer *and* be polite enough to wrap it in red and green foil for me.

In the afternoon, Helena and I spend at least an hour personalising a cardboard box that contains a wooden motorcycle for my godson. I do this not only because of my instinctive aversion to the Aryan families with which toy manufacturers insist upon adorning their products, but also because young children are usually more interested in the box than the present itself. And why wouldn't they be? After all, the packaging costs the manufacturer far more than whatever is in the box. I replace the photo of Mr and Mrs Master Race with a picture of Helena and me. Then I cut out a picture of my godson's mother and turn her into a helmeted motorbike rider. Finally I cull all the blond bobbed boys on the packaging and replace them with an assortment of apes. Helena can't quite understand the inordinate pleasure this brings me but, then again, what does she know about presents?

After a brief conversation about precisely what Helena would like for Christmas (which is a bloody chandelier, if you can believe it!), I tell her about the job in London. The exchange goes something like this:

'Helena, I've been offered a job in London.'

'Oh?'

'Yes, you remember London, don't you? It's the place at the other end of the Euro tunnel.'

'Yes, I remember London. It's the city where it costs €60 to get on a bus which was built back when you still had an empire, isn't it?'

'Er, yes, that's right. But it's also the place where Nathalie lives and, as far as I can remember, lives quite happily.'

'I know where my cousin lives, thank you.'

'Wouldn't you like to live near Celeste, Léonie and Arsenal?'

'Who?'

'Celeste, Léonie and the new baby.'

'It depends.'

'On...?'

'What we'd be doing over there.'

'Working. We'd be working. At least, I'd be working. You'd be looking after the baby and spending a lot of time with Nathalie and her kids. If you wanted to, that is.'

Helena looks at me, the word suspicion writ large across her forehead. 'So what's the job?'

'Is that the time?' I'm sidling out into the kitchen by now. 'I'd better get dinner on.'

'I don't want us to end up in a tiny flat in a big city, with you working all hours at a job you despise and never seeing your son.'

'Sorry Helena, I can't hear you. You haven't seen the sausages, have you?'

Ali Baba and the forty thieves, December 21st

I've given up on the idea of buying Helena a present unaided and beg her to tell me where I can find a chandelier. The only place I can remember seeing one is over at the presidential palace but Helena has advised me against pilfering government property and adds helpfully that they're available at every flea market in Paris. I agree to go with her and try to look delighted at the prospect even though I'd rather spend the morning unblocking the drains.

But the flea market turns out not to be quite the ordeal I'd feared. Of course, there's nowhere to park, it's freezing cold, the stuff on sale is completely knackered and the stalls are all manned by people who ought to be in jail for grand larceny. But other than that it's OK. We've chosen the flea market at Porte de Vanves, at the southernmost tip of the *périphérique*, because Helena says it's the cheapest.

It takes us more than an hour to get there and the first stall we come across is run by a cheerful bloke from the Maghreb. Not that it makes a blind bit of difference where any of these market traders come from – an excess of unfounded cheer and a conniving grin are the only prerequisites for setting up stall, whether the market is in Manchester, Marrakech or on Mars. Anyway, it turns out that this particular criminal does have a chandelier, although it's in five pieces and covered in about three centuries worth of grime. Inexplicably, this only adds to the charm as far as Helena's concerned and the trader can tell that we're interested which must be why, when I ask him the price, he conjures up a wince and tells me it's €350. Naturally I chortle and return the entrails to the pavement whence they came and head to the next stall, assuming that Helena will not be far behind. Wrong again. Now, she's tugging at my sleeve, telling me that that's what these things cost and asking me to imagine what it will look like after it's been cleaned up. I assure her that, even if an army of professional cleaners were to work on it for a week, this particular artefact would still resemble a piece of mangled scrap metal. I politely inform her that I'd prefer to insert my money into the nearest drain than let this unscrupulous bastard get his hands on it. 'It's because you're English,' Helena says urgently, 'they think they can charge what they like. Keep your mouth shut from now on. I'll do the negotiating.' Now I remember the first time I came to the flea market with Helena (which I swore would be the last) when she talked me into parting with my life savings in exchange for a pair of mildewed old armchairs.

As I reminisce about the friendly old ladies of the *Galeries Lafayette*, I try to keep any thoughts of murder to myself because it's clear that Helena's enjoying herself for the first time in weeks and hasn't once mentioned the extra weight she's carrying as we amble from one stall to the next. She's more than cordial with the traders, when all I want to do is have them arrested. But I content myself by keeping my mouth shut and my hands deep in my pockets (just to make sure that there's no room for theirs).

By the time we reach the very last stall at the market, my teeth are beginning to chatter and I'm not feeling quite so well disposed towards the world as I was half an hour ago. I get there before Helena and, to my surprise, find what looks like a chandelier, hanging out of the back of a white van. I try not to stare at it and do my best to look like a French person by pursing my lips and indulging in a series of futile, calorie-burning gestures. Eventually Helena arrives and I point discreetly at what looks like being her last chance of getting what she wants for Christmas. She likes it and we open the bidding with the stall holder, who isn't at all cheerful. In fact he's a miserable old sod who isn't prepared to negotiate as much as one centime. My sole contribution to the bargaining process is 'Let's just pay the old bugger and get out of here,' but Helena's having none of it. According to her, bartering is all part of the charm of the flea market. She wants the chandelier all right, but not if she has to pay what he's asking for it. I protest that this model is barely a third of the price of the other, that it's still in one piece and may actually work. But I'm ignored by both Helena and the miserable one.

Providentially, the wife of the stall holder appears in the nick of time. It turns out that her cadaver of a husband doesn't understand the magic of the market any better than I do and she's only too happy for us to try and negotiate the price down to something which probably approximates to what they wanted for the piece all along.

Right! Can we go home now, please? Not quite. The woman turns out to be every inch as cheerful as the rest of her market brethren and now she's noticed that Helena's pregnant. How it took her so long, God alone knows. Maybe she just wasn't prepared to acknowledge the fact until the haggling was complete, lest any human emotion adversely affect the financial transaction. Now she wants to talk to Helena, minute by minute, through the births of each of her three girls. Halfway through the second of them, Mr Misery Guts and I exchange silent, meaningful glances and I realise he doesn't want to be stuck here listening to this any more than I do. Another place he wasn't too keen on being, some thirty-five years ago, was the hospital delivery room. He was there for the birth of his first daughter alright, but according to his wife, he found it so disgusting that halfway through the ordeal he left the mother of his children in the hands of the midwife and didn't return until all the blood had been wiped off the walls. Judging by the tone of his wife, he has yet to be forgiven for this and, as the rest of her tale unfolds, he shifts from one foot to the other and pretends to polish up a piece of old brass. Suddenly I'm keen to put some distance between myself and the absconder, just in case something rubs off and I end up beating the same cowardly retreat.

It's a long way home from here, but who cares? As far as I'm concerned, it's mission accomplished and I'm stuffed with the straw of false pride. For the first time ever, I've bought Helena a present that she won't be sending straight back to the manufacturer. After all, there'd be little point, as whoever made this particular artefact has been dead for at least a century. Just one pleasure remains before I can say goodbye to all flea markets forever: as we pass the original stallholder, I can see he's failed to flog the tangle of wires and broken brass he's been trying to pass off as something worth hanging from a ceiling, so naturally I pause at his stall with enough of our own purchase removed from its plastic bag to ensure he can see it.

Back home, the damned object offers no clue as to how it was ever hung from a ceiling but luckily for me, the labourers in the apartment below are putting in a bit of illegal Sunday overtime and Helena bribes one of them to come up and do the job for us before some friends arrive for dinner. To reach the light fitting, he has to stand on our table, which in turn, requires the removal of his boots. Just as the sun is setting on this, the shortest day of the year, he finishes the job. The only problem now is that the apartment smells like an abattoir in Hell and I need to scrape the remnants of his acrylic socks from the table before our guests arrive.

The mother of all pains, December 22nd

Back at the maternity hospital, we're learning more about how to cope with the trauma and aftermath of childbirth. Today's exciting instalment is called *l'enfantement*, so I'm not expecting to provide much more than a bit of moral support and the odd unwelcome rejoinder as Helena is taught to breast feed, change nappies and the right way up to hold a baby. But it turns out that, rather than kicking back on the sofa while she gets on with the job, *l'enfantement* translates roughly as giving birth and, all too soon, we're reintroduced to our old friend, the detachable pelvis.

As the midwife starts forcing the ethnically correct doll through the plastic pelvis, I'm busy observing the sprinkling of my fellow fathers who've turned up to watch that which we'll never have to go through. Arranged on the brightly-coloured floor mats, most of them can hardly bear to look and, sure enough, they soon start writhing and squirming as pointlessly as an earthworm stranded on the central lane of a motorway. So it's not just me, which is vaguely encouraging. I focus again on the midwife and she explains that the baby may descend the *canal de naissance* any way he damned well chooses and, although most emerge head first, she shows how it's possible for them to arrive at the big party buttocks to the fore.

Over the course of the twelve hours which it takes to deliver a first child, the contractions gradually increase in both frequency and intensity and so, inevitably, does the pain. I remember again Cécile telling us how it became so unendurable that she implored the midwife to slaughter her right there in the delivery room. I've tried to imagine this scene but I can't, or maybe I daren't. I've also asked Helena whether she has thought much about it, but she just shrugs her shoulders and says it's something every woman must resign herself to. I'm convinced that such suffering must change your outlook on life irrevocably. Once they've been through these agonies, it's no wonder that women scoff so readily at the things which have most men howling – an unexpectedly large credit card bill, being passed over for promotion at work, the common cold or losing on penalties in the World Cup semi-final.

Happily, there's always the option of the epidural, which can be taken until relatively late in the day and Helena has decided that this is the way to go – to see how much pain she can bear before seeking assistance. She'll have to judge it carefully though, because the time comes when it's too late for the release of anaesthesia and, no matter how hard you're begging for death, the job has to be finished without it.

My sister gave birth to both David and Lily without an epidural. When I asked her why she'd want to do such a thing, the answer she gave was short, sharp and just a little sour: She wanted to give birth naturally and, in the process, anoint herself to martyrdom. Of course, most women will tell you that the moment the baby is out, the pain is as easily forgotten as yesterday's bread. I've no idea how such a thing is possible but then again, there are quite a number of things I've yet to comprehend when it comes to women.

The midwife then demonstrates a variety of different positions the mother may adopt in order to push the baby out of its uterine comfort zone. I thought the only way to do it was flat on your back and howling for the duration. Not so, it seems, as babies can be pushed out lying on your side or even stretched out on your front. A popular variant at this hospital is for the man to sit behind the woman for support and for a rolled-up sheet to be wrapped around both partners as the woman hangs on to the ends and pushes for all she's worth. Practising the manoeuvre, we look like an Oxbridge boat crew arguing over who should make the bed and it occurs to me that, despite the disposable nappy, the proliferation of the *iPod* and all those other wonders of our ever-advancing civilisation, giving birth remains just as primitive as it was when Eve bit into an early *Golden Delicious.* The bottom line is that the minute you stop pushing, the baby's preferred course of action is to beat a hasty retreat back to the Garden of Eden whence he came.

Once the reluctant one has finally been expelled from his kingdom, he remains attached to the mother ship via the umbilical cord and, according to the midwife, any partners who have survived the ordeal thus far are invited to cut it themselves. I freeze on the spot as that alien, quivering blue object so clearly visible on the photos of Inès returns to haunt me. A brief glance around the room reveals that I'm not the only one horrified by the prospect of slicing through live tissue, although I'm determined not to let it show. I don't want my son to be met by a look of total disgust on his father's face and, to alleviate the tension building up in my belly, I ask whether we're expected to bring our own scissors.

After the session, I wonder, once more, whether I'm truly

prepared for what will come to pass in a little more than a month. If I'm honest, the answer has still got to be 'No', although I don't know what else I can do to get ready. Was it not Helena's paediatrician father who told me that it's the men who claim to be shocked by nothing who invariably end up out for the count in their very own hospital bed?

From the hospital, we take a taxi straight to the station at St Lazare and, by some miracle, we end up in the only compartment not stuffed as full as a jar of Spanish anchovies, thus enabling Helena to stretch out across three seats. A ferocious-looking Frenchwoman in the seat opposite checks out Helena's belly, gives me a quick, filthy look and immediately strikes up one of those we-women-who've-been-through-it-all-before-type conversations with Helena. I've observed this phenomenon with increasing regularity over the past few weeks. It wasn't just that woman at the flea market who allowed her professional façade to slip at the sight of a heavily pregnant woman. I've watched on amazed as the deep-frozen faces of supermarket cashiers, scowling bank tellers and even the murderous and deeply deranged French post office clerks all melt into something approaching compassion at the mere sight of a pregnant woman. Maybe it's nothing more than complicity over all that pain, but I've seen, with my own eyes, how women will bare their canines if a pregnant sister is in any way threatened by a stray, inconsiderate male.

Late night drinking and the prospective father, December 23rd

At the other end of the line, Helena's family is waiting for us under a Christmas tree and, as the cab grinds to a halt in the drizzle, we're greeted by Pierre, Clément and rabbit, all of whom have driven from one end of the continent to the other to show off the new baby. Ever since he was betrayed forever by his mother over the birth of his little brother, young Clément has been clinging onto his father for all he's worth.

I register the pain and disappointment written all over his pale and injured little face. Like a favourite pair of jeans, he'll be wearing the same expression throughout Christmas.

The great usurper himself is lying on the sofa, gurgling away quite happily. Maxime is three months old and completely unaware of the way in which he has ravaged the life of his elder brother. I take my first good look at this small, wriggling package of arms and legs. Despite three ultra-sounds and all those assurances that he'll be fine, I have yet to think beyond the birth or dared to wonder what my own son might look like. But now, as Maxime stares at me through trusting, grey-blue irises, I allow the question to filter through my defences, beyond my gnawing fears and the deep blue yonder of the impending birth. What will he look like? I don't really care, because all I really want is a healthy, happy baby like Maxime.

As I sit on the floor beside him, the baby's limbs describe a series of short, involuntary jerks during one of which he accidentally encounters my wrist. He clutches at it hard and I can feel a tiny fingernail digging into my skin. I had no idea they possessed cutting edges at such a tender age.

'Ah! I see you two have met.' It's Cécile, followed closely by Helena.

'Look at this!' I say, pointing with astonishment at the bundle of velour on the sofa.

'Yes, it's a baby. Haven't you seen one before?'

This makes me more than a little indignant. Of course I've seen babies before, but this time it feels different and I think I know why. 'Yes, but I never realised they looked so, you know, so human!'

'What did you think they were then?' asks Cécile.

I want to say lizards or reptiles. That would be the truth, after all. But I'd better not. I'm just pleased that the next few days will give me an opportunity to study the whole business of babies and parenthood in a bit more detail and, dispensing entirely with the customary courtesies, I rudely fire off some preliminary questions.

'How often does he eat?'

'As often as he can get away with it, but generally about every four hours.'

'Are you still breastfeeding?'

'Yes.'

'What about sleeping?'

'He does more of that than in the beginning, when he was waking up three times a night.'

'Three! Are you sure?'

'Yes, quite sure.'

'Why?'

'Some babies have a problem digesting their food. It was giving him a bit of a stomach ache, so he kept waking up and crying.'

'So that's not always the case then?' I try to eliminate any overly hopeful tone from my voice.

'No, it didn't happen with Clément.'

'So with some babies you, um, they get to sleep the night through?'

'Not for the first couple of months, they don't.'

'No? What do they wake up for then?'

'Breast feeding, a good cry, or just to check you're still there.'

'I see. But if it's for a feed, there's not much Pierre can contribute, right?'

'He's there to provide moral support,' interjects Helena pointedly.

'Maybe, but he can't do a great deal on the breastfeeding front, can he?'

'There's more to it than getting your breasts out.'

Cécile quickly nips our argument in the bud by explaining that Pierre helps out in the morning before leaving for work, at the mention of which, I decide this would be an opportune moment for me to lug our cases up to the bedroom.

By the time I get back downstairs, the rest of the family

is beginning to assemble around the tree. Aunt Helena is playing with Clément and talking to Cécile, and Pierre is making tea for his parents. And Maxime? Well, Maxime is still lying on the sofa writhing like a caterpillar in a set of itchy woollens.

Christmas Eve in Caen

I'm awakened by the sound of Clément crying. He has a temperature and a bit of a cold. I've yet to forget what happened the last time Clément fell ill and a hand goes straight to my stomach to check for premature contractions.

I've taken but one bite of my morning croissant when I get another disturbing peek at the future. Now Maxime is crying because he needs to be fed and Cécile is trying to get down at least one gulp of coffee before she morphs into a mobile cafeteria. Clément is still crying, partly because he's sick, but mainly because Pierre is trying to keep the inconsolable Maxime busy until the nipple arrives. Pierre continues to rock the Maxime while Clément hangs onto his father's leg – this limb being the only available body part from which he can extract some form of comfort.

Cécile explains that this is the general morning pattern. Alarmed, I glance at Helena but she's already crashed on the sofa, exhausted after consuming an orange juice and a couple of bread and jam *tartines*. Pointing at the pallid, inconsolable Clément, I ask how he's coping with having a brother. 'He must be jealous,' I say in my first statement of the blindingly obvious this morning. Cécile rolls her eyes and relates Clément's horror on his first visit to the hospital after the birth – he hadn't quite understood how that bump in mummy's tummy could be a baby that would one day burst out into an extremely needy and quite unwanted little brother. Perhaps that was just a story his mother had told him to make him smile, as she did every evening before bedtime? But then again, it was now indubitably the case that the bump underneath her dress had disappeared and a small blotchy stranger was now occupying his favourite spot right underneath mummy's earrings. That couldn't possibly be a permanent addition to the family, could it? Not when he'd envisaged that it would forever be just the three of them and the faithful Quito?

Cécile says that right then and there, in that scrubbed Spanish hospital, the penny finally dropped for young Clément. He turned to his mother and looked deep into her soul. She says it was the worst moment of her life, that she could read the hurt and betrayal in the eyes of her son, even though he was unable to express it in words then and may never be able to do so. Since that hideous moment, which taught Clément more about the unfairness of life than he could possibly want to know, he's put quite a distance between himself and his deceitful mother. That's why he clings hard to his father, who at least shows no propensity to hide unwelcome family members inside his clothes, even if he devotes unseemly amounts of attention to them the minute they drop from the skirts of the treacherous one.

Naturally, this is the story of every eldest child that's ever been born and, as an eldest child myself, I've seen enough to remember that my earliest thoughts were dedicated to fratricide. I finish my breakfast quickly and leave the young family to establish the patterns which will dictate family life for the next decade or so.

For as long as I can remember, Christmas has left me feeling vaguely dissatisfied and slightly apart from all that family cheer. Throughout the festivities, I'd try to remain suitably anaesthetised and tell anyone stupid enough to listen that I hated Christmas. Maybe I did, although it's more likely that the time of the year forced me to reflect on my life and my relationships with those closest to me, and I didn't like what I felt. Don't ask me why, but it feels different today. I called my sister last night and she's celebrating with David and Lily at my mother's place. I told her I was sorry I couldn't be with them and the minute the words were out of my mouth, I knew that I meant it. I sent them all their presents a few days ago – nothing much really – just a few bits and pieces with silly jokes written on the labels. More than anything else, I wanted to be able to watch the kids' faces as they tore into the wrapping paper.

Christmas Eve is the main event in France and, downstairs, preparations for our formal dinner are well under way. Pierre has gone to the station to pick up his younger brother, Helena is playing with Clément and it turns out that the most helpful thing I can do is to try to entertain little Maxime. So I pick him up and plonk him onto my knee. He gazes up at me and I stare back at him. OK, so now what? We can't just spend the next hour gawping at one other and a game of *Scrabble* is out of the question. I try a variety of objects but none of them holds his attention for longer than a couple of seconds. For some strange reason, he seems to find my facial features more gruesomely fascinating than any of the glittery Christmas decorations with which I endeavour to distract his attention. He attempts to unscrew the nose off my face, sticks his uncoordinated fingers into my mouth and eyes but he's never happier than when I purse my lips, emit a low buzzing noise and generally behave like an aeroplane spiralling out of control. In fact, he likes this so much that he's even prepared to delay his next feed by a good quarter of an hour in order to watch me behaving like a airborne prat. This is how I discover that Maxime has a wide, gumless smile and that we're perfectly capable of sharing a little pre-prandial banter. He gurgles and I burble. He giggles, I chortle. He gets hiccups and I reciprocate with a few beetly clicking noises. He farts and I, well, never mind.

Then, just when I believe we are on the verge of establishing a firm friendship, young Maxime bursts into a series of staccato sobs closely followed by a bit of uncontrollable howling. Just like Agathe, his deceptively small podgy frame houses a sturdy pair of lungs. At first I'm convinced I've said the wrong thing, made an unacceptable face or grunted in an inappropriate fashion, but no, Cécile informs me there's absolutely nothing to worry about – he just needs to be fed. What, just like that? I'm stunned. How can the weather change so quickly from clear blue skies to *donner und blitzen*? But as she shovels a spoonful of something the colour of Kryptonite into Maxime's mouth, Cécile confirms that there's no gradual, subtle increase of appetite in babies – either they're contentedly gurgling to themselves or they're screaming for food.

We say goodnight to the kids before dinner and gather around the Christmas tree for an aperitif. As far as the kids are concerned, the tree is just an oddly located, blinking conifer. Even Clément is too young to realise that the packages underneath its moulting branches contain gifts intended for him, and while I can't say he goes to bed without a whimper (he still has a temperature and is completely exhausted), he does put up less of a fight than expected.

It's well past midnight by the time we round off an excellent dinner with a Yule log steeped in crème fraîche and espresso. It's time to get started on a rather strange set of French rituals. At first I think the party's over, because everyone disappears upstairs, but this turns out to be nothing more than a spot of last minute gift wrapping. Meanwhile Helena's mother starts organising the presents into a series of small anthills under the tree. Then I'm asked to remove one of my shoes which I'm naturally reluctant to do until I notice that everyone else has already removed one of theirs – They are required to identify to whom each pile of presents belongs. Why the French don't invest in a few of those snowman-shaped sticky labels is beyond me, but for the rest of the night, the entire household is limping in an unnecessary and slightly unhygienic fashion.

Everyone is then called, in ascending order of age, to open their presents in front of everyone else. Thus Helena's little brother is first, followed by his girlfriend and so on, until the tribal elders are finally reached at about five in the morning. This gives me a little time before my own turn in the spotlight during which I reflect gratefully upon the fact that I've not repeated my attempts to buy Helena some French lingerie. Somehow I wouldn't have fancied her unwrapping it, centre-stage, in front of her parents and having the whole family exclaim over its transparency or erotic quotient while I die of embarrassment or hide in the rubbish bin with the shells of the oysters we ate with an aperitif. Funny people, the French!

But one moment of anxiety passes only to be replaced by another, as I suddenly remember that Helena's chandelier is already attached to the ceiling back in Paris. Now the whole family is going to think that I simply haven't bothered to buy her anything and as Pierre takes his turn up front by trying on a pair of ski goggles for all to admire, I whisper urgently to Helena and attempt to hand her a short speech which I've penned to explain my dilemma. But she's next up herself and in the excitement leaves my carefully constructed set of excuses and what remains of my dignity among the growing pile of Christmas wrapping paper on the carpet. Ah well! I've already demonstrated a lack of respect for Helena, her parents, the French language, French culture in general and the institution of marriage. Now the whole world will think that I'm too mean to buy her a present.

Every church has a back door, December 25th

Clément and Maxime are a little sicker. Both have a temperature and noses set on thick, green dribble for the entire day. Clément has finally discovered his own mound of presents and, much in the style of his aunt, has rejected all but one of them – a wooden workbench with an assortment of tools. For two hours he bangs away with a clunky hammer and a set of wooden nails while I assume the role of willing yet incompetent assistant as the rest of the crew drifts gradually from the construction site. Next week he'll be two years old and he's already far better at DIY than I'll ever be. As he begins to tire he looks for his parents but they are nowhere to be seen and he starts to cry. My immediate reaction is one of panic, but then I spot our mutual friend Quito, lying in the corner of the room, bum to the wind. I'm sure that the stuffed toy will offer greater comfort than I can, but dare I pick the wretched thing up? Clément's father and I have been circling each other a little warily ever since I arrived and I don't want to do anything that will endanger our truce. With my luck, Pierre will enter the room the minute I touch the accursed object and I'll be convicted of assault and rabbit battery, and incarcerated forever. Luckily Cécile's finely tuned child antennae have picked up the distress signals before I can make any false moves and I'm saved from the cells for another day.

I take a walk in the fresh air and my feet (or perhaps a part of me not identified in the annals of anatomy) take me back in the direction of the *Abbaye aux Dames*. As I push on the heavy wooden door, it swings wide open and only once I've stepped inside do I realise that I've flattened a small French woman who must have been standing the other side of several centuries of solid French oak. I apologise as best I can before she pushes something into my hand. To my horror I realise it's a service sheet for Christmas mass and now I feel obliged to take it from her.

Inside the abbey, I shuffle to the fringes of the winter-coated congregation. There's quite a gathering, but a few spare chairs are still available right at the back. The priest giving the service is a small round man who, were it not for the robes, would look exactly like the cue ball on a snooker table. Because the abbey is a rather large, cavernous building of damp yellow stone, he's forced to use a microphone to transmit his Christmas message to the assembled throng, which unfortunately lends him the air of a *Railtrack* employee mumbling his way through an excuse for yet another train that's disintegrated overnight in the sidings at Crewe. I'm not sure whether the faithful understand a word of what he's saying but I certainly don't and perhaps this is why I allow a sense of serenity to sneak past my natural defences. I wonder if this is how it usually happens? One day you end up in church by accident, at a moment when your natural resistance to the idea of a power greater than yourself is temporarily weakened, because you've watched too many seasonal sitcoms, say, or because you've caught young Clément's cold and, either way, you're just too embarrassed to walk out before the ceremony ambles to a close.

This reminds me of a story about Cousin Nathalie which Helena told me only last week. Apparently Nathalie has taken to visiting her local church in Tottenham, although she was at pains to explain that this is not because she's fallen prey to organised religion, but rather because the local vicar happens to be an effusive gay man who makes the congregation giggle with his camp and vaguely risqué sermons. It's quite evident from her tone that Helena has swallowed this story whole and doesn't doubt the word of her cousin. What's not so clear is whether Nathalie believes it herself. After all, if it's a good laugh she's looking for, then surely she'd be better off down at her local comedy club? When I suggested that Nathalie may find more in the church than an effete vicar Helena immediately poured scorn on the idea but, then again, Helena is an agnostic whose favourite subject happens to be the history of the world's religions. Or consider the case of my grandfather; an avowed atheist. Once retired, he spent most of his time travelling Europe and visiting sites of historical interest. His favourite destination? Right! The churches and cathedrals of Europe. Shortly before his death, this highly rational man possessed one of the largest collections of postcards in Britain and, at a rough guess, at least 75 percent of them were photographs of buildings erected to the glory of God.

Staring at the magnificent arches in the abbey (purely for their architectural merit, of course), I've been so lost in thought that I barely realise what's going on when a large black man suddenly thrusts his hand into mine and vigorously shakes the pair of us awake. I catch only a few words of what he says – something about 'welcome', 'Christmas', homecoming', and possibly 'turkey meatballs' – and the only thing I can think is to wish him a 'Merry Christmas' in English. Then it's all over and everyone is filing out of the place to the thunderous sounds of an excitable octogenarian organist and some almightily heavy bells. I've no idea whether I'll ever be back, but I do know that it felt more like Christmas in here than it ever did back home in England, watching Steve and all the other McQueens on the telly and stuffing my face with mince pies and brandy disguised as butter.

Back home, Helena and the others want to know where I've been and I'm not sure quite what to say. Publicly I state that I've been for a walk. In private, I confess to Helena that I went to the abbey because I'd heard the priest was an Old Testament homosexual with a nice sarcastic wit and a thriving sideline in rubber cassocks. Helena looks at me suspiciously and orders me to help with the washing up.

After lunch I offer Cécile a brief reprieve and prise Maxime from her arms. He's a little drunk on his mother's milk as I lay him gently in my lap and allow his head to come to rest on my bony, protuberant knees. He stares up at me quite contentedly. For such a tiny creature, Maxime either possesses the most unbelievable powers of concentration, or he suffers from a complete inability to turn his head to the side, but as I try not to listen to Helena and Cécile striking up yet another conversation about childbirth, his eyes drill into mine. Before this unnerves me completely, I ask Cécile to what degree she was scared when the contractions started. But she says she was calm, prepared and felt only a degree of apprehension before each of her two births. I notice again how she skips over the pain part, in an effort, I suppose, to avoid scaring Helena. She does say it must have been hard for Pierre to watch her suffer like that, but reiterates how all is forgotten the minute the cord is cut. Then, with barely a pause for thought, Cécile tells us how she'd love to have a daughter. The very idea has me squirming and jiggling little Maxime on my knees as he grips onto one of my fingers for dear life. I look down into his unblinking eyes once more – they're like two little compact discs loaded up with a million songs.

Fatherhood and the law of averages, December 28th

After another lengthy and untroubled sleep I'm up early to pore over the holiday season football results. Helena's father is the only other person out of bed and he's still smiling to himself at the idea that anyone might want to read a newspaper entirely dedicated to sport. Personally, I find Proust a little heavy going before breakfast.

Cécile and Pierre are supposed to be leaving for the Alps this morning although one look at the kids is enough to suggest that they won't be going anywhere. Neither parents nor children have had much in the way of sleep and before Helena's father can leave for his clinic in town there are a couple of consultations to make at home.

As breakfast descends into chaos, I notice how neither Cécile nor Pierre gets a moment's peace now that the size of their family has been increased by precisely two dirty buttocks and one extra soul. Cécile explains that when it was just Clément, one of them would often find the time to do something other than change a nappy, wipe a nose or read a story. But once the second child arrives, she says, you can forget all about any such extracurricular activity – it will be several years yet before the boys are up to entertaining one an other or spending a quiet afternoon at the public library.

We idle away the last hours of our Christmas break in much the same way as those that preceded it: cooking, talking and playing games. Stories are read to Clément as I hide behind the sofa and listen in an attempt to improve my French vocabulary and Helena tells me she has never seen me with such a smile on my face. The truth of it is that I cannot remember a finer Christmas and, after a dinner of pork stuffed with prunes, we all retire to the living room for a last game of *Scrabble*.

In the hope of avoiding another mauling, I persuade Helena to play as my partner. I know she'd rather resume life as an embroidered cushion on the sofa, but I'm desperate to avoid another humiliation and persuade her to stay vertical for another hour or so. Our start to the game is unspectacular and Helena keeps us in touch with the early leaders by putting down another solid and, to me, entirely unfamiliar verb. But halfway through the game, she suddenly rises from the table muttering about the pressure. I protest that this isn't the time to start wilting – not now, when we're still in with a chance! But she means the pressure being imposed on her bladder by the little fellow, which at least gives everyone a moment of light relief from the intensity of our late-night contest.

Reluctantly, I haul a few more letters out of the bag and try to arrange them into some sort of order. As they dance before my eyes like unruly Germans at a student disco, something lurks at the back of my mind. I'm almost sure that I can see this motley collection of letters trying to form itself into a genuine word... Yes, there it is! The word is 'steroid' and it uses all seven letters. My heart leaps. That's an extra fifty points if I can get the thing down whole onto the board. Then I remember that the French spell it with an extra 'e' at the end and my heart stops leaping and starts sinking. To my left, Helena's father takes his turn. He leaves an 'e' in one of the corners at the bottom of the board. There are seven spaces above that 'e' and one of them just happens to be a triple word score hole. Two more players are to have their turn before us. Ah, forget it! It's too much to hope for...

Helena returns from the bathroom. She's never heard of a steroid and fails to understand why I start slapping her wrists when she tries to rearrange our letters.

One more player before it's our turn again. Pierre hesitates and looks at 'my' space on the board. I can't bear it. This one word would put me, Helena and the little fellow so far into the lead we'd be out of sight. Pierre winces and shuffles a few letters across the edge of the board and into no man's land. I've no idea what this word is or where he finally intends to place it. Again he hesitates before, unbelievably, he shoves his collection of consonants into the dense forest at the centre of the board. Our turn! Fingers shaking, I get my letters down faster than a sprinter running the home straight full of nandrolone. I look up to see everyone staring at me aghast. 'How on earth do you know a word like that?' asks Helena's father. 'It just goes to show,' I explain, 'that there are some benefits of reading *l'Equipe* every day'.

I'm not quite ashamed enough to admit that this is probably my favourite moment of the entire holiday, even if we still lose the game and everyone else has forgotten about it by bedtime.

The baggage, December 30th

Another year has almost passed and Helena is looking forward to the most momentous month of her life, while I continue to look back over my shoulder at the vertiginous peaks and bottomless troughs of all those that have gone before. Everyone says that the last few weeks of pregnancy are the worst and now we're finding out why. Sleep is systematically eluding Helena and she's exhausted by her efforts to drag an extra twenty kilos wherever she goes. She's fed up of wearing jogging pants, her morale is low, her temper high and she describes it all as like being stuck in an uncomfortable, drafty waiting room with no onward train for the next thirty days. She just wants to get on with it which must be why she's already packed her bags for the hospital and, poking out of her unzipped suitcase, are a nightgown, slippers, cotton wool, baby clothes, cosmetics, a packet of nappies and a luxury hairdryer.

I notice how worn and ragged a lot of Helena's clothes

have become and I'm suddenly overcome by a wave of sympathy for the woman with whom I share my life. It's been a hell of year for Helena and all I want to do is tell her not to worry because everything will be alright. But those would only be words. Words issued by the same mouth that has already promised a great deal and delivered very little.

Paris, NYE

All our talk has now turned towards getting through the next twenty-four hours without champagne. If I make it tonight, this will be the first time I've passed into the New Year in a state of full consciousness since the age of sixteen. In the past, the challenge was how to get more fired up than on an average Friday evening and the answer was never going to meet with the approval of the government's Chief Medical Officer. At least we're not going out tonight. What would be the point? Helena doesn't feel up to it and I don't want to spend the evening watching people doing what I've done to myself for almost a quarter of a century.

As evening falls, I walk down the Rue des Martyrs to buy food. This is the place where the cash-rich bohemian bourgeoisie, or *bobos,* of the ninth *arrondissement* come to shop and the street is lined, top to bottom, with the purveyors of excellent and hugely expensive meats, fruits, vegetables and cheese. But tonight I don't care – I'm going to cook whatever Helena wants for dinner and what she wants is a bucketful of scallops. That's why I'm freezing my butt off in the scrum outside the *Poissonnerie Bleue*. I'm a regular customer here but that does me no favours tonight, despite all the extra staff laid on to deal with the crabs and oysters spilling out onto the pavement. I'd no idea the French like to celebrate the New Year with seafood, but I won't forget it again. It feels as if the whole street has been transformed into a beach restaurant in the middle of winter. Dozens of cod, salmon and trout are lolling about on beds of shaved ice. Staring at me through glassy, bloodshot eyes are langoustine, prawn and live lobster on an inestimable number of cracked, spiny legs, as well as pomfret, sea bass, whelk, monkfish, tuna, turbot and skate. The crew of the *poissonnerie* are shouting, gutting, de-scaling and waving live crustaceans above the heads of tinselled customers as we all slide about on a deck of wet sawdust and fish guts and, by the time I haul my catch up the road, I'm as exhilarated as the survivor of any shipwreck.

I've never prepared live scallops before. They are highly muscular and obstinately defensive beasts and the first one I try to prise open immediately slams shut again on my jittery frozen fingers. With the aid of an oyster shucker and plenty of the French vernacular, I eventually relieve the slippery little bastards of their armour plating and get them cleansed of grit and inedible parts. Then I throw them into a bowlful of lime juice, coriander and chilli and leave them to choke to death in the spicy marinade before joining Helena on the bed for a rest.

'What are we going to do tonight?' I ask.

'Eat dinner!' says Helena with all the enthusiasm of a blue whale closing in on a massive shoal of plankton.

'Yeah, I know, but what else?'

'What do you mean "what else"?'

'Well, it's New Year's Eve. We ought to be celebrating.'

'Like dancing, you mean?'

'Yes.' Helena glances quickly at the free-form belly dancer to whom she will be playing host for another thirty days, before asking me what I used to do for New Year back in London.

'You don't want to know!'

'Yes I do. Tell me.'

I cast my mind back to two years ago. It takes a while before I'm able to locate a shadowy figure in a darkened corner of south-east London.

'Last time I was with Vincent and a group of his friends from France.'

'Where did you eat?'

'Eat? You don't eat in London on New Year's Eve.'

'You must have eaten something?'

'OK then, we ate about six pints of beer and then we went out for a drink.'

'Out where?'

'To a club.'

But no further details of that night come to mind, such as what time or how I got home and I try to divert the conversation back to this evening: 'But I want to do something different tonight.'

'Like what?'

'Like reflect on the year that's passed and look forward to the next. I don't know, maybe write a list or something... ' I'm on dodgy ground here, given all the stuff I've put Helena through in the past twelve months but to my surprise, she agrees. Then I go back into the kitchen to pay my respects to the newly deceased shellfish.

We settle down to dinner around nine. To me, it still feels weird – this business of celebrating with a bottle of lemon-twist *Perrier* while the rest of the world is out there getting hammered. But once the scallops have slipped neatly down our throats and on into the crustacean hereafter, we launch ourselves into a fresh fruit salad and some *Häagen-Dazs* ice cream – the vanilla one with pecans in it, which Helena temporarily confuses with 'toucans'. It's another two hours till midnight and we lapse into silence once more until Helena can bear it no longer and suggests a bit of music.

I'm not in the mood for anything remotely danceable, so we opt for an old Cannonball Adderley album which kicks off with a beautiful, bitter-sweet version of the old Cole Porter tune 'Autumn Leaves', with Cannonball on sax and Miles Davis on trumpet. We listen to the song three or four times and stare at the candles. I find myself thinking about last year when we were in the Alps with Helena's family. It was snowing hard and I'd wandered down to a small church wedged into the side of a mountain. I'm not the type that prays, but I do remember asking somebody or something for a bit of guidance that night. It was as if I could sense what was coming.

'Come on, Helena,' I say, 'let's get cracking!'

She scurries into the bedroom to look for her list. I can tell she's been looking forward to this. Maybe she's taken her chance and compiled one long catalogue of my shameless behaviour and maybe this wasn't such a good idea after all. We begin with a minor argument about the order in which the lists should be read, although I eventually persuade her to read our choices in ascending order of importance. I guess that's just the way in which a mind diseased by football and *Top of the Pops* works, so what's the point in me fighting it?

I've written mainly about recovery from alcohol poisoning, rediscovering Helena, my family and those few parts of myself that may yet be worth preserving, while Helena hasn't even mentioned the source of my shame. Instead she has written about learning to trust me again and, to my surprise, we even concur when it comes to the biggest event of a year which will come to a close when we blow out the candles in a couple of hours' time: I describe it as the chance to become a father, but what Helena has written – 'to be living with your child in my belly', has me swallowing hard to remove a temporary and inexplicable obstruction in my throat.

As for the New Year that's about to dawn? Well, the most fervent wish of the mother is that our baby 'is as cute as all other babies', mine merely that he's born safely and in good health. Helena has made no mention tonight of the aborted marriage (neither did I, although that's slightly less surprising). As she gets ready for bed, I sit with old Cannonball in the living room a little while longer. I stare at my list and reflect on the miracle which has befallen me. Had I been offered all this a mere eight months ago, I'd have snatched it faster than a pickpocket on Oxford Street.

We're still half an hour shy of the New Year yet both of us are having trouble keeping our eyes open, so I turn to the mother and child combination next to me which now claims at least three quarters of all of our bedroom territory.

'Helena, you do know why I didn't marry you, don't you?'

Helena turns her head slowly towards me although the majority of her remains tilted at the ceiling. 'I think so, yes.'

'Go on then. Tell me.'

'You're a scaredy-cat coward who can't commit.' She pauses to look somewhere deep beneath my skin.

I give her the chance to say more, but she lapses back into silence and I watch as her eyes close once more. 'There is perhaps one minor item you seem to have overlooked.'

'Oh?'

'Yes, I lost my way. I can't tell you exactly when or how it happened, but by the time I realised I'd taken the wrong path, it was too dark to find it again. I'd lost all trust in myself and ended up asking all the wrong people... ' My story tails off and I notice Helena's profile dancing slightly in the candlelit bedroom. There's no change in the steadiness of her breathing.

'And do you think you might be finding your way back home any time soon?'

I nod slowly in the dark just as the hands of the clock finally crawl past midnight.

A new pair of genes, January 1st

Who knows what the New Year will bring? It will certainly be different from all those that have gone before. I'm awake before Helena and tiptoe into the kitchen to make a cup of tea and, to my amazement, I catch sight of a series of heavy snow flakes sliding past the window pane. It's still early and with the snow muffling all sounds of life outside, the silence is almost complete. Sitting there, with nothing but a chipped teacup for company, I spend the best part of an hour watching as the snow falls. It won't settle here in the city, but it's calming to watch and indulge this feeling that, somehow, the world has changed overnight and become a more welcoming place.

When Helena emerges, it's with a face that suggests she's been disturbed in the midst of a deep midwinter hibernation. I tell her to look out of the window and observe as a look of childish delight flashes across her face. Helena loves the snow. She loves it so much that she's even willing to forgo breakfast in order to get out and feel the flakes melting against her hot face. As one who likes the idea of snow more than the reality of it, I protest. But she wants to know whether the Bois de Boulogne will be carpeted in white this morning before insisting that I drive to the western perimeter of the city to find out.

It has gone ten by the time we venture outside, but the streets remain completely deserted beneath the ochre sky. There is but one light burning in our entire neighbourhood and I'm no longer surprised to discover that it belongs to the *boulangerie*. So we set off for the Bois with a couple of warm croissants while the rest of Paris sleeps off its hangover.

But Helena was right. In the woods we wander slowly through a light dusting of snow and we're among the first to leave a set of scuff marks upon the New Year. As we turn back for the warmth of the car, it dawns on me that the month in which I'll become a father has arrived.

In the afternoon, I leave Helena to rest and take the metro to the ragbag of stuffed animals and bones at the *Galerie de l'Evolution*. I first visited this place shortly after the death of my father and came here in the belief that there were more differences between us than similarities. Yet the longer I stayed, the more I realised that the truth was precisely the opposite. Now I suppose I've come back to look for the link to a third generation.

My father was never able to fully break free of the nightmare of his own childhood. It scarred him and left him with depressive tendencies that blew in and out in his life as freely as a prairie wind drives through an open barn door. But I didn't understand that when I was a child. All I felt was a nameless hole in the place where there should have been something else and most of my childhood was already gone by the time I understood what it was. In the end, it was only words which failed him and maybe this accounts for my own fears of inadequacy as I look towards the birth of my son.

With the temperature in freefall, I continue to ponder the mysteries of the twisted double helix which links father to son. The other day I got a spooky email from my brother in which he wrote that our 'little boy loves us already' and that we need to remember that he has specifically chosen Helena and me as his parents. My brother often comes out with this sort of stuff – part wishful thinking, part psycho-babble. But, in spite of myself, I can't help feeling that there may be some truth in it, or at least something I ought not to overlook and resolve to ask him why he chose our father in preference to, say, John D. Rockefeller. Because, given the choice, I think I might have plumped for someone slightly more filthy rich than our own, modest parents.

Middle of the night, January 3rd

I'm throwing a party. My old boss is sitting alongside me, listening as I extol the virtues of sobriety. But at the same time as talking, I'm taking deep slugs from a pint of darkish bitter. I wake up with a start and in a cold sweat. I must try to remember that, like my son, I'm really only at the very beginning. I fall back to sleep, but my subconscious won't leave me alone. This time I'm on a horse ploughing a lonely furrow around the race track at Longchamps. The snow is gone and I'm getting bogged down in the mud. I'm completely unable to make out the spectral form of the main grandstand through the fog. Instead, my exhausted steed and I are trying to reach the finish line by following some hoof marks in the mire. Then, without warning, a line of horses, straining to their fibrous limits, comes bursting out of the fog, whipped hard by energetic jockeys in electric silks. I thought we were almost home, but these horses are not coming from behind us at all, but rather head on and right at us! I must have got it all wrong again and can only cower as they thunder past, sweating and snorting enormous plumes of steam. Suddenly I'm in the grandstand being given a tip for the next race by a rather shady-looking Frenchman. He tells me it's a 100–1 shot, but certain to win. The horse wins. I go to collect my winnings on a €50 bet, only to find that I've forgotten to place it in the first place.

Childbirth – a game of two halves, January 4th

I can't help feeling there's still a large gap between what I am and what I'd like to become. But lying here in bed isn't going to solve the problem and Helena wants the baby's room finished by the time Cécile and Pierre arrive back from their holiday in the Alps. I'd prefer to finish my film script before the baby is born, but the two activities don't mix and I don't waver long before deciding that the baby's room is easier to fix than the script.

Under the supervision of his mother, I assemble our son's little wooden cot, trapping my fingers no more than twice in the process. I shift his wardrobe from one side of the room to the other and my desk in the opposite direction. Helena's ceramics oven is way too heavy to shift from the room, so we cover it with a piece of chipboard and some brightly coloured fabric. Then I put up a string of lights in the shape of sheep as Helena hangs a set of baby-friendly pictures on the wall. Still she's not happy. She wants my desk moved to the living room. I argue that I'll never get any work done from such a central position in the house and she looks at me as if to say that I never get any work done anyway.

As Helena puts the finishing touches to the room, I open

a web report on an obscure ice hockey fixture deep in the Carpathian Mountains. On top of the oven, she's arranged some toys, a bottle of baby shampoo, a box of cotton buds and a musical monkey box that Cécile gave us for Christmas. This makes me feel as if we're counting our chickens prematurely and I start to fret and hop agitatedly from one foot to the other.

'I wonder what he'll look like,' she says, pinning a mirror to the wall.

'I don't really care.'

'What's the matter?' I can tell from her tone that she's shocked at my brusqueness.

'Nothing!'

'What do you mean you don't care?' Helena carefully places two pairs of woollen purple pants, knitted by her mother, on top of the oven.

'I mean I care too much.' I watch her as she folds a tiny T-shirt with a small bear on the left breast.

'You're looking at his stuff as if it doesn't belong here.'

'That's because it doesn't. Not yet anyway.'

'Oh, you're so superstitious!' Helena, who is not superstitious, laughs a little.

'Of course I'm not. Look at this... Chelsea lost. They're seven points adrift now.'

'He's going to be alright, you know.'

'I hope so, because that's all I want. I really don't care what colour his eyes are.'

'So, you don't mind if they are brown, like mine then?'

'Well, that would be unfortunate, but I guess it can't be helped.' Damn it! She's made me grin. I'm serious about this. The only thing I really care about is whether the little fellow makes it safely through the earth's atmosphere.

But later in the evening, over a dinner of *boudin noir* (a delicious black pudding made with chestnuts and onion), baked spuds and apple sauce, it's Helena's turn to show the strain:

'I'm afraid.'

'Don't be. People have been eating pig's blood for centuries... '

'Not of the *boudin noir*, you idiot! Of the birth.'

'What about it?'

'I don't know. The pain, I suppose.'

I don't know what to say next, but I'd better think of something and preferably something comforting although 'There's always the epidural' is the best I can manage. Not that Helena appears to be listening – she's just forking a piece of broccoli aimlessly around her plate.

'It's not so much the pain I'm afraid of. More the fear of being afraid.'

Ah! Fear of fear. This sounds much more like my home territory. 'Are you going to eat that black pudding?'

'Er, no. You can have it.'

'It's perfectly normal, you know.'

'What is?'

'Being afraid – it's your body's way of preparing itself for the birth.'

Helena looks at me with a trace of hope in her eyes, although she says nothing. I can tell she's waiting to be convinced. I search for an appropriate metaphor and, needless to say, the only one I can think of is related to my favourite sport.

'When I was a kid, I used to get scared before playing football.'

'How can you think of football at a time like this?' Helena looks at me, her eyebrows arching murderously.

'Hang on Helena, let me explain. Every Saturday, before we ran out onto the pitch I was nervous to the point of throwing up. I wanted to hide in the showers and forget all about the game, a game I loved... '

'Love!' Her features relent slightly under the incessant downward pressure of gravity.

'OK, *love*. Every time I pulled on my boots, I was overcome with fear, but the point is this – the minute the referee blew his whistle to start the game, my fear vanished completely.'

'Are you trying to convince me that playing football for an hour is the same thing as squeezing another human being out of your body?'

I can see that I'm about to lose Helena here and push on before all is lost. 'Had I gone into battle without a trace of nerves, I'd have been knocked straight on my arse. You need that adrenalin running around your system and you feel it as fear, but as soon as you go into labour, you'll just be getting on with the job.'

'And you'll be there too?'

'I'll be there. I may be struggling myself, but I'll be there. I promise.'

Helena smiles. A little weakly perhaps, but it's still a smile and I feel like a football manager who has helped a star striker overcome a morbid fear of taking penalties.

We're interrupted when a call comes in from Dirk who has an announcement to make and it takes a couple of seconds before I twig that my job is to sound surprised. I remember this when I hear Carla in the background, buzzing about as excitedly as a road runner that's tripped over an electrified fence.

'Guess what!'

'I can't, Dirk. Do tell.'

'Carla's pregnant!'

'Nooooo!'

'Yes, really!'

'And how do you feel about that Dirk?' (as if I didn't already know).

'I'm total... '

'Get off the line, Dirk and let me speak to Carla. Is she alright?'

Carla is so excited about reaching her third month that we're given a blow-by-blow account of the past ninety days: she's feeling sick; no – it doesn't show yet; she can't believe it; she's getting nervous; it's a miracle; she can't eat anything; can't keep anything down; but she wanted us, and Helena in particular, to be the first to know. Well, believe me, we were, and it's hard when you're trying to sound surprised not to betray the fact that you aren't. But I'm delighted for Carla and in the midst of it all this chaos, I realise this must mean that I'm also delighted for myself.

All too soon, the irrepressible Dirk is back on the line. It seems he has a fear of his own and it's a big one:

'I've just had a horrible thought!'

'What's that, then?'

'I might have a daughter.'

'What's wrong with that? I quite wanted a daughter.'

'But you're having a son.'

'So?'

'So, if you're having a son and I'm having a daughter, I just wouldn't like them to meet down the line, that's all.'

'You're a sick man, Dirk. Many congratulations.'

The thing within, January 6th

The company in London has come back with a new and improved offer. It's sitting in front of me right now and the dollar signs are dancing in front of my eyes like a gaggle of voluptuous belly dancers. My eyes may be agog, but my heart weighs a ton. I really don't want to leave Paris, not even for Toulouse. I've yet to discuss this with Helena but this is not so surprising, as I've only just admitted it to myself.

There's no doubt the job is a good one. On top of the salary, they're prepared to replace our battered old *Clio* with something new, shiny and German, there's a pension, health insurance and the promise of a full military burial. First they want me in London for an interview, although I'm stalling on that one until I've had lunch.

When the doorbell rings I'm in the kitchen cooking up noodles with pork, lime, chilli and coconut milk, because I tend to find that kind of thing easier than thinking or telling Helena the truth. I open the door only to find that there's nobody there. Then I hear a small sound from somewhere between my knees. Almost lost in the carpet is a mass of blond curls, which eventually asks for Helena. It's Clément, back from the Alps, but where are his parents? I try asking Clément whether he's walked from the Haute Savoie by himself but all he can say is 'Helena?' I tell him she's in the bedroom and he rushes past my saucepans to find his favourite and, to be perfectly frank about it, only aunt.

Eventually we're joined by Cécile and Pierre who've been outside all along, trying to find a parking place for their car, which, on a Monday morning in Pigalle, is a bit like searching for the Holy Grail in Chelmsford. It's good to see them again and Pierre embraces me warmly. Does this mean my entirely self-inflicted problems with Helena's brother are now at an end, or can he just smell the food in the kitchen?

The excitement forces Helena out of bed and she's starts to play building sites with her nephew. But Clément is no longer content to play with the set of toy tools his parents gave him for Christmas. Over the course of the past week, he's graduated to the real thing and, right now, he's hammering one of Helena's fingers into our coffee table. She just gazes at him adoringly as blood oozes from beneath one of her fingernails.

After lunch, Cécile and Pierre want to leave and it takes almost half an hour before we can separate Clément from a pair of pliers, the hammer and a fistful of dangerously long nails and say our goodbyes.

I make some coffee and corner Helena in the bedroom:

'I've got an offer.'

'A good one?'

'Very good.'

'I see.'

'It means we would have to move back to England'

'When?'

'Probably next month.'

'Is it a job that you really want to do?'

'It's a job I can do and one that will keep your son in shoes for the foreseeable future.'

'Our son.'

'Yes sorry, our son. But how do you feel about moving to London?'

'I'll go if you want to go.'

'I don't. I think I want to stay here.' Helena interrupts the passage of a whole string of noodles by decisively truncating them with her teeth and I watch as they slither back to join their fellows in a sea of coconut gravy.

'I see. Well, that's settled then. We'll all stay here!'

The year in which nothing much happened in Paris or anywhere else

I don't want to think about my job situation, I don't want to check email, I don't want to go back to work on the script, I don't want to think about Helena's continued refusal to pay the rent (nor face the fact that this foolhardiness will get us thrown out on the street) and I especially don't want to think about my promise to stop smoking, once and for all, before the baby is born. I'm just lying in bed, avoiding the truth in a pleasant, semi-conscious state when our doorbell rings for the second time in two days. This is a little odd as the doorbell never rings in Paris because every apartment block in the city has a quintuple set of door codes and nobody bar the local criminal fraternity can ever remember the numbers. This means it's harder to surprise your friends at home than it is to break into the Bank of France. Take our very own code which happens to be 1807. In order to commit this number to memory and gain entry to my own building, I had to ask Helena (the history teacher) to provide me with a memorable event from that year and guess what? – absolutely nothing of significance happened in the year 1807 and should I forget this absence of interesting historical fact, I'm liable to lose touch with all my personal possessions forever.

If you want to visit a close friend in Paris, you have to give at least six years advance warning. There's none of that informality so typical of London: '*Awright mate? Jus' fought I'd give yuz a bell... See if ya fancied a coupla sherberts.*' Forget that! Here, the rule for making even the most casual of appointments is to call months in advance and hang on the phone while your bosom buddy pretends to shuffle through an entirely empty personal organiser. If he's playing the game properly, he'll tell you he's way too busy to make the first three appointments you suggest and, after a few good sighs and one final tut, he'll offer to call you back the following week. That way, you get to play the game too and the closest of friends can steer clear of each other for generations at a stretch.

Anyway, one glance at the slumbering figure of Helena reveals that she's not expecting anybody today so there's nothing for it but to pull on some jeans and drag my aching carcass to the front door. It's Russell, the Kiwi who's now on the verge of marriage to Ophélie. I feel a familiar pang of guilt as soon as I see his sheepish, goateed features looming in the doorway. I gesture at him to enter and because he's essentially of good, Anglo-Saxon stock, put the kettle on without even asking whether he wants a cup of tea.

Before I've even rustled up a couple of teabags, Russell is pressing a wedding invitation into my hand. I'd quite forgotten that he'd called a couple of weeks back to warn us that the official invitation was still stuck at French customs. The poor sucker! He thought it would be a good idea to get the invitations printed cheaply in New Zealand, but he forgot to remind his dozy down-under mates to read the date on the proofs sent over by his mother-in-law. Once the catatonic Kiwis had finally finished the printing, they compounded the error by slapping an unnecessarily high value on the package which was then seized by French customs who, in their own sweetly bureaucratic way, took an age before deigning to inform Russell they had even arrived on the Old Continent. Russell is breathless as he tells me all this, which does at least give me a bit of time to search for some biscuits and study the invitation: the RSVP date on the front passed almost one month ago and, when I ask Russell what the mother of the bride thinks of this delay (a formidable French lady, every detail of whose life is run with the efficiency of a military manoeuvre), he rolls his eyes to the heavens before taking a long, hearty slurp of Darjeeling.

The wedding will take place at a château about an hour outside Paris and Russell says that a room has been booked in our name if we are able to make it. This is only ten days before the birth, but Russell tells me there's a maternity hospital barely fifteen minutes drive from the castle at St Germain-en-Laye, a leafy suburb of Paris to which the French aristocracy decamped en masse shortly after they all lost their heads in the French Revolution.

The gratitude list, January 10th

Quite shamelessly, I've started writing to just about everyone I know in an attempt to rustle up a bit of work and avoid becoming the unemployed father of a newborn son. The fact that this will inevitably drop me back into the shark tank of marketing services seems, well, just a little less important than it did forty-eight hours ago. Not that there's anything to report. Once I'd said 'no' to London, I sat by the phone for a few days but the only person who called was a man who wanted to service the gas fire in our living room and he said he didn't need any help with that.

By the middle of the afternoon, my perilous situation is beginning to weigh a little too heavily on my mind. As is my custom when my emotional barometer takes a nosedive, I begin to go through my bank statements and wonder what happened to all of my savings. I know damned well that I spent most of the money in those damned pavement cafes, but this is a truth I'm still not entirely ready to face. So I go through the statements one more time, in the hope that the bank has made an error on my account roughly the size of a small family inheritance. But I can't even find a 20-cent cock-up and I'm just about to resort to a full afternoon of self-recrimination when an email clicks into my inbox. It's from someone who says she's looking to get a bit of work done in Paris. She wants to know if I'm interested.

I mull over the request for about as long as it takes a Sputnik to orbit the M25 and, before I can even think about changing my mind, I fire off an email to the effect that I'm ready to confirm my interest in blood or the bodily fluid of her choosing. The phone rings again and the same woman asks me to get on a train for London and subject myself to a preliminary interview.

Somewhat dazed, I put down the phone and stumble into the living room. I want to explain the latest developments to Helena, but she's not concentrating because Clément has arrived for one last audience before returning to Spain. I try to get some of Helena's attention, but all she will say is that Cécile and Pierre will be with us in an hour. I know what that means – while she and Clément continue nailing one another to the floorboards, I'm expected to start cooking lunch.

Lunch does include some sausages, lentils and a bit of spinach, but it's mainly about photography, speeches and how the next time we all meet, Clément and Maxime will have a little cousin. Just for a moment, I forget myself completely and ask how come. But, other than that, I think I acquit myself adequately and even shoot a few rolls of film of Helena kissing her nephew. After the goodbyes and good lucks, they're off and driving all the way back down to Mazagón on the southernmost tip of the continent. It'll take them a full two days behind the wheel to get there and, as soon as I close the door on little Maxime and his European rallying family, I feel more than a little lost. We liked having them around and not only because they provide a timely reminder that the infinite business of pregnancy does eventually yield an end product.

Helena doesn't know what to do with herself once they've gone. Our spanners and screwdrivers are spread across the floor but there's a small, blond hole in her life. She doesn't say so, but she's getting desperate to fill the space with her own little creation. So she makes her umpteenth tour of the baby's bedroom, just in case there's anything she's forgotten and, in an attempt to cheer her up a little, I persuade her that we should go to the cinema. I'm sure it will do her good to get out, but her eyes fall automatically to that provisional balcony which casts a shadow over her toes. Before she can refuse, I tell her I'll book the entire row at the cinema. She still makes a face but I sweeten the deal by suggesting a pizza immediately afterwards. The very prospect banishes all thoughts of hardship and she acquiesces as easily as four cheeses melting gently onto a nice crusty base.

After the film, Helena wipes an excess of popcorn salt from the corners of my parched cracking lips and we are joined by a couple of friends for dinner. To my immense relief, we can't get in at the first pizza joint we try and I live briefly in hope that I'll be able to divert our party away from the idea of a slice of overrated cheese on toast altogether. But Helena, for whom any kind of pizza is preferable to no pizza at all, stands firm and, before you can say Antonio Vivaldi, she's polished off all four seasons plus a side order of garlic bread.

Over dinner we exchange 'how we met' stories and I find out how little I know of our friends' marital life. As the last of the diners start to ebb from the restaurant, they explain that they met at a dinner party and their relationship almost failed to get off the ground because she was living on one continent and he on another. Unlike Helena and I, however, they did not wait four years to give each other another chance and were married before coffee and dessert. Naturally enough, this leads on to a series of detailed questions from one woman to another about the baby, as two grown men study the restaurant décor. To my amazement, I learn that they'd like to have a baby themselves. At this point, I risk a quick glance at my friend. We've known each other for several months and not once have we talked of such things. I never thought to ask whether they were planning a family. I suppose my blinkered assumption was that they were happy with life as it was and would want to avoid such a fate as much as I did. How little I know, and how far from the truth! Two years ago, she'd even fallen pregnant, although it wasn't to be.

I watch my friend as he listens to his wife relating part of his own story. He removes and then carefully polishes his glasses before replacing them once more and I imagine I can see the light fade briefly from his eyes. I can't help but think back to my own reaction when Helena first told me she might be pregnant and an army of shame trudges heavily across my chest. How I wish I could take back those minutes and hours when I didn't want to hear what she was trying to tell me. How I struggled against becoming a father and the idea of growing up. I stare at the bubbles as they rise to the brim of my glass of mineral water. Why has it taken me so long to see the truth about the gift we are soon to receive?

Why we all get the family we deserve, January 11th

I start the day with a whirlwind tour of the Bois de Boulogne. Dressed like a fluorescent penguin, I think I look ridiculous until I see my bike mate Thierry, who not only looks like he'd be more at home swimming with a shoal of tropical fish on the Great Barrier Reef, but has also attached what looks like a small dental mirror to the side of his crash helmet. I'm not sure quite how this helps him as we splash through the park, but at least he won't have mud on his teeth by the time he gets home.

After a quick shower to unfreeze my toes and jaw, we swallow a quick lunch over which I tell Helena about my trip to London for the interview. She agrees that the best thing is to make the necessary arrangements in the morning and get it out of the way as soon as possible.

She awakens me from a post-lunch snooze by shouting that my brother is on the line. My what? She must be mistaken. My brother never calls, except once earlier this century to ask whether I'd be the godfather of his son. I only consented because I thought it would be like having my own son, only without all the arse-wiping.

'Which brother?'

'How many have you got?'

'One'

'Well, I guess it must be that one, then.'

'From Thailand?'

'Yes, from Thailand. Hurry up.'

My brother is an unfortunate sod. He's a prawn farmer, which means he's virtually obliged to live in that sweaty tropical belt which adheres obstinately to the equator. Years ago, he set up hut as far as he possibly could from the distinctly temperate zone of our Hertfordshire home, to which he hardly ever returns and, like I said, he never calls. But then again, my brother has always differed a little from the rest of our oddly materialistic, human race: He's never felt the need to rush to the sales twice a year, nor to pay over the odds for a cup of coffee at *Starbucks*. He doesn't look to see whether his shower gel is flavoured with green apples or goat urine and he couldn't give a toss whether his bottle of lager has been imported from a trendy ex-Soviet satellite or boring old Burton-upon-Trent. In fact, he appears to be quite happy with a lifestyle which would have most of what passes for Western civilisation reaching for a fistful of *Prozac*. Now, he and his family live (in terrible hardship) on paradise island, surrounded by white sand, pineapples and coral. The first thing he tells me is that it's 32° centigrade where he is, parked in front of the TV set with a can of beer, 98° longitude east of Greenwich, somewhere in the middle of the Andaman Sea. He also happens to be watching Arsenal versus Middlesbrough.

'So who's winning?' I demand.

'Nil-nil, but Thierry Henry's just missed a sitter.'

'But that's not why you called.'

'No, but I thought it might be worth mentioning. How are you?'

'I'm fine. How's my godson?'

'We're all fine. We've just had a barbecue on the beach and when the sun went down we thought we'd give you a call to find out how the baby's coming along.'

'We're almost there, just two more weeks now.'

'Good. How's Helena?'

'She's overweight, fed up and frustrated. She can't sleep, can't walk, can't talk, at least not about anything but the baby, but other than that she's as well as can be expected.'

'Glad to hear it. Have you got a job yet?'

'I've got an interview in London next week. Haven't you got something to offer me out there? I'll do anything you like – serve the cocktails, scrub the barbecue, shoot cockroach.'

'How are your references?'

'Good, I... '

'Penalty!'

'What?'

'Thierry Henry's gone down in the box. Penalty to Arsenal.'

I'm then subjected to the bizarre, global phenomenon of my brother in Thailand pressing the telephone receiver close to his tropical TV set in order that I, shivering my butt off in minus 5° in a small apartment in the northern hemisphere, can hear the nasal drone of Martin Tyler describing a penalty kick in Teesside. Luckily it goes in, which means that I can relax a little and continue to chat idly to someone with whom I shared almost all of my childhood mishaps and triumphs and who, if I really think about it, I suppose I still miss.

Then he tries to put my godson on the line: 'Come here and talk to your uncle for a minute.' But his son has yet to get over the fact that I've only sent him one present in almost three years and grunts an emphatically negative reply.

'Ah well,' says my brother, 'maybe next time.'

'When will that be?' I wonder out loud.

'I don't know,' he says, before starting to wind down the conversation. 'We may be in Europe this summer... '

'Hang on! There was one more thing I wanted to ask you.'

'Don't worry, it's still one-nil.'

'No, not that. Do you remember the last email you sent me?'

'No.'

'Well, most of it was utter rubbish, but you did say one thing that interested me.'

'I did?'

'Yeah, that thing about babies choosing their own parents. Do you really believe that?'

'Of course I do!'

'So how come you chose Mum and Dad, then?'

My brother hesitates for a minute. Maybe he wasn't expecting me to come at it from that angle and maybe one of the reasons he's spent so much of his life on the far side of the planet is that there are elements of our childhood he'd happily consign to one of those landfill sites which are rapidly consuming the corner of England in which we grew up.

'Well, Dad introduced me to that guy who gave me my first chance on a fish farm.'

'Yes?'

'Well that's probably why then, isn't it?'

'I've no idea. It's your theory.'

I put down the phone, safe in the knowledge that my brother has been in the sun far too long, which enables me to dismiss the notion that my son has chosen me for any particular reason and, therefore, that I won't be letting him down before he's even born.

We're joined for tea by Agathe and her parents, who look exhausted. I assume this is down to little Agathe still not sleeping through the night but the real reason is that, in his attempts to leave behind the world of the moving stairway,

Mr Escalator has just finished another round of interviews with the driverless train people. In the great French tradition, he has now been interviewed at length by everyone at the company except the tea lady and he still has no idea whether they intend to offer him the job.

I retire to my son's bedroom with Inès and her daughter for a quick nappy-changing lesson. I stare at Agathe's little face. As the packaging suggests, she really is the perfect line extension of her parents – she possesses the colouring of her mother and the eyes and bald patch of her father, something which causes me to reflect further on my brother's sophisticated genetic theories. But no matter how long I stare, I can't quite figure Agathe as a featureless squiggle, swimming about in the chromosome pond for centuries, just waiting to be born into a family of moving staircases.

But at least I've safely negotiated my first attempts at wiping a baby's bum and Inès duly declares to her cousin that I'm as ready for fatherhood as I ever will be.

Paris, January 13th

It hasn't stopped raining for almost a week and that small piece of sky which leaks down between the five-story buildings crowding our courtyard is so sodden and damp that I have the feeling we're living in a large and particularly mucky aquarium. Collar turned up against the damp, I scurry back from the *boulangerie*, close the curtains on the tearful city and give thanks that I don't need to go out again for the rest of the day. I spend most of the morning on the phone to England, getting briefed on what it is that the Londoners want done in Paris. It seems they already have a small, loss-making office here and they would like to turn it into a large and highly profitable one. They need to know whether that's something I can engineer overnight. I doubt it but decide it may be more circumspect to say that I do. Then I agree to catch the *Eurostar* and submit to a good grilling at their offices near the City.

No problem then, until I discover, to my horror, that my passport expires the day before I plan to get on the train. Not an auspicious sign, nor the hallmark of someone trying to ooze efficiency and competence to a prospective employer. I call the British Consulate in Paris and attempt to explain my situation to a civil servant with a personality as brittle as a china tea set. She tells me that if I can present myself tomorrow with a ticket that I've already purchased they may be able to assist with my trip. Does that mean they will *definitely* be able to assist me with my trip? No, it most certainly does not. What it does mean is that they'll help me with my trip if they bloody well feel like it. I want to know what the alternatives are, but there's only one – get on the *Eurostar* and hope that UK customs don't notice my passport has already expired. I fancy my chances of making this work on the outward journey but I don't like the idea of getting stuck in London just as Helena is going into labour. Helena likes the sound of it even less, which means I'm left with no alternative but to chance my arm at the Consulate.

Paris, January 14th

I try explaining my situation to another minor civil servant with megalomaniac tendencies and the first thing that she tells me (in a voice which appears to dam an awful lot of hysteria just below a strangely prominent Adam's apple) is that I'm a very naughty boy to have gone out and bought a ticket when I knew damned well that my passport had already expired. How did she know I'd done this? I've no idea, but I deny it vehemently. Then she tells me that it will take at least five working days to get a new passport and this is before she notices the stamp which declares my passport may not be renewed without reference to Singapore where the damned thing was issued in the first place. So what are my chances now? Officialdom is not given to such speculation and I'm told to come back again tomorrow morning.

I get back on the phone to forewarn London of any possible failure to appear for the interview and this is the moment Helena chooses to tell me that, if I plan on raising any objections to the name she has selected for our son, I'd better raise them before the end of the week, otherwise the whole naming process will have gone too far to be reversed. I ask her to remind me of the name in question and receive a slap in the face of the sort which would make any Consulate official salivate with jealousy. I complain that the decision is too difficult, that I can't make up my mind until I see his face. 'Impossible,' says Helena. But I can't understand why, if babies get to choose their own parents, they can't just choose their own bloody names while they're at it. Maybe I'm getting just a little stressed, so I decide to keep my thoughts to myself and disappear into the courtyard for a cigarette, only to remember that I've given up smoking yet again and that the familiar oblong box is missing from my trouser pocket.

Paris, January 15th

The day on which I'm supposed to be speeding to London finds me back at the Consulate clutching a set of colour photographs. The bureaucratic weasel behind the bulletproof glass is clearly delighted to inform me that she hasn't heard back from Singapore and waves me into a hard plastic chair while she talks to a colleague to see whether anything can be done. I'm not quite sure how long she plans to be on the phone to Her Majesty but I do know that my train leaves in less than three hours. I inform her of this in the politest tones I can, but my impertinence only serves to further delay the process.

Eventually I'm called back to the window which separates the malicious android from us maggots on the other side and she informs me that the Consul has agreed to extend my existing passport for a further year and I should count myself very lucky. Just in case the automaton changes its mind, I adopt a suitably contrite expression and fold my hands behind my back like some Italian footballer guilty of a testicle-grabbing challenge from behind. Then I'm dispatched back to the sin bin for another wait of indeterminate duration.

Once I've digested all the available literature on what happens if you are caught smuggling tobacco or aliens into Britain, I'm called back to the window where, with the greatest reluctance, my friend and servant of the British people hands me a brand spanking new passport. I'm dying to ask how, if it normally takes five working days, this feat has been accomplished in less than thirty-five minutes, but I keep my mouth shut and smuggle its cargo of amalgam past the metal detector for approximately the sixth time in two days.

Two hours later, I'm safely ensconced in a window seat as the *Eurostar* pulls clear of the sunny Parisian suburbs and prepares for the rain in London. I barely had time to check in with Helena, but she promised not to give birth before I get back to Paris, then handed me a ham and Gruyère sandwich and wished me luck as I rushed out of the door. I finish the sandwich before the train has outrun the tentacles of the city and now there's nothing for it but to pull out a pen and a pad of paper and try to remember everything I ever knew and loved about marketing services.

London Waterloo, January 16th

Back on the *Eurostar*, Paris-bound and completely buggered. Suit rumpled, mouth dry, tongue suspended three feet from rest of my mouth, eyes unable to focus (even on the sports pages of today's *Guardian*). May be able to string a few consonants together, but vowels have gone missing altogether. Too tired to sleep, brain telling legs to go fetch coffee, legs can't be arsed. What have I done? I feel like one of Pavlov's dogs, only without the biscuity rewards. I think I may have agreed to do some work for the company, although I can't be sure. Hang on, let's try another shot of caffeine...

Almost instantaneously, the rocket fuel connects my misfiring synapses and I can pick up my story where we left off yesterday afternoon. From Waterloo, I went straight to the first part of the interview, which wasn't too painful, I suppose, with just the twelve inquisitors firing questions at me from all four sides as well as the ceiling. Considering I haven't done this sort of thing for the best part of a decade, I thought I did alright, although, by the end of the afternoon, I was almost ready to swim home to France. Then the bastards asked me to come back again today, so I took the tube down to Clapham, where Vincent was waiting for me in a pub. He was drinking *Coca Cola* and I ordered one for myself, before we embarked on a game of pool. At least there was no need to talk, which left me free to watch the balls rolling silently across the baize. Vincent won, as he always does, and then we went back to his place, dangerously close to the party zone in Brixton. I'd already made it very clear that there was no way I was going out on some all-night narco-fest, although I needn't have worried – he'd been partying all weekend and was in no mood for another instalment. All he could manage was a bit of frilly soft porn dressed up as classic BBC drama on the telly and even that failed to keep him awake.

Vincent had already left by the time I poked my head round the kitchen door this morning to check that none of the actors were still kicking around from last night. They weren't, although I did find one pair of knickers which Vincent had presumably left on the toaster to impress me. I had a quick cup of tea and went back to bed for half an hour before taking a long shower with some good old-fashioned English peppermint, molasses and donkey dung shower gel from *Sainsbury*'s. I wanted to leave plenty of time to get into town as my faith in the public transport of Britain has been somewhat eroded since the Romans managed to connect Epping Forest to Ealing Broadway with a nice piece of straight red railway track.

If you've ever lived in London, you don't need me to tell you about how I spent the next half hour on the Northern Line platform; waiting and watching as twelve tube trains passed through the station. Each one was a piece of performance art in its own right. So many people were pressed into each carriage that, had they been anchovies in a tin can, they would surely have sued. The trains stopped for the doors to open alright, but nobody could get on or off. It was all mere ritual and, as the passengers exhaled, briefcases, umbrellas, legs, arms, buttocks and, for all I know, sanity all started to spill from the carriage while the commuters attempted to avoid touching each other in ways they'd regret for the rest of the week. Then, it was 'mind the gap,' and everyone inhaled for all they were worth and all those little air pockets were removed until the next stop. I didn't bother trying to get on and watched as the trains moved off with the passengers frozen into whatever ridiculous gesture they'd assumed ahead of the next reshuffle. They looked exactly like pickles in a jar only without the comfort that comes from knowing you're already dead.

By now I was so late that I didn't bother making the change onto the Bakerloo Line. Instead I got off at Elephant and Castle, which is no more than a sustained two-mile sprint from my final destination. When I got there the boss of the company was staring dementedly at the empty chair in which I was supposed to be sitting. When I started to tell her about the tube she just waved a hand at me, although it wasn't clear whether this meant that I was to leave immediately or that there was really no point in apologising on behalf of the Northern Line.

She showed me the schedule for the day and pointed at a large flask of coffee. I was expected to meet five people in the morning and remember all of their names. The boss herself would be back in the early afternoon to take me out to lunch which, by my reckoning, was a good four and a half hours' talking away. There was no mention of the toilets, so I just let it dribble discreetly down my leg. Then we were off and running.

Despite all my preparation, the only thing interviewer number one wanted to do was to talk about my film script. I'd forgotten I'd even put it on the CV (in a lame attempt to make my life sound a little bit less like a new anti-anxiety prescription). Anyway, it turns out that he'd tried his own hand at a couple of books and I suspect he wanted to find out what would have happened had he stuck at it. I guess the answer was slumped pathetically right in front of him. Anyway, we had some fun before he was called away to a meeting about baking some right-sized numbers into a cake, while I helped myself to a second cup of coffee.

Number two was their healthcare expert. All he wanted to talk about was doctors, chemists and my knowledge of the pharmaceutical sector in France. God knows how I managed to spin that conversation out for over ten minutes, but by the time he got fed up with it, I was feeling knackered so I swallowed down another two cups of coffee.

Number three was Mr Technology – all packet switching, gigabyte motherboards, reverse proxies, site multihorning and other inedible farmyard animals of the future. I had almost no idea what he was talking about although I did manage not to slouch in my chair and made an attempt to sound vaguely amused, if not entirely interested. Halfway through our conversation I noticed that the coffee pot was at an alarmingly low level and that all the chocolate *Hobnobs* had already gone. It was another two hours till lunch and I was starting to drool. 'Right, yes. You were saying? Ah, yes, the potential use of WAP-enabled mobile phones to interview a representative sample of horny housewives in Weybridge? Funny you should mention that; I was thinking about them on the train over from Paris... '

I don't recall anything much about number four. I think he was larger and slightly rounder than the other three and had the beginnings (or perhaps the end) of some sort of pimple on his chin. I used this blemish to give me something to focus on when my concentration started to wander out of the sixth floor window. We talked about the financial industry rather than the pimple, or at least I think we did.

By the time number five arrived and threw me completely, the coffee pot was completely drained and I was operating my mouth without any recourse to my rapidly dimming brain cells. The main problem was that he was American and, by now, I was too far gone to adjust my conversation from one side of the Atlantic to the other. Instead, I just stared while he tried to impress me by quoting some spurious nonsense he'd read in a Victorian textbook about the reserve of the Brits and their inability 'to say what they think and mean what they say'. His face continued to fade in and out of focus and, after about ten minutes, I became convinced that his moustache was on the move. First it inched its way up to his forehead, then it slid down one of his cheekbones before finally coming to rest behind his left ear. As I searched for the one question that would keep him talking for the rest of the morning, or at least until the ambulance arrived, I could feel my eyeballs rocking and rolling in their sockets and became aware that I was emitting a low and involuntary droning noise.

Before lunch with the boss, I finally got to relieve my bladder of half the annual Colombian coffee harvest. Outside I gulped at the air like a goldfish that's thrown itself out of its bowl, and tried to recompose myself for one last conversation. I vaguely remember the boss offering me a glass of *Pinot Grigio* and I think I refused, although a significant part of me wanted to tear the entire bottle from the waitress's hand. The boss wanted to know what I thought of her team and I said I thought that they were all fine, upstanding individuals. I even managed to eat a little lunch. Then she asked me whether I'd consider jotting down a few ideas about helping them set up an office in Paris and I agreed to that too. I know I should take it as an encouraging sign but, to be honest, I'd have agreed to anything so long as I didn't have to answer any more questions.

We said goodbye at one of the many bridges which cross the Thames and lead to the serious money in the City. I set off aimlessly in the direction of St Paul's Cathedral, then I cut back westwards, along Fleet Street and into Holborn. In Covent Garden a couple of beggars looked up at me hopefully as I passed, but I had that look in my eye and they recognised it immediately. From there, I made my way south again and sat on a bench by the river for a while. Eventually I called Vincent. He said he was on his way into town after work and wanted to know if we could meet for a drink before I got back on the *Eurostar*. I agreed, subject to two conditions – no coffee and no questions. When he arrived, the first thing he said was 'The next time I see you you'll be a papa'. I just nodded.

Paris, halfway between the past and the future

Midnight has been and gone as the *Eurostar* steals back into Paris. Helena's still awake and she wants to know how I liked the ham and Gruyère sandwich. Her question elicits no response. It feels like a year since I ate that sandwich and I've been fuelled by nothing but coffee and adrenalin ever since. Never mind, I'll get up in the morning, eat a large breakfast and go back to bed for the rest of the day. I put my hand on Helena's belly and ask her whether everything is alright with the little fellow. My eyes are closed already but Helena is still trying to make contact with my receding consciousness.

'Wassamatter,' I say from somewhere far beneath the duck feathers. But she won't be deterred and continues to poke at my skeleton:

'You haven't forgotten about tomorrow, have you?'

'Hhrrrfuurrr? I need a chance to forget about today first.'

'The wedding of Russell and Ophélie'
'Hhrrrfuurrrck!'

Weddings and other propellants, January 17th

Ophélie and Russell are getting married in a small town called Saint Martin, about an hour's drive outside Paris. After breakfast, Helena eases herself into the *Clio*. She's not in the best of moods and looks about as enthusiastic as a lamb that's seen a full bowl of mint sauce. She's not looking forward to the drive or the ceremony and, above all else, she doesn't want to wait another ten days to see the face of our baby. She's had enough of talking about it, of waiting, of overbalancing on the pavements of Paris and I'm beginning to suspect that she's had more than enough of me. Through incessant drizzle, we slide out of Paris in a north-westerly direction and in silence.

I do sense a slight improvement in Helena's mood the minute we leave the *périphérique* behind and the water-coloured fields begin to stretch out before us. I tell her about the interviews in London and how I have to write a proposal which, if the company bites, may mean the three of us will all get to live on something other than breast milk and bread. Helena is still not talking to me although I sense that she may now be listening. I explain that the job would mean staying in Paris, before suggesting that we find a house with a garden in the suburbs. Helena just sighs and continues to look at out of the window as we roll gently through the sodden countryside.

It's lunchtime as we arrive at the château in which the reception will take place. The marriage itself will take place in a church at the other end of the village but not until four in the afternoon. I promised Helena we'd get here early for something to eat and a bit of a rest. A gravel driveway leads across an old stone bridge, over the moat and into the grounds of the château, each corner of which is topped with a small, fairy-tale turret. The minute Helena sees it her face is filled with enchantment. Never mind tiny Parisian apartments or mud huts in suburbia, this is the kind of place she fancies living in. I wouldn't mind myself, but I've never bothered with lottery tickets.

Because Helena is pregnant, we've been given one of the best rooms, high up in one of the turrets. We have two rooms to ourselves plus a palatial bathroom, all of which adds up to a space which is double the size of our place back in the city. Helena can no longer maintain her silence and purrs with delight. From the window, I can see a few carp lazing around in the moat. Helena slips under the perfect white bed sheets while I go to find something to eat. When I get back from the village she's sitting up in bed with a copy of *Elle* magazine and playing to perfection the role of Snow White (to my seven dwarves).

I'm starving and cut roughly through the crust of an olive and anchovy pizza. Helena tells me to be careful, as she has just read some statistics in *Elle* which suggest that men are more liable to injure themselves in the weeks immediately preceding the birth of a first baby. As I look at her in disbelief, she explains that they break legs or fall onto sharpened kitchen knives because, subconsciously, they're afraid of the birth.

'Sounds like a load of old nonsense to me. The birth doesn't scare me.'

'Are you sure about that?'

'Of course I'm sure,' I scoff before hiding my face under a layer of shaving foam in the bathroom.

But the reflection in the mirror tells me the truth, which is that there are just one or two minor details about the birth which are worrying me sick. These include the onset of contractions, how we will know when to leave for the hospital, getting to the hospital (will I be able to drive without smashing into every oncoming vehicle?), the sight of the delivery room, the stirrups and all that other apparatus, the anaesthetic, the anaesthetist, the midwife, the birth itself, the umbilical cord, the placenta, not to mention the baby and whether he will emerge whole or in several Francis Bacon-like pieces. The very thought of it has me breaking out in a cold sweat. I'd love to tell you that I'm taking it all in my stride, but the truth is that I've lost more than a stone in the last two months and I'm beginning to look like a stick insect that's sworn off the leaf.

'Don't you want any pizza?'

'Coming,' I say, in a voice three octaves higher than usual. I rinse my face with cold water and try to manually readjust my features into a slightly less panicked expression.

'What are you doing in there?'

'Nothing, just cleaning my teeth.'

By the time we arrive, the church is packed to its elegant, oak rafters. Helena and I squeeze onto the end of a row and settle down for what is likely to be a long service with plenty of jumping up and down between hymns, readings and homilies. Perhaps this is why Helena was in two minds about coming to the church. But as we stand and wait for the bride, it suddenly occurs to me that there may just be one other, small reason she doesn't want to attend a marriage ceremony with me. I find her hand just as a veiled and utterly radiant Ophélie sweeps into the church and the congregation heaves a collective sigh.

The ceremony lasts two hours and Helena almost makes it to the end. She particularly enjoys the priest's speech which, as usual, is all about how marriage, like wine, can only improve with age. I'd love to be able to give you the detail, but I wasn't listening too hard, just in case he said something I didn't want to hear. Helena hasn't been jumping up and down every thirty seconds like the rest of us, but once she sees people getting up for communion and moving about freely, I feel her fingernails through the sleeve of my suit and I know it's time to leave. I guide her through the peachy throng and we make our way back to the car. We have an hour or so to while away before cocktails are served back at the château and Snow White wants to spend a little time growing her hair before the party begins. I'm only too glad to escape a little early as the stress of the last two days in London is beginning to catch up with me.

As Helena sinks into the bath, I put my head down on the sofa. Just for a couple of minutes, mind! I'm not going to sleep or anything. I'll be as right as rain in a few minutes. I just need a bit of peace and quiet. I'm not even going to close my eyes...

I'm still debating whether to have a swim or to pluck the last remaining ripe pineapple from the palm tree on my personal Caribbean beach when I'm rudely awakened by the sound of Helena using words you would not normally associate with a member of the educational establishment.

'*Merde, putain!*'

'Whasup?' The coral beach retreats slowly from my consciousness to be replaced by the rapidly reddening features of Helena.

'*La marche. Putain!*'

'Step? What step?'

'That step, there!' Helena is pointing to an area between the bedroom and the reception area of our luxurious, temporary home.

'I nearly fell arse and tit.'

'It's arse *over* tit, and where did you learn an expression like that?'

'You taught me.'

'I did? Shit, I fell asleep. What time is it anyway?'

'Late. What time are the cocktails?'

I pick up my watch from the bedside table. Forget cocktails, we've almost missed dinner! I scramble back into my suit and Helena daubs on a bit of mascara. We got away with leaving the church early, but being late for dinner would undoubtedly constitute one of my more spectacular breaches of French etiquette.

Downstairs, the champagne is flowing and, thankfully, dinner is even later than we are. I leave Helena with a glass of mineral water and a fistful of hors d'oeuvres and check out the seating plan. The tables have all been named after famous Parisian landmarks and, even if I think it's a little odd that Helena and I have been seated at different tables, I'm not going to make a fuss about it. At least our tables are adjoining and perhaps Russell has decided to put me with his male friends from New Zealand so that Helena gets to sit with all the French women. Quite considerate of him, really.

The only other person sitting at my table is a twelve year-old French girl and she doesn't look unduly perturbed when I take my appointed place in the seat next to hers. She offers to pour me a glass of *Pepsi* and I'm only too happy to accept. At the next table, Helena is chatting to a woman from New Zealand who is almost as pregnant as she is. They ask whether I'm sure I'm at the right table. I shrug my shoulders as the women are joined by an assortment of couples and laid back Kiwis while I'm joined by a couple of bridesmaids and three pageboys. Between us we decide to crack open a can of *Orangina*. Helena points at an empty chair next to hers and gestures me over, but I'm the kind of pre-teen who lives in fear of the wrath of his parents and always does as he's told. Besides, I don't want to offend my young friends and wave away her protests. I do find it a little strange that the seat next to my girlfriend remains empty, but she's 'Arc de Triomphe' and I'm definitely 'Place de la Bastille'. It says so on the seating plan.

It's not until my starter of chicken nuggets arrives that I'm prepared to entertain the thought that Russell has either made a mistake or that this is some kind of joke. Maybe he's come to the conclusion that the English winning the Rugby World Cup is worthy of at least minor retribution, I don't know, but by now, Helena is gesturing at me frantically – she has so little understanding of the English capacity for self-imposed embarrassment and suffering. Ah well! One more gulp of fizzy pop and I take leave of my little buddies and reluctantly rejoin the real world.

Conversation at the table is dominated by two women exchanging pregnancy tales. The Kiwi lives in London and doesn't speak a word of French. Helena may have got used to my English but she's a little confused by the bent and twisted vowels from down-under, but there's no need to intervene as they both speak the international language of motherhood, one which is mastered exclusively by bringing a child to term and one which no man can speak, however long he may press his nose against the expansive display in the shop window.

Russell's father gets to his feet to kick off the evening's proceedings. He's a big, bearded gentleman who moves like a bear and, when he talks, the sound and general effect is not unlike taking a shower under a powerful waterfall. He calls all the male Kiwis up to his table to perform a Hakka and then recites a poem which he composed on the twenty-four-hour flight from Auckland. It's littered with passionate, male adjectives such as crashing, banging and walloping, and leaves no room for the doubt or hesitation in which certain men specialise. Next, the bride's father gets to his feet and gives a classical French display of reserve, subtlety and understatement. They may come at it from different angles, but both reach the same conclusion – that this is a marriage of contrasts, as well as one which was born of chance (Russell and Ophélie met on a flight between London and Paris). The fathers are agreed that the odds against the union were large, but once the wheels were set in motion, nobody could stop it happening. I personally know of at least one person who could have stopped it happening and so, of course, does Helena.

Next up is Russell himself, overcome with emotion and fatigue. He talks in a mixture of French and English, thus ensuring that only 50 percent of the guests can understand him at any one time. Halfway through his speech, at about that point when he wishes to describe the beauty of his wife, he dries up completely, although you can tell what he wants to say just by looking at the milky firmament in his eyes. None of us really needs to hear the words but, as one, we will them out of him anyway.

Later in the evening, Havana cigar in hand, Russell has relaxed sufficiently to add a few details to the story about that chance meeting on the plane. What his new father-in-law had neglected to tell us was that Russell had been up partying until all hours the night before. It was ten in the morning when he boarded that flight to Paris and all he wanted to do was curl up with his copy of the duty-free catalogue and get a bit of kip. But shortly after take-off, Ophélie made her momentous appearance, as if from the cumuli cloud enveloping the plane. Russell's hangover was all for telling her the seat next to his was occupied, but his romantic nature won the day. Fifty minutes later, Ophélie was offering to show him a few of the sights of Paris and the boy was completely besotted. No wonder he can't tell the difference between the Arc de Triomphe and the Bastille.

Helena is still holding out at midnight, which is when all the action starts at a French wedding. This reminds me of a call we received, from a shocked cousin Nathalie, shortly after she'd attended her first English wedding. She wanted to know why everybody was drunk by 9.30 p.m. and why nobody wanted to dance until dawn as they do in France. 'Think of it as a night in the pub,' I told her, 'only everyone's in their Sunday best and all the rounds are on the bride's father. Yes, that guy over there in the corner, shivering like a chihuahua soaked in *Brut* aftershave.'

French weddings are, well, just a little different. For starters, the food is edible (unless you land on the kids table) and, other than the obligatory alcoholic uncle, nobody gets pissed. The next thing you're likely to notice is that the vast majority of French men are not totally obsessed with trying to get it on with the bridesmaids. The dancing itself generally starts around midnight with a waltz and tonight, for the first time in eight months, I take Helena's hand and lead her to the dance floor. She protests that she can't move, let alone dance, but I take her anyway. I can't help myself when I hear a bit of Strauss – the sound of all that unadulterated happiness just grabs me by the passionate bits and, for a full five minutes, forces me to behave with all the chivalry of a faithful, medieval knight. We're not the most agile of dancers this evening and no matter how hard our feet try to insist, my son ensures that we're never less than a kilometre apart, but it does bring a smile to the face of Helena and at least the little fellow has had his first waltz.

Next the wedding guests all dance what the French know as *le rock* and the rest of us call the jive. This is a curious phenomenon, not only because its popularity in the rest of the world began to wane around forty years ago, but also because, in France, it cuts across the generations and provides arthritic old men like me with one of a dwindling number of opportunities (perhaps even their last) to dance with women half their age. Even the alcoholic uncle gets a look in at this point. But tonight Helena and I remain on the sidelines and watch as the baton is passed from generation to generation. My friends with the *Orangina* were nowhere to be seen when their grandparents were embarrassing them with their Viennese high-stepping, but they're not so young that they can't appreciate the comedy value of Uncle Claude getting his goolies in a twist thanks to *le rock*. They'll all be at it till the wee hours, long after Helena and I are slumbering heavily in our turret perched high above the moat, in anticipation of the many sleepless nights to come.

St Martin, January 18th

I hear Helena ordering room service but continue to doze under the sheets as we are brought orange juice, a pot of coffee, a small mountain of croissants and freshly baked bread. She's in her element and asks once again whether I've noticed the difference between this castle and our apartment. Let me think... I know there aren't any carp swimming about in the streets of Pigalle and I haven't seen any prostitutes wandering the hallways of the castle. But that isn't what she means:

'Listen,' she suggests.

'To what?'

'That's precisely what I mean. The silence.'

I can see where this conversation is heading and try desperately to avoid the inevitable but I might just as well try diverting the Seine through London. 'I can hear a few birds,' I say, more to test my luck than anything else.

'Yes, but birds aren't industrial dishwashing machines and they don't use jackhammers and drills.'

'Birds get up pretty early in the morning, you know.' Outside our room, I can hear only one pretty lame blackbird on the scrounge for an earthworm. The only other sound is that of the croissants sighing as they cool off after a spell in the oven.

'It makes a difference, doesn't it?' says Helena, before getting out of bed and theatrically wrapping herself in a couple of kilometres of virgin white towel. 'I'm going for a bath. Enjoy the peace and quiet. And the birds!'

This is nothing but the latest instalment in an argument that started as soon as Helena got pregnant. How often has she been brought to tears by the workings of the Danish restaurant beneath our apartment – the clatter of plates and orders for dessert, as well as other, more obscure Scandinavian activities, such as the slaughter of large shoals of herring before dawn. I block it from my consciousness and no longer hear a thing but the faster the birth approaches, the more sensitive Helena's ear becomes. My attempts to placate her, with such classic examples of male understanding as 'Why don't you try not to listen', have all backfired in woeful fashion. What she really wants is for me to admit that the situation is totally unbearable, to nip downstairs, blow up the restaurant and book us into the presidential suite at the *Sheraton* for a spot of the happily ever-afters.

Ah well, there's nothing I can do about it now, so I might as well attack the pastries and see if any of last night's footie is on the telly. Otherwise I might have to start listening to all that silence or thinking about the fact that there are no further landmarks between here and me becoming a father in roughly ten days' time.

I've just about worked my way through a large pot of coffee when I hear Helena calling from the bathroom. So much for a peaceful breakfast! Despite nine hours of sleep, my senses still feel dulled by the trip to London, so I put down my cup and tell it to stay where it is because I'll be back in a moment.

Roughly halfway between the bedroom and the bathroom, however, my mission is rudely interrupted. I haven't seen that damned step and my big toe meets it full force and in mid-stride, sending me straight to the deck with half a baguette coated in butter and strawberry jam wedged sideways into my mouth.

'*Merde, putain!*'

'*Qu'est-ce-qui s'est passé?*'

'*Merde,* my foot!'

Like an ornamental swan, Helena emerges from the bathroom while I continue to grovel and writhe around on the carpet like a poisoned caterpillar, attempting to reach my toe but not daring to touch it. 'What happened?'

'That fucking step! I tripped. *Merde!*' By now my foot is steadily dripping blood onto the pastel soft furnishings.

'You mean the step I warned you about yesterday?'

Helena looks at my toe and then at my face. She wants to laugh and checks to see whether she'll get away with it. She won't. I scramble onto my one remaining foot and head to the bathroom where I continue cursing in a mixture of French and Old Norse. Not until I've squeezed the toe into my boot and attempted to hobble downstairs does Helena remember the article in *Elle* magazine, at which point she can restrain herself no longer and fills the old castle with peals of Sunday morning laughter.

Old wives tales and the modern mother, January 19th

Monday morning dawns grey and heavy with rain clouds. I've been asleep since we got back from the wedding, yet I still feel as lethargic as a sloth after a Sunday roast. My toe is throbbing, my chest is heavy and, after two cups of finest Brazilian roast, my nervous system is still refusing to respond. It could be the thought of a bit of work, I suppose, as I know that I'm going to have to open my laptop and start thinking about the document I promised to write for London.

I'm supposed to send my proposal to the suits by the Thames before the end of the week, so I may not have long but that's still long enough not to get started right away. First, I'll make another pot of coffee. That should do the trick. As the thick, black liquid percolates upwards and my nervous system kicks into gear, I find myself staring through an object in our kitchen which would like to think of itself as a window, although the description is way too grandiose for a tiny pane of glass, criss-crossed by four regulation prison bars. It overlooks a small roof and the guttering which drains the city rain from our apartment building, a place where the filthy Parisian pigeons come to crap. On the other side of this void, slightly below the level of our apartment, is another kitchen window through which I can surreptitiously observe the comings and goings of a neighbouring family. They don't seem to mind, just as I don't mind if they're watching me stir up a cheese omelette for Helena or singing along to an old Chet Baker tune.

The family opposite comprises a young couple and their two sons. I like to watch the mother in the morning as she prepares breakfast for her boys, clad in her big, white dressing gown. She's always the first out of bed and bears all the hallmarks of a good mother. Next to appear, in his own forest green dressing gown, is her husband. Each of them will choose a kitchen appliance upon which to lean as they chat for a few minutes and plan their day. Next to arrive on the scene is their youngest son, dressed in pyjamas covered in *Disney* cartoon characters. At a guess, he's about twelve years old. Mummy always stops fiddling with the toaster when he appears and turns to give him a kiss as he wipes the sleep from his eyes. Then he waddles happily into the dining room to eat a bowl of cereal, taking comfort, no doubt, in the metronomic steadiness of his parents. Last out of bed on a daily basis is the eldest son, now in the full throes of puberty. He lopes into the kitchen, arms and hair swinging low, wearing nothing but a pair of track pants. When his mother's back is turned, he'll burst into an air guitar riff or play a short but violent drum solo on an itinerant biscuit tin. For him, there's no kiss from Mummy – not any more – but there are always a few tender words. She seems to be quite capable of maintaining radio contact with a young man who is already as tall as his father. Sometimes I think I can see a look of concern on her face as their son sweeps into the dining room and on out of sight. I couldn't tell you where in their apartment he eats his toast once he's wandered out of range, but it's all too easy to read the look of untainted admiration on the face of his younger brother as he follows the rebellious progress of his personal superhero around the flat. I can't hear anything that's said within their four not-so-private walls, but I appreciate the way this family handles itself. They never seem to argue or throw cereal at one another, I could set my watch by their rhythm and maybe I'm imagining it, but I'm sure there's a fair bit of love between each of the family members. One day we'll be gone, or perhaps they'll leave first, but I like to think that I'll remember them as my son grows up.

The coffee has rendered me sufficiently conscious to boot up my computer and the rest of the day is spent writing and watching the rain as it slides down the window pane. When a slightly darker shade of grey signals the onset of evening, I stop and print what I've written so far. Then I shuffle out of the room to see how Helena's doing. She's been asleep most of the day and needs a bit of conversation as much I do. There's only one thing on her mind and it certainly isn't my document:

'There's a full moon on Wednesday.'

'Oh?'

'You know what happens when there's a full moon, don't you?'

'The werewolves go carol singing?'

'No.'

'What then?'

'Women give birth to babies.'

A surge of panic rises in my chest. Is this true? I don't want it to be – not yet anyway. 'Isn't that just an old wives' tale?'

'I don't know.'

'I guess we'll find out soon enough. How are you feeling about it all?'

'Don't know. You?'

My instinct is to play the fearless male, but I can't be bothered and end up telling the truth: 'Frightened, I guess.'

'Me too! I don't know if I can go through with it.'

'It's a bit late to back out now.' This is a hopelessly inadequate response, but I don't know how else to reassure her. 'When are you going back to the hospital?'

'The last antenatal appointment is tomorrow.'

'You should talk to them about it,' I say, in an attempt to deflect some of the pressure in the direction of people better equipped to deal with it than I am.

'What am I going to tell them?'

'Just tell them you're scared. I'm sure you're not the only one.' Damned right! There's me, for starters. I'm petrified.

'Alright. Can you take me in the car? We'll do a dry run for the hospital.'

'Sure. I might even have a chat with the midwife myself.'

'What about?'

'Oh nothing! Just to check that we've got everything we need.'

Sex and the heavily pregnant woman, January 21st

I'm even more tired than yesterday and it's still raining in the morning when we drive to the hospital. As usual, I can't remember which turning to take once we leave the main drag east. Helena is unimpressed but my mind just seems to go blank once we get to within spitting distance of the place where the fallout from the collision between our chromosomes will finally become visible to the naked eye.

Helena is almost too large to squeeze into the cramped hospital lift. She's lost most of her flexibility and all of her mobility, and I'm concerned that this may be a problem when it comes to the birth. The lift groans a little under the undulating load but successfully delivers us to the fourth floor of the hospital. A sign above the door reads, '*blocs operatoires*'; I don't like the way that sounds – it makes me feel queasy and apprehensive. We ring the doorbell and wait. Waiting – that's all we seem to be doing.

I've promised to leave Helena alone with the midwife and she's promised me that she'll discuss her fears with the professional. I beat a retreat back to the vending machine near the lift shaft, where my own fears will just have to be swallowed along with a cup of reconstituted coffee. Then I do a bit more waiting.

Quarter of an hour later Helena joins me: 'Well? How'd it go?'

'She says I'm too tense.'

'You too, eh?'

'What?'

'Nothing. Anything else?'

'The baby's too high in my belly.'

'So?'

'So they're going to do a bit of acupuncture'

'Needles! What good will they do?'

'They'll improve my knitting – what do you think they'll do?'

The thought races through my mind that no one in this hospital has the faintest idea what they're talking about. They're supposed to be enticing a baby out of the womb, not subjecting its mother to an ancient Chinese ritual one week before it's due. I'm on the verge of sweeping downstairs and offering to deliver the baby myself when the midwife appears in the doorway, all smiles, and asks whether the human pincushion is ready. I snap my jaws shut just in time.

More waiting. I read a long article on the state of the rap scene in France. I retain none of it but note that the term 'motherfucker' has effortlessly crossed the Channel to take up residence in the French language. When Helena reappears she looks a little less tense than she did and a whole lot less than I do.

'Well? Where did they stick the needles?' (I hate all needles, so there's no right answer to this question.)

'One here,' she says, gesturing at the upper tier of her belly, 'two here' (the lower), 'two in the top of my legs and one in each foot.'

'Why on earth are they sticking needles in your feet?'

'Calm down, will you?'

'I'm perfectly calm!' I scream, with enough force to awaken the newborn on the floor below and disturb their mothers in the midst of their yoga.

'Yes, the needles follow the energy lines in your body and it works!'

'It works?'

'Yes. I feel better.'

'You feel better?'

'I do.'

'You do?'

'Yes. Are you going to repeat everything I say this evening?'

'What about the other thing?'

'What other thing?'

'The birth, the pain, the fear and all those other good reasons we came here in the first place.'

'Oh that,' says Helena as if the birth of our son were an afterthought, a mere piece of candied peel buried deep in a bulging Christmas cake, 'They said not to worry.'

'Well, that must have helped. Even I could have... '

'*Calmes-toi* and I'll tell you exactly what they said.'

For the thirty seconds it takes Helena to relate how the midwife has reassured her, I do, for once, manage to keep my mouth shut. They've told her to have confidence in herself, that she can do what every woman, on every continent and through out the ages, has done before her. She just needs to relax and believe it. That's all.

I can't believe that Helena has been reassured by a speech of so little weight and substance. She can do it because everyone else has done it? In her shoes, I'd be looking for a bit more content than that. But it does seem to have done the trick and as the lift door closes in my face, I resign myself to the fact that this is just one more little secret passed from one woman to the next in a way that men will never need to understand.

The fact that the baby is sitting too high in the womb also means that the little fellow is unlikely to be born before next week, full moon or no full moon. I find this vaguely heartening and go back to work on my document. Late in the evening, I stop to fry up a couple of herring for supper.

'How's it going?' Helena leans on the kitchen door.

'OK. You?'

'I'm fine.'

Then she gives me a look which I've not seen for a while. In fact, I haven't seen it for so long, that, at first, I fail to recognise it: 'The midwife did mention one other way to induce the baby.'

'Let me guess. Aromatherapy? Astral travel?'

'No. More down to earth than that.'

'Oh?'

'Sex.'

'Sex!' My mind gropes around in an effort to relate the word to a distant stirring in my loins.

'Yes, the sperm acts upon the uterus and causes it to contract.'

'That's enough to put me off dinner, never mind a bit of rumpy-pumpy.' I take a step back to assess Helena's figure. She's so large that, from where I'm standing, sex looks like a logistical impossibility even if I could remember which bits are supposed to go where. Like a surveyor, I study the problem from a couple of different angles, before pausing to scratch my head.

'What are you doing?'

'Calculating my approach.'

'Come here. We'll figure it out as we go along.' She takes my hand and leads me to the bedroom.

'What about the herring?'

'Tell them to wait.'

Midnight snack

In the middle of the night Helena wakes me up to tell me she's caught a cold, but I'm barely alive and I fall straight back into a horrible dream: I'm in South East Asia again, travelling with an old friend. It's hot and I'm sweating. The friend takes me to a restaurant and we sit down to eat. I ask him what's good and he tells me not to worry – he'll order for both of us. But when the food arrives, I can make out the shape of what I'm being asked to eat through a light coating of batter – one lizard, half a turtle and a couple of snakes. The dish may have been fried, but the animals are quite clearly not yet dead. Unable to refuse, I pick up a knife and watch the lizard squirm as I slice into its body. After dinner, the friend, who is about to be struck from my address book forever, offers me a glass of chilled pepper vodka and intimates that he has a bag of magic mushrooms in his alligator skin briefcase. I refuse immediately and suddenly I'm awake again, panting in the moist night air. Where did that come from? For once I'm relieved to hear the rain pattering on the roof outside our bedroom window. When I close my eyes, I can still see those cold-blooded animals, writhing and squealing under the pressure of my serrated knife. I'm desperately tired but my mind won't stop racing as it tries to make sense of the dream.

Conception – don't blink or you'll miss it, January 23rd

Huddling next to our gas fire as dawn comes, I remember, all over again, the trip to London on which we found out that Helena was pregnant. It was Vincent's birthday. Helena was still in Paris and I'd arranged to meet some friends for a drink in a bar near Clapham Common. I was still hung over from the night before and I knew the only thing that would make me feel better was a good stiff drink. I ordered a large vodka and tonic and was instantaneously transformed from a state of fatigue into one of advanced loudness and overbearing. As I reached the ice cubes at the bottom of my drink, I was already talking a lot of bar-stool bullshit that I wouldn't remember in the morning. I drained the glass, ordered another and, for a split second, caught sight of myself in the mirror behind the bar, surrounded by people and row upon row of bottles and optics. In a single moment of fractured clarity, a wave of shame and loneliness rolled over me. I've no idea what my friends thought as they finished their drinks and took their leave. I didn't ask. But I knew what I was thinking alright – I could no longer accept the person I'd become. In fact, I wanted him dead. Then, just as easily as it had come, that fleeting moment was gone again and another vodka was pressed into my hand. Helena was preparing to leave for London and although I didn't yet know it, she was already bearing that tiny seed in her belly – the secret that was to change my path and give me a reason to live.

Full moon has been and gone and it's still pissing with rain. I still feel uncomfortable looking back on that evening, but now I must stir myself and face the truth, otherwise there'll be no peace and I'll never be able to look my son in the eye. Sometimes it feels as if the only thing that's changed is that I'm more tired and less sure. Anyway, I won't be getting any more sleep this morning, so I settle down with a cup of tea to finish off the document for London.

Istanbul, January 24th

Helena's had another session of acupuncture but has yet to show any signs of going into labour or doing the washing up. My document has finally gone to London and I'm lying on the sofa wondering what we'll do this weekend, presumably our last before we're overwhelmed by nappies and bottles. I close my eyes and try to imagine another person sharing the sofa with me, even a very small one. But I still can't do it.

Helena drifts into the room and as if she's been reading my mind asks precisely the wrong question:

'Can you believe that this time next week, you'll have a baby on your knee?'

'No. Can you?'

'No way.'

We're interrupted by the sound of broken glass beneath our apartment window. It's Friday night and the restaurant is opening for business. Helena's face crumples like a piece of waste paper.

'We have to move,' she says, blinking back the tears.

'I know, but now's not a good time.'

Helena nods forlornly. Then she goes upstairs to visit a neighbour with double-glazed windows. She wants to know whether he too can hear every single plate being washed up, rinsed and stacked in the galley below. She disappears and I close my eyes once more, grateful for a couple more minutes without having to say anything.

Before I relinquish my grip on consciousness altogether Helena is back, explaining that our neighbour upstairs has gone to Brazil for a month. It registers but I fail to react until she tells me that the new tenant upstairs is a Zulu.

'A Zulu, huh?'

'No, he's not a Zulu. *Il sous-loue.* He's subletting.'

Opening a single eye, I catch Helena trying to stifle a laugh. She's still angry about the restaurant, but she can't quite contain herself and bursts out laughing so hard I'm afraid she'll give birth on the spot. Of course she sets me off and it feels like the first time I've laughed in months.

We're still cackling away when the phone rings. It's Dirk and he wants to know if there's any news. 'No news,' I snigger. Then Dirk wants to know why I'm snorting and snuffling like a pig after a truffle and I try to explain. But his French is about as good as my Swahili and he won't get any sense out of me for at least another week, so he asks me to call back when we have news. I put down the phone and it rings again. This time it's Cécile. I put Helena on the line to make sure she gets the lack of news in full detail.

What do you do on the weekend before life changes forever? Do you go to a nightclub and dance? Do you go for a long walk along the banks of the Seine, take in an exhibition or go out for dinner? Not if you're me, you don't. The only thing I can think of is to work myself up into a right old lather and I start by questioning Helena yet again about what she's packed for the hospital. Then I start worrying about where the car is parked. After all, someone might have stolen it overnight. Helena thinks it unlikely but I prefer to check for myself. Of course, it's still in exactly the same spot where I parked it three days ago, nose pointed straight at the hospital. I catch myself wishing that someone would steal the damned thing and then at least it would be some taxi driver's responsibility to get us all safely there when the time comes. Eventually Helena can stand it no longer and sends me to find out what's on at the cinema. I protest that we shouldn't be going anywhere with her at such an advanced stage of pregnancy. But she's having none of it and underlines her determination by telling me I can choose what we watch. I opt for a Turkish film which won something at the Cannes Film Festival. I've no idea what it's about. All it says in the listings is that it contains long periods of silence. At least that way I'll be able to keep an ear cocked to Helena's breathing.

The movie is playing at an art house cinema which means I'm to be deprived not only of ice cream but also of ice cream advertising. Instead, we're surrounded by the Parisian intelligentsia with their bifocals strapped irritatingly around their necks, shushing anyone with the temerity to breathe once the film has already started, even though fuck all happens for the first fifteen minutes. To tell the truth, there's more entertainment value in watching my neighbour trying to chew his way through a packet of *Rolo*'s without moving any of the muscles in his lower jaw.

But slowly I fall under the spell of this gentle film and its tale of a Turkish peasant who arrives in the big city looking for work. He moves in with his lone-wolf of a cousin, a photographer who at first appears glad of a little company. But this doesn't last long because the world-weary cousin doesn't want to share any part of his life with another human being. We learn that he was once married, but that relationship ended when his wife fell pregnant and he insisted she have an abortion. They still call each other but she lives with another man. Perhaps she still loves him and maybe he still loves her, but their lives were permanently fractured by that one simple decision. Briefly, I remember how I was prepared to go to almost any lengths to preserve what men like to call their independence. But it's snowing in Istanbul and the ill-clad country cousin can't find any work. The camera trails behind him as he wanders the lonely cityscape, following single women through the slush and buying toys to send to his niece back home in the fields. He has outstayed his welcome and his host wants to return to a life of isolation. The strain between them mounts slowly and reaches breaking point when a mouse becomes trapped in the apartment. As it begins a painful, undignified death, its tiny feet stuck to a nicotine-yellow floor trap, the photographer shows no mercy and instructs the country cousin to put the dying animal out with the rubbish. He does as he's asked because he still feels indebted to his host, but when he sees a pack of cats approaching the blue bin liner in which the mouse lies dying, he takes pity on the animal and kills it before the alley cats can tear it to pieces. The final scene of the movie is unforgettable – the cousin has gone and the photographer sits alone on a bench in the middle of the Istanbul winter. Life goes on around him, but he's not part of it. In silence he smokes a last *Marlboro* and we can only guess at his thoughts. The credits roll and I feel the warmth of Helena's hand in mine. I could so easily have taken one more wrong turning and ended up on that same park bench. I've no idea what kind of father I'll become, but at least my resistance to the process has finally come to an end.

We're hungry and take a booth at a Tex-Mex restaurant opposite the cinema. It's Saturday and the place is full of young lovers preparing for a long night out. We're surrounded by plastic cacti and bathed in an eerie neon light which only serves to heighten the feeling that I'm living a dream. What am I doing here so close to the birth of my son? Shouldn't I be somewhere else? I don't know and I'm too tired to care. The burritos may well be the worst I've ever eaten and the glutinous rice has certainly never seen a paddy field, but the waitress is friendly enough. When she smiles and apologises for spilling the coffee, it's enough to reassure me that I'm still part of the human race. It's going to be a long time before Helena and I are able to do this again. When we finally stumble home to our bed, I fall quickly into deep, dreamless sleep.

In the waiting room, January 25th

The sun has disobeyed the orders of General January and burst through the cloud cover. It's still early and Helena and I are back in the car although we're not yet bound for the hospital. Instead we're on our way out to the Bois de Boulogne because the hospital hippies have told Helena to do a bit of walking in order to shake the little fellow out of his comfort zone. I'm hoping a bike ride will ease the tension building steadily in my chest, which feels as if it's in the grip of a monstrous boa constrictor. I reassemble my bike in the car park and watch as Helena disappears into a stand of dormant rhododendrons.

The park is full of young children and their parents. If the doctors are to be believed, I'll become one of these people in around forty-eight hours' time. As I push on through the naked trees, I try to understand why this idea seems less and less likely, the closer we get to the due date. Me, a father? The whole thing feels more preposterous than ever before and, just to make sure, I checked Helena's belly again this morning. But it wasn't a dream. There's something in there alright.

I reach my favourite spot in the Bois where a small lake is surrounded by old beech trees and dare myself to try and look forward to the birth. What will it be like? I've absolutely no idea. I saw all those women giving birth on the hospital videos but this will not be 'those women', this time it'll be Helena up on the slab and going through agony. As for life after birth, well, I still lack the audacity to anticipate my son's personality and it pisses me off when anyone asks me to try. I don't want to think about it. I just want him to be born safely. I'm doing my best to keep these fears to myself and maybe Helena is too. All she will say is that the baby is strong and that he'll be OK. But how can she have such confidence?

All I can think about is what can go wrong, and as I start another lap of the lake, I begin listing them all over again – stuff with umbilical cords, oxygen, anaesthesia, the mistakes that doctors can, and sometimes do, make. After every ultra-sound they've told us that everything is OK. But what if they're mistaken or lying? What if there's something wrong with my boy? I must have been through this damned list a hundred times, but it never gets any shorter. When I do get to the end, I go straight back to the beginning and start all over again. What if I never get to bring him to this lake? Will he ever be able to see the ducks, ride a bicycle and feel the wind against his face?

By now I'm circling the lake like a vulture that hasn't eaten for months. I've lost all track of time and it's not until I almost run over a small, blonde girl that I realise I was due back at the car park ten minutes ago. I take the shortest route to find Helena waiting by the car. Her eyes are closed against the weak winter sun and the wind has ruffled her hair.

'Helena, are you alright?'

'There you are. I was beginning to wonder what had happened to you. Are you alright?'

'Who me? Yes, of course!'

The hunter and the hunted, January 26th

I'm camped in the jungle now. I don't know how I got here or what I'm doing. The only sound is the squealing of monkeys and I'm beginning to lose it. My brother's here too, on some sort of an assignment, but he refuses to give me any details. We have to leave, he says, packing his gear in a tearing hurry. Thank God! I've had enough. The mosquitoes are eating me alive, it's stinking hot and the sweat stings in the open sores all over my body. I jump on a motorbike and turn the throttle as hard as I can. I've got to get out of this putrid forest. The hanging vines are whipping my face and arms and I'm convinced that scores of animals are keeping pace alongside me in the foliage. I can't see them. I just know that they're there, hunting me. My brother is nowhere to be seen. The sweat is pouring into my eyes, but now I think I can see something up ahead. I can almost make it out through the dust. I'm approaching it fast, far too fast, but it's not moving. What is it? What's it doing in the middle of the dirt? As I begin to brake, it just sits there, staring. I'm too close – get out of the way! I'm going to hit it! Pulling desperately on the brakes, I feel my rear wheel as it tears through the desiccated ruts beneath me. I close my eyes tightly against the impact and the engine chokes. Slowly the dust settles and, fearing the worst, I open my eyes. Through eyes of gold, the lynx stares back at me and refuses to flinch.

As Helena arrives in the bedroom, I'm still hiding under the blankets, sweating and disoriented.

'Good morning!'

'Huh?'

'Thought you might like a cup of tea.'

'Where are we?'

'At home. Where do you think we are?'

'Thank God! I thought I was still in the jungle.'

'No jungle here. Just planet Pigalle.'

Helena gives me a strange look, puts the teacup down next to the bed and leaves. She's probably gone to call the psychiatric ward.

I lie there for a moment trying to piece it all together. Has she had the baby already? If so, where is it? She doesn't want me to see it. She's hiding it from me. That's it! I knew there was something wrong. No, wait a minute! That can't be right. She still had her belly when she brought the tea. I must have been dreaming, but about what?

Half an hour later I'm almost entirely back in the land of the living, though I'm not quite sure what to do with myself, so I decide to clean the oven. This is an odd decision, because we've been living in this apartment for a year and a half and, in all that time, it hasn't once occurred to me to clean the kitchen, never mind the oven. I don't think Helena knows what to do with herself either, because she's standing over me as I fill the apartment with toxic fumes from an aerosol can.

'Why are you doing that now?'

'Because it's dirty.' And to prove the point, I start scrubbing even more furiously at the burnt-on residue of a thousand pizzas. But this proves to be another mistake as I catch a finger on something sharp lurking underneath the grime and it slices into my skin. Helena watches as I pull my hand out of the oven and blood drips slowly onto the kitchen floor. She looks at my white face and walks out. She doesn't laugh. Not this time.

For the rest of the day, I try to keep out of trouble and while away the hours reading by the light of the 40-watt bulb on my desk. At some point Helena enters the room looking a bit shocked. She tells me she's seen blood and I look at my finger. But she's not talking about my finger. This time it's her that's bleeding. I want to know why. She doesn't know. I tell her to call the hospital. They tell her she has just lost something called a *bouchon*. What's that? Helena doesn't know the word in English but it all points to an impending birth. When? She doesn't know that either.

We don't do much for the rest of the evening, other than eat a thick fish soup with some cheese and croutons. Then Helena watches some television while I go outside and check the oil in the car.

Antipasti, January 28th

At 5.30 in the morning Helena wakes me up to tell me that the contractions have started.

'How do you know they're contractions?'

'Because I've had them before.'

'Do they feel any different this time?'

'No, just more frequent and a bit more painful.'

'How frequent?'

'About every twenty minutes.'

We sit in the dark. There isn't a sound outside the apartment. Eventually I ask Helena whether she wants to go back to sleep. She doesn't and neither do I, so we just lie there and wait for something to happen.

But nothing happens until about 8.30, when I decide to go to the *boulangerie* for a loaf of bread. Then I squeeze some oranges, make some toast and give Helena breakfast in bed.

'How do you feel?'

'Same.'

'Does it hurt?'

'Only when the contraction comes, otherwise not.'

'Shouldn't we be checking the frequency or something?'

We both know the rules of the game by now – there's simply no point in rushing straight to the hospital. Today is her due date but if we arrive too soon, they'll only send us back home. What we have to do now is wait until the contractions come every ten minutes.

After breakfast Helena asks whether we should call the hospital. I can't see the point but I'm not the one suffering an acute pain because something wants to escape from my body. She makes the call and is told to relax and to take a bath. But we don't have a bath and neither of us is able to relax. I tell Helena to try to get some more sleep and she gives me a look that could turn Michelangelo's David to dust, so I start preparing lunch. It's almost 10.30 in the morning.

In the mailbox, I find a letter from London. It states briefly that my proposal has been approved and that I'm expected to start work next month. But the words do not penetrate and I put the letter to one side and continue shelling peas.

Helena attempts to eat some fish but she's forced to stop when her body is overtaken by pain. I stop eating too and watch as the contractions pass in and out. Then she picks up her fork and slowly resumes spooning the buttery haddock into her mouth. She tells me that the contractions feel like bad stomach cramps which return each time with a higher payload of electrical pain.

By the middle of the afternoon, the interval between contractions has decreased to around fifteen minutes. Between them, we chat inconsequentially. I'm still finding it hard to imagine everything that may happen today. Helena tells me she'd like to go for a walk, so we bundle up against the cold and leave the apartment behind. I'm not sure this is a good idea but the walk does put a temporary halt to the contractions. As we round the block, I glance at the *Clio* one more time, but it just shrugs its shoulders as if to say there's no way of hurrying these things.

As soon as Helena gets back into bed the contractions resume, only now they are occurring every eight minutes. I ask her if she'd like to go to the hospital. She says no. Then I ask her what she wants for dinner and, for the first time ever, Helena tells me she's not hungry.

I prepare some tagliatelle in an olive and tomato sauce. It's one of her favourites but, when she gets to the table, Helena looks every bit as pale as the pasta and merely stares at the sauce. I wait for her to start eating but, before she's even picked up her fork, she says firmly, 'Let's go!'

'What, now?'

'Yes, now!'

'But it's the middle of the rush hour,' I cry. 'Can't you wait?'

But Helena has no intention of waiting. You can take my word for that. Quickly, I fill the gaping hole in the middle of my face with a ladleful of tagliatelle and gather Helena's bags which seem to have been lying in the bedroom for almost an eternity. I'm convinced this is a false alarm; that we'll be home in time for the news and a cup of cocoa. Perhaps that's why I feel so calm.

The *Clio* growls into action and I pull the car up in front of our building. Then I go back upstairs to find Helena. The contractions are coming every five minutes now and we don't say much on the way to the hospital. Helena doesn't ask me to drive more quickly or more slowly and I manage to keep the car off the pavement, out of the Canal de l'Ourcq and headed in the general direction of the hospital.

We arrive shortly after 8.00 p.m. and get straight into the elevator. The sign on the fourth floor still says '*blocs operatoires*' and I still don't like the way it sounds. I ring the bell and the midwife still takes an age to answer it. She asks Helena for her name, something that strikes me as a little unnecessary, considering that the girl is clearly about to drop a baby onto the floor. But, after this brief bureaucratic interlude, we're shown directly into the *salle de preparation*, where Helena is wired up to a monitoring machine. The baby's amplified heartbeat booms into life and oscillates between 96 and 160 beats per minute, which seems to be far too fast, though barely faster than my own. Sometimes the pulse disappears altogether, forcing me to hold my breath as I wait for the thunder to come back into range. Every time this happens I glance at the midwife, but she looks unconcerned. Then she tells us she'll be back in about fifteen minutes to examine Helena and leaves us alone in a clinical white chamber that resounds with the erratic pounding of three hearts.

It's going to be a busy night at the hospital. On our way into the room, I saw another expectant father. I know that's what he was because he was wearing thin, blue plastic galoshes over his shoes and looked like he was about to keel over. I guess his wife must already be in the delivery room. In passing, I asked him how it was all going and he just looked right through me.

We wait the full fifteen minutes. Then another fifteen. Still no midwife. It's about 9.00 p.m. now, and I don't really know what else to say. Every five minutes, her face alternately tightens and then crumples as she's attacked by another set of convulsions. I can't ask her yet again how it feels, but what else can I say? I doubt she's interested in anything that's going on outside this room and it's really not the time for small talk

('Did you notice the other letter which arrived this morning, Helena? Yes, the one from the estate agents which threatens eviction if you persist with your rent strike?'). Instead, I remain focused on the heartbeat monitor and try to discern whether there's any pattern to the fluctuations of my son's heartbeat. But if one exists, I certainly can't figure it out.

Another fifteen minutes passes. For some unaccountable reason, I'm beginning to feel deathly tired. But how can that be? I know we were up early this morning but, after nine months of anxiety, this is hardly the moment to start falling asleep. For the first time tonight I fish a few grubby coins out of my pocket and pay a visit to the coffee machine located on the ground floor. Then I step outside for a cigarette. The streets are calm and there's a bitterly cold wind whistling between the apartment buildings. A few stragglers are hurrying home late from work, collars upturned against the cold. I notice the dull yellow light glowing in the apartments surrounding the hospital and imagine the residents watching the evening news and getting ready for bed. I can almost hear them yawning. I envy them the certainty of their sleep but I'm starting to shiver, so I drain my coffee, throw my cigarette butt into the gutter and head back inside. As I wait for the lift, the night watchman at the hospital stares at me for a moment before nodding once. He's seen my type pass this way before.

By the time I get back to the fourth floor, a nurse is examining Helena. She confirms a dilation of a rounded four centimetres. Helena looks at me, then at the midwife.

'Does that mean...?'

'Yes, you're going to have your baby tonight.'

I wasn't expecting that. I was so sure we'd be sent home. Tonight? That can't be right, can it? Surely not tonight? I sit down on the only chair in the room. It's made of a dull metal and feels cold beneath my tremulous bones. The nurse leaves the room and I look at Helena. 'Tonight!' I say.

'Yes,' says Helena, as a small tear forms in the corner of

her eye.

Then the nurse is back, asking whether Helena would like an epidural. Helena says she'd like to see how it goes for a while and checks to make sure that she's allowed to change her mind. She is. Then the nurse sticks a needle into a bluish vein in Helena's hand and leaves the room once more. It's about ten in the evening.

For a while, not much of anything happens. I sit with Helena and watch as the contractions continue to grip her body. Each one lasts about forty-five seconds and there's nothing I can do but sit there, squeeze her hand and wait for it to pass. Why do I feel so tired?

The next time the midwife visits she's accompanied by a doctor who starts asking Helena a lot of questions. I try to follow what they're saying, but they despatch me from the room and I head back downstairs for another smoke. This time the night watchman has to unlock the door to let me out. In the fresh air, I allow myself to think about how I feel. I'm calmer than expected, which is probably a good thing, but I'm still overwhelmed with fatigue, which isn't.

At 11.00 p.m. Helena is moved into the delivery room and I'm told to don my own pair of blue galoshes. This room is incredibly bright and hotter than a tropical beach at midday. But Helena says she's cold and the nurse unfolds a thick woollen blanket over her legs. Is that a bad sign? My eyes dart nervously over the equipment in the room. I don't know what any of it's for, but I'm not in the least comforted by the flashing lights and balletic needles etching their way across everlasting sheets of graph paper. An oxygen mask hangs from the ceiling and my mind jumps to those safety videos which the airlines insist upon showing you every time you board a plane. They always strike me as unnecessary and absurd. Why don't they just tell you that if the plane goes down, you might as well prepare for death, rather than spending your last few seconds groping around for some superfluous, surgical mask. I'm just about to share this thought with Helena when

I remember how much she hates flying.

At 11.30, the midwife is back. She's not that friendly and, to be honest, I don't like her at all. I don't think Helena likes her much either, although no words are exchanged on the subject. After all, this isn't the supermarket, where you can change lines if the cashier looks like the kind of person who keeps a snarling dog tied up in the basement. Then Helena tells her she'd like the epidural and, maybe I'm imagining it, but I think the midwife gives her a bit of a sullen look. Then she leaves us alone once more.

Snowfall in Paris, January 29th

Midnight has been and gone. Helena's laboured breathing is punctuated only by the spasms which signal the onset of another contraction. It's now taking a full minute for the waves to subside and each one only heightens my sense of futility. The heat in this room is making me delirious and all sorts of absurd thoughts are pulsing through my head. What has my son been eating in the womb? How does he breathe and does he know what's about to happen? Is he awake and what would he like for breakfast? How come I know so little of how all this works and, above all, why ever did I stop reading *Future Maman*? Mercifully, Helena derails the train by asking me to pull the blanket tighter over her legs. Then she goes back inside to talk to our son and the room falls silent once more.

The anaesthetist arrives to administer the epidural. Once again I'm sent from the room and catch the lift back downstairs to the vending machine. The night watchman is watching a French soap opera and I ask him to unlock the door. He wants to know why. I stare at him malevolently. I'd have thought it was bloody obvious why... My girlfriend is about to give birth and this has never happened to me before. I'm totally stressed out and I need a cigarette. Now unlock the door, you fucker! He tells me this will be the last time tonight and I glare at him for a few seconds. Then he turns the key in the lock and I escape into the night.

On the streets of Paris it has begun to snow. I wasn't expecting that. I allow the big, heavy flakes to fall on my face and pray they will go some way towards waking me up. A thin white veil has drawn across the eleventh *arrondissement*, which appears to be otherwise deserted. Inhaling deeply, I watch as the snow begins to settle on the cars parked outside the hospital. I ask whoever may be listening whether everything is going to be alright. No one answers and I'm not sure if I want to go back upstairs or not.

Half an hour later, another midwife enters the delivery room. She smiles and says her name is Adèle. She wants to know how Helena is feeling. Then she tells us she will be overseeing the birth and I'm pleased. I don't know where the unfriendly one has gone but I hope she stays there. Adèle smiles again and I sense that Helena is just as relieved as I am. Adèle manipulates Helena's lower belly and tells us the baby is still sitting too high in the womb. She says there's a lot of work to be done if we are to share breakfast as a family of three (although not by me, which is just as well as I can feel my eyes beginning to close once more). I tell Helena that I'm going to nip out to the waiting room by the lift and shut my eyes for a few minutes but Adèle says I can lie on the floor and offers me a foam mattress. I refuse. How can I fall asleep as Helena goes into labour? That would be ridiculous behaviour, even by my own exacting standards. But Helena intervenes and instructs me to do as I'm told. She says it will be easier for her to breathe without having to see my fearful features every time she goes through a contraction. It's well after one in the morning and, reluctantly, I admit defeat.

I drift in and out of consciousness for an hour or so before falling asleep. In my dreams, Helena and I are inhaling and exhaling in unison. Every so often Adèle comes back into the room and even if I'm completely incapable of movement, I still know she's there. I've forgotten to tell Helena about the snow, but I can't open my mouth. My head feels like a piece of lead buried deep in the mattress and my limbs have lost radio contact with my central nervous system. I no longer have any choice – I've been buried alive and the worms and the soil are working me further and further away from where I need to be.

At 3.30 in the morning, I hear Adèle instructing Helena to breathe deeply. I open my eyes and try to focus on my surroundings. Adèle tells Helena that it's time for the real work to begin. I draw my fingers close to my face and study them. They're responding, so it must be time to get off the floor. Quickly I force my body into an upright position and stow the mattress at the side of the room. Then I move silently round the bed and take up a position next to Helena. 'It's snowing,' I say. Helena looks at me and I think I discern a weak smile on her face. Then Adèle tells her to push and I feel Helena's fingers close around mine.

The contractions are rolling in like waves off the Pacific. Each time they ripple through Helena's body, Adèle urges her to push and she does. Then she stops briefly and pants hard, before pushing again and then a third time, but as soon as the contraction comes to an end, her arching spine collapses back onto the bed and Helena gasps for air. I spray her face with water from an aerosol can and watch the strain on her features as she licks her cracked lips. There is no more talking between contractions – just waiting and spraying, tensing and pushing.

It has gone four o'clock when Adèle declares that Helena must try harder. She urges Helena, imploring her to push harder, much harder. Each time she does, Helena takes my forearm and grips it. Her fingernails tear at my flesh but I say nothing. I don't even feel it. I wonder how much more of this Helena can endure.

Adèle says that our son is ready and Helena must make her last effort now, otherwise the baby will not come. There's no time to consider the meaning of these words and I don't think Helena even hears them. She's not listening any more. All she can do is to push and I don't think she can do that for very much longer. I'm not sure if she's still conscious, or even human. All she is now is a set of contradictory muscles, forcing, pushing and contracting. There's no space for anything else – no feeling, thinking or processing. Everything she ever was has come down to this single supreme effort. I lean close and whisper into her ear that she must push. I tell her she can do it, just like her mother did and her grandmother before that. Can she hear me? I doubt it. Her eyes are closed and I can see the tension in every last fibre, straining and fraying like a cord at maximum load.

Adèle says she can see the baby's head and implores Helena to push again. I see it too, but only for a moment. Then Helena stops pushing and he disappears again. 'Come on, Helena. Push for your grandmother. Please!' The baby's head reappears and both Adèle and I beg her to try harder. I bend close to her face – 'Helena, it's true! I can see him.'

Several times I see the head of my son slithering free, only to watch in agony as he slides back inside. I know this is the hardest part. Once the head is out, Adèle will twist his shoulders round and it'll be over. But Helena is unable to force him clear. There must be something wrong, I'm sure of it. How much longer can this go on? I look at Adèle, but still she's calm. The pain comes again. 'Come on, Helena, come on. For the love of God, do it now!'

The head appears once more. I can see it quite clearly this time, covered in fine hair and matted with blood. But he makes no sound at all. Why can't I hear him? He should be crying. I'm sure of it. 'Push, just one more time,' cries Adèle, 'push!' Out of sheer necessity and with an almighty groan, Helena forces the baby's head clear of her body and collapses back onto the bed. I watch as Adèle takes the head in her gloved hands. Still no sound. Even Adèle says nothing as she works to free his shoulders. The baby's not moving. He's lifeless and utterly silent, and an overwhelming sadness settles in my heart.

I look at the baby's body as Adèle wrestles him free. He's pale, a ghostly white colour and big too, much bigger than I expected. Perhaps that was the problem. I don't know. It takes an age to pull his legs free and still Adèle says nothing. He's dead, I'm quite sure of that. But what am I going to say to Helena?

There's a little blood on his motionless body, but Adèle wipes him clean and says something to Helena. I think she's telling her the baby has arrived, that she can have him now. Then she lifts his limp body towards the light and frees the umbilical cord. I watch in shock as Adèle passes him up the bed towards Helena's outstretched arms. My son's face is turned directly towards mine. I can feel my soul jangling in the pit of my stomach. It wants to scream, but I've lost the ability to make any sound at all and I've stopped breathing. The baby is laid upon Helena's breast and I notice how his ears are streamlined against the side of his head. They're a funny shape, too, like the perfectly formed wings on the feet of Achilles. How beautiful he might have been!

I can no longer look. I turn away and exhale a lifetime of breath. Time seems to have ground to a complete halt. I search for a neutral point on which to steady my gaze but my eyes return to the prostrate body of my son at the very moment he opens an eye. I don't understand. How can that be? I thought... Mouth open wide, I look round and see Adèle grinning at me. I try to say something, but the words still won't come.

'Your boy is fine,' says Adèle, 'just fine.' Then she gets up and mumbles something about leaving us alone for a time.

I turn to Helena, who has started to cry. Our son opens another eye, which is just as large as the first and quite possibly blue. He chokes once or twice and then he, too, starts to cry. I may even be at it myself by now, but I'm sure you don't want to hear about that.

EPILOGUE

Dear E,

Tomorrow, I'll be driving to the hospital one last time to pick you up. You're coming home with me and Mummy.

I've just come back from the town hall where I registered your birth. I'm afraid you've only got two names – my name, which you've inherited, and the one chosen by us. We thought about giving you a third, but decided not to weigh you down with things you won't need.

When I left the town hall, the sun was shining and the air was so warm it felt like the first day of spring. Yet you were born in the middle of a snowstorm. How funny!

On my way back to the hospital I stopped for lunch and the thought about all the things I'd like to tell you. I could wait until you're a little older, of course, but I'm afraid I won't be able to remember them, that I might not be able to find the right words, or even that my mouth may be a little dry.

You were born at 4.27 in the morning. You cried, but only a little. Then I took you in my arms and carried you carefully out of the room. The nurse weighed you in at exactly four kilos and told me to give you a bath. To be honest, I was a little nervous as I lowered you into the water. You clenched your fists and for the first time I noticed the size of your hands. Maybe you were scared too, I don't know, but you seemed to like the water alright. Of course, you kept an eye on me, just to make sure I didn't do anything silly while your mother was lying in the bed, too tired to talk or even lift her head.

Then you and I talked a little. I told you a bit of a story. A story about a man who'd waited a long time to see his son and thought the day would never come. Even when it seemed that it would, things kept happening along the way and there were times when it looked like things might not turn out the way he'd hoped. I'll get round to telling you the rest of the story one day, but right now, I just want to take you home.

★★★

Acknowledgements

I would like to express my thanks and gratitude to those who encouraged, inspired or simply endured, especially the following:

Janet and Douglas the Scot; Matt and Joss; Sam, Natty and little Tiggys everywhere; Isabel, José and the Family Genis Drujon; Michele Ainzara; Horace; Hilary and the Lees; Franck and Fabienne; Douwe and Claudia; The Family Kobi; Charlie, John H., David de la P., Jonathan F., Majid, Frederica and friends; H.P.; the City of Paris; and, of course, my editor Anthony Nott, without whom all would have remained mere possibility.

James Briggs